This book may be returned to any Wiltshire
library. To renew this book phone your library
or visit the website: www.wiltshire.gov.uk

Wiltshire Council
Where everybody matters

No
Echo

ANNE HOLT is Norway's bestselling female crime writer. She spent two years working for the Oslo Police Department before founding her own law firm and serving as Norway's Minister for Justice between 1996 and 1997. She is published in 30 languages with over 7 million copies of her books sold.

Also by Anne Holt

THE HANNE WILHELMSEN SERIES:

Blind Goddess
Blessed Are Those Who Thirst
Death of the Demon
The Lion's Mouth
Dead Joker
No Echo
Beyond the Truth
1222

THE VIK/STUBO SERIES:

Punishment
The Final Murder
Death in Oslo
Fear Not
What Dark Clouds Hide

No
Echo

Anne
Holt

Translated from the Norwegian
by Anne Bruce

CORVUS

First published in trade paperback in Great Britain in 2016 by Corvus, an imprint of Atlantic Books Ltd.

Originally published in Norwegian as *Uten Ekko*. Published by agreement with the Salmonsson Agency.

This translation has been published with the financial support of NORLA.

10 9 8 7 6 5 4 3 2 1

A CIP catalogue record for this book is available from the British Library.

Trade paperback ISBN: 978 0 85789 815 9
Paperback ISBN: 978 0 85789 230 0
E-book ISBN: 978 0 85789 237 9

Printed and bound by CPI Group (UK) Ltd, Croydon, CR0 4YY

Corvus
An imprint of Atlantic Books Ltd
Ormond House
26–27 Boswell Street
London
WC1N 3JZ

www.corvus-books.co.uk

Hairy Mary could hardly remember her real name. She came into the world in the back of a truck in January 1945. Her mother was an orphan aged sixteen. Nine months earlier, she had sold herself to a German soldier for two packs of cigarettes and a bar of chocolate. Now she was on her way to Tromsø. Finnmark was ablaze. Having pushed out in freezing temperatures of minus twenty-two degrees Celsius, the baby was swaddled in a moth-eaten blanket and then turned over to a married couple from Kirkenes. They were walking along the road holding a child of five by the hand, and barely had a chance to gather their wits before the truck with the sixteen-year-old was gone. The baby girl, two hours old, got no more from her biological mother than her name. Mary.

Incredibly enough, the family from Kirkenes managed to keep the infant alive. They held on to her for eighteen months. Before Mary reached the age of ten, she had put four new foster families behind her. Mary was quick-witted, remarkably lacking in the beauty stakes, and what's more had sustained an injury to one leg during her birth. She walked with a limp. Her body twisted halfway around every time she set down her right foot, as if scared that someone might be following her. If she had problems moving about, she was all the faster at shooting her mouth off. After two combative years at a children's home in Fredrikstad, Mary headed for Oslo to take care of herself. She was then twelve years of age.

Hairy Mary certainly did take care of herself.

Now she was the oldest street hooker in Oslo.

She was an exceptional woman in more ways than one. Maybe it was an obstinate gene that had helped her survive almost half a century in the trade. It might just as easily have been downright defiance. For the first fifteen years, alcohol had kept her going. In 1972 she became addicted to heroin. Since Hairy Mary was so old, she was one of the very first people in Norway to be offered methadone.

"It's too late," Hairy Mary said, and hirpled off.

At the start of the seventies she had her first and last dealings with the social-welfare office. She needed money for food after starving for sixteen days. Only a few kroner; she was fainting all the time. It wasn't good for business. A humiliating ordeal of being sent from one social worker to another, which only ended up with an offer of three days' detox, ensured that she never set foot in a social-welfare office again. Even when she was granted disability benefit in 1992, everything was organized through the doctor. The physician was a decent guy, the same age as her, and had never let a single unkind word fall from his lips when she came to him with swollen knees and chilblains. There had also been the odd sexually transmitted disease down through the years, without his smile growing any less sincere each time she limped into his warm surgery on Schous plass. The disability benefit managed to cover house rent, electricity, and cable television. The money from street work went on drugs. Hairy Mary had never had a budget for food. When things became chaotic, she forgot about the bills. The debt collectors came to the door. She was never at home, and never protested. The door was sealed, her belongings removed. Finding a new place to live could be difficult. Then it was a hostel for one or two winters.

She was worn out now, completely worn out. The night was bitterly inclement. Hairy Mary was wearing a thigh-length pink skirt, laddered fishnet stockings, and a long silver-lamé jacket. She tried to wrap her clothes more snugly around herself, but that wasn't much help. She had to get inside somewhere. The City Mission's night shelter would be the best option after all. Admittedly, admission was refused to anyone under the influence, but Hairy Mary had been high on drugs for so many years that no one could tell whether she was clean or not.

She took a right turn beside police headquarters.

The park surrounding the curved building at Grønlandsleiret 44 was Hairy Mary's place of refuge. Conventional citizens gave it a wide berth. An occasional dark-skinned immigrant with wife and countless children sometimes sat there in the afternoons while the kids kicked a ball about and sniggered in terror at Hairy Mary's approach. The winos were the trustworthy sort. The cops didn't bother her, either; it was ages since they had stopped harassing an honest whore.

On this particular night, the park was deserted. Hairy Mary shuffled out from the beam of light shed by the lamp above the entrance gate to Oslo Prison. That night's honestly earned fix was in her pocket. She just had to find somewhere to shoot up. Her steps were on the north side of the police headquarters building. They were not illuminated and never used.

"Fuck! Bloody hell."

Someone had taken the steps.

That was where she planned to shoot up her fix. That was where she was going to sit and wait until the heroin had reached a proper balance in her body. The steps around the back of police headquarters, a short stone's throw from the prison wall, those were her steps. Someone had taken them.

"Hey! You!"

The man made no sign that he had heard her. She tottered closer. Her high heels ground into rotten leaves and dog shit. The man slept like a log.

The guy might be good-looking. It was difficult to say, even when she leaned over him. It was too dark. A huge knife was sticking out of his chest.

Hairy Mary was a practical creature. She stepped over the man, sat down on the top step, and fished out her syringe. The pleasant, warming feeling she craved hit her before she had got as far as withdrawing the needle.

The man was dead. Probably murdered. Hairy Mary had seen murder victims before, even if they had never been as expensively dressed as this one. Attacked, probably. Or maybe the guy was a faggot who had taken too great a liberty with one of those young boys who sold themselves for five times the price of a blow-job from Hairy Mary.

She stood up stiffly, swaying slightly. For a moment she studied the corpse. The man had a glove in his hand. Its partner lay to one side. Without any appreciable hesitation, Hairy Mary crouched down and appropriated the gloves for herself. They were too big, but were real leather with a wool lining. The guy had no more use for them. She pulled them on and began walking to catch the last bus to the night shelter. A scarf lay on the ground a few meters from the body. Hairy Mary had hit the jackpot tonight. She wound the scarf around her neck. Whether it was the new clothing or the heroin that helped, she had no idea. In any case, she did not feel quite so cold. Maybe she should even splash out on a taxi. And maybe she should call the police to let them know they had a dead body in their back garden.

All the same, the most important thing was to find herself a bed for the night. She didn't know what day it was, and she needed to sleep.

S anta Maria, Mother of Jesus.

The picture on the wall above the bed reminded her of one of her forgotten scraps from childhood. A pious face gazing down above hands folded in prayer. The halo around her head had long ago faded to a vague cloud of dust.

As Hanne Wilhelmsen opened her eyes, she realized that the soft features, narrow nose, and dark hair with severe middle parting had led her astray. She saw that now, though she did not understand why it had taken such a long time. It was Jesus himself who had watched over her every single night for nearly six months.

A ribbon of morning light fell across the shoulder of Santa Maria's son. Hanne sat up and her eyes squinted against the sunlight forcing its way through the gap in the curtains. Stroking the small of her back, she wondered why she was lying crosswise in the bed. She could not remember the last time an entire night had been lost in deep, undisturbed sleep.

The cold stone tiles on her feet made her gasp for breath. In the bathroom doorway she turned to study the picture again. Her gaze swept over the floor and came to a sudden halt.

The bathroom floor was blue. She had never noticed that. She put the knuckle of her index finger against one eye and stared down with the other.

Hanne Wilhelmsen had lived in this spartan room in Villa Monasteria since midsummer. It was now almost Christmas. The days had been drab, just as all other colors were absent in and around this huge stone building. Even in summer, the Valpolicella landscape outside the enormous window on the first floor had been monotonously free from true colors. The vines clung to golden-brown trunks and the grass beside the stone walls was scorched.

A chilly intimation of December struck her half an hour later when she opened the double doors leading out to Villa Monasteria's gravel courtyard. She ambled aimlessly across to the bamboo woods on the other side, maybe twenty meters away. Two nuns stood in animated conversation on the path that divided the grove in two. They dropped their voices as Hanne approached. When she passed the two older, gray-clad women, they bowed their heads in silence.

The bamboo on one side of the path was black. On the other side the stalks were green. The nuns were gone when Hanne turned around, perplexed about what had caused the inexplicable difference in color between the slender plants about the thickness of her thumb on either side of the path. Hanne had not heard the familiar shuffling across the gravel yard. She wondered fleetingly what had become of the nuns. Then she let her fingers brush over the bamboo stalks as she scurried up to the carp pond.

There was something going on. Something was about to happen.

In the beginning the nuns had been friendly. Not particularly talkative, of course: the Villa Monasteria was a place of contemplation and silence. Sometimes a brief smile, perhaps at mealtimes, a quizzical look above hands that gladly poured more wine into her glass, and an odd softly spoken word that Hanne could not understand. In August she had almost made up her mind to spend the time learning Italian. Then she had dismissed the idea. She wasn't here to learn anything.

Eventually the nuns had realized that Hanne preferred complete stillness. Even the astute manager. He accepted her money every three weeks, with no more than a simple *grazie*. The fun-loving students from Verona, who sometimes played records so loudly that the nuns came running within a few minutes, had spotted a kindred spirit in Hanne. But only in the beginning.

Hanne Wilhelmsen had spent six months being entirely alone.

She had in the main been left in peace to her daily battle not to bother about anything. Recently, nevertheless, she had been unable to divert her curiosity from the obvious fact that something was about to happen at Villa Monasteria. *Il direttore*, a slim, omnipresent man in his forties, raised his voice increasingly often to the nervously whispering nuns. His footsteps pounded harder than before on the stone floors. He dashed from one incomprehensible task to another, immaculately dressed and trailing a whiff of sweat and aftershave. The nuns were no longer smiling, and fewer of them assembled at meal-times. However, they sat increasingly often in silent prayer on the wooden benches in the small chapel dating from the thirteenth century, even when there was no Mass. Hanne could see them from the window as they padded, two by two, in and out through the heavy timber doors.

It was difficult to tell the depth of the carp pond. The water was unnaturally clear. The fishes' plump movements along the bottom seemed repellent, and Hanne felt a trace of nausea at the thought of them swimming around in the convent's drinking water.

She sat down on the wall surrounding the pond. Heavy oak trees, almost bare of leaves, were outlined against the wintry sky. A flock of sheep grazed on the northern hillside. A dog was barking in the far distance, and the sheep huddled more closely together.

Hanne yearned for home.

She had no reason to yearn for home. All the same, something had happened. She didn't know what; nor did she know why. It was as if her senses, blunted through a conscious process over several months, were no longer lurking in enforced hibernation. She had started to notice things.

Six months had passed since Cecilie Vibe died. Hanne had not even attended the funeral of her partner of almost twenty years. Instead she had shut herself into their apartment, numbly registering that everyone had left her in peace. No one rang the doorbell. No one had attempted to come in. The phone was silent. Only junk mail and bills in the mailbox. And eventually a settlement from an insurance company. Hanne had had no idea about the policy Cecilie had taken out years before. She had phoned the company, got the money paid into a high-interest account, written a letter to the Chief of Police, and applied for leave of absence for the rest of the year. Alternatively, the letter could be considered her resignation.

She had not waited for an answer and instead simply packed a bag and boarded the train, heading for Copenhagen. Strictly speaking, she did not know whether she still had a job. It was of no concern to her, at least not then. She had no inkling where she was going or how long she would be away. After a fortnight of traveling haphazardly through Europe she had stumbled across the Villa Monasteria, a run-down convent hotel in the hills north of Verona. The nuns could offer her tranquility and home-made wine. She signed in late one evening in July, intending to move on the following day.

There were prawns in the pond. Small ones, admittedly, but prawns all the same: transparent and darting by fits and starts in flight from the indolent carp. Hanne Wilhelmsen had never heard of freshwater prawns. Sniffing, she wiped her nose with the sleeve of her jacket and let her eyes follow *il direttore*'s car along the avenue. Four women dressed in gray stood under a poplar tree gazing up at her. Despite the distance, she could feel their eyes on her face, sharp as knives in the drizzly air. When the manager's car disappeared out on to the highway, the nuns wheeled around abruptly and bustled toward the Villa Monasteria without a backward glance. Hanne got up from the wall. She felt cold and rested. A huge raven, flying in oval circuits below the low-lying clouds, made her shiver.

It was time to go home.

3

Housing one of Norway's three major publishing companies, the anonymous building was nonetheless modestly tucked away in a back street in the city's most unprepossessing district. The offices were small and uniform. No history of the publishing house decorated the walls, and no dark furniture or plush carpets graced the interior. Along the glass walls dividing the office cells from the endless corridors hung newspaper clippings and posters, evidence of a memory that only extended a few years back in time.

The conference room in the Literature Section, reminiscent of a lunch room in a social-welfare office, was situated on the second floor. The table was pale veneer and ordinary office standard, and the orange upholstery on the chairs belonged more to the seventies. The publishing company was Norway's oldest, founded in 1829. This publishing company *had* history. Serious literary history. The books on the cheap IKEA shelves lining one wall, however, looked more like mass-market paperback novels. A random selection of that autumn's publications was displayed with front covers facing out; they looked as if they might topple at any minute and clatter to the primrose-yellow linoleum floor.

Idun Franck stared absent-mindedly at Ambjørnsen's most recent bestseller in the *Elling* series. Someone had turned it upside-down and the dust-jacket was torn.

"Idun?"

The Senior Publishing Manager raised his voice. The five others in attendance sat with expressionless faces turned to Idun Franck.

"Sorry—"

She leafed distractedly through her papers and picked up a ballpoint pen.

"The question is not really how much this project has cost us to date, but whether the book can actually be published at all. There has to be an ethical consideration of ... Can we publish a cookery book when the chef who wrote it has been stabbed to death with a butcher's knife?"

The others seemed unsure whether Idun Franck was joking. One of them gave a slight smirk, before swiftly smothering it and staring at the table top as a red flush spread over his face.

"Well, we don't know whether it was a butcher's knife," Idun Franck added. "But he certainly was stabbed. According to the newspapers. In any case, it would be considered rather tasteless to follow up a gory murder by publishing an account of the victim and his kitchen."

"And we don't want to be tasteless. We are, after all, talking about a cookery book," Frederik Krøger said, baring his teeth.

"Honestly," muttered Samir Zeta, a dark-skinned young man who had started in the Information Department three weeks earlier.

Krøger, the stocky Senior Publishing Manager, who tried to hide his bald pate under an awe-inspiring comb-over, made an apologetic gesture with his right hand.

"If we can go back and examine the actual concept for a moment," Idun Franck continued on her own initiative. "We were definitely on the track of something. A further development of the trend in cookery books, so to speak. A sort of culinary biography. A mixture of cookery book and personal portrait. Since Brede Ziegler has for several years been the best—"

"At least the most prominent," Samir Zeta interjected.

"... the most prominent Norwegian chef, he was a natural

choice for a project such as this. And we had come quite a long way with it."

"How far?"

Idun Franck was well aware what Frederik Krøger was querying. He wanted to know how much the whole thing had cost. How much money the publishing house had thrown out the window on a project that, in the best-case scenario, would have to be put on ice for some considerable time.

"Most of the photographs are done and dusted. Also the recipes. However, there's an appreciable amount of work to be undertaken with respect to Brede Ziegler's life and personality. He insisted on concentrating first on the food, and then we were to follow up with anecdotes and reflections on his life connected with each individual dish. Of course, we've chatted a great deal, and I have … notes, a couple of tapes, and suchlike. But … the way I see it today … Can you pass me the pot?"

She tried to pour coffee into a cup without a handle, decorated with the Teletubbies. Her hand was shaking, or perhaps the thermos coffee-pot was too heavy. Coffee spilled across the surface of the table. Someone handed her a blank sheet of paper. When she placed it over the spillage, the brown liquid seeped out along the edges and ran across the table, dripping on to her trousers.

"As I was saying … We could of course make use of what we have for a straightforward cookery book. One among many. The pictures are good, for that matter. The recipes are fabulous. But is that what we wanted? My answer would be—"

"No," Samir Zeta said, feeling too warm in his sweater.

Frederik Krøger pinched the bridge of his nose and hiccuped.

"I'd like you to put that down on paper, Idun. When I … With figures and all that. We'll take it from there. Okay?"

No one waited for an answer. Chair legs scraped across the

floor as they all scuttled out of the conference room. Only Idun
was left sitting there, her eyes fixed on a black-and-white photograph of a cod's head.

"Saw you at the cinema yesterday," she heard and looked up.

"What?"

Samir Zeta smiled and ran his palm over the door frame.

"You were busy. What did you think?"

"Think?"

"About the movie! *Shakespeare in Love!*"

Idun lifted the cup to her mouth and swallowed.

"Oh. The film. Excellent."

"A bit too theatrical for my liking. Movies should be movies,
in a sense. Even if the actors are wearing costumes from the six-
teenth century, they don't need to talk like that, do they?'

Putting down her Teletubbies cup, Idun Franck rose and
tried, to no avail, to wipe a dark stain from her trouser leg. Then
she looked up, smiling faintly as she collected her papers and
photographs, paying no heed to the spilled coffee that had stuck
two large color photographs of fennel and spring onions together.

"Actually I really liked the film," she said. "It was ... warm.
Tender. Colorful."

"Romantic," Samir said, grinning. "You're an absolutely hope-
less romantic, Idun."

"Far from it," Idun Franck said, closing the door softly behind
her. "But at my age that would be permissible anyway."

4

Billy T. was fascinated. He held the glass up to the light and studied a ruby-colored spot wedged inside pink pack-ice. Russian Slush was most certainly not the best drink he had tasted. But it looked beautiful. He twisted the glass toward the chandelier on the ceiling and had to screw up his eyes.

"Sorry—"

Billy T. held his hand out to a waiter in blue trousers and immaculate collarless white shirt.

"What is this, in actual fact?"

"Russian Slush?"

One corner of the waiter's mouth tugged almost imperceptibly, as if he didn't quite dare to smile.

"Crushed ice, vodka, and cranberries, sir."

"Oh, I see. Thank you."

Billy T. drank, though strictly speaking he might be said to be on duty. He had no intention of presenting the bill to the Finance Section; it was seven o'clock on a Monday evening, December 6 to be precise, and he could not care less. He sat on his own, fingering his glass as he scanned the room.

Entré was the city's new, undisputed "in" place.

Billy T. had been born and raised in Grünerløkka. In a two-room apartment in Fossveien his mother had kept him and his sister, elder by three years, in line while she worked her fingers to the bone in a laundry farther up the street and spent her nights mending clothes for extra payment. Billy T. had never met his father. It was still unclear to him whether the guy had done a runner or his mother had turned him out before their son had arrived into the world. Anyway, his father was never mentioned. All Billy T. knew about the man was that he had been six foot six in his stocking soles, a womanizer of the first order, and an out-and-out alcoholic into the bargain. Which had in all likelihood led to an extremely premature death. Somewhere far back in his memory, Billy T. had gained an impression that his mother had one day come home surprisingly early from work. He could only have been about seven years old and kept off school because of a bad cold.

"He's dead," his mother had said. "You know who."

Her eyes forbade him from asking. He had gone to bed and had not got up again until the following day.

There was only one picture of his father in the apartment in Fossveien, a wedding photograph of his parents that had, surprisingly enough, been allowed to remain on display. Billy T. suspected that his mother used it to prove that her children had been born in wedlock, if anyone should be impudent enough to assume any different. If a stranger were to set foot inside the front door of their overcrowded apartment, the wedding photograph was the first thing they spotted. Until the day when Billy T. had come home in his stiff uniform, having passed his exams at what was then called police college. He had sprinted all the way. Beads of sweat hung from the synthetic fibers of his clothing. His mother refused to let him go. Her skinny arms were locked around her son's neck. His sister sat laughing in the living room as she opened a cheap bottle of sparkling wine. She had become a fully qualified nurse two years earlier. The wedding photograph had disappeared that same day.

Billy T. had not acquired a taste for alcohol until he reached the age of thirty.

Now he was over forty, and weeks could still pass between the occasions when he drank anything other than cola or milk.

His mother still lived in Fossveien. His sister had moved to Asker with her husband and eventually three children, but Billy T. had remained in Løkka. He had experienced all the ups and downs of the district since the start of the sixties. He had grown up with an outside toilet, and been at home on the day when his mother, tearful and proud, had run her fingers over their newly installed WC in what had until then been a closet. He had seen the urban regeneration program break the back of one housing cooperative after another during the eighties, and had lived through trends and fashions that came and went like birds of passage in Cuba.

Billy T.'s love for Grünerløkka was anything but trendy. He was not someone who had only recently fallen in love with Thorvald Meyers gate's tiny, jam-packed bars and cafés. Billy T. lived outside the Løkka community that had formed in the course of the past four or five years. It made him feel old. He had never been in Sult waiting an hour at the bar for a table. At Bar Boca, where he had once ventured for a glass of cola, his eyes had stung after only a few minutes of claustrophobic posturing at the bar counter. Instead, Billy T. took his youngsters to the McDonald's across the street. The world outside his windows had become something that did not impinge on him at all.

Billy T.'s love for Grünerløkka was connected with the buildings. With the houses, purely and simply, the old workers' apartment blocks. Below Grüners gate, they were built on clay soil and had unexpected cracks in the middle of their façades. As a little boy, he had thought that the houses had wrinkles because they were so old. He loved the streets, especially the short and narrow ones. Bergverksgata was only a few meters long and came to an end at the slope down to the Akerselva river. The current can take you away, he remembered; you mustn't venture into the water, the current might take you away! His body turned red with eczema every summer. His mother complained and scolded and smeared liniment on his back with furious hands. The boy jumped into the polluted water just the same the very next day. Summer after summer. It was a holiday as good as any.

Entré was located on the south-west corner of the intersection between Thorvald Meyers gate and Sofienberggata. A department store full of old-fashioned women's clothes that never sold had resisted the forcible modernization of Løkka for years. However, big business had won out in the end.

He was sitting on his own at a table just beside the door. The restaurant was crammed, despite it being a Monday. The make-shift sign on the door had been written with a marker pen that had scored through the paper. Billy T. could read the reversed lettering from where he was seated:

THE RESTAURANT'S OWNER AND CHEF, BREDE
ZIEGLER, HAS PASSED AWAY. IN MEMORY OF
HIS LIFE AND WORK, ENTRÉ WILL REMAIN
OPEN THIS EVENING.

"Fuck!" Billy T. said, gulping down an ice cube.

He should not be sitting here. He should be at home. At the very least, Tone-Marit should have accompanied him if he was going to eat in a restaurant for once. They hadn't been out together since Jenny was born. That was almost nine months ago now.

A molar was causing him extreme pain. Billy T. spat the ice cube out into his half-clenched fist and tried to drop it unnoticed on the floor.

"Anything wrong?"

The waiter bowed slightly as he placed a glass of Chablis on the tablecloth in front of him.

"No. Everything's fine. You ... you're staying open today. Don't you think many people will feel that's ... disrespectful, in a way?"

"The show must go on. It's what Brede would have wanted."

The plate that had just landed in front of Billy T. looked like an art installation. He stared in bewilderment at the food, lifting his knife and fork, but had no idea where to begin.

"Duck liver on a bed of forest mushrooms, with asparagus and a hint of cherry," the waiter clarified. "*Bon appetit!*"

The asparagus was arranged above the liver like an American Indian tepee.

"Food in a prison," Billy T. murmured. "And where the hell is the hint?"

A solitary cherry sat in splendor at the edge of his plate. Billy T. pushed it in and sighed in relief when the asparagus tent collapsed. Hesitantly, he cut a slice of liver.

Only now did he catch sight of the table beside the massive staircase leading up to the first floor. An enormous picture of Brede Ziegler was displayed on an immaculate white tablecloth flanked by two silver candlesticks, a black silk ribbon draped across one corner. A woman with an upswept hairdo approached the table. She picked up a pen and wrote a few words in a book. Then she held her hand to her forehead, as if about to burst into tears.

"You'd think the guy was a royal," Billy T. muttered. "He hadn't done anything to deserve a bloody book of condolence!"

Brede Ziegler had looked anything but regal when the police had found him. Someone had phoned the switchboard and slurred that they ought to check their back steps. Two trainee police officers had gone to the bother of following that exhortation. Immediately afterwards, one of them had come running, out of breath, back to the duty officer.

"He's dead! There *is* a guy there! Dead as a—"

The trainee had stopped at the sight of Billy T., who quite by chance had popped into the duty office to collect some papers, bare-legged and wearing only a singlet and shorts.

"Doornail," he had finished the sentence for the young man in uniform. "Dead as a doornail. I've been exercising, you know. No need to stare like that."

That had been eighteen hours ago. Billy T. had gone straight home without waiting to find out anything further about the dead man. He had taken a shower, slept for nine hours, and arrived at work one hour late on Monday morning in the forlorn hope that the case would end up on some other chief inspector's desk.

"Great minds think alike."

Billy T. looked up, at the same time struggling to swallow an asparagus spear that could never have been anywhere near boiling water. Severin Heger pointed at the chair beside Billy T. and raised his eyebrows. Without waiting for a response, he plumped himself down and stared skeptically at the plate.

"What's that?"

"Sit on the other side," Billy T. spluttered.

"Why's that? I'm fine here."

"Bloody hell. Move yourself! It looks as if we're—"

"Boyfriends! You've never been homophobic, Billy T. Take it easy, won't you."

"*Move yourself!*"

Severin Heger laughed and lifted his rear end slowly off the seat. Then he hesitated for a second before sitting down again. As Billy T. brandished his fork, something stuck in his throat.

"Just joking," Severin Heger said and got to his feet again.

"What are you doing here?" Billy T. asked, once his throat was clear and Severin was safely seated on the opposite side of the table.

"The same as you, I assume. Thought it would be a good idea to get an impression of the place. Karianne has interviewed a whole load of these people today ..."

He used his thumb to point vaguely over his shoulder, as if the staff were lined up behind him.

"… but it's helpful to take a look at the place. Check out the ambience, in a manner of speaking. What's that you're eating?"

The food had been reduced to a shapeless jumble of brown and green.

"Duck liver. What do you think?"

"Yuk."

"I don't mean the food. The place!"

Severin Heger rapidly surveyed the room. It was as though his many years in the Police Security Service had enabled him to look around without anyone even noticing that his gaze had shifted. He held his head absolutely still and half-closed his eyes. Only an almost invisible vibration of his eyelashes betrayed that his eyeballs were actually moving.

"Strange place. Fancy. Hip. Trendy and almost old-fashioned sophistication at the same time. Not my cup of tea. I had to flash my police badge even to get through the door. Rumor has it there's a waiting time of several weeks to book a table here at weekends."

"Honestly. This food is awful."

"You're not supposed to mash it all up into a mush, either, you know."

Billy T. pushed his plate away and took a gulp of white wine from the huge glass with a splash of liquid at the bottom.

"What can I say?" he murmured. "Who could be interested in killing this Brede Ziegler?"

"Aha! Numerous candidates. Just look at the guy! He's … Brede Ziegler was forty-seven and a social climber all his life. In the first place he had an amazing favorite hobby: picking fights with everything and everyone in the Norwegian culinary milieu. Secondly, he's achieved great success in everything he has—"

"Do we actually know that?"

"... both economically and professionally. This place here ..."

Now they both had a good look around.

The Entré restaurant represented the fashion pendulum's swing back from the minimalist functionalism that had dominated the business in recent years. The tablecloths were voluminous, white, and swept the floor. The candlesticks were silver. The tables were placed asymmetrically in the room, some of them on small podiums ten or fifteen centimeters above the rest. From the first floor a staircase flowed down, reminiscent of something from a Fitzgerald novel. The interior architect had understood that nothing should block the massive sweep of old, ornamental timber, and had created a wide corridor of open floor space all the way to the entrance. Four crystal chandeliers of varying size were suspended from the ceiling. Billy T. fidgeted with a rainbow-hued reflection of light shimmering on the tablecloth in front of him.

"... was a success from day one. The food, the interior, the ambience ... Have you not read the reviews?"

"The wife," Billy T. said wearily. "Has anyone spoken to his wife?"

"Farris mineral water, please. Blue. No ice cubes."

Severin Heger nodded to a waiter.

"She's in Hamar. Went to her mother's before any of us had managed to talk to her properly. The clergyman arrived, the girl cried, and an hour later she was on the train. It's understandable to some extent that she might need some motherly comfort. She's only twenty-five."

"Twenty-four," Billy T. corrected him, polishing off the last of the wine in his glass. "Vilde Veierland Ziegler is only twenty-four years old."

"Which means that our friend Brede was pretty well exactly ... twice as old as his wife."

"Almost."

The waiter, who had just removed the catastrophic remains of the first course, made a fresh attempt. The plate was bigger this time, but the food was equally impregnable. Islands of mashed potato were arranged into a defensive fort around a piece of Dover sole decorated with thin strips of something that had to be carrot and something indefinably green.

"It looks like a fucking game of Pick-Up Sticks," Billy T. said despondently. "How on earth do people *eat* food like this? What the hell is wrong with steak and French fries?"

"I can eat it then," Severin offered. "Thanks."

The waiter deposited a glass of Farris with a sprig of mint hanging on the rim in front of him and vanished.

"No, you bloody won't. That dish cost *three hundred kroner*! What are these green streaks in the sauce? Confectioner's coloring?"

"Pesto, I think. Go ahead and try it. They had only been married for six or seven months."

"I know. Do we know anything about his assets, inheritance, will, and so on? Does everything go to his wife?"

Severin Heger's gaze shifted to a couple in their forties who had lingered for some time at the condolence book. The man was wearing a tuxedo, the woman an eggshell-colored dress that would have been more appropriate at another season. Her skin looked dull and pale against the heavy silk fabric. When she turned around, Severin could see that she was weeping. He looked away when their eyes met.

"You haven't ordered *red wine* with the sole?"

The waiter poured another glass without blinking.

"My sister says you can drink red wine with white fish," Billy T. said stubbornly and took a demonstratively large swig.

"Cod, yes! Halibut, maybe ... But Dover sole? It's up to you. And no, we know next to nothing about money and suchlike.

Karianne and Karl are working their socks off. We'll know a lot more tomorrow."

"Do you know that his real name is Freddy Johansen?" Billy T. said with a grin.

"Who?"

"Brede Ziegler. He was damn well called Freddy Johansen until he was grown-up. What a show-off. Pathetic. Changing your name – honestly. Especially for a man—"

"And you say that, though you dropped your own surname twenty years ago!"

"That's different. Completely different. This is tasty, in fact."

"It looks good. Wipe your chin."

Billy T. unfolded the stiff linen napkin and rubbed his jaw.

"I spoke to Forensics this afternoon. Ziegler was very unlucky. That knife wound—"

He raised his own knife and directed the blade at his chest.

"It struck here approximately. If it had gone in just a couple of centimeters farther to the right, then Ziegler would still be alive."

"Oh, shit."

"You can well say that."

"Did they know anything more? Force – I mean, above and down, the other way around, left-handed murderer, small man, strong man. Woman? That sort of thing."

"Nothing at all. They're not clairvoyant, either, you know. But *something* more will be forthcoming. Eventually. Aren't you going to eat at all?"

"I've eaten. But you … My goodness, there's Wenche Foss!"

Severin Heger spoke in a whisper and tried to avert his eyes.

"Well, then," Billy T. said. "She is allowed to go out, you know. What did you mean when you said that everyone and his aunt could have had a motive for killing Brede Ziegler? Apart from that the guy had a career, I mean."

"I thought she only went to the Theater Café."

"Hel-lo."

"Sorry. I've spoken to Karianne—"

Severin tried to keep his eyes fixed on Billy T.

"And got some kind of summary of the witness statements up till now. Although we're used to everybody jabbering away about 'oh, so shocking' and 'no, I can't think of anyone who would want to kill the man' and … This case is entirely different. The witnesses seem shaken, of course, and that sort of thing, but all the same, they are … Not exactly shocked. Not the way we're used to. They all have thoughts about who might have done it. They speculate indiscriminately without batting an eyelid."

"That could have more to do with the witnesses themselves than our homicide victim. Many of the people who surround a guy like Ziegler are attention-seekers. They just want to make themselves seem interesting."

The First Lady of the National Theater had positioned herself at the condolence book, together with a young curly-mopped actor.

"Is it permissible to read what people write in that book over there, do you think?" Severin Heger asked.

"No. For fuck's sake, you've become fixated on celebrities! Get a grip."

"We should've had Hanne Wilhelmsen here," Severin Heger said all of a sudden as he straightened his back. "This case is just up her street."

Billy T. laid down his cutlery, clenched his fists, and smacked them down on the table on either side of his plate.

"She's not here," he said slowly without looking Severin in the eye. "She's not coming, either. There's you, me, Karianne, and Karl, as well as five or six other investigators if it turns out we need them. We don't need Hanne Wilhelmsen."

"Okay, then. I was just trying to make conversation."

"Fine," Billy T. said, sounding exhausted. "The syringe. Have you found out anything else about that?"

"No. It was lying right beside the body, and looked as if it had just been dropped there. It doesn't need to have anything to do with the murder. Or have you heard anything different from Forensics?"

"No."

The dessert was microscopic and devoured in thirty seconds flat. Billy T. waved for the bill.

"We're leaving," he said as he paid in cash. "This place isn't for the likes of us."

He came to a sudden halt at the exit door.

"Suzanne," he said softly. "Suzanne, is it you?"

Severin Heger stopped as well, his eyes appraising the woman. Tall, slim bordering on morbidly skinny, she was dramatically dressed in a blue-and-black outfit. Her face was pale and narrow, and her hair drawn back from her forehead. She looked as if she wanted to offer Billy T. her hand, but changed her mind and instead gave a perfunctory nod of her head.

"B.T.," she said quietly. "Long time no see."

"Yes, I ... What are you doing ...? Lovely to see you."

"Could you please decide whether you're coming or going?" the head waiter, a strange-looking man with an over-large head, said with a smile. "You're blocking the door standing there."

"I'm coming in," the woman said.

"I'm going out," Billy T. added.

"Hello," Severin Heger said.

"Perhaps we'll bump into each other another time," the woman said, disappearing into the restaurant.

The December night was unusually mild. Billy T. turned his face up to the black sky.

"You look as if you've seen a ghost," Severin Heger said. "Someone who's allowed to call you B.T., eh!"

Billy T. did not answer.

He had more than enough to contend with, struggling to keep his body calm. He held his breath to avoid gasping. Suddenly he broke into a run.

"Bye, then," Severin shouted. "See you tomorrow morning."

Billy T. was already too far away to hear.

Neither of the two police officers had noticed a young man peering into the restaurant through the window that overlooked Sofienberggata. He was holding his hands like a funnel around his eyes and had been loitering there for some time.

Severin Heger had turned his back on Billy T. and started to walk east. If he had taken the opposite direction, an automatic reflex might have made him talk to the boy.

At least he would have, if he had seen the young man's face.

* * *

Interview with witness Sebastian Kvie, edited extract

Interviewed by police officer Silje Sørensen. Transcript typed by office colleague Rita Lyngåsen. There are in total two tapes of this interview. The interview was recorded on tape on Tuesday December 7, 1999 at Oslo police headquarters.

Witness:

Kvie, Sebastian, ID number 161179 48062
Address: Herslebsgate 4, 0561 Oslo
Employment: Entré Restaurant, Oslo
Given information about witness rights and responsibilities. Willing to provide a statement.
The witness was informed that the interview would be taped, and a transcript produced later.

Interviewer:

Can you first of all tell us something about what you do? About what connection you have with the deceased and that sort of thing? *(Coughing, some unclear speech.)*

Witness:

I've worked at Entré since it opened. That was on March 1 this year. *(Paper rustling, mumbling in the background.)* I qualified in catering at Sogn High School in the spring of '98. I worked for a few months at the Hotel Continental immediately afterwards. Then I was traveling in Latin America for a while. Nine weeks, in fact. Brede Ziegler said that he'd heard about me from others, and wanted me for Entré. It goes without saying that I fucking wanted the job. I was really happy that a guy like him had heard about me as well. The pay is shit-awful, but it always is when you haven't yet made a name for yourself.

Interviewer:

How ... did you like it?

Witness:

Basically, I've worked non-stop since I started. For instance, I didn't get a summer holiday this year. I'm meant to be off every Monday and every second Wednesday. But that's only in principle. But what the fuck – I really enjoy it. Entré is the most exciting kitchen in the city right now. Both because ... I mean ... *(Unclear speech.)* Although I really only have to do what I'm asked, I learn a huge fucking amount. The head chef is very efficient, and quick to praise those of us who put in a bit of extra effort. Actually, all of us do that on the whole. Brede isn't scared to lend a hand, either. He's worked in the kitchen himself, five or six times at least. That's bloody brilliant, when you think about all the other things he has to attend to. I mean, he fucking owns the whole place. Most of it, anyway. That's the impression I've got, at any rate. I've heard that he owns a lot of other stuff too, but I'm not really sure what.

Interviewer:

I don't like to be prudish, but it would help matters a great deal if you didn't swear so much. This interview is going to be written down word for word from the tape recording. It actually looks pretty stupid in print.

Witness:

Oh yes. Sorry. I'll be more careful.

Interviewer:

Did you know Brede Ziegler well?

Witness:

Well ... well? He was my boss, of course. Chatted to me quite often, at work, I mean. But know him ... *(Longish pause.)* He was older than me, you see. Much older. So we weren't exactly friends. I can't really say. It wasn't as if we would go for a beer or to a football match together. *(Laughter.)* No. Not like that.

Interviewer:

Do you know who the deceased was actually friends with?

Witness:

Everybody! *You name 'em! (Loud laughter.)* There were loads of celebrities around Brede. They attached themselves to the guy. There was something about ... Of course, I was quite shocked when I heard that Brede had been murdered. But he was really pretty controversial, you know. In the trade, I mean. He was so fucking ... so damn successful! *(Feeble laughter.)* Apologies. Won't swear. Sorry. *(Pause.)* Brede was the very best, you know. There must have been an incredible number of people who were jealous. It was as if everything he touched turned to gold. And loads of people out there are quite petty, you know. In our trade there's a lot of jealousy. More than most, anyway. At least that's my experience of it.

Interviewer:

Do I interpret you correctly if I say that it seems as if you ... admired Brede Ziegler? Almost a bit star-struck?

Witness:

(Soft laughter, changing to coughing.) I read an article about Brede Ziegler in one of my mother's weekly magazines when I was eleven. He's kind of always been my hero, I guess. My greatest wish is to be like he was. Hugely accomplished and generous with it. For instance, I've heard he was thinking of giving each of us our own Masahiro knife for Christmas. With our name on it and all that. Sort of engraved on the handle, you know. Maybe it was only rumor, but I've heard that anyway. It would be just like Brede. *(Lengthy pause, paper rustling.)* He always remembered names. Even the people who come and go in the dishwashing section, he talked to them as if he knew them well. I will say that Brede Ziegler had great insight into people. And he was the best chef in Norway. Without a doubt, if you ask me.

Interviewer:

Did you know the deceased's wife?

Witness:

I met her only once. I think, anyway. She's called Vilde or Vibeke, or something like that. Much younger than Brede. Pretty. She popped in once a couple of months ago to pick him up. Didn't get any particular impression of her. I've no idea if she's in the habit of eating at Entré, since I'm in the kitchen all evening, and it's rare for me to get time to peek out into the restaurant. That day she came to collect Brede, we weren't open yet. I was standing talking to Claudio, the head waiter. She didn't say hello to us. Maybe seemed a bit high-and-mighty. Maybe she was just in a hurry.

Interviewer:

Have you—

Witness *(interrupts)*:

You really shouldn't ever listen to rumors. But I've heard that Brede snatched the girlfriend from a boy who's not so very much older than me. Twenty-five or -six, maybe. I don't know the guy, but he's called Sindre something-or-other and works at the Stadtholdergaarden. Smart guy, I've heard. But that's just rumor, you know.

Interviewer:

What do you think, then? *(Pause, sound of chair scraping, somebody entering the room, sounds of something being poured into a glass.)*

Witness:

About what?

Interviewer:

About this whole business.

Witness:

I've no idea who killed Brede. But if I were to take a guess, it's most likely that it has something to do with jealousy. Crazy, of course, totally crazy to kill someone just because you don't like them being successful at this or that, but that's what I believe anyway. As for myself, I was in the kitchen at Entré on Sunday evening. I arrived between two and three o'clock in the afternoon, and didn't go home until after two that night. I was with other people the entire time, apart from the three or four times I had to go for a pee.

Interviewer's note: The witness gave a good, coherent statement. The witness was provided with coffee and water during the interview.

5

"*Stazione termini. Il treno per Milano.*"

The manager had followed her to the taxi that was waiting outside the gate beside the dry-stone wall. He chided the driver and expressed concern about Hanne Wilhelmsen's sudden departure.

"*Signora*, why can't you wait – very good flight from Verona tomorrow!"

But Hanne couldn't wait. There was a plane to Gardermoen from Milan that same day. The train from Verona to Milan took less than two hours. One hundred and twenty minutes closer to home.

At passport control she felt faint. Perhaps it was her travel jacket. It had belonged to Cecilie. Like a vague memory, she caught a scent she had thought gone. Leaning against the counter, she waved on the people behind her.

The apartment.

Cecilie's things.

Cecilie's grave – she didn't even know where it was.

An official handed her passport back. She could not summon the energy to take it. Her arm would not rise. Her elbow on the counter was aching. She counted to twenty, pulled herself together, snatched the burgundy-red booklet, and legged it. Out of the queue, out of the airport terminal, off the road leading to home.

Hanne Wilhelmsen was back in Verona. She had followed her very first impulse. From Verona there would be a flight to Oslo via Munich the next day.

She had hardly seen anything of the city. She had confined herself to the Villa Monasteria and the hills around the old convent since she had arrived in July. To begin with, the students had tried to entice her to Verona at weekends; it took less than fifteen minutes by car. Hanne had never succumbed.

The long series of days from brownish-yellow summer to wet December had assuaged some of the pain that had paralyzed her the night Cecilie had died. In a way, Hanne had moved on. All the same, she needed more time. Just twenty-four hours. In twenty-four hours she would board the flight to Norway.

She would go home to the apartment with all Cecilie's more or less half-completed renovation projects. Hanne would go home to Cecilie's clothes that still lay neatly folded and sorted in one half of the wardrobe in their bedroom, beside Hanne's unsystematic chaos of trousers and sweaters.

She would search out Cecilie's grave.

Hanne stood in Piazza Bra in Verona, struggling to shut her ears to the clamor of the city. When she reluctantly listened, it was composed only of voices. The city traffic was shut off from the extensive square. The shouts ricocheted off the ancient marble walls surrounding the Arena di Verona in the center of the city and reverberated back across all the market stalls, at which hundreds of vendors sold sausages and crockery, car vacuum cleaners and gaudy finery *per la donna*.

Her rucksack chafed her shoulder. She wandered aimlessly, away from the teeming crowds of humanity, into the shade; a side street. She had to find a hotel. A place where she could leave her luggage, spend the night and prepare herself for the long journey home. She wasn't sure whether it had already started.

6

The morning meeting should have commenced twelve minutes ago. Billy T. had not yet shown his face. Karianne Holbeck had fixed her gaze on a hook screwed into the ceiling just above the door, trying to avoid looking at the clock. Sergeant Karl Sommarøy had pulled out a Swiss knife and was gently whittling the bowl of a pipe.

"Far too big," he explained to whoever was interested. "Doesn't sit well in my hand."

"Do you use studded or unstudded tires?"

"Eh?"

Glancing up, Karl Sommarøy brushed some shavings from his trousers.

"I'm not giving up studded tires, anyway," Severin Heger commented. "I'm going to pay the fucking fine for as long as that's allowed. Yesterday morning, for instance, when I was going out—"

"Good morning, folks."

Billy T. crashed through the door and slammed a ring binder down on the desk.

"Coffee."

"Say the magic word," Severin commanded.

"Coffee, for fuck's sake!"

"Okay, okay. Here you are! You can have mine. I haven't touched it."

Billy T. raised the cup halfway to his mouth, but put it down again with a grimace.

"Let's summarize what we have, and then divide up the assignments for the next forty-eight hours. Something like that. Severin. You go first."

Severin Heger had traipsed around on the very top floors of police headquarters for years on end. He had enjoyed working for the Security Service. It was exciting, varied, and gave him a sense of importance. An exhausting period of scandals and carpet-bombing from a unified Norwegian press corps had not eradicated his enthusiasm for the job that he had aspired to ever since he had been old enough to understand what his father did for a living. Severin Heger enjoyed the work, but nevertheless always felt scared.

At the age of eighteen he had reluctantly reconciled himself to the idea that he was gay. It would not prevent him from reaching the goals he had set for himself. On his twentieth birthday – after a puberty filled with competitive sports, soccer, and incessant wanking – he decided never to tell anyone, never to show anything that might betray what would cause his father to kill himself, if he ever got to hear. His father had sailed with Shetlands Larsen during the war, and had been highly decorated for his efforts for his homeland. In the fifties and sixties he had worked for the Police Security Service. That was when Communists lurked in every trade union, and the Cold War was truly icebound. Severin was an only child and a daddy's boy, and only once did the façade crack, when he had attempted to chat up Billy T. He was solicitously rejected, and since then Billy T. had never uttered a single word about the episode.

The Head of Security Services had been forced to resign in the wake of the Furre scandal, when Berge Furre, a respected historian and former Socialist Left politician, was himself investigated by the Security Service while serving on the Lund Commission, set up to look into the activities of the self-same Security Service.

This resulted in the appointment of the first female boss of the Police Security Service, though her tenure proved short-lived. Before she left, though, she had managed to summon Severin Heger to her office and declare: "It's not a security risk that you're gay, Severin. What's suspicious is that you put so much energy into hiding the fact. Give in. Look around you. We're approaching a new millennium."

Severin recalled that he had stood up without giving an answer. Then he had gone home, slept for a long time, got up, taken a shower, and, smelling sweet, had paid a visit to the gay club Castro that same evening. After spending a night making up for lost time, he requested a transfer to the Crime Section. His father had died two years earlier. Severin Heger finally felt liberated.

"All we know for certain are the following—"

He tapped his fingers one by one on the edge of the table.

"The body is Brede Ziegler. Born 1953. Recently married. Childless. When he was killed, he had a wallet with more than sixteen thousand kroner in banknotes on his person. Sixteen thousand, four hundred and eighty-two kroner and fifty øre, to be painfully precise."

"Sixteen thous—"

"Plus four credit cards. No less. AmEx, VISA, Diners and MasterCard. Gold and silver and platinum, and God knows what."

"That sends the robbery motive up in smoke," Karianne murmured.

"Not necessarily."

Severin Heger adjusted his glasses.

"The thief might have been surprised by passers-by before he got hold of the loot, so to speak. But *if* it was a thief, he chose a strange murder weapon. A Masahiro 210."

"A what?"

Karianne swallowed the sugar cube she had been sucking.

"So he was really stabbed to death? A Massa-what?"

"Masahiro 210. A knife. An expensive, beautiful knife. It should really have been listed in the weapons register. A particularly dangerous kitchen implement."

"That was what the kitchen boy was talking about," Silje Sørensen said eagerly. "They were each to get one at Christmas or something!"

Billy T. gave Karianne a vexed look.

"If you can't be bothered coming to the meetings, but are instead more preoccupied with interviewing peripheral witnesses, then for God's sake you'd better find out exactly what was said."

"But … it was actually *you* who turned up late—"

"Cut it out. We discovered that yesterday."

He forced out a smile. Karianne chose to interpret it as some kind of apology, but did not relinquish eye contact until he averted his eyes and pressed on: "By yesterday morning, a message was relayed from Forensics informing us that it said 'Masahiro 210' on the knife blade. We should have had that information right away. Sunday night. As soon as they pulled the knife out of his ribcage. Maybe sometime in the next thousand years we'll manage to get those bloody medics to understand that they need to communicate with us."

"You were fast asleep then," Karianne muttered, barely audible.

Severin Heger stood up and flung out his arms dramatically.

"My friends. Greatly esteemed colleagues. How can we possibly solve this case if we're more obsessed with cutting one another's throats?"

"I'm very happy – no problems!"

Silje Sørensen smiled broadly and raised her coffee cup in a toast. She was a newly qualified officer from that year's litter, and delighted to have landed right in the middle of the Crime Section. Her fellow-students were plodding the streets in the uniformed branch.

"You, yes. But our Chief Inspector here …"

He put his hand on Billy T.'s shoulder, but Billy T. shook him off.

"… he's in a terrible mood. I don't know why, but it really isn't very productive. And you, dear lady …"

He pointed his finger at Karianne Holbeck and drew a spiral in the air.

"… you seem to be going through a somewhat delayed revolt against authority at the moment. Is it hormonal or what? PMS perhaps?"

Karianne blushed deeply and was about to protest. Billy T. gave a smile, a far more genuine one this time.

"Dare I suggest that we call a truce, that Karl puts down his dainty handiwork, that somebody puts on more coffee, drinkable this time, and that I am then permitted to sit down quietly to share a bit more of my knowledge about the murder weapon with this truly eminent, if rather grumpy, group of investigators?"

He smiled at each and every one of the six others in the room. Karianne's face was still bright red. Silje Sørensen concealed a smirk behind her hand. On her ring finger sparkled a diamond that must have been worth half a police officer's annual salary. Karl hesitated, but in the end folded his pocket knife and stuffed the pipe into his jacket pocket. Annmari Skar, the Police Prosecutor, who until this point had been sitting immersed in her documents and obviously could not care less about the whole debacle, stared at him with a look he was not quite sure how to construe. Then, to his surprise, she burst into peals of laughter.

"You're a treasure, Severin. You really are a treasure."

Sergeant Klaus Veierød had already headed for the coffee machine.

"How many want some?"

"All of us," Severin said mildly. "We all want coffee. So—" He resumed his seat and took a deep breath.

"It says something else on the blade of the knife."

He leafed through his papers and held a slip of yellow paper up to his face.

"I really must learn to use my glasses. 'Molybdenum Vanadium Stainless Steel'. In plain Norwegian that means something like aerospace steel. Strong and unbelievably light. Monobloc. All the classiest restaurant kitchens have such knives. These are considered to be the hottest. The best. They cost one thousand and twenty-five kroner and eighty-two øre, to be exact, at GG Storkjøkken, the catering suppliers in Torggata. In other words, you're unlikely to find this sort of knife in our canteen here."

He pointed at the ceiling with his thumb.

"Anyway, Entré uses these knives exclusively. The problem is that so do ten or twelve other restaurants here in the city. At least. Incidentally, the knife blade measures two hundred and ten millimeters. Eighty-two of them were inside Ziegler's body. The tip had only just perforated the pericardium."

He fell silent. No one said a word. The hum from the dilapidated ventilation system was giving Billy T. the beginnings of a headache, and he rubbed the bridge of his nose.

"Light," he said with a sigh. "The knife is also extraordinarily light?"

"Yip. I called in at GG's yesterday to feel one. It's unfortunately outwith my budget, but *my God*, what a knife! I've always thought Sabatier was the only acceptable brand, but now I know better."

"Light," Billy T. repeated, grimacing this time. "In other words, we can't exclude a female killer."

"We can't do that anyway," Karianne said, clearly straining not to appear ungracious. "I mean, a knife doesn't ordinarily weigh so much that a woman couldn't wield it as a murder—"

"Or a child," Billy T. interrupted pensively.

"Exactly. The weapon actually tells us very little, other than that the killer is either extremely well off or belongs to the restaurant fraternity."

The blush crept over Karianne's face again. She ran her finger vigorously across one cheek, as if trying to wipe it away.

"The restaurant fraternity," Karl reiterated. "Or someone who simply wanted it to look like that."

"As usual."

Billy T. stroked his neck with his pass as if he were shaving.

"But of course it's quite encouraging all the same—"

Silje Sørensen had raised her hand in the air, though that wasn't necessary.

"I mean, it would've been a lot worse if the knife had been from IKEA or some such. There has to be a far more restricted number of these knives here in Norway, doesn't there? Do we know anything about fingerprints?"

"Yes," Severin Heger said. "Though Forensics are dilatory as usual, I've put a rocket under Kripos to get an answer. Nothing found as yet. The handle is clean, apart from some blood and trace fibers of fine paper. Wiped with a paper handkerchief, if you ask me." Since responsibility for the scientific and technical aspects of police work had been centralized at Kripos, Norway's National Criminal Investigation Service, obtaining the results had become a notoriously slow process.

"And I am," Billy T. said. "How long is the DNA-analysis going to take?"

"Too long. Six weeks, they're saying now. But I'll get that cut down as much as possible. Also, they haven't found any other stab wounds on Ziegler's body. However, there were fingerprints on the syringe. Kripos are running them through our records. I don't think we should raise our hopes too high. But apropos of nothing,

Forensics said something about Ziegler's complexion being an odd color. The doctor asked whether he was a drinker. Do we know anything about that?"

They all stared at Karianne, who had been assigned responsibility for coordinating the tactical investigation. She shook her head gently.

"We've conducted twenty-four interviews and I still couldn't say whether or not the man was a drinker. This new system whereby we record the interviews on tape is all well and good, but it becomes fairly difficult when there aren't enough people to type them up. There are only three transcripts available at present. Silje and Klaus have done a fantastic job, and we've got through more interviews in a single day than I can ever remember doing before now. But what good is that when they're just on a brown tape! Now I can't be bothered doing any more interviews until we've got transcripts for the ones we already have!"

"Of course you can be bothered." Billy T. looked straight at her as he continued: "I appreciate the problem. I'll see what can be done. But you must go on with the interviews as long as I tell you to. *Capice?*"

"Guys," Severin Heger said in a warning tone. "Now we're not going to continue where we left off, are we? What do you say, Karianne, do you know absolutely nothing about Ziegler's alcohol consumption?"

Karianne Holbeck's cheek muscles contracted in knots before she went on: "Some say that he drank every day. Not plastered, but more ... continental drinking habits. Some say for the most part he would take only a glass or two, whereas others say he poured it down his throat."

The door opened. A gust of fresher air blew into the windowless room, and Hans Christian Mykland, Chief of Police, followed it. Chairs scraped on the floor.

"Just sit down," he muttered as he took a seat beside the coffee machine, after flashing Billy T. a smile.

The Chief Inspector straightened his back almost imperceptibly and indicated with a hand motion that Karianne should continue.

"Now you have to understand that I haven't *read* the interview transcripts," she said, before looking in the direction of the Police Chief, adding: "There's nobody to type out the tapes, so—"

"We've heard that," Billy T. said flatly. "Go on."

"But I have now formed some kind of picture of the guy. I mean to say, I *haven't*."

She touched her neck and twisted her head from side to side.

"It's so difficult to get hold of who he really was. For example … At least half of the witnesses claim to be close friends of Ziegler. When we press them harder, it turns out that they've met him – I mean properly – only two or three times in recent years. And then there's this business of his wife. Hardly anybody even knew they were going out together, until they arrived back from Milan with gold wedding rings and were suddenly married."

"Was that chunk of gold a *wedding* ring?" Billy T. asked, taken aback. "That huge thing with a red stone in it? Do we have …? Is there a Norwegian embassy in Milan?"

"Maybe the Italians have different rules from us," Karianne said tartly. "Maybe, for example, they don't demand a residence permit. Maybe it's just a case of traveling to Italy and getting married. If you live in a European Economic Area country, perhaps. You possibly know that we are affiliated to the European—"

"Cut that out, now!"

Annmari Skar had become visibly more animated in the presence of the Chief of Police.

"Continue with what you were telling us."

"Okay then," Karianne said, with a sharp intake of breath. "I'm just answering questions from my boss. As far as the wife is concerned, Vilde Veierland Ziegler, then I'm pretty discouraged, to be honest. I spoke to her twice on the phone yesterday. Both times she promised to come to Oslo as soon as possible. She hasn't turned up yet. If she doesn't attend as arranged at twelve o'clock today, I'll go to Hamar to talk to her there. But—"

She brightened and thrust her index finger in the air.

"I've checked the register of nuptial agreements in Brønnøysund. Nothing is recorded for the Zieglers."

"Joint ownership, then," Annmari Skar said slowly. "The lady inherits everything. He doesn't have any children."

Different variants of *aha* combined in a babble of voices across the table.

"Wrong," Karianne said. "At least not entirely correct. Maybe the young widow won't be particularly happy, because she doesn't get the restaurant."

"No?"

Chief of Police Mykland raised his voice for the first time since his arrival.

"Why not?"

"No—"

Karianne Holbeck hesitated.

"I'm not entirely familiar with this aspect of law, but ... There's apparently something called a deed-of-partnership agreement. Can that be right?"

Annmari Skar and the Chief of Police both nodded.

"Anyway, it says the following."

Karianne grabbed a blank sheet of paper and quickly ripped it in two. She waved one piece as she went on: "Ziegler owned fifty-one percent of Entré. The rest, that is to say forty-nine percent ..."

Billy T. rolled his eyes. Karianne waved the other piece of paper.

"... was owned by the head waiter, Claudio—"

She was forced to glance down.

"Claudio Gagliostro. What a name! Hardly any of the witnesses had any idea what his surname was. Nobody really knew that he had such a large stake in the business, either. Claudio is the head waiter and day-to-day manager, and in the partnership agreement it says that each of them will inherit the other's shares in the case of death prior to December the thirty-first, 2005."

"So it's our friend Claudio who'll grow rich," Karl Sommarøy said. In distraction he had resumed whittling the pipe bowl.

"Huh," Karianne said. "We don't yet know what the place is actually worth. In any case, there's plenty left over for the wife. The apartment in Niels Juels gate was purchased in '97 for over five million. The mortgage is about three million, but we haven't got round to checking with the bank how much of this sum had actually been repaid. There'll be a substantial amount of money left over, anyway. In addition, the bank hasn't been very forthcoming. It's possible we might have to ask for help from the court."

"Why a knife?" Silje mused softly, as if she really had no wish for anyone to hear what she was saying.

"Eh?"

Karl Sommarøy squinted in her direction.

"I mean … Brede Ziegler was murdered with a knife. A very special kind of knife. And only one stab wound. One single stab. Knife killings are usually very violent. Forty-two stab wounds, I read in another case the other day. The perpetrator is furious and stabs over and over again. Usually, I mean. This guy only stabbed once. With a very special knife. That has to mean something, surely?"

"Fuck," Billy T. muttered, shaking his head abruptly. "It's unfathomable that nobody can get this ventilation system to work. You get a headache just from thinking in here. Continue with what you're doing. Severin … You and I are going to go for a jaunt to Ziegler's apartment. Karl, put some pressure on Kripos and Forensics."

"I forgot something," Karl Sommarøy said with a start, dropping his pipe on the floor. "Insignificant, maybe, but—"

He lifted his backside and produced a folded sheet of A4 paper that had assumed the shape of his back pocket.

"Other finds at the crime scene," he read out. "Two used condoms. Sixteen cigarette butts of miscellaneous brands. Four beer cans, Tuborg and Ringnes. A pocket handkerchief, yellow and used. A large piece of giftwrap with a blue ribbon. A scrap of ice-lolly wrapper, Pin-up brand."

He refolded the sheet of paper and, satisfied, pushed it back where it had been.

"Thanks for nothing," Billy T. said. "Do you have an archive in your ass, or what?"

Then, nodding to Severin Heger to accompany him, he raised his hand to take his leave of the Chief of Police, and disappeared from the room.

"What's actually wrong with the guy?" Karianne said, before providing the answer herself. "He's suffering from post-Hanne-Wilhelmsen-syndrome. Isn't it about time he got over that woman?"

No one responded. She bitterly regretted her outburst when she felt the Police Chief's eyes on her.

"I think you should confine yourself to matters you know something about," he said, unruffled. "That'd be the best course of action."

It was Tuesday December 7, 1999 and, outside, it had started to snow.

7

Hanne Wilhelmsen did not wear black because she was in mourning. It's simply that it was so practical. Her leather jacket had four capacious pockets, making it unnecessary to carry a handbag. When she had left home, she had thrown two pairs of black jeans and four dark T-shirts into a bag together with underwear and socks. It was mainly because she had nothing else that was clean, and also because she had no idea when she would have the opportunity to wash clothes when traveling.

She caught sight of herself in a shop window.

Her hair had grown long again. A few months earlier, she had begun to comb her fringe back. At long last her hair had grown long enough to sit properly in the new style. The reflection on the glass showed her someone she barely recognized.

She shifted her focus from the strange mirror image to the shop itself. A clothes shop. They did not have especially much on sale. The interior was simple and severe, with a few garments hanging on a steel frame. Two slim headless mannequins were dressed in tight trousers and crop-tops. A pair of bright-red gloves took center stage on a small high-legged table.

She went inside.

They were the reddest gloves Hanne had ever seen.

Slowly, paying no attention to the young woman who was presumably asking if she needed any help, she tried them on.

They were made for her, enveloping her hands like a second skin. Hanne, feeling warmth spread along her arms, touched her face.

"*Duecentomila lire*," she heard someone say.

Without answering and without removing the gloves, she produced her wallet and handed over her VISA card. The woman smiled expressively and said something, possibly an acknowledgment of the customer's taste and choice. Hanne was still wearing the gloves as she signed the receipt.

When she left the shop, she noticed for the first time the gentle breeze sweeping through the narrow streets. High above the terracotta-colored buildings she could see the sky turning blue: an unfamiliar summer hue, out of place in December. She stared at her gloves and started to walk.

The gloves were all she could think about.

Suddenly a rectangular piazza opened out before her. A marble fountain was surrounded by sidewalk restaurants, open even now, well into the Advent season. She took a seat at a table beside the wall and ordered a cappuccino.

Momentarily she felt something reminiscent of peace. Animated voices, laughter and unceremonious scolding, clinking of glasses, and rasping sounds of opera from the loudspeakers above her head all blended together into something that epitomized Italy, the Italy she had sought refuge from, in months spent off the beaten track. She fished out a cigarette, still wearing her gloves. As she coaxed a flame from her lighter, she heard a voice.

"*Scusi—*"

Hanne slowly lifted her eyes from her own cigarette. They stopped at a pair of red hands. She was taken aback for a second. She had to cast about, to find out where her own hands were, whether they were still hers.

Someone held a cigarette between two fingers, asking for a light. The hands were wearing the same gloves as Hanne's. Exactly the same snug-fitting, fiery-red calfskin gloves for which she had just paid a small fortune.

"*Scusi—*" she heard once more, and looked up.

The woman was gazing at her and smiled. When Hanne showed no sign of sparking her lighter again, the stranger took the unfamiliar gadget from her hands and helped herself. She lingered. Hanne stared at her. The woman was no longer smiling. Instead she stood with the cigarette in her hand, untouched, until there was nothing left but a baton of ash.

"Can I sit here?" the stranger eventually asked, dropping the cigarette end on the ground. "Just for a minute?"

"Of course," Hanne replied, pulling the adjacent chair out from the table. "Please do. Sit. Please."

Then, leisurely, she drew off her gloves and stuffed them into her pocket.

8

Brede Ziegler's apartment in Niels Juels gate was located in a pale-gray anonymous block in the functionalist style of the 1930s. Billy T. clambered out of the patrol car and peered up at the façade. A button on his pea-jacket fell off and disappeared into the slush underneath the vehicle.

"We can't park here," Severin Heger said.

"Help me, won't you? My button's somewhere under here."

Billy T. groaned and stood upright again, drying his hand on his trousers.

"Bloody hell. Now Tone-Marit will change all the buttons. I like these ones. See if you can find it for me."

"We can't stay here," Severin reiterated. "The car's blocking the vehicle entrance."

"I'll stay wherever I fucking want," Billy T. said crossly. "Besides, it's mid-morning and this is a residential property. Nobody will go in or out of here at this time of day."

He slapped the police ID on the dashboard, clearly visible through the windscreen, and locked the car.

"How many apartments are there here, actually?"

Severin Heger shrugged, appearing to contemplate moving the car himself.

"One, two, three—"

Billy T.'s right forefinger ran from window to window. Several of them had no curtains, and the building seemed dazzled by the low winter sun that had just broken through the cloud cover.

"I'll bet there's two on each floor," he said, as he set off, jogging across the asphalt driveway. "That makes eight apartments, plus Ziegler's big penthouse at the top."

Beside the double glass doors at the rear of the building, the doorbells were marked with brass nameplates.

"No temporary paper labels here, eh?"

Billy T. fumbled with a bulky bunch of keys. Finally he found the right key and let them in. The hallway brought to mind a small hotel reception. The floor was covered in azure and gray tiles and there was a faint smell of ammonia. The walls were primrose-yellow with three lithographs in severe black frames. On the opposite side, mailboxes were built into the wall and labeled with brass plates similar to the ones on the doorbells. An enormous leather winged armchair and a sideboard had obviously been placed here so that residents could sort their mail before going out or going home. A manila-fiber wastepaper basket, half-filled with advertising flyers and empty envelopes, capsized as Billy T. tried to inspect the contents. He righted it carelessly, leaving three colorful ICA supermarket-chain leaflets scattered on the floor. He stretched out to reach a small box fixed to the cornice directly above the chair.

"CCTV," he said eagerly. "Get somebody to secure the tapes, Severin. Today."

"There should be a sign on the door advising people of that. Both because it's a legal requirement and because part of the point must be to scare layabouts from trying anything. And while we're talking about rules and regulations, Billy T., do we actually have permission to do this?"

Severin Heger leaned against the wall beside the framed lithographs, with his hands thrust deep inside his pockets as if to distance himself from the entire enterprise. Billy T. waved the bunch of keys.

"His wife said yes. As for Ziegler himself, well, asking him is a bit more difficult."

"Did his wife really agree that we could enter the apartment without her being present? That's obviously Ziegler's own bunch of keys you have there."

"Yep. But I phoned the lady. On her cellphone. She was on her way to Oslo. She said it was fine."

Severin removed his glasses and placed them in a brushed-metal spectacle case.

"Can't get used to these," he said glumly as he stepped into the open elevator. "I would never have let anyone like us into my apartment if I weren't absolutely obliged to. Do you have the code to go all the way up?"

A small metal plate was hooked on to the key ring. Billy T. squinted at the tiny figures and tapped a five-digit number into the display on the door.

"Crazy to have the number attached to your keys, don't you think?"

"Oh, good Lord," Severin exclaimed.

Billy T. gave a long-drawn-out whistle as the metal doors opened soundlessly.

The elevator went directly into the apartment. From where the two police officers were standing, the distance to the opposite wall must have been at least thirty meters. The floor was glossy black and Billy T. could count four doors on either side of the wide corridor that opened out into what had to be the living room.

"Black lacquer," he blurted in excitement. "The guy's damn well lacquered the whole floor!"

"Floor paint," Severin Heger mumbled. "It's just floor paint. I've never in my life seen a coal-black floor in anyone's home."

"Smart! Really smart!"

Billy T. strode into the apartment with his boots on, his footsteps clearly delineated in the light from the spots running along the perimeter of the high ceiling. They had switched on automatically as the elevator doors opened. Severin Heger removed his shoes.

"Check out this kitchen," he heard Billy T. yell. "Mini-kitchen! I thought chefs had gigantic kitchens."

Severin found himself tiptoeing as he crept along the corridor. He felt just as awkward every time.

"Oh, good Lord," he repeated as he turned the corner and peered into the diminutive kitchen. "Well, it might be small, but no expense has been spared."

The refrigerator looked like a bank vault. Constructed of solid steel, it was divided vertically, with the freezer on the left side and the fridge on the right. In the freezer section a built-in dispenser displayed buttons for ice, crushed ice, water, and carbonated water. The fridge gave the impression of being a fortress around an abundant storehouse of food, but turned out to contain three rolls of film, a table-pack of butter, and two bottles of champagne.

"*Besserat de Bellefon*," Billy T. read aloud. "*Brut. Grande Tradition*."

"That's not too bad a drink. But look at that!"

Severin pointed at the actual kitchen fittings, while Billy T. surreptitiously tucked the rolls of film into his pocket.

"I'll bet that's German."

Severin caught hold of an arched steel handle and opened a drawer.

"Feels expensive," he said as he peered at a label, discreetly attached to the inside of the drawer. "Poggenpohl. The best there is."

"But that there is more like a canteen—"

Billy T. wrinkled his nose and pointed at the stainless-steel cutlery, all arranged in perfect order, as if a photographer from an advertising bureau was expected at any minute.

"In that case it must be the canteen in the royal palace," Severin said. "This is Italian designer steel. There's not a single item here that doesn't match."

If the kitchen was minuscule, the living room on the other hand measured more than a hundred square meters. The walls and ceiling were chalk-white and the beams were black like the floor. The entire room centered on a seating arrangement comprising two five-seater settees facing each other, separated by at least four meters. Billy T. picked up a deluxe edition about Indian temple monkeys from the table and leafed through it indifferently. Tossing it aside with a thump, he pointed at an oil painting on the gable wall behind one of the settees.

"Look at that red color at the bottom there. It matches the settee! He's bought a fucking picture to match the furniture!"

"Or the other way round," Severin said, as he approached the enormous abstract painting. "Gunvor Advocaat. I think it's the other way round, Billy T. First the picture, then the furniture. Incredibly stylish, with that red against the black!"

Billy T. did not answer. He struggled to open a door in the south-facing glass wall that gave on to a magnificent roof garden.

"Locked," he said superfluously as he gave up. "Let's take a look at the bathroom. Bathrooms are always mind-blowing."

He trudged back to the long corridor between the living room and the elevator. Suddenly he halted, squinting at a series of fifteen to twenty photographs framed behind glass and hanging in three rows on the wall.

"Brede Ziegler and … Here's something for you, Severin. Brede and Wenche Foss!"

Severin Heger grinned as he pointed at the next picture.

"Catherine Deneuve! That's Brede Ziegler and Catherine Deneuve!"

"And Brede eating with Prime Minister Jens Stoltenberg!"

"And that's … Who the fuck is that?"

"Björk," Severin said. "That's Ziegler and Björk in a car!"

"Jaguar," Billy T. murmured. "Who's Björk?"

Severin laughed so hard he began to hiccup.

"And you say I'm star – hic – struck!"

Billy T. thumped him on the back and leaned closer to the picture on the lower right.

"It can't be," he exclaimed, smacking his index finger on the glass.

"Do you see who Brede is shaking hands with there?"

Severin tried to hold his breath and talk at the same time.

"The Pope," he groaned. "Brede is being intro – hic – duced to the Pope."

"Take a glass of water. That gizmo on the fridge looked classy."

Billy T. let his hand slide across the wall to the first door beyond the photographs. The handle felt cold and heavy against his hand. He pressed it gingerly and nudged the door open.

The bedroom was similar in style to the rest of the apartment. The floor here was lacquered in brilliant white. A double bed with a brushed-steel frame was placed in the center of the room. The bed linen had been stripped, and the quilts and pillows were neatly folded at the foot of the enormous mattress. The bedside tables were also white, with frosted glass drawers. A book by an author unfamiliar to Billy T. lay on one of these. The other was bare, apart from a table lamp with a globe shade fashioned of the same glass as the drawer fronts. The bedroom walls were stark and unadorned. The wardrobe sliding doors were of smoked mirror glass. Billy T. stared at his reflection for a second or two, before drawing one door aside.

"This is perverse," he said in an undertone to Severin, who was standing in the doorway gulping a glass of water. "There must be fifty here."

A broad tower of shoeboxes, each one with a Polaroid photograph attached, was stacked inside. Billy T. opened the box at the top of the pile. The front picture showed a pair of lady's red stiletto shoes. The contents matched. The next box was labeled with a photo of men's black dress shoes. The contents were exactly as expected.

"An archive of shoes," Severin said, impressed. "He had quite a sense of order, our friend Brede!"

"But look here—"

Billy T. opened the closet on the other side, where three columns of wire baskets stood side by side.

"Two baskets of women's stuff," he said, lifting a black bra between his thumb and forefinger. "The rest is men's clothing. You'd almost think the woman didn't live here. Look at this—"

He opened the middle of the wardrobe. A clothes rail extending for at least three meters was crammed with hanging suits, trousers, blazers, and shirts. At the far end beside the shoeboxes dangled a gossamer party dress, a maxi-skirt, and two blouses.

"Is it just me, or is there something creepy about this whole place?" Billy T. asked. "It looks like something in an expensive showroom. The only thing approaching any kind of personal touch in the entire apartment is a really tacky wall covered in celebrity photos and a wardrobe that could be put on sale in the Ferner Jacobsen department store. Was he never at home, or what? And Vilde, then … Did she actually even live here?"

"This stuff's not Ferner Jacobsen," Severin said, running his hands lingeringly over a cashmere jacket. "This hasn't been bought in Norway at all. The bathroom – you said that we ought to take a look at the bathroom."

"If we can find it," Billy T. mumbled, closing the bedroom door behind him. "What about this door here?"

Stepping into Brede Ziegler's workroom was like moving

from one world into another. The walls were decorated with deep-red silk wallpaper in a pattern Severin chose to call lions' paws. Fifteen to twenty lithographs and three oil paintings hung close together, some in semi-darkness, others below their own brass picture lights. The flooring was dark and partly covered with an oriental rug. In the corner farthest from the door stood a marble statue of Aphrodite on an open shell, measuring one and a half meters high. The writing desk was roughly rococo style: shiny lacquered wood with an inlaid sheet of green felt as a writing pad. A Mont Blanc fountain pen lay diagonally on the felt, beside a matching glass inkwell, black and yellow. A telephone with a mahogany case sat beside an answering machine that looked as if it came from some time in the seventies. The air was oppressive and clammy. Severin poked his nose forward and sniffed loudly.

"Do you smell it?"

"Mmm. Pot."

"I agree – and listen, my hiccups have stopped."

"Good for you. What do we have here?"

Billy T. picked up an onyx owl, set it to one side, and riffled quickly through the papers it had held down on the desktop.

"A bill from the phone company: eight hundred and fifteen kroner and fifty øre—"

"Not particularly chatty, in other words."

"An invitation to … the Chinese embassy. Dinner. And this—"

He unfolded an A4 sheet of paper. "Eh?"

"This is too stupid," Severin said.

"Some kind of—"

"Threatening letter. For fuck's sake, it's a threatening letter."

Billy T. roared with laughter.

"The daftest threatening letter I've ever seen! Take a look at this!"

He laid the paper carefully on the green felt and produced a pair of thin plastic gloves from his pocket. The paper was yellow, with pasted letters that at first sight looked as if they had been clipped from a magazine. The sender had been generous with the paste, and individual letters were almost drowning in goo:

ThE CheFs GoOse iS CoOkEd
RegGArDs
IRoN FiSt

"Turn round with your hands in the air. Nice and slowly."

The voice sliced through the heavy, marijuana-laden atmosphere. Billy T. wheeled around and automatically threw himself to one side when he had completed the move.

"Stand still!" the voice in the doorway yelled. "I told you both to stand still."

"It's Securitas," Severin said, crestfallen, as he stretched out his hands.

"Securitas?"

Billy T. ran his fingers over his skull and grinned at the terrified young man holding a Maglite, for want of any other weapon.

"Take it easy. We're from the police."

Billy T. took one step forward.

"Stop right there!" screamed the Securitas guard. "Let me see your ID! Easy now!"

"Relax, for fuck's sake!"

Billy T. patted the pockets of his jacket.

"Shit! My police ID's in the car. The car parked outside here. Maybe you saw it? Right in front of the entrance?"

Severin Heger produced a plastic card from his wallet and held it out invitingly. The security guard hesitated, before stepping three paces into the room and snatching the ID.

"That adds up," he said with a faint smile to his colleague. "He's from the police. You should have switched off the alarm."

"Alarm? I didn't hear shit."

Billy T. put on the plastic gloves and folded the extraordinary letter, before dropping it into an evidence bag and tucking it in his inside pocket.

"Silent alarm. It's not intended that you should hear anything. Will you be staying long?"

"No," Billy T. said tartly. "We're leaving now. Then you can sort out that alarm shit on the way out. Severin, give me the tape from the answering machine."

The car was still parked where they had left it. Someone had attached a penalty ticket under one of the windscreen wipers. Farther up the street stood two traffic wardens, notepad and pen in hand, beside a truck with front wheels on the pedestrian crossing.

"Hoi, you," Billy T. yelled. "You up there! *Didn't you see the police badge or what?*"

"Forget it," Severin Heger advised him, tapping impatiently on the roof of the car. "We don't have permission to park here anyway."

The traffic wardens did no more than glance in his direction before continuing with their issue of another ticket. Billy T. vented a series of expletives from the time he opened the vehicle until he started the engine.

"I *hate* folk in uniform," he snarled. "Be it Securitas clowns or ..."

He rolled down the window on Severin's side as they passed the traffic wardens.

"... the assholes from the Traffic Department!" he shrieked.

He narrowly avoided crashing into a bright-yellow Polo.

"Had Brede Ziegler reported anyone for making threats before now?" Severin Heger asked, wiping condensation from the front windscreen.

"Parking-meter morons," Billy T. replied.

9

Daniel regretted leaving his winter boots behind. It was the evening of Tuesday December 7 and the temperature had dropped again. The last few days had alternated between snow, rain, and sunshine. Now his good leather shoes were splashing through ice-cold slush, and he clenched his legs to keep warm.

He was running short of time.

The IKEA bus arrived. The people around him at the bus stop in front of the Law Faculty scuttled into the warmth, and Daniel looked at his watch.

She could not stand him turning up late. That's the way it had been ever since he was old enough to go to the theater. Thale always wanted him to see the third performance after the premiere. By then the production still had something about it that his mother called "creative tension." At the same time the first-night nerves had gone, and mistakes that had only been discovered with exposure to a real audience had been smoothed away.

Watching Thale's performances was a duty.

It fell into the same category as emptying the dishwasher after school and scrubbing the floors every Friday. Washing the stairs had been discontinued when he moved to a student bedsit two years ago. The obligatory theater visits would stick to him like glue for as long as his mother could stand upright on a stage. Fried eggs and hot chocolate at the kitchen table after the show were also so inescapable that he had never dared to protest. Not even the time when his girlfriend's twentieth birthday fell on the same day as the third performance.

"She can come with you, of course," Thale had said unflappably. "You'll be coming in any case."

When he was younger, he had believed his mother had done this for his sake. That was what she said. He would benefit from going to the theater, she claimed. Only recently had he realized it was a tradition that actually ministered to her own need to have someone to talk to.

Thale always chatted energetically after performances. She related to her roles, the characters in the plays, as if they were close friends. Apart from that, she was reluctant to discuss other people. She said very little at all, except for those nights when they drank hot chocolate with a skin on top and ate eggs and tomatoes with English toast until he could not bear any more and simply had to sleep.

Daniel turned up his jacket collar more snugly around his ears when he felt the wet snow against his neck. He felt it was childish of him to wait for her to say something. On the other hand, he felt a sort of adult defiance: she ought to appreciate that he was having problems. She had not spoken a single word about the incident. When he had phoned her earlier that day, her only concern had been that he should make it to the performance.

"Egoist!" he said under his breath, startled by his own remark.

Now he was really having to rush. He scanned up and down Karl Johans gate, but could not find what he was looking for. He glanced again at his watch. In five minutes' time he absolutely *must* go.

Daniel had always known that his mother was not like other mothers. The mere fact that she insisted on him calling her Thale, rather than Mum, had made him feel different as early as kindergarten days. Mostly she left him in peace. She never asked him about his school work. She rarely showed any interest in who he was mixing with. Throughout his upbringing she had been strict about what time he came home and about theater visits, and moreover taught him that he should always keep his promises. Apart from that, she let him do as he pleased.

She had not said anything.

It wasn't so strange, but he felt offended all the same.

It was even worse that Taffa had not phoned. That was also far more significant. Perhaps she would phone him tomorrow. Or call in.

"Hi! Sorry I'm late."

Daniel nearly jumped out of his skin and dropped the envelope he was clutching tightly. Quick as a flash, he bent down to retrieve it from the slush.

"It's okay. Here. A thousand kroner. You'll get more in a fortnight."

"A thousand—"

The other young man screwed up his nose.

"I've no more just now," Daniel said, taking a deep breath. "And anyway, I've got to run. A fortnight. I promise."

He punched his companion lightly on the shoulder and sprinted across the street. His shoes were squelching. He just managed to find his seat in the National Theater before curtain-up, aware that he was about to succumb to a heavy cold.

10

The snow had arrived that same night. Silence reigned. The clamor of voices, children crying, and the clatter of footsteps on the cobblestones had all disappeared. Hanne closed her eyes and listened, but could apprehend no more than a regular tapping from the bathroom pipes.

She had gone.

It must have been about six o'clock when she slammed the door behind her. Hanne was not entirely sure. It meant nothing. She had been there. Her scent still wafted from the bedclothes. She had disappeared around six.

"It's not true, you know," she had said before she left. "That Venus doesn't smile in a house of tears. She does!"

Hanne got out of bed and drew back the curtains. The sunlight, strongly reflected on the snow, assaulted her eyes. She felt faint. She felt light-headed. Everything was white, and her mind turned to Cecilie.

Nefis Özbabacan was her name, and she had only just run her index finger over Hanne's lips in farewell.

Hanne dressed without showering and crammed the rest of her luggage into her bag. Today she would succeed. Nefis had made it possible for her to travel home to everything that had been Cecilie. Hanne Wilhelmsen snatched her key from the bedside table and slung her bag on her back. She thought of Nefis's parting words as she drew on the red gloves when she was seated in the taxi headed for the airport.

* * *

Interview with witness Vilde Veierland Ziegler

Interviewed by police officer Karianne Holbeck.
Transcript typed by office colleague Rita Lyngåsen.
There is in total one tape of this interview. The interview
was recorded on tape on Tuesday December 7, 1999 at
Oslo police headquarters.

Witness:

Ziegler, Vilde Veierland, ID number 200576 40991
Address: Niels Juels gate 1, 0272 Oslo
Informed about witness rights and responsibilities.
Willing to give a statement.
The witness was informed that the interview would be
taped and that a transcript would be produced later.

Interviewer:

Let me first of all offer my condolences on *(cough, indistinct speech)* of your husband. We're working hard to solve this case, and we are dependent on ... If we're to find the perpetrator, we need to know as much as absolutely possible about your husband. That can seem unpleasant, but unfortunately it is ... *(Scraping sounds, indistinct speech.)* Eh ... It can certainly be difficult when—

Witness *(interrupts)*:

Yes, I understand that. It's okay.

Interviewer:

Then we can begin. First something about yourself, perhaps. What work do you do?

Witness:

Well … No … *(Clears throat.)* A bit of modeling. Bridal shows and that sort of thing. And I'm taking prelim exams in the spring.

Interviewer:

Do you earn anything? I mean, what do you earn from that?

Witness:

Not much. Brede … *(Indistinct speech, cough?)* … what I need. Sixty thousand, maybe? I think I earned something like that last year.

Interviewer:

Who have you worked for? In the modeling business, I mean.

Witness:

Various. Had an assignment for *Tique* last summer. *KK*, for example. I was in a kind of stable at Heads & Bodies before, you see. That's a model agency. But now … I sort of get more direct approaches. It's not so important, really. It's not as if I'm dependent on it, you see. It's just for amusement. I'm going to study languages. French and Italian was what I had planned. Or maybe Spanish. Haven't quite made up my mind.

Interviewer:

Did you have anything to do with the running of the restaurant?

Witness:

No. Brede didn't want that. I said several times that I could do some work there … And that sort of thing. He didn't want that.

Interviewer:

How long had you known Brede?

Witness:

About two years, I think. Of course, I've kind of known who he was, for a long time. More than two years, I mean. But it's about two years since we got to know each other. Sort of properly, if you know what I mean.

Interviewer:

When did you get married?

Witness:

In May. May 19. This year, that is. It was the day before my birthday. I got a bit kind of … a bit cross with Brede. He forgot my birthday. He always said it was childish. Bothering with birthdays, I mean. He didn't want to celebrate or mark it in any way. Not his own, either. That was for children, as far as he was concerned.

Interviewer:

Childish … *(Coughing.)* Did he say that often? That you were childish? Of course, there was quite a big age difference and—

Witness *(interrupts)***:**

No. Not exactly that. But he did make most of the decisions. That was only natural, I think. You see, he had lived … He had money and all that. He worked extremely hard and long hours, while I … *(Pause.)*

Interviewer:

How did you meet?

Witness:

At a party. Or a function, really. A friend of the guy I was with before was going to open a new eating place, and then ... *(Inaudible.)* ... Sindre and I split up. He took it quite badly, since ... *(Lengthy pause.)* I was with Brede after that party. *(Brief laughter, giggle?)*

Interviewer:

Do you know anyone in Brede's family?

Witness:

Mrs. Johansen. His mother, that is. Or ... *(Pause.)* I don't really know her. But I've met her a few times.

Interviewer:

How do you get on?

Witness:

Get on? What do you mean? Get on ... Well, fine, presumably.

Interviewer:

Fine? Presumably?

Witness:

I mean ... She was ... is, I mean. She's a real mother hen. The sort that almost seems head over heels in love with her own son. You know the sort of thing I mean.

Interviewer:

Not entirely.

Witness:

Yes, you do ... Everything was absolutely splendid with Brede. The way she saw it, he could never do any wrong. She ... I will say that she worshiped her son. And that made it not so easy for me to … *(Long pause.)* But everything went well, all the same.

Interviewer:

(Paper fluttering.) Brede's father died when he was small, and according to what it says here, Brede was both an only child and childless. Did he have any other relatives that you know of?

Witness:

No. Can I have a pastille?

Interviewer:

Go ahead. No relatives. Friends, then?

Witness:

Loads.

Interviewer:

Such as?

Witness:

The list's enormous. Do you want me to write them down?

Interviewer:

We'll see. But who was closest to him, in your opinion?

Witness:

No idea.

Interviewer:

Don't you have any idea who your husband's closest friends were?

Witness *(raising voice considerably)*:

He knew everybody. Everybody. He had an unbelievable
number of friends. It's not so easy to … Claudio, then. If you
absolutely need to have a name.

Interviewer:

Claudio. The head waiter? Claudio Gagliostro?

Witness:

Yes. He's the day-to-day manager of Entré. He's known Brede
… forever, so it seems. He owns a share of the restaurant as
well, I think. I know that he's part-owner of Entré. Anyway, he
was the only one who knew in advance that we were getting
married in Milan. In addition to the two from *Se og Hør* magazine, anyway. The ones who were there to do the reporting.
They paid for the whole thing.

Interviewer:

Did *Se og Hør* pay for your wedding? *(Pause.)* What did you
think about that?

Witness:

Don't know … *(Indistinct speech.)* … such things. Brede was
dependent on the publicity. He said that he always had to put
himself forward, or else no one would accept the food he had
to offer. That was how he put it. Fair enough, really. They just
took lots of photos. Brede knows loads of people in Milan that
we met down there. Of course they chatted to one another in
Italian, so it was actually fine for me to have someone to talk
to in Norwegian.

Interviewer:

Now that your husband has passed away … do you know anything about the more … financial consequences for yourself? I'm sorry, but …

Witness:

No, I … *(Sniffling, sobbing.)* He once said that we should have separate ownership, but … *(Pause, indistinct speech, and sniffling.)* I'm not sure if that had been arranged yet. He had a pile of papers that he wanted me to sign, but I don't actually know what they were. *(Pause.)* Do you know what happens now? With the apartment and that kind of thing?

Interviewer:

You … Brede Ziegler most certainly had a lawyer who organized the business side of things for him. Do you know who that might be?

Witness:

No … He knew a number of lawyers. Celebrities. They … *(More sobbing.)*

Interviewer:

Listen to me. You'll need to get in touch with a lawyer yourself. Someone who will represent you, and only you. Then it will all get sorted out. *(Violent sobbing, presumably from the witness.)* Shall we take a break, then? Then you can have some coffee and maybe something to eat. Does that sound okay?

Witness:

Mmm. Yes. *(Violent sobbing continues.)*

Several seconds had passed since he had said "excuse me" and rapped his knuckles on the open door. The woman at the writing desk sat with her back to him, still with no sign of turning round, even though she must have heard him.

"Excuse me," Billy T. repeated. "Can I come in?"

She was wearing an apple-green sweater and appeared to be holding her breath.

"What a fright you gave me," she said finally as she slowly swiveled round. "Honestly, you gave me such a fright."

"Apologies."

As Billy T. held out his hand, she stood up and grasped it. Her handshake was firm, almost too earnest.

"Billy T.," he introduced himself. "I'm from the police. And you are Idun Franck?"

He pointed at the sign on the door in the glass wall dividing off the corridor.

"Yes. Take a seat."

There was barely room for him. One of the longer walls was covered from floor to ceiling with packed bookshelves. On the floor beside the doorway sat an enormous stack of books that the office was too small to house. An incredible quantity of papers, stashed among pens and cups full of pencils, lay on the broad desk under the window. A grubby plush Moominpappa soft toy perched on the far edge of the table, the brim of his top-hat torn, and stared vacantly at a colorful Gustav Klimt poster. A bulletin board plastered with cartoons, a couple of photographs, and three newspaper cuttings hung crookedly above Billy T.'s head. Idun Franck removed a pair of gold-rimmed glasses and polished them with her sweater sleeve.

"How can I help you?"

"Brede Ziegler."

Feeling claustrophobic, Billy T. tried to reach the handle of the door he had just closed behind him.

"I can open the window," Idun Franck said with a smile. "It gets a bit stuffy in here."

A puff of cold, exhaust-laden air forced its way into the room.

"Not much of an improvement, I'm afraid."

Nevertheless she left the window open.

"I did realize it would be about Brede Ziegler," she said pointedly as she put her glasses on again.

"Yep. I've learned that you're working on a book. About Ziegler, I mean."

"Do you usually interview witnesses at their place of work? I had anticipated some kind of summons. I thought that was how you normally went about these things."

The woman did not seem hostile, despite her appropriate reprimand. Billy T. scrutinized her while scratching his thigh. She must be around fifty. Although she could not be described as fat, she was certainly well built. Her breasts strained behind the green sweater: the stitches were stretched, revealing her black underwear. She peered at him over her glasses, as if she did not quite know what to make of him.

"You're right," Billy T. said, grinning. "It is slightly irregular. But I was in the neighborhood and thought I might as well pop in and see if you were here. You don't need to talk to me at all. In any case, you will be called for interview later. For a formal interview, I mean. And if you—"

He started to rise from his chair.

"Stay seated."

Her voice reminded him of his mother's. He did not know whether he liked that or not. He sat down again.

"Officer," she began.

"Chief Inspector, in fact, though that's not so important."

"I didn't catch your surname."

"That's not so important, either. Billy T. is plenty. Is it true that you're writing a book about Ziegler?"

Idun Franck removed the elastic band holding her hair back in a ponytail. Only now did Billy T. notice that she had thick streaks of gray in her ash-blond hair. However, her face looked younger with her hair loose; her cheekbones no longer seemed so school-teacherly severe, beneath her unusually large eyes.

"Well," she said, her mouth contracting into what might be some sort of smile.

"Well?"

"I wasn't actually writing a book about Brede Ziegler. I'm an *editor*, not a writer or an author."

"But—"

Billy T. produced a newspaper cutting from his inside pocket and spread it over his knee.

"This was in *Aftenposten* three weeks ago or—"

"That's right. We had planned to publish a culinary biography. A kind of odyssey through Ziegler's life and work, if you like. With recipes and anecdotes, his life story, and pictures. Unusually, I was to do the writing, but the plan was that this should be a sort of autobiography. A hybrid, so to speak. In several places the text would be written in the first person. Is this important?"

Again the corner of her mouth tugged into what might be construed as a smile. Her face took on a slightly mocking aspect, and

Billy T. felt his armpits sweat. He pulled off his jacket, though he had no idea what to do with it.

"Did you already know Ziegler?" he asked, dropping the jacket on the floor.

"No. Not before I met him in connection with this project."

"But you *now* know him well, isn't that so? I mean, how far had you got with this ... cookery book?"

Idun Franck suddenly got to her feet and used both hands to brush her tweed skirt.

"I should have offered you coffee, of course. Sorry. Black?"

She grabbed her own mug and disappeared without waiting for an answer. The phone began to ring. Billy T. stared at the apparatus. The sound was unusually discordant: an old-fashioned, piercing ring that made him rise to pick up the receiver. As he hesitated momentarily, it fell silent.

"Are you looking for something?" he heard at his back and wheeled round abruptly.

Idun Franck had returned with two cups of coffee and was staring at him with an expression he interpreted as somewhere between irritation and curiosity.

"The phone," he said, pointing. "The ring was so damn loud. I thought I should answer it, but then it stopped. Bloody awful noise."

Idun Franck's laughter was unexpectedly deep and husky. She snaked her way past Billy T., handed him a cup, and fished out a cigarette from a pack of Barclay extra-mild in a drawer.

"Does it bother you?" she asked, lighting the cigarette.

"No, it's fine."

"Where were we?"

Once again she stared at him over her glasses. For the first time it struck Billy T. that he found this somewhat overweight fifty-year-old woman attractive. She made him feel hesitant and awkward. He had to pull himself together to avoid his eyes lingering on her bust.

"How well did you know the man?" he repeated, shuffling his feet. "How far had you reached in the work on this book?"

"It's actually difficult to say. People have a tendency to think that a book project is like ... a fifty-kilometer ski race, for example."

She took a long drag, betraying that she was used to far stronger cigarettes.

"It's surprising how many people believe that a book is completed by placing one stone on top of another. It's not normally like that. The process is more ... organic, you might almost say. Unsystematic. So I can't ..."

Billy T. again felt the gaze above her glasses that forced his eyes to stray to the Moominpappa, which had now toppled on to its back and was staring at the ceiling.

"... say how far we had reached."

"Okay, then," Billy T. said, clearing his throat. "That's fine. But can you tell me whether, through the work you've done to date, you've learned anything about who ... or what – whether he had difficulties with anyone? Conflicts above and beyond the everyday?"

Idun Franck took a gulp of coffee and a last puff of her cigarette, before stubbing it out and dropping it into a Farris bottle. She leaned across the desk and closed the window. Afterwards she remained seated with her eyes half-closed, as if thinking through a lengthy exposition.

"Billy T.," she said quizzically.

He nodded.

"Chief Inspector Billy T.," she said long-windedly. "You are intruding on an extremely problematic area now. I am actually an editor. As you almost certainly know, that gives me certain editorial responsibilities. I can't say just anything to just anyone.

You are asking me about things that I might *possibly* have learned from a source I have spoken to, in connection with work on an as-yet-unpublished book."

"So what?"

Billy T. opened out his arms expressively, narrowly missing a mind-your-own-business potted plant on an adjacent sideboard.

"Confidentiality of sources," Idun Franck said, smiling. "Publisher's ethics."

"Confidentiality!"

Billy T.'s voice rose to a falsetto.

"The guy's dead, and you're not bloody working for a national newspaper! Of all the preposterous things I've heard – and believe me, there's been a whole *fucking lot* of those over the years – you've got the nerve to tell me you plead confidentiality for your sources, in connection with a *cookery book*! What the hell kind of book is it, then? Full of secret recipes or what?"

Idun Franck used her coffee cup to heat her hands: broad hands with short nails. On her left hand she wore a large ring of Viking design. She tapped it against the cup in a regular nerve-racking beat.

"If you reflect on it, I think you'll understand the problem. I've initiated a collaboration with a man who is going to tell me about his life, so that I can obtain enough material to publish a book. What would be printed of what he has told me was to be decided much later in the process. Everyone we obtain material from, whether it is authors or anyone else, is assured that what gets published will only go to print with their full agreement. I'll permit myself to refer you to both the *Criminal Procedure Act*, section 125, and to the *European Convention on Human Rights*. Article ten, if I'm not entirely mistaken. If I gave you information now, under cover of the fact that Brede Ziegler is hardly in a position to protest ..." She stopped and held her breath for a moment or two before continuing: "… then none of my authors would be able to trust me in future. It's as simple as that. I had a purely professional relationship with Ziegler. Talk instead to those who knew him personally."

Billy T. thought he detected a touch of vulnerability about this person who had sat with her back turned and let herself feel alarmed at his approach.

"How wrong can you be?" he said, retrieving his jacket. "You want to play hardball. Okay then. We too have lawyers to deal with that sort of thing."

There was nothing more to be gained here. As he headed for the door, the phone rang again. The window opened by itself, and a strong blast of air lifted four sheets of paper from the desk. All of a sudden Billy T. was aware of a whiff of perfume from Idun Franck, a fragrance he had not encountered for a long number of years. It made him dizzy. When he irritably raised his hand in some kind of farewell gesture to the publishing editor as she spoke on the phone, he narrowly avoided colliding with a young man. Billy T. thought he recognized the boy.

"Authors just keep getting younger and younger," he muttered, pulling on his jacket as he strode off.

12

Thomas needed to pee. If he did not think about it too much, he might manage to reach all the way home before he came to grief. Even though he was seven and a half, he sometimes wet his pants. Yesterday he had met a man with a blue nose. The man was terribly old and his awful stink extended as far as the electricity substation where Eirik, Lars, and Thomas were doubled-up with laughter, yelling and jeering from their hiding place as they stared at his huge bright-blue nose. When the man had crossed Suhms gate at the gas station, Thomas had been left standing with a wet patch on the front of his trousers and a yellow puddle at his feet. Running home with the hilarity of his pals at his back, he nearly got knocked down by a car.

Now he stood on tiptoe at the gate with his legs crossed. His mum preferred him to wear the key around his neck. Dad had given him some sort of janitor's gizmo at Christmas: a metal key ring that could be fastened to his belt. Thomas had to stand on tiptoe to make the key's cord long enough. At last the key slipped in and the gate slid open. Thomas rushed into the entrance.

"Somersaults, sandcastles, sardines."

That usually helped. Long strings of words with difficult S-words. He had posted a list in his room, and constantly added new and increasingly difficult words that he could learn by heart.

He came to a sudden stop before he reached the front door. The witch was on the prowl. Thomas Gråfjell Berntsen never walked past Tussi Gruer Helmersen of his own free will. Mrs. Helmersen on the first floor was the only person in the whole world of whom Thomas was really scared. Once she had bumped into him on the stairs and made him fall. Not that he hurt himself at all badly, but since then he had suffered nightmares about her yellow eyes. If she came upon him unawares – something that happened increasingly infrequently – she was in the habit of pinching him hard on the cheek in some odd kind of greeting.

Thomas could not hold out any longer. He stood behind the garbage bins, not daring to move a muscle, with tears welling up in his eyes.

Mrs. Helmersen was wearing her dressing gown, even though the weather was quite chilly. That probably meant she was heading straight back up again. Thomas closed his eyes and sobbed through gritted teeth: "Go away. Go away!"

But Mrs. Helmersen stood still, with only her head moving, as if she were looking for something.

"Pussy! Here, puuuuusssy! Come on, pussy-cat!"

Mrs. Helmersen did not have a cat. She hated cats. Thomas knew she had complained to the management. About Helmer, a ginger tomcat that Grandma had given Thomas for Christmas two years ago. Actually he had wanted a dog, but dogs were not allowed.

"Clever puss," he heard Mrs. Helmersen say. "Drink it all up, that's right."

As Thomas held his breath, he peeped out from behind the garbage bin. Mrs. Helmersen was crouching over Helmer, who was lapping milk from a saucer.

Finally she moved away. She really did not seem human and instead reminded him of some kind of robot, her movements were so stiff and frightening. Thomas's teeth were chattering, but he was reluctant to creep from his hiding place until he was certain that Mrs. Helmersen had returned all the way up to her apartment.

Eventually he felt reasonably safe. His trousers chafed on his crotch as he sneaked up on Helmer, who was still licking a white saucer decorated with tiny sprigs of flowers. He picked up the cat.

"Did Mrs. Helmersen give you some food?"

The soft cat's ear against his mouth made him burst into tears. When he arrived at his own apartment and managed to strip off his clothes, he was still freezing cold. He knew he ought to wash, but wanted to wait for his mum. He crept into bed, pulling the quilt over himself and Helmer. The cat was whimpering softly. Thomas fell asleep.

When he woke just before five, when he heard that his mum had come home, Helmer was dead.

13

Only afterwards did he notice the warning on the package. He had taken two Paracet tablets an hour ago. Now he had swallowed down another two and the bitter taste burned his throat. He read the warning yet again, shaking his head.

"If only this damn tooth would let up."

It was not going to let up. Lately it had throbbed whenever he drank or ate anything either above or below body temperature. This evening the toothache had taken complete hold. Billy T. did not want to visit the dentist. Admittedly, the tooth was a goner. The dentist would take one look at the damage and suggest a crown. Three thousand four hundred kroner for a single crown. Out of the question. To put it mildly, Billy T. could not afford it. Jenny would need a pushchair soon. Four child-support payments in addition to Jenny made him sick every time his paycheck arrived. The pay rise that had accompanied his temporary appointment as chief inspector in charge vanished in one huge gulp.

He needed money. As far back as he could remember, he had been short of cash.

The toothache sneaked up the left side of his face and ended as a shooting pain somewhere deep inside his head. He wrung out a dirty cloth and pressed it against his eyes. The faint reek of baby poo made him snatch it off again.

"Shit. *Shit!*"

He snarled at his reflection in the mirror. The fluorescent light made him look more pallid than he actually was, and he stood there rubbing his temples as he struggled to squint away the bags under his eyes. It was past midnight and he really ought to grab some shut-eye while Jenny permitted it.

Warily, he opened the bedroom door.

Jenny was lying on her back in the cot with her arms out-stretched, the quilt in a tangle at her feet. She resembled a sun-bather in blue pajamas. Billy T. carefully covered her with the quilt and pushed the grubby yellow rabbit into its usual place in one corner.

He felt Tone-Marit's warmth on his back when he lay down gin-gerly in the double bed. The toothache did not ease off. Instead, it grew worse.

Even though he had already sired four children, the two girls in the bedroom were his first real family. Since he had left home, anyway. At this very moment he would prefer to be alone, however. Then he would have flicked on all the lights, drunk himself to semi-oblivion from the cognac bottle that remained untouched after a business trip to Kiel two years earlier, turned *Il Trittico* to full volume, and waited for the pain to subside.

He wanted to be alone.

Life had been uncomplicated as a young guy and weekend dad. After a bit of early fuss with the youngest child's mother, the arrangement had gone well. He did not interfere in how the boys fared with their four different mothers. For their part, they involved themselves only minimally in how the boys got on at his house. As long as his sons seemed congenial and healthy, he found no reason to meddle with a setup that worked. Now and again the boys sulked a little because he did not attend end-of-term functions and that sort of thing, but eventually they had grown used to it all the same. If they had football matches or other activities while staying at their father's, then naturally he accompanied them. When all was said and done, he was having a great time.

This was something altogether different.

Jenny had not slept through one whole night since the day she was born. She bawled and screamed and demanded to be fed. Before her hunger was assuaged, the last feed was running out the other end. The apartment was too cramped to escape it. A few times Billy T. had spent the night with friends in order to get the peace he craved, but then he mostly lay awake thinking about Tone-Marit having to cope with it all on her own.

The apartment was quite simply too small, but they could not afford to do anything about it.

The bedroom was chilly and he pulled the quilt up to his chin. His feet protruded from the bottom and he curled up. Jenny made gurgling noises, and like an echo, he heard a whimper from Tone-Marit.

The only woman he had never actually abandoned was his mother. Each time their relationship ran into difficulties, he simply lay low for a while. Then it was smoothed over. Billy T. had never understood the expression "to work at a relationship." A relationship was not a job. Either you saw eye-to-eye, or else you didn't.

The encounter with Suzanne had been just what he didn't need.

When he had sprinted home from Entré on Monday night, he had wanted to cry. Instead he had blamed the toothache and had gone to bed before Tone-Marit. He had lain awake that night too.

It must have been twenty years since he had last seen Suzanne.

He got up carefully, dragging his quilt with him.

The boys' beds were too small.

He lay down on the settee. Truls had broken his earphones last weekend, when the youngsters had agitated to play *Star Wars* and Truls was made to be Princess Leia because he was the youngest.

Eighteen years had gone by since he had heard from her, when he made a precise calculation. He did not want to; he wanted to think about something else.

He had been twenty-two then, and his first year at police college was almost over. She had phoned him to help her return to the acute psychiatric wing. After that she had simply disappeared. As far as he was aware, she had later moved to France. It was of no concern to him and he had forgotten all about her.

Alexander wanted nothing but a PlayStation. He was the only boy in his class who did not have one. A PlayStation cost as much as what Billy T. had to spend on all four boys added together.

He closed his eyes and pressed his jaw shut to ease the tooth-ache. It grew worse. Now the pain was gripping the back of his head tight; it felt as if half his head was being unscrewed from his body.

Hanne Wilhelmsen had left him.

She was the one who had left him, not the other way around.

He did not want to think.

The phone rang.

Billy T. jumped up, dashed into the hallway, and threw himself at the apparatus before it had time to ring again. He stood stiffly to attention and listened for sounds from the bedroom.

"Hello," he almost hissed into the receiver.

"Hi. It's Severin."

"It's … it's nearly one o'clock, for fuck's sake!"

"Sorry, but—"

"I've a wee baby here, you know!"

"I've said sorry, but there's something I was sure you'd want to know right away."

"What's that, then?"

Billy T. pushed his thumb into his eye socket and pressed hard.

"Brede Ziegler was murdered twice."

Car tires screeched outside the window, followed by the noise of a violent collision. Billy T. held his breath and sent up a silent prayer.

Jenny wailed.

"Shit," he said. "The baby's awake. What did you say?"

He moved to the window and looked out. A taxi driver was arguing with a young woman who was in floods of tears. Two Mercedes had taken an enormous mouthful from each other's front end.

Jenny was screeching like a stuck pig.

"Wait a minute," Billy barked into the phone.

Tone-Marit was about to lift the baby when he entered the bedroom. Half-asleep, she handed him the child without protest, before quite literally diving back into bed.

"Hush, my little one. It's Daddy. Nothing's wrong."

Clamping his daughter to his chest, he tottered back to the living room to pick up the receiver again.

"What did you say?" he mumbled.

"Brede Ziegler was in fact killed twice."

Jenny gurgled and grabbed her father's nose.

"Twice," he said in a monotone. "He was killed twice. Well, well."

"Do you remember Forensics wondering whether the guy was a drinker? Because his complexion was such a strange color?"

"I think so."

As the sound of howling sirens approached, Jenny clung to his neck. She began to cry again. Billy T. pushed a pacifier into her gaping mouth.

"It wasn't alcohol. It was paracetamol. Brede Ziegler was poisoned. Stuffed full of paracetamol."

"Paracetamol? You mean … like ordinary Paracet, the kind in the orange wrapper?"

"Extremely dangerous in large doses. That's why you can't buy more than one pack at a time in the pharmacy."

"But … did he die of that? Was he already dead when he was stabbed?"

"No, the other way round. He died of the knife wound, but would probably have died later of poisoning anyway. If he hadn't received hospital treatment, that is. In time."

"Oh, fuck."

"You can say that again."

"We'll discuss this in the morning."

"Fine. Hope I haven't spoiled the night for you."

"Spoiled nights are my specialty," Billy T. murmured as he dropped the receiver on the floor.

When the vehicles outside had been towed away and Jenny had fallen asleep at last, it was past five o'clock on the morning of Thursday December 9. Billy T. laid the child down in bed and padded out to the bathroom. He ran the bath water and decided to go to work as soon as he was dressed. It was all the same to him. If he fell asleep now, he would never be able to get up again. As the bath filled, he pressed the nine remaining Paracet tablets out of their foil and flushed them down the toilet, where they vanished in a rush of blue water.

At least his toothache had gone.

14

One of the many snippets of information Vilde Veierland Ziegler had withheld from the police was that she mainly stayed at Sinsen, where she had a two-room apartment in Siloveien. The second room, strictly speaking, was no more than a hole in the wall with space for a broad single bed. The apartment did contain a toilet, but the shower was in the hallway and shared by three apartments.

Brede sometimes needed peace and quiet – that's what he had said, at least. After all, he was an artist. In the beginning the arrangement had seemed prudent. He simply asked now and again to be allowed some space, every second week or so. Just for a couple of days. Later it grew longer. For the past three months she had noticed that, without really thinking it through, she had moved all her clothes and personal possessions into the poky apartment. That was where she lived. She still kept the key and code for Niels Juels gate, but she had hardly spent a night there for several weeks.

Vilde had no idea who owned the apartment in which she was living. Brede had taken care of it all. It had not meant anything, and he always arranged everything. Now things had become more difficult. She sat curled up in bed with her knees tucked under her chin, completely in the dark as to who was the owner of her home. The police would almost certainly find out where she really stayed. Maybe she ought to move down to Niels Juels gate at once. She had already considered that when she had left police headquarters, but something held her back. Niels Juels gate was more like an exhibition space. Brede had been so hysterically terrified that she might make any change whatsoever to the interior decor. She had felt as though even her wardrobe was a hindrance to what Brede liked to call "an overall manifestation of aesthetics."

Vilde felt more at ease in Sinsen.

When she inherited Niels Juels gate, she would sell the vast apartment. She would buy herself a little house, maybe in a terrace, in Asker or Bærum, with a small garden and money to spare. She would study. Do some traveling. Quite a lot, when she came to think of it. Traveling was the best way to learn languages.

Vilde burst into tears, clutching her own knees as she rocked back and forth. Brede was dead. The policewoman had been nice enough, but it seemed exactly as if she had seen right through her. She had spotted the concealments lodged inside her throat and made her start to tell lies. They had taken a break three times, and each time Vilde had been offered coffee and bread rolls. She didn't succeed in swallowing a single morsel.

The noise of the doorbell ringing made her bump her knees on her chin. She bit her cheek and was immediately aware of the taste of blood. The digital alarm told her that Thursday had barely begun; it was twenty minutes to six. She remained seated, completely motionless. Someone must have pressed the wrong button; it happened quite often. It rang again.

She would not open the door.

If she sat quite still and pretended not to be at home, then whoever was trying to get hold of her would disappear.

Someone pressed a finger on the doorbell and refused to let go. The shrill sound reverberated through her apartment for a long time. Vilde closed her eyes, holding her hands over her ears.

After a couple of minutes she struggled to her feet and crossed to the window. Slowly, taking care not to be seen, she peered out between the window ledge and the drawn curtains. A male figure, obviously drunk, staggered away along the path. When he reached the bench at the roadside, he leaned against it and turned to face the apartment block. Quick as a flash, Vilde pulled back. She had recognized the man's jacket. Not at all strange, since she had given it to him as a present less than two years earlier, when they had been madly in love and planning to marry.

15

She just wanted to turn back. Momentarily she regretted not wearing the jacket with big lapels that she could have turned up, or maybe a hat. Something to hide behind.

Grønlandsleiret 44 was exactly as before. In one or two windows an optimistic officer who still believed in Christmas had lit a candle to create something of an Advent atmosphere. Apart from that, everything was gray, the way it had always been. The slope up to the main entrance of police headquarters was just as grueling as ever, and she buttoned her jacket as she walked. She stopped at the massive familiar steel doors. She could still turn tail, but she knew that would only be a postponement of the inevitable. Taking a deep breath, she pushed against the door and stepped into the foyer.

The smell made her gasp.

Hanne Wilhelmsen had never thought about police headquarters having a smell, an almost imperceptible scent of office building and sweat, of fear and arrogance, papers, metal, and floor polish. It reeked of the police, and she crossed to the elevator.

"Hanne? Hanne, is it you?"

Erik Henriksen's shock of red hair was as untidy as ever, and his mouth fell open.

"The one and only."

Hanne really made an effort to smile. She felt her leather jacket sticking to the back of her shirt, and most of all wanted to do an about-turn and vanish.

"Where have you ...? Where have you been? Are you back ... for good, I mean? How are you doing?"

The elevator pinged. Hanne snaked past her former colleague, sending up a silent prayer that the doors would close before it entered his head to follow.

"Speak later," she mumbled, and her prayer was answered.

It seemed as though the rumor had traveled faster than the elevator. On the sixth floor, she had the impression that everyone was staring at her. At the canteen entrance, five people stood silent, but made no move to go inside for lunch. She nodded halfheartedly at one of them as she passed. Their eyes burned into her back as she continued along the gallery toward the Chief of Police's office. The faint whispering rose to animated discussion as she moved off.

In the end she could not restrain herself.

She wheeled round and suddenly the five officers rushed away.

When her gaze swept down over the galleries on the other side of the six-story foyer, she caught sight of him. On the second floor, blue zone. Stopping suddenly, he leaned against the banister and squinted up at her. He was too far away for her to read the expression on his face.

All the same, it was impossible to mistake.

Billy T. shrugged and turned his back on her.

As for herself, she called in to see the Chief of Police, to find out whether she still had a job.

16

" I thought the woman was mentally disturbed, so I did. At least, that's what I'd heard. Admitted to Gaustad psychiatric hospital and that sort of thing. Committed, or so they say."

Beate from reception adjusted her dress strap with a giggle, before taking a far too generous swig of the aquavit. A fine shower of alcohol sprayed across the table, and Karianne swiftly drew back.

"Somebody said she had gone to China to adopt a child. Somebody who knows her really well, that is. So I'd thought she might be on some sort of maternity leave, or whatever they call it these days ..."

Karianne Holbeck's appearance had undergone a transformation that caused a couple of police trainees to force their way down to their table. Normally she hung about in clothes from the Lindex fashion chain, which revealed no secrets other than that she was heavily built. She never wore make-up. Her face was usually pale, with almost-white eyelashes and brows. Her annoying tendency to blush was afforded plenty of leeway. Her colleagues had begun to give her the nickname "Traffic Light" when they thought themselves out of earshot.

She was unrecognizable. A well-fitting dress of gray velvet skimmed over rounded hips and thighs. Her ample breasts had uplift. Her hair usually hung loose, presumably because it was the only cover she could hide behind when her face turned red. Now she had clearly paid a visit to the hairdresser, since the ingenious hairstyle could not possibly be her own handiwork. Or the make-up, either: it looked as if she had just taken part in some gala TV show.

"I think I'm overdressed," she whispered to Severin Heger, tightly clutching her beer glass. "Look at them all!"

He sat beside her with his arm around her bare shoulders. Karl Sommarøy stood at the bar counter discussing cars with a colleague. He had just bought a four-year-old Audi A6 and was complaining that the turbo was smoking after only two days. His shirt tail was hanging out and he was dressed in jeans. Admittedly he was wearing a tie for once, but it was already loosened and would almost certainly end up adorning his head within the hour.

"You look fabulous," Severin whispered in her ear. "The most beautiful woman here. The others are making fools of themselves. Not you. You are ... stunning! Cheers."

Her complexion was approaching purple as her fingers squeezed the glass even more tightly.

"This place is different from how I ... from what I expected, you see."

She stammered as she stole a glance around the room with her head bowed.

"Not exactly the Ritz, no. Hoi! You, Karl!"

Sommarøy turned around, showing his irritation.

"Don't you have anything else to wear?"

"Just give over, won't you! I thought we were going for a pizza!"

The run-down restaurant in Brugata was located only four or five siren-blasts away from police headquarters. The Christmas Party Committee had chosen the place from sheer laziness. Brown tables, red checked tablecloths, and candles planted in old Mateus Rosé bottles were in all likelihood intended to give the illusion of a French bistro.

Karl Sommarøy stuck his pipe in his mouth and plumped himself down at the table.

"As to food, what do you think?"

No one felt called upon to pass any remark about the black charred sheep heads, mostly untouched when they had been carried back to the kitchen nearly half an hour ago.

"But didn't you *see* Hanne Wilhelmsen today, then?"

Beate from reception had begun to slur her words.

"I saw her, so I did!"

Billy T. sat sulking at the far end of the table. He had hardly spoken a word since his arrival, halfway through their meal. He did not have much to drink and looked at his watch every ten minutes. Now he leaned back and folded his arms across his chest.

Sergeant Klaus Veierød laughed all of a sudden.

"I've heard she's writing a crime novel! Isn't that what most folk do nowadays, eh?"

Veierød was probably the most experienced investigator of them all, having served in every single department in police headquarters. Three years ago he had been transferred from Finance to Violent Crime. He was thorough, punctilious, and completely lacking in imagination. A long time had elapsed since he had realized he would never become a chief inspector, but that did not matter. He could retire on full pension in six years' time, if he wanted to. Then he would be able to devote all his time to his collection of old war mementos. He was gradually beginning to form a plan of building a little museum in the ancient barn beside his cottage so that he could be his own boss, with no interference from anyone.

The breathless pace of the Violent Crime Section did not suit Klaus Veierød. Least of all did he like the inner circle that surrounded Hanne Wilhelmsen, Billy T., and Håkon Sand. When the clique had been disbanded – first by Sand being appointed a public prosecutor, and later by Hanne Wilhelmsen disappearing once the case involving the homicide charge against Chief

Public Prosecutor Halvorsrud had been finally solved – Klaus Veierød had been only too pleased. Admittedly he had never questioned Wilhelmsen's abilities. Privately he considered her the best detective the Oslo police force had ever seen. It was the feeling of being excluded that he could not stand. As long as Billy T. and Hanne Wilhelmsen were only sergeants, things had gone fairly smoothly. As chief inspectors, however, they were both useless. Skulking about here and there, whispering and harboring all sorts of secrets. That's not how things were supposed to be.

"Billy T.," Klaus Veierød said, leaning across the table. "Can't you tell us where she's been, eh? After all, you know her so well!"

The Chief Inspector looked at his watch again, before staring absent-mindedly into his glass, half-full of flat beer.

"Do you know," Silje Sørensen said, installing herself on the lap of one of the police trainees, "I think we'll soon be able to wrap up the whole investigation. It's my belief that Brede Ziegler committed suicide."

An awkward silence spread around the table where eight people now sat on six chairs.

"Exactly," Severin murmured.

"Right enough," Karl Sommarøy said, sucking his pipe.

"But think about it," Silje insisted. "He was, after all, full of—"

"Honestly," Severin interrupted. "You don't really *mean* that someone has committed suicide by using a knife to stab himself through the heart on the steps outside police headquarters, do you?"

Silje waved her right hand, where the diamond ring twinkled in the subdued light.

"What have we got, then? Ziegler had bought the knife himself. Wasn't that what you found out this morning, Karl?"

Karl Sommarøy nodded, struggling to relight his pipe.

"So," Silje went on, taking a breath. "Brede had purchased his own murder weapon two days prior to his death. The shop assistant recognized him, and they hadn't sold a knife like that for a few weeks."

"We don't *know for sure* that it was the same knife," Severin protested. "Although they're extremely dangerous, they're not numbered or anything of that nature."

"Hel-lo!"

Silje rolled her eyes.

"It's quite likely, though."

"And then the guy wiped off his fingerprints," Severin said into his beer glass. "After he died, of course—"

"I wish you wouldn't smoke so much."

Silje rummaged in her handbag for a handkerchief; a solitary tear was running from her left eye. She seemed seriously disconcerted. The blond police trainee, who was obviously enjoying having her on his knee, roared out a command for someone to open the door for some air. No one responded.

"Brede's fingerprints were on the knife blade anyway," Silje Sørensen continued. "So it's established beyond all doubt that he *had* taken hold of it. He may have worn gloves, for instance, he—"

"… his hands were bare."

Severin signaled to the waiter for more beer.

"Okay," Silje said. "But … it's remarkable then that the guy was stuffed full of paracetamol, don't you think? I mean, according to Forensics, he had ingested around fifteen grams. Only people intending suicide do that. I'm willing to bet that he *wanted* to die, and then was so disoriented that he plunged the knife into himself. Maybe by accident. Or to make sure of dying. Who knows."

Karl stroked his hand over what little he had of a chin. His entire jaw seemed to disappear under his thumb.

"She has a point, you know … Brede Ziegler's liver was quickly progressing toward total collapse and he must have been suffering pain for hours on end, perhaps for twenty-four hours or so. Odd that he didn't consult a doctor."

"We don't know whether he did."

This was the first contribution Billy T. had made all evening. He stood up and disappeared in the direction of the toilet.

"The man who died twice," Klaus Veierød said. "Wasn't that a film?"

Severin Heger stood, making a move to leave. "I think you're all crazy. Bloody hell, I—"

"Hang on a minute," Karl said soothingly, pulling him down again. "Everything certainly points to Ziegler being in that area of his own free will. His car was found in the vicinity. In Sverres gate, neatly parked and locked, with no sign of any attempted break-in or hot-wiring."

Karianne Holbeck no longer regretted her outfit or hairstyle. Everyone wanted to drink a toast with her. On several occasions she had felt tentative strokes on her neck as someone walked past. Someone was conducting a hesitant flirtation with her under the table, but she did not dare to discover who it was.

"Now you really need to sharpen up," she said, more abruptly than usual, as she put her hand on Severin's shoulder. "No one – absolutely no one – has claimed that Brede Ziegler was depressed. We've conducted twenty-seven or -eight interviews to date, and the words 'depressed' or even 'fed up' haven't been mentioned a single time."

Silence descended on the table. Unexpectedly Billy T. returned and resumed his seat. However, it still seemed he had no intention of joining the discussion.

"On the contrary," Karianne added. "Even though it's almost impossible to form a picture of the man from our interviews ..."

She straightened a lock of hair and sipped her aquavit.

"Is it possible to get some red wine instead?" she said, smiling at Klaus Veierød, who seemed the likeliest suspect in relation to the flirting foot.

He shrugged.

"You'll have some red wine," Severin said, grinning, as he attracted the attention of a passing waiter. "Red wine for the lady! I'm paying."

"It's exactly as though he has been a … an amoeba. Or a … an image in one of these telescopes we had as children, you know. The ones that show a picture, but when you give it to someone else to see the same one, it's all changed."

"A kaleidoscope," Severin murmured. "I know what you mean."

Karianne pushed her glass away, pulling a grimace, and glanced across at the bar, where someone was roaring with laughter at a coarse story about their boss.

"During the interviews, of course, we've also concentrated on charting Ziegler's final movements. We know he left his apartment at 19.56 precisely. That can be deduced from that leading-edge alarm system of his. But not a single soul has clapped eyes on him after that. When we ask people about his habits, whether he exercised, or liked to go to the cinema, or went after women—"

"Or if he drank," Severin offered helpfully.

"Exactly. Then we get just as many answers as the various interviewees. To be honest, I've learned more about the guy from reading all his press interviews. There's an unbelievable number of them. At least then he's answering for himself."

"With regard to that, Billy T., have you had any more discussion with that woman at the publishers?"

Severin smiled at the thunderstorm brewing at the end of the table.

"I don't think a Christmas party's the place for discussing a murder case," Billy T. said as he got to his feet, downing his beer in one gulp. "I'm going."

"Good Lord," Klaus Veierød exclaimed. "Was that sheep's head poisonous, or what?"

Billy T. was actually the only one who had eaten the head down to the bone, including the wretched animal's eyes.

"Admit, at the very least, that it's a sound theory," Silje Sørensen said with a note of resignation, shifting to another lap. "It's essential to keep all possibilities open, I think."

A commotion made them all suddenly turn toward the bar.

"... fucking don't!"

One of the police trainees aimed a blow at an equally youthful colleague who had just scrambled to his feet after tripping over a table covered in glasses and ashtrays. He brushed shards of broken glass and fag ends off his jacket and slurped the blood gushing from his nose.

"... and that's *not* why," yelled the other boy as he crashed sideways into the bar counter.

"And you're going home, I think."

From behind, Severin Heger grabbed the young lad by the shoulders and locked his arms. Karl Sommarøy pushed the other one roughly toward the toilets.

"*Let me go, you fucking faggot!*"

"There, there. Take it easy, my boy."

Severin tightened his grip and the trainee screamed louder.

"*Bloody hell*, I'm certainly not your boy!"

"You'll only regret it all in the morning," Severin said, maneuvering the boy across to the exit. "Shut up, won't you. That'd be for the best."

Two minutes later he returned.

"Hailed a taxi," he said, wreathed in smiles, and smacked his hands together triumphantly in a dashing gesture. "He won't feel too well in the morning."

"At last this is starting to look like a Christmas party," Karl said contentedly. "Another couple of hours now and we'll have enough to keep us gossiping through till March."

"You'll have to continue your gossiping without me," Severin said, taking hold of Karianne's hand. "Shall I see the princess home, or will she manage by herself?"

Karianne laughed and let him kiss the back of her hand.

"I think I'll stay a bit longer," she said. "But thanks very much for the offer."

When she withdrew her hand, she sat pressing the back of it to her nose. The faint scent of Sergio Tacchini wafted in the air. Now she was the only person in this whole disreputable premises who was dressed for a party, and she felt pleasantly warm, with no desire to go home just yet. A lot might still happen. Karianne Holbeck wanted to participate in all the gossip, all the way through till spring.

* * *

Interview with witness Sindre Sand

Interviewed by Police Sergeant Klaus Veierød. Transcript typed by office worker Pernille Jacobsen. There is one tape of this interview. The interview was recorded on tape on Saturday December 11, 1999 at 10.00 at Oslo police headquarters.

Witness:

Sand, Sindre, ID number 121072 88992
Address: Fredensborgveien 2, 0177 Oslo
Employment: Chef at Stadtholdergaarden restaurant, Oslo, phone no. 22 33 44 55
Given information about witness rights and responsibilities. Willing to provide a statement, and gave the following explanations:

Interviewer:

Well, the tape recorder is running now, so we can make a start. Have you ever given a statement to the police on any previous occasion ... ehh ... do you know the procedure?

Witness:

No, I've never had any dealings with the police before. Other than having reported a stolen bike a couple of times, that is to say *(indistinct speech)* ... can ask me whatever you want. But I'm pretty tired, you know. Worked late yesterday, and then there was something afterwards.

Interviewer:

As you know, this has to do with the murder of Brede Ziegler. We're trying to speak to everyone who knew him or—

Witness *(interrupts)*:

I know that.

Interviewer:

Fine. You ... *(Telephone rings.)* I just need to switch ... The interview recommences at 10.15 hours. The witness has been given coffee. Sorry about that phone call, now I've given instructions so that we won't be disturbed again. Where were we? ... You knew Brede Ziegler, is that right?

Witness:

Yes.

Interviewer:

For how long?

Witness:

A really long time. I began as an apprentice with Brede when I was seventeen.

Interviewer:

And you're now ... Born in 1972, I see. That would make you ...

Witness:

I'll be twenty-eight next October.

Interviewer:

How well did you know Brede Ziegler?

Witness:

(Brief laughter.) That depends on what you mean by *well*.

Interviewer:

I suppose ... Did you know him as a boss, or did you socialize at all? Of course, he was considerably older than you.

Witness:

Don't think that meant much to Brede, exactly. Anyway, we can just get straight to the point. Brede was a scumbag. That's probably what you want to know, I assume. What I thought of him, I mean. A good old-fashioned scumbag. Of the very worst kind.

Interviewer:

Scumbag. It was then ... Go ahead and smoke. You can use the coffee cup as an ashtray. How ...? What do you actually mean by the description "scumbag"?

Witness:

There aren't really so many ways of being a scumbag. I mean the whole caboodle. Brede Ziegler used people, trampled on them, swindled them, thoroughly cheated them. Didn't give a fuck for anybody but himself. As long as Brede got what he wanted, everything was okay. *(Pause, clears throat, indistinct speech.)* … greedy. He was incredibly greedy.

Interviewer:

I see. *(Pause.)* What do you think about him being dead, then?

Witness:

Suits me fine. I'll be totally honest with you. When I got to hear that someone had done him in, first of all I felt nothing. I wasn't even shocked. Then, in fact, I became … *(Long pause, scraping sounds.)* Not exactly happy … More satisfied, in a way. If I knew who the killer was, I would send him flowers.

Interviewer:

Him. Are you so sure it was a man?

Witness:

Whatever. I've no idea.

Interviewer:

I think we'll go over all this from the beginning. How did you get to know Brede Ziegler?

Witness:

I already told you. During my apprenticeship. He was the head chef at the Continental. First of all I was on work-placement from school, and then I got an apprenticeship there. Everyone wanted to work with Brede at that time. He was, like, the hottest chef in the whole city. For the first year I did a lot of the dirty work. Washing up. Peeling and chopping. Rinsing. The usual. But then my father died. *(Some indistinct speech.)* … I got compassionate leave for a week, and everybody was decent when I came back. Especially Brede. Then he called me *talented. (Affected, contorted voice.)* It wasn't until a good while afterwards that I got the picture.

Interviewer:

The picture? Was he—

Witness *(interrupts)*:

(Brief laughter.) No, no. He didn't lay a finger on me. Not on me. Not on boys at all, as far as I know. He laid his fingers on money. On my money, too. *(Pause.)*

Interviewer:

Did you have money? When you were … eighteen?

Witness:

Nineteen. My father died, and I became rich. My mother had died when I was five, and I didn't have any brothers or sisters. Dad had sold two supermarkets and a clothes shop in Lillehammer three months before he died. He was only sixty, and the sale realized more than twelve million kroner. He had scrimped and scraped and worked insanely hard all his life. *(Pause.)* Intended to enjoy himself in his old age. And also there would be something to leave behind, as he used to say. But then he had already worked himself to death … *(Extremely lengthy pause.)*

Interviewer:

And then ... *(Pause.)*

Witness:

Brede had somehow got to know about that money. There was gossip, I suppose, so it's probably not so strange. There were a number of people at work who knew that my father had money, you see. So one day Brede invited me out to dinner. I was super-happy. I felt ... sort of cool. He chatted and picked up the check. Then ... *(indistinct speech, yawn?)* a project in Italy. Milan. In with the big boys, in a manner of speaking. He was going to put in twenty million himself, he said. If I wanted, I could go in with them. It was a sure thing. I was young and stupid and ... *(Pause, then a bang, flat of hand on table?)* Anyway, there's nothing more to be said about it. Other than that Brede came back four months later and said the money was gone. All of it. He apologized and moaned about it, but that was how things were. Then he smiled. He had a certain way of smiling that made people ... I don't know exactly. Feel inferior. The worst of it is that I never got any proof that he had really invested twenty million himself. He said it, at that time. But all I ... I should have gone to a lawyer. I should have made life hell for him. But I was actually fucking ... devastated. Really down in the dumps. *(Lengthy pause.)*

Interviewer:

I'm beginning to understand why you weren't very enthusiastic about the man. Have you ever—

Witness *(interrupts)*:

He stole my girlfriend, too. You must know about that.

Interviewer:

No, I—

Witness *(interrupts)*:

You'll find out about it, anyway. Let's put it like this: there's probably at least a hundred people in Norway alone who could have killed Brede. But there probably aren't very many who had as good a reason to do it as me. He took my money, and he snatched my girlfriend just before we were to be married. Besides, I'm pretty sure that, little by little, he made it difficult for me to get new jobs. He … Can I have another cup? With fresh coffee, I mean?

Interviewer:

Of course. Here. Take this one. I haven't touched it.

Witness:

Thanks.

Interviewer:

What would you say … if you were to …? Would you say that you *hated* Brede Ziegler?

Witness:

(Laughter.) It doesn't matter what I feel. The point is that Brede was a freeloader and a charleetan …

Interviewer:

Charlatan.

Witness:

Whatever. As I said at the start: he was a scumbag.

Interviewer:

At least you appear to be honest. A lot of people wouldn't quite dare to say that they didn't like someone who's been murdered, before …

Witness:

Before the murderer's been found, you mean? I understand that pretty well. The point is that I've got an alibi. *(Loud laughter.)* Watertight, in fact. Brede was murdered on Sunday night, according to the newspapers. I was at the NRK broadcasting studios from eight o'clock that evening. We were recording a TV program that will be shown next Friday. Some sort of food show. I turned up at eight o'clock with a pal of mine, got make-up on at nine, the recording started at quarter to ten, and we were finished at half past eleven. Since we … We were six chefs in two teams, you see, and … Anyway, we had prepared a fucking huge amount of food, and so we had a sort of party afterwards. Ate all the food with the technical team. The cameramen and the program host, and so on. We weren't finished until around one o'clock. Then I went out on the town with three of the others. I was with them until four o'clock in the morning. One of them stayed overnight at my place, since he lives and works in Bergen. Petter Lien, if you want to check that.

Interviewer:

You can be sure we will.

Witness:

I don't have anything to worry about.

Interviewer:

When did you see him last?

Witness:

Brede, you mean?

Interviewer:

Yes. Have you seen him recently at all?

Witness:

Well, it depends what you mean by recently. Don't remember. A good while ago, I think.

Interviewer:

You think? Don't you remember? *(Telephone rings, pause, indistinct speech, on the phone?)* Apologies again. I had given instructions, but that was something urgent. Is it all right if you …? Would you be able to come back in a couple of hours?

Witness:

Not really. I'm bloody exhausted, and have to go to work tonight. Need to catch some sleep, to be honest. It was hard enough to drag myself here so early on a Saturday morning.

Interviewer:

Then I'll see you later. *(Pause.)* Let's say two o'clock?

Witness:

(Lengthy yawn? Sigh?) Okay then. Two o'clock.

Interviewer's note: The interview was terminated because of other pressing business. The witness was cooperative, but obviously affected by tiredness. He seemed somewhat distressed when speaking about the deceased. In one instance

– when talking about the money that by his own account was swindled from him – he had tears in his eyes. The interview will resume at two o'clock.

17

The winter sun that suddenly broke through the heavy clouds did little to help. The room remained gloomy. A solitary 25-watt bulb with no shade hung from a cable in the center of the ceiling. Thale stepped over cardboard boxes on the floor and sat down on the bed. It creaked noisily.

"I don't understand why you don't just move back home. This place is miserable, to put it mildly. Fourth floor without an elevator and hardly any furniture. Besides, it stinks ..."

She sniffed the air.

"Mold. This place must be a health hazard."

She rubbed the sole of her foot on the grubby wall-to-wall carpet and pulled another grimace. Daniel sighed demonstratively as he set down the last packing case. Perspiring from all the heavy lifting, he ran his index finger along his top lip.

"Thale, listen to me. There was some trouble over the rental contract in Bogstadveien and—"

"I could at least feel that you were safe there. Nice and bright and orderly. Why on earth, at the age of twenty-two, you had to find yourself a landlady who doesn't allow girls to visit or the use of the toilet after nine o'clock at night is beyond my comprehension, Daniel. You're more than welcome to move back home. Any time you like. It would be cheaper for you too. This dreary room is so ... You're always so *impractical*, Daniel. In fact, you always have been."

"This place is cheap. And it is *practical* not to spend very much money on rent."

It came out more sharply than he had intended. He smiled and added: "Anyway, it's pathetic to move back into your childhood bedroom after you've left home."

Thale, standing on the bed with her shoes on, was about to take down a picture of a gypsy woman smiling seductively over the edge of a tambourine.

"You simply can't have this hanging here."

She unhooked the picture resolutely, unaware of her son's irritation. Daniel was not particularly enthusiastic either about the gypsy women or about the elk in the sunset hanging on the opposite wall, but his mother could at least have asked. He choked back a protest and scratched his neck. This was how things had always been. Thale made decisions. His mother was not particularly quarrelsome. She was just thoroughly unsentimental and had an extremely practical disposition. It was as if all her emotions were used up in the theater; as if she had to operate at a minimum level for the remainder of the day in order to come to life on stage. Even when, at the age of fourteen, they had thought he was going to die, all that Thale had talked about was how things should be arranged. She had decided that the boy would recover his health, and so that was how it turned out. She browbeat, organized, and bullied the doctors, and Daniel got well again. His mother took it all as a matter of course. Later, Daniel had often wondered why she did not show more gratitude to Taffa. Admittedly Taffa was Thale's sister, but that still didn't make it inevitable that she would be there for her, the way she was. It was Taffa who had sat at his bedside in the evenings, who had comforted him and read to him and stroked his hair, even though he was in ninth grade by then. Only on one occasion had he been able to discern genuine anxiety on his mother's face. That was in the middle of the night, after a performance. Thale had crept into the hospital, thinking Daniel asleep. He had seen her face in the subdued light from the bedside lamp and realized that his mother was scared to death. He grasped her hand and called her Mummy for the first and last time. She let him go, smiled encouragingly and left. Immediately after that, Taffa had arrived and she had stayed until he fell asleep again.

His mother was putting on her coat.

"There's nothing more I can do here. But I still can't understand why you're so hard up that you have to stay here. Is that three or four jobs you've got now, as well as studying?"

"Two, Thale. Two decent part-time jobs."

"Well, you should be able to manage to pay for a reasonable place to live."

Thale always looked at something else whenever she spoke to him. She had put on her coat and was now rummaging through a packing case.

"Are these Grandfather's books?"

She picked up a small book.

"*Catilina*. Impossible play. No good roles for women."

The gloves she had tucked under her arm while she leafed through the book dropped into the case, but she did not notice.

"This is a first edition. The original one, from 1850. Do you know how much this is worth? It's fortunate there wasn't a bank-ruptcy hearing."

She put down the book and caught sight of her gloves. Daniel felt more than anything that he wanted to cry. He gnawed the inside of his cheek and raised his voice.

"I'm not selling any of Grandfather's belongings. Okay? He wanted me to have the things he left behind. Then it turned out that the house at Heggeli was mortgaged to the hilt. So what? Grandfather had these books at least, and he'd be turning in his grave at what you're saying. He loved his book collection. *Loved*, do you understand that?"

Thale spread out her arms in despair.

"The man had promised you the value of a colossal villa, Daniel. He let you down, you know. Instead of securing his only grandchild's future, he chose to ... *gamble away* ..."

She spat out the words, as if the mere thought that her own flesh and blood, her father, had been a notorious gambler made her feel sick.

"Thale, can't we go out for something to eat? Have a chat?"

Daniel ran his fingers over his eyes and tried to take hold of her arm, but she twisted away and pulled on her gloves.

"Go to a café now? No. I need to go home for a nap. I've a performance tonight, you know that."

She blew him a kiss. Then she vanished without another word. The door was left open behind her. Daniel picked up Ibsen's first play. He knew that the book was valuable, but had never dared to investigate more closely how much he might get for it. The gods must know he needed money.

He needed it desperately.

18

The Chief of Police was right. Of course she should have given some kind of advance warning. She could simply have phoned, he had said as his evasive eyes glanced at her in mild reproach. He was right, of course he was, from a purely objective point of view. She could have sent a letter or made a phone call. The Police Chief was not to know that something of that sort had been impossible. Not until she was in Norway at least, and then she felt she might as well turn up in person.

The new office was located in the depths of the red zone, distant from all the others in the section. She had accepted the key without a murmur. The room was stripped of everything other than an office desk with a chair and a shabby enamel metal shelf unit. In addition, a computer sat on the floor beside a jumble of cables unconnected to anything whatsoever. An almost imperceptible odor of ammonia and dust told her that the last occupant had moved out long ago. The window refused to budge. The frame was probably warped. All the same, she lit a cigarette. Since there was nothing resembling an ashtray, she used the floor.

The assignment had obviously been engineered by Billy T. to keep her here. Hanne Wilhelmsen was to read through all the written material in the Ziegler case. Analyze it. Come up with suggestions for further interviews or alternative steps in the investigation. Write notes. In a best-case scenario they would hardly need to meet. She had carried a half-meter-high stack of documents along the corridor from the waiting room without anyone so much as looking in her direction. Now the papers sat like a wobbly model of the Postgirobygget skyscraper on the other side of the desk. Hanne lit yet another cigarette and rubbed her eyes. It was Saturday December 11, and she had spent six hours skimming all of it.

Perhaps she needed glasses.

The apartment was like a mausoleum. She had endured it for all of ten minutes, just enough to scrape together a few items of clothing, fill a suitcase, and book into a hotel. The Royal Christiania was within walking distance of police headquarters. It would be best to take one thing at a time. She had wondered initially about going up to Håkon and Karen in Vinderen. They had a large house and plenty of space. Something stopped her. After having seen Billy T. turn his back on her, she realized what it was.

She had never spared them a thought.

When Cecilie died, the others were as nothing. Even Cecilie's parents were insignificant. Cecilie's death was Hanne's sorrow, Hanne's misfortune. The others could take care of the funeral, gravestone, and obituary in *Aftenposten*. Hanne did not even know if she had been mentioned in that. In all likelihood she had been; Cecilie's parents had always been friendly, never disapproving. In her most lucid moments, Hanne could see that all they had wished for, through almost twenty years, was that *she* would accept *them*.

Hanne had not given them a thought. Not her parents, not their friends. Cecilie's death was her death. There was no room for anything else. That her parents might want something of their daughter's – a piece of jewelry or a picture, the antique vinaigrette that Cecilie had inherited from her grandmother and that had been her dearest possession, or the photograph of Cecilie as a newly qualified doctor wearing her white coat and holding her stethoscope and diploma triumphantly aloft – the thought had not entered her head. The apartment was untouched. Cecilie's parents did have keys: they had been given a set when Cecilie was at her most poorly. They could have let themselves in and taken whatever they wanted. No one had been there. Hanne knew that the moment she opened the front door. It was her own sorrow that filled the rooms, untouched by all the others.

There was a knock at the door.

Assuming she had misheard, Hanne opened a ring binder without answering it.

Another knock followed and the door opened ever so slowly. A woman warily popped her head inside.

"Sorry! Am I disturbing you?"

Hanne Wilhelmsen looked up and blew cigarette smoke through gritted teeth.

"Not at all. Come in, if you can stand the smoke."

"Actually, I can't really."

The woman was young and slender, almost frail-looking. When she tottered across to the window on the highest heels Hanne had seen outside Italy, it struck her that the girl was unlikely to be a police officer. An office worker, probably. Or one of those clerical assistants who typed up interviews, and that sort of thing.

The window relented and she threw it wide.

"There's a knack, you see. It's something to do with the settlement of the whole building. You have to press just *here* ..."

She smacked the bottom corner lightly with her fist. Then she opened her slim hand and held it out it to Hanne.

"Silje Sørensen. Police officer. Nice to meet you!"

Hanne half-rose from her seat and took her hand.

"Hanne Wilhelmsen. Chief Inspector. In name only, that is."

"I know! I've heard about you, you know! Everybody has."

"I'm sure."

Hanne made great play of lighting another cigarette with the old one.

"I was really only delivering these to you," Silje Sørensen said, slapping a green folder down on the desk. "Have they not even given you an extra chair? I'll bring you one."

"No, not at all. I'll do it later. Here, take this one."

Hanne pushed her chair halfway round the desk and found a comfortable spot for herself to perch on the window ledge.

"I didn't mean it like that," Silje Sørensen said, remaining on her feet. "As I said, I was only supposed to give you these ..."

She pointed again at the papers in the green cover.

"More interviews. And then I just wanted to say that ... that it's lovely to have you back, you see. Of course I'm new and all that, but ... That was all. Welcome back."

She headed for the door, but turned around after only a couple of steps.

"Tell me, where have you been, in actual fact?"

Hanne burst out laughing. She lifted her face, turned to the snowy weather outside the window, and laughed out loud. For a long time. Then she dried her eyes and turned to face the room again.

"You may well ask. I must tell you this. I've not spoken to many people since I got home, but they at least have better reason to ask than you. But you're the first one. In fact."

She gasped and tried to pull herself together.

Silje Sørensen sat down. She crossed her legs, tilted her head, and asked again: "But where have you been, then? I've heard so many strange stories."

"I'm sure you have."

Hanne's laughter continued. She tried to catch her breath and tears ran down her face. Then she fell totally silent. She held her breath and closed her eyes to ward off a violent headache crawling ominously up her neck. It would take complete hold if she did not relax.

"What have you heard?" she eventually asked.

"Lots of weird things. Different things."

"What, then?"

"Where have you been? Can't you just tell me?"

Hanne reopened her eyes. Silje Sørensen's face was still not visibly affected by police work. She did not hide herself. Her big blue eyes were genuinely curious. Her smile was authentic. There was not a trace of cynicism in the graceful features of her face.

"Jesus!" Hanne muttered.

"What?"

"Nothing. You remind me of a picture I ... Nothing. Beautiful ring."

She pointed at Silje Sørensen's right hand.

"Got that from my husband." Silje was whispering, as if the ring were an embarrassing secret.

"Everything's fine. Don't bother about the people here in police headquarters. They're chronically bitter about the levels of pay and can't bear anyone else having money. I've been in a convent."

Hanne's heels hit the floor. Then she left the room. First of all she went to the toilet to swallow down three Paracet tablets with a glass of water. Then she checked four offices before she found a chair that she could appropriate without too much of a guilty conscience. On the way back she balanced a ceramic ashtray on top of a half-full cup of coffee in one hand, as she dragged the chair behind her with the other.

"You're still here," she said dully to Silje Sørensen as she closed the door behind her.

"A convent," Silje said slowly. "Is that true? Have you been ...? Have you become a nun, or what?"

"No. Not quite. I've been staying at a convent hotel. In Italy. It's quite simply a place where you can take some time to yourself in order to ... have some time. Think. Read. Get your strength back. Eat simple food and drink simple wine. Try to find your way back to ... simplicity."

"Oh."

"I don't suppose that's what you had heard. Lesson number one for every detective: don't believe everything you hear. Or everything you see. Understand?"

When Silje did not answer, Hanne opened one of the document folders spread out in front of her.

"Silje," she said deliberately, as if not entirely sure whether she liked the name. "We're both working on the same case, I see. Has it struck you that this investigation is sprawling in all directions?"

"What? Pardon?"

"I can't seem to be able to get a grip of ... They *say* so little, these witnesses. It strikes me that it's not only because they have so little to tell, but more that ... They haven't been asked!"

"But it's—"

"Don't take it personally. You're totally new, and your interviews are all right, but look ... Look at this, for instance. This is an interview that Billy T. conducted himself."

Hanne Wilhelmsen dropped her cigarette on the floor before realizing that she had brought an ashtray. Ignoring the fact that Silje bent down to peer underneath the desk, she produced the report of the conversation with Idun Franck as she ground the cigarette butt into the linoleum.

"This Franck woman is, in my opinion, one of the most important witnesses we have in this case. She has spoken intimately with the deceased over a period of several months and has in her possession notes, tape recordings, and God knows what. And then she gathers up all this stuff and protects it under her duty of confidentiality. Billy T. must have become terribly interested in law recently. His special report looks most like a legal dissertation. He lets the woman chatter away about the *Criminal Procedure Act*, section 125, and her right to refuse to give a statement and blah, blah, blah. It seems a bit strange to me that an editor in a publishing company, who should first and foremost have knowledge of language and literature, starts to refer to the *European Convention on Human Rights* ..."

Smacking her lips, Hanne shook her head as she let her finger run across the paper.

"Here. Article ten. How does she know all this? Police Prosecutor Skar is still poring over it to work out that whole legal mush, and she's a lawyer after all! Idun Franck couldn't have known ... It's advanced expertise for a publishing editor, I must say. And here ..."

Hanne produced yet another cigarette, but refrained from lighting it.

"Why hasn't he asked how they work at the publishing house? Whether there are others who had contact with Brede? It seems there were loads of photographs taken at the restaurant, but Billy T. hasn't enquired about who took them. Information like that at least can't be covered by this ... *duty of confidentiality*! Besides, why hasn't the lady in question been called in for formal interview?"

She tapped the cigarette filter on the desktop.

"Am I being very instructive now?" she said to Silje with a smile.

Silje shook her head and seemed to be longing to ask a question. She closed her mouth with a little click.

"And here," Hanne said, opening a brown envelope.

She withdrew three sheets of A4 paper.

"These are copies of the threatening letters Brede Ziegler received. They were found in a drawer with a complaint, somewhere in the

blue zone yesterday. Yesterday! Five days after the murder! And
then it turns out that they were given due prominence in *Se og Hør*
magazine less than two months ago. Does nobody here keep up
with what's going on, or what?"

She waved the gossip rag, in which a deeply concerned Brede
Ziegler graced half of the front page under the headline "Death
Threats Time after Time."

"We don't exactly read *Se og Hør* regularly here, you know."

Silje Sørensen tugged at her dark hair and leaned closer to look
at the copies.

"Surely you do," Hanne Wilhelmsen mumbled. "Look at these
ridiculous words: *'One, two, buckle my choux, dead pastry-chef.'*
'By hook or by crook, I'll kill that stupid cook.' And then there's
this signature, *'Iron Fist.'* What's that supposed to mean? The
point is … All famous people receive threatening letters of some
kind or other. It's seldom that anyone needs to bother much
about it. There are plenty of harmless nutters out there, in a
manner of speaking. This rhymesmith here might well be one
of them. But for crying out loud, we need to have a system that
identifies such complaints when people actually end up getting
murdered!"

"Don't get mad at me!"

Silje Sørensen smiled like a little girl, as if disclaiming all
responsibility for everything. Hanne had no idea why she was
talking to this young police officer. At present she had not dem-
onstrated anything other than that she was a rather sweet and
probably spoiled young woman. But there was something about
her eyes. They reminded Hanne of something she had lost or forgotten long ago.

"One more thing."

Hanne let the still-unlit cigarette spin between the index and
middle fingers of her right hand.

"Why has no one done any more about finding the person who discovered the body?"

"Discovered the body? We were the ones who discovered the body. Two policeman who—"

"No. Someone phoned."

"Yes, but it was just a very short message and—"

"That person might have something to tell us. He or she could have—"

"It was a she. Of course we've listened to the tape, and it's a woman. Probably."

"I see. And do we know anything more than that? Age, background, accent? The lady might have seen something. Found something. Stolen something. God save us, the woman could be the murderer, for all we know. And in all this material here ..."

She rubbed the bridge of her nose as she stared at Silje.

"... there is nothing whatsoever to indicate that anyone has done anything about finding her."

The door opened with a crash.

"So this is where you are," Billy T. said grumpily to Silje as he held the door open with his hip. "I've been looking for you. Do you think this room's a café? But for all I know maybe you've already been to the security firm and picked up the video cassettes from Niels Juels gate?"

Silje got to her feet and hovered, at a loss. Billy T. was blocking the doorway.

"No, but I'm on my way there and ... Was just having a chat with Hanne."

"Get your ass in gear, Silje. This case won't be solved by chatting."

Silje dashed to the door as Billy T. stood aside, making a pretense of sweeping her out of the tiny office.

"Very smart, Billy T.," Hanne Wilhelmsen said tersely. "Push Silje around, when it's me you're mad at."

"Ground rules," he replied vehemently, banging his fist down on the desk. His face was only fifteen to twenty centimeters from Hanne's as he continued: "*One*: I'll leave you in peace. *Two*: you leave me in peace. *Three*: and then you'd *fucking better* leave my investigators in peace as well, so that they can get on with their work."

Hanne did not relinquish eye contact.

After that ill-fated night when they had turned to each other in their shared misery about Cecilie – only a couple of months before she died – he had gone around like a frightened dog. Not once had she glanced in his direction. She had punished him severely for a crime for which she herself was responsible. It was essential: nothing sufficiently agonizing existed to make amends herself. Not until Cecilie died could she make a start on her own atonement. He had begged for reconciliation before she left. Now he was rejecting her with every move he made, with every fiber of his being.

"Is it at all possible for the two of us to talk?" she whispered.

"No! You took off, Hanne. You ran away. You didn't give a shit about me or any of the others, you just … Who was it who had to …? *No!* We've got nothing to talk about."

Her ears were ringing when he slammed the door behind him. She could not even muster the energy to weep.

19

"We must report her. Really and truly."

The cat's body was properly buried in a decorous ceremony at Thomas's grandmother's house. Helmer's mortal remains lay under almost ten centimeters of frozen earth beside a leafless oak tree. Thomas himself had constructed the cross and painted it green with red stripes.

"For what?"

"What do you mean? For what? For killing the cat, of course!"

Sonja Gråfjell smacked the newspaper on her lap as she continued: "The woman's stark staring mad! To think of killing ... To think of *poisoning* Helmer! Next time it might be—"

"We don't *know for sure* that Helmer was poisoned."

Bjørn Berntsen whispered and pointed at the door of the bedroom where Thomas should have gone to sleep ages ago. Repeated scraping sounds told them that he still hadn't even gone to bed.

"Of course he was poisoned. Thomas saw for himself that Mrs. Helmersen coaxed Helmer to come to her for some food. Why on earth would she do that? She *hated* that cat!"

"Maybe she'd discovered they were related," Bjørn Berntsen said drily. "They have almost the same name, after all."

"Don't joke about it."

Sonja Gråfjell stared skeptically into the depths of her redwine glass, as if she suspected Tussi Helmersen of tampering with that too.

"Until now, I've just regarded her as an annoying, eccentric old lady. But *murder*!"

"Sonja! We're talking about a cat!"

"A living, breathing creature that Thomas loved dearly. I'm just so … *furious*."

Bjørn Berntsen moved closer to her on the settee. He kissed his wife on the head and let his mouth linger on her hair.

"I am too, darling. You're quite right that it probably was Mrs. Helmersen who poisoned Helmer. But let's not blow this out of all proportion. We're talking about a frail old lady who was fed up with Helmer yowling and peeing on the landing. Nor can we prove anything whatsoever. The saucer's gone, and Helmer's dead and buried. You were the one who insisted on that cere-mony there."

"It was important for Thomas," she said curtly, moving away. "If you won't come with me, I'll go to the police by myself."

"With what? Do you really think the police can prioritize a dead cat, in a city where people are being murdered and raped and—"

"I suppose you're right."

Sonja Gråfjell stood up. Thomas had opened the door and was standing in the doorway tugging at his pajamas.

"I can't sleep," he whimpered. "Can't I stay up for a while?"

"Of course you can," said his mother, taking him by the hand. "Come over here, then, and we'll see if there's anything worth watching on TV."

When the Gråfjell Berntsen family woke on Sunday morning, nobody said any more about going to the police. Instead they took a trip out to Bygdøy and picked up a new kitten, as Thomas's mother had promised. The cat was ginger, just like Helmer.

"I'm going to call him Tigerboy," Thomas said.

20

I dun Franck gave her reflection a skeptical glance. She was wearing a pair of black trousers and a gray V-necked sweater. Everything was shades of gray and black at present. It did not suit her. All the same, she couldn't be bothered doing anything about it. She could barely be bothered with the thought of going to the theater. She ran her hand through her damp hair and came to a decision for the third time.

"Straight to the theater, straight home."

She drew on her sheepskin coat and pulled a woolen hat down over her hair. The wall clock showed quarter past five. If she hurried, she could walk instead of taking the tram. In fact she could not stand Saturday performances. They began as early as six o'clock, so that the audience could eat dinner afterwards; people in party mood who clapped enthusiastically whether the performance was good or bad. Idun went into the bedroom to fetch a pair of socks. She had put on her outer layers and forgotten she was still barefoot after her shower.

"Straight to the theater. Straight home."

The green-and-mauve Indian silk scarf would break the drabness of brown, gray, and black. A faint whiff of perfume rose from the empty bottle tucked between panties, socks, and dress scarves. Idun grabbed a pair of brown toweling socks. She nearly fell over as she put them on. Her hands then rummaged through the rest of the drawer contents. The Indian scarf was missing. Irritated, she snatched up another one, the red-and-yellow scarf she had bought in Paris several months earlier. When she finally locked the door behind her, it dawned on her that she had left the ticket on the kitchen worktop.

Tears threatened to spill over when, at last, she was able to run downstairs with the ticket in her hand.

"Straight home afterwards," she repeated in an undertone, and it occurred to her that she had forgotten her purse.

It did not matter. She was going to walk there and back in any case.

* * *

Interview with witness Signe Elise Johansen

Interviewed by police officer Silje Sørensen. Transcript typed by office colleague Pernille Jacobsen. There is in total one tape of this interview. The interview was recorded on tape on Sunday December 12, 1999 at Oslo police headquarters.

Witness:

Johansen, Signe Elise, ID number 110619 73452
Address: Nordbergveien 14, 0875 Oslo
Phone no.: 22 13 45 80
Status: Retired
Made aware of witness rights and responsibilities, willing to give a statement.
The witness is the mother of the victim. Explained as follows:

Interviewer:

Well, I've pressed the button now, so we've started. The time is … 14.17. As I just said to you, we record what you say on this tape for purely practical reasons. Then I don't have to write while we're talking. The police are very pleased ... hm ... I mean thanks for making the time to come. I know that it must be difficult for you.

Witness:

It's absolutely dreadful! *(Very loud voice.)*

Interviewer:

(Crackling.) ... just move this slightly. There's good sound on this ... You don't need to speak right into the microphone, Mrs. Johansen. You can just use your normal voice.

Witness:

Oh, sorry. I'm not used to these modern contraptions. But it's absolutely dreadful ... I can't take it in *(quiet sobbing)* ... that Brede is dead. He's never done anything wrong, you know!

Interviewer:

Maybe you could speak even more softly. I'd just like to say ... that we're working hard to find the person who has done this. But perhaps we should begin—

Witness *(interrupts)*:

And I don't get to know anything at all. I've still not had a message about when he can be buried. I expect it's someone from medical ... I've forgotten what it's called. The people who decide these things, I mean.

Interviewer:

Forensics. First of all they have to complete the postmortem, before the undertakers can take over. Unfortunately, that takes some time.

Witness:

But that's absolutely dreadful. To think of where he is now ... I just can't cope ... *(Sobbing.)* The undertakers say they need to speak to Vilde to get everything arranged. But she's not answering her phone.

Interviewer:

Isn't she answering her phone? Hasn't she called you?

Witness:

It's so awful. All of a sudden I have to make an appointment with a complete stranger about how I can bury my own son!

Interviewer:

But Vilde Veierland surely isn't a complete stranger. After all, she's your daughter-in-law.

Witness:

She's in her twenties, and I've met her three times. I've thought this through in the past few days. I've met her three times. *(Pause.)* But you see I've heard from Brede that things weren't as they should be in that marriage. Coming home suddenly like that and being married. It's not like my Brede. There must have been something ... something else. A matter of honor, if you understand what I mean. He would never have married her if he didn't have to. But then it didn't come to anything ... It's not the first time someone's been duped like that.

Interviewer:

Yes, well, hm ... Do you mean that Brede married Vilde because they were expecting a baby?

Witness:

Yes, no … He's never said anything, you see. Brede would never have done that. Difficult things, he always kept them to himself. But of course I've lived long enough to understand one thing and another, you see. It wasn't so difficult to see that it wasn't easy for him. Brede always had so much responsibility. But I couldn't understand why he absolutely had to take on responsibility for that girl as well.

Interviewer:

But if he didn't say anything, how did you …? Well, I mean … How did you know what their marriage was like?

Witness:

It's easy for a mother to see that there's something wrong. For example, she never came with him when he visited. She's only been to my place in Nordbergveien once! *(Quiet clearing of throat.)* Brede was always so considerate. He came every Sunday. Yes, well … maybe not every single Sunday, then … *(Rasping sound, asthma?)* For dinner, you understand. He liked so much for me to set the table for Sunday dinner, like in the old days. When Brede was a boy and … Yes, poor Brede, it wasn't always so easy for him to get away. All the same, he came faithfully for dinner every Sunday. Yes, you know … With so many staff and other people who continually wanted to get hold of him, it wasn't easy for him all the time. But he knew that everything was ready for him. Home-made roast pork with prunes and caramel pudding. I wanted it to be like that. That he was always expected, I mean, if he had a moment to spare.

Interviewer:

But how often did he come then?

Witness:

Yes, no, I don't suppose it was *so* often. Often, of course, but maybe not every Sunday. He had so many other things to do. Look after his health. He used to go swimming on Sundays. At the Grand Hotel. And then sometimes he met business contacts, or other artists. People he needed to talk to. Then it wasn't so easy for him to make it to his mother's, even though he really wanted to.

Interviewer:

I understand. But you mentioned his health … Did Brede have any health problems?

Witness:

Certainly not! He was just as fit and healthy, before he … *(voice indistinct)* as when he was twenty years of age. He has always been strong, Brede. He was careful about his health. Kept himself fit – is that what they say? He didn't smoke and couldn't abide other people doing so. Yes, I really enjoy an occasional cigarette myself, but I refrained when Brede was around. Since it bothered him, I mean. When I was expecting him to pay a visit, I aired the place out and did without a smoke.

Interviewer:

Did you sit there gasping for a cigarette, with the place well aired, even though he didn't turn up?

Witness:

Sometimes he came, you see. Often. But Brede was so particular about things. He was so aesthetic. The press has also always emphasized exactly that. You've probably read about it. The pure and the beautiful, that was his sort of credo. *(Lengthy pause.)* Brede has such an assured sense of taste. He involved himself in making sure that everything was neat and tidy in my home as well. Inferior art, for example ... It gave him the shivers. *(Witness gives a little laugh.)* I had an Alexander Schultz painting at home; as a matter of fact, it was a portrait of Brede's father. Yes, sadly, Brede lost his father when he was quite small – it hasn't been easy for him. But Brede always said that it was such a terrible painting. Father deserved better, Brede thought. It did actually look nicer in the living room when we took it down. He bought one of these modern silk-screen prints for me instead.

Interviewer:

Yes, his father ... Was your husband's name Ziegler?

Witness:

Oh, you're wondering why I'm not called Ziegler? My maiden name was Kareliussen and my married name Johansen. But Brede was so creative and he adopted the name Ziegler when he was in his twenties. He changed both his first name and his surname, in fact. He was christened Fredrik, of course, but my late husband ... *(Brief laughter?)* He managed to ... make it shrink, in a manner of speaking. To Freddy. *(Indistinct speech.)* ... before he died. Not very pretty, if you ask me. Naturally I never used it, but his friends, and at school ... I suggested that he should go back to Fredrik, since that's both attractive and ... Anyway. I thought that I should take the name Ziegler as well, to sort of keep the family ... *(indistinct speech, coughing, asthmatic wheeze?)* but he thought that was a bad idea. It was a bit odd to begin with ... I mean, to call your own son by something different from what you've become used to over the years. His entire upbringing. I asked to be allowed to continue with the old name, but ... Brede wanted to be called Brede. He insisted. I got used to it eventually. It is a lovely name too.

Interviewer:

But you're quite sure that Brede didn't have any health problems? Headaches, for instance? Did he take any medication?

Witness:

No, never. I can be quite categorical about that. He often said to me that I mustn't take such things. Pills and suchlike. He was very principled. Thought it was better to put up with some pain. Everything passes in the end. Even though I do in fact suffer sometimes. Yes, my joints ... They bother me sometimes. But he always said, "It's better not to take anything, Mother."

Interviewer:

Did you know any of his friends? Who were his close friends, do you think?

Witness:

Oh, there were so many!

Interviewer:

But were there any that you knew well – childhood friends, for instance?

Witness:

No, Brede wasn't like that. He looked forward, did Brede. Never back. Yes, of course he had lots of friends at school, but Brede has always gone his own way. When his friends got married and were picking up their children from kindergarten, and that sort of thing that men do nowadays, well, that wasn't anything that appealed to Brede. He was always in the company of such interesting people. He told so many amusing stories about the people he met.

Interviewer:

But was there nobody you were acquainted with?

Witness:

No, Brede always kept extremely private.

Interviewer:

Did he have any enemies?

Witness:

No, certainly not. Everybody liked Brede, you can see that from all they said about him in magazines and everything.

Interviewer:

Did you know that he had received threatening letters?

Witness:

Threatening letters? Oh yes. Those dreadful letters that they wrote about in one of those magazines – I don't remember all of it. That was absolutely ghastly. It must have been somebody who couldn't stand Brede being so talented. He was quite exceptional. Whoever wrote that dreadful *(unclear voice, indistinct)* ... it must have been an abnormally jealous person.

Interviewer:

What did he say himself about these letters, then?

Witness:

Say himself … *(Clearing her throat.)* Actually, I can't remember that we ever talked about that particular subject. No. I don't think we did.

Interviewer:

Why not?

Witness:

It wasn't really a very pleasant topic to discuss over Sunday dinner, do you think?

Interviewer:

When did you actually last see your son, Mrs. Johansen?

Witness:

Last … I can't honestly remember. It can't possibly have been very long ago.

Interviewer:

Was he there last Sunday? A week ago, the day he …

Witness:

(Lengthy pause, crying, new sounds reminiscent of asthmatic wheezing.) No. He wasn't. He … *(A great deal of indistinct speech, coughing, and crying.)*

Interviewer:

But is it possible to say when you saw him last? What did you talk about then? *(Still violent weeping.)* We'll soon be finished now, Mrs. Johansen. We can take a break anyway *(Rustling.)* … I'd like you to look at this personal property report with me.

It lists here what your son had in his possession when he …
Can you take a look at this and see if there's anything unusual
here? Anything that might be missing?

Witness:

(Tearful.) Yes, I'll do the best I can. Could I have some water,
by the way? *(Rustling, indistinct sounds.)*

Interviewer:

I think we'll turn this off for the moment, and then we can
come back when you've had a look at this. The interview is
terminated at, let's see … 14.48.

Interviewer:

The interview is continued: the time is 15.12. The witness has
had a break and gone to the toilet. She has looked at the personal
property report. Do you have any comment to make about the
clothes or items that were found on Brede?

Witness:

No, it seems entirely normal. The camel coat – he always suited
that … *(Mumbling.)* The tie pin, the watch … There is one thing,
though. He always used to wear gloves. He was so careful about
wearing gloves, even in the spring. Didn't like to get dirty, Brede.
It says a scarf there, but no gloves.

Interviewer:

Thanks, Mrs. Johansen. You've been a great help. The interview
is concluded at 15.16.

21

Daniel stayed at home. It was Sunday evening and he ought to do some reading. He was straggling far behind with the reading list and had a subject exam coming up in January. The books were stashed in an unopened cardboard box behind the door. Daniel lay on his back in bed, trying to shut out the odor of mold. It smelled as though the damp stuffiness had worsened since he had moved in, and now it was forcing itself upon him like the stench of putrefaction. The entire week had been spent achieving nothing. Apart from moving house, that is. Since he hardly owned more than a stereo system and a few boxes of books and CDs, it had all been done and dusted on Saturday morning. Actually he should have been at work on both Tuesday and Thursday, but he had phoned in sick. Because he was not a permanent employee at either workplace, he lost money. He needed money.

A week had elapsed since Brede Ziegler's murder, and Daniel began to cry. At first the tears came quite quietly. Then his throat tightened. Sobbing, he used his hands to cover his face.

Not even Taffa had said anything much.

It was fine that Thale grasped none of it. That was how it always was. Daniel sat up in bed to catch his breath. Snot ran from his nose and, gasping, he wiped it with the back of his hand before stuffing his hand under his T-shirt and letting his forefinger slide across his dry skin. He should really use cream more often. He suffered from eczema when he forgot those damn lotions.

Taffa usually understood. Taffa could read him the way other people's mothers normally did. He had gone to see her and made eye contact, just as he always did when he wanted her to see.

Maybe she didn't want to.

Maybe she didn't understand any of it, either.

Daniel tossed and turned in bed, stretching his arms above his head, and cried through yet another night.

22

It was the morning of Monday December 13 when Hanne Wilhelmsen rewound the tape for the twenty-first time.

"Police, central switchboard."

"Eh, hmnnn ..."

The sound of violent, prolonged coughing crackled through the loudspeaker.

"Hello? Hello? What's it about? Who's calling?"

"... dead man. On your steps."

"Can you speak more clearly?"

"Outside. Oh, fuck!"

Something dropped to the floor.

"Bloody hell, outside at your place, I told you already. You can't be so slow on the uptake! A dead man. Outside at your place. Go round the back of the police station, then."

That was all. Hanne switched off the tape player. She turned to face university lecturer Even Hareide, who had been unable to hide his enthusiasm for the task. He had reported to the duty desk a mere half-hour after Hanne's phone call.

"Vika dialect," he said firmly, clasping his hands round his knees. "Good old east-end dialect. The inflection is very characteristic. A number of points. It's almost impossible to learn as an adult."

Hanne closed her eyes as she listened to the long-winded lecture that followed about knowledge of regional variations and sociolinguistics, dialects, and sociolects. The man did not come up with anything she herself had not understood when she first heard it. The bill for the linguistics researcher's unnecessary input would cause Billy T. to explode.

"Thanks," she said suddenly, interrupting him. "Have you any idea how old this person might be?"

"A worn-out, old person. Obviously."

"Yes. I can hear that too. How old, do you think?"

"She's lived quite a while."

"I'll tell you what I think," Hanne said in desperation. "And then you can tell me if you agree, okay? In the first place ..."

She sniffed, resisting the temptation to light a cigarette. The university lecturer looked as if he had come straight from the woods, with old-fashioned student glasses and an open-necked flannel shirt, military boots on his feet, and an enormous diver's watch round his right wrist.

"... the woman smokes. Red Mix or Teddy without filters. The tar is thickly coated on her vocal cords."

Even Hareide nodded contentedly, as if Hanne were a diligent student taking an oral examination.

"She's probably a heroin addict," she continued.

Hareide's eyes opened wide, but he did not say anything.

"I can hear that from the characteristic ... pressure? Can you call it that?"

Hanne pinched her fingers around her own larynx and squeezed out the next sentence.

"The voice is sort of pushed over and sometimes up into a falsetto. You can hear it most when she swears. There, when she drops something or other."

"Yes, I guess so."

The university lecturer no longer seemed quite so certain.

"The slurring might be caused by intoxication, either alcohol or heroin, or both," Hanne said. "Agreed?"

"Yes," Hareide conceded. "Then we have a heroin addict,

advanced in years, who is a woman and lives in Oslo. That must be—"

"An old hooker, no less. Since we know that the phone call came from … Thanks, Hareide. You've been a great help."

When the man had shut the door after establishing where he should send his account, Hanne felt better within herself. Fortunately a bright spark at central switchboard had secured the tape when Brede Ziegler was found dead. Someone had listened to the tape on the Monday morning, the day after Ziegler's murder. After that it had lain forgotten, untouched and wrongly filed in the evidence room. It had taken Hanne two hours to find it.

"An old hooker," she whispered softly.

23

The massive stone villa was situated on an incline set back from the street. A lilac bush grew right beside the entrance, concealing the number on the door. There was no sign to say what the house contained, and no name displayed under the doorbell. The merchant who had built the house in the thirties had held his dinner parties under the shelter of thick stone walls and protective lead-glass windows. Later, a clergyman had moved in with his wife and three little girls. They can hardly have imagined that the place would end up as a homeless shelter for Oslo's most decrepit prostitutes.

Hanne Wilhelmsen jogged up the last few steps.

The police, of course, were familiar with the address of the City Mission's night shelter. However, they rarely came visiting. Some time ago the neighbors had grown tired of finding discarded hypodermics in their gardens and gravel paths. The police had eventually raided the place. They made sure to arrive at eleven o'clock in the morning, when all the overnight guests were long gone and only the cleaning staff were busy about their work.

"You know I can't answer that. I can reel off the conditions I adhere to. But you know them perfectly well."

The manager had led Hanne Wilhelmsen into one of the two spacious living rooms, each divided off from the other by a sliding door. The room was bright and cozy, although the interior decor showed signs of a strict budget. The leather settee and the Stressless chair were ill-matched, and the floor had acquired cork tiles since the merchant's days. Flowerpots on the windowsills and a bookcase chock-full of the last ten years' Book Club editions lent the room some warmth, all the same. Hanne gazed at the manager over her coffee cup.

"This is a murder case. I need to remind you of that."

"It doesn't make any difference. You know that only too well."

The woman with responsibility for running the night shelter had come into the public spotlight as leader of the advocacy group for sex workers many years earlier. For a long time it had amused her that journalists thought she was a prostitute herself. Anyway, she had done next to nothing to refute the rumor. These days, hardly anyone speculated about it.

"The girls have to be able to rely on me. You understand that. Besides, we don't know who's going to be here at any particular time."

"Don't know?"

Hanne put down her cup and squeezed her eyes shut again.

"Don't you have any kind of registration system?"

"Yes, of course. The girls have both names and numbers. But if they register under the name Lena, we accept that their name is Lena. Even if something totally different is stated on their birth certificate, as it were."

"But you must get to know these girls over time."

The manager smiled. Her clean bare face caught the sun from the pale wintry day outside. A slight draft from the gap at the window brought with it the scent of spruce branches. Two figures in the garden were busy changing light-bulbs on a bushy Christmas tree.

"Lots of them. They are regulars."

"Listen to me now. Someone must have—"

The shouts of the two people decorating the garden for Christmas intruded into the room, and Hanne stood up to close the window.

"We know the call was made from your staff phone. Somebody must have let someone into the office to make the call. Unless the person who phoned was a—"

"A member of staff?"

The manager's smile and soft south-coast accent began to irritate Hanne.

"For example. No. It didn't sound like that. Unless you've got extremely worn-out members of staff. Extremely worn-out."

"I can't give you any information. I ... My loyalty's with the girls. That's the way it has to be. If you get a legal order that insists on us saying any more, then of course I'll consider it. It's not a clear-cut thing. Not even then, I mean."

Hanne Wilhelmsen sighed theatrically.

"Have all the witnesses in this case been studying law in their spare time, or what?"

"Sorry?"

"Nothing. Forget it."

Hanne looked at the settee, hesitating. Then she leaned across quickly and retrieved her jacket from the arm.

"Gorgeous gloves," the manager said. "Red. Original! I'm sorry your visit was a wasted journey."

She escorted her out and closed the door behind her. When Hanne heard the lock click, she stopped suddenly and stood squinting at the sky. It really seemed as if the Goddess of Justice had decided to torment her. First of all, Idun Franck had buttoned her lip, citing a variety of paragraphs, and now here was this city missionary invoking every possible justification – and a few more besides – in order to avoid uttering a cheep.

"Inger Andersen," Hanne said slowly, without knowing why.

Inger Andersen had gone to police college two years before Hanne. Later she had studied law. After eighteen months as a police prosecutor, she had changed her mind. Fed up to the back teeth with legal paragraphs, she wanted to return to what she called real police work. Eventually she was put in charge of the Prostitution Surveillance Group – Prosspan. That was before the police had given up and closed down the entire section at the end of the eighties. Everyone had protested. The Violent Crime Section had tenaciously attempted to argue for the maintenance of the group; the intelligence gleaned there had proved useful to them also. The Child Welfare Department, which had looked after young teen-agers and at the very least succeeded in keeping them away from the red-light district until they were a couple of years older, had almost screamed themselves hoarse. The hookers themselves had protested. Nothing helped. Prosspan was shut down, and Inger Andersen and her colleagues were allocated other assignments. Inger knew the environment better than anyone. The last Hanne had heard of her, she was working at Manglerud police station.

Hanne got into her car and inserted the cellphone earplugs in her ears. Then she produced an address book from her inside pocket. After being sent from pillar to post, she finally got Inger Andersen on the line. The Police Sergeant had been transferred to Stovner, where she was working on preventive measures with children and teenagers.

"The oldest hooker in the city," Inger Andersen repeated on hearing Hanne's question. "Hairy Mary. Mary Olsen. She was already the oldest at that time, and the woman has nine lives. If she's still on the game, she has to be the oldest street hooker in Northern Europe. It wouldn't surprise me in the slightest."

"Hairy Mary," Hanne reiterated slowly. "Where would I find her?"

Inger Andersen laughed so loudly that Hanne had to pull out her earplugs.

"Find a hooker? In the red-light district, of course. If Hairy Mary's still alive, you'll find her there. Good luck."

24

"It took ages. We had to wait more than an hour for the last witness. Do we have any spare tights?"

Karen Borg hobbled over to the counter as she examined the back of her left leg. Three stitches had run, forming a broad ladder from the tendon at her knee all the way down to her shoes.

"And those documents from the records office in Brønnøysund that I requested, have they arrived yet?"

The phone rang.

"Ms. Borg's office. No, unfortunately she's not in yet. Can I take a message?"

The secretary held her hand over the receiver and whispered as she nodded at a filing cabinet in the corner.

"Third drawer on the left-hand side. Tights. The papers are on your desk. And here ..."

She held out a sheaf of Post-it notes.

"Thanks," she continued the phone conversation. "I've taken a note of the number."

The secretary disconnected the call. Karen Borg leafed quickly through the messages.

"Four messages from Claudio Gagliostro. Impatient guy."

"I'd prefer to describe him as furious, I'm afraid. He's phoned eight times. In the end I couldn't be bothered writing any more messages. It would be a good idea to call him before your next appointment. It's ..." She squinted at her wristwatch through a pair of reading glasses balanced on the end of her impressive nose.

"... sixteen minutes until Vilde Veierland Ziegler is due. This Gagli ... Galci—"

"Gagliostro."

"Exactly. He's threatening to report you to the Norwegian Bar Association."

Karen Borg chuckled.

"He can report me to the King if he wants, if only he'll answer my questions. I'll give him a call. And you ..."

She struggled to haul her academic gown, briefcase, coat, new pair of tights, and cup of coffee into her office. The cup fell on the floor.

"Shit! Sorry."

"I'll fix it. Just go in."

Johanne Duckert was more than twenty years older than her boss. She was the lawyer's next-door neighbor in Vinderen, and had accepted her offer of a ten-till-three job during a garden party last summer. Mrs. Duckert had never worked outside the home, but there were limits to how much time could be wasted in her well-maintained garden. After her husband had died two years previously, she had often thought of finding herself something else to do. It did not come to anything until Karen happened to mention that she had a pressing need for help, but was short of money.

"I've more than enough money," Mrs. Duckert said happily, and moved into the office in C. J. Hambros plass with her flowerpots and photos of her grandchildren.

When, many years ago now, Karen Borg had been a partner in a major commercial lawyers' firm in plush premises in upmarket Aker Brygge, she'd had two secretaries. They were young, had qualifications and education, a command of four different word-processing programs, and flirted discreetly with the clients. Mrs. Duckert had hardly touched a typewriter until she was sixty-one years of age, but her spelling was awe-inspiring, she had a colorful turn of phrase that it had taken Karen some time to get used to, and in addition she remained at work until six or seven o'clock in the evening without ever asking for overtime pay. Mrs. Duckert had blossomed in tandem with the roses that flourished in plant pots and containers all over the outer office.

Karen Borg's clients were no longer men in tailored suits. Their wives, on the other hand, did come to her. Shuffling into the office, they dissolved into tears with violins playing in the background. After thirty years of marriage they were being replaced by someone younger, smarter, more beautiful; they were in a state of collapse over a demand for an unequal division of assets from their spouse, who wanted to uproot them and at best install them in an apartment in Groruddalen. They sat on a chair in Karen Borg's office with a box of Kleenex on their lap, having just learned that their husband, after a long life and three grown-up children, was of the opinion that he had finally found love with a twenty-eight-year-old.

These clients did not need any flirtation. They needed Mrs. Duckert's tiny cakes and coffee with a little dash of something stronger, just to steady the nerves of course. They needed the clasp of Mrs. Duckert's warm hand, and a reassuring conversation about gardening and daughters-in-law, and finally to remember those beautiful grandchildren!

The men who came to see Karen Borg hardly knew what flirting was. They had skinny legs in tight trousers and arms covered in needle marks. They too were given coffee, cakes, and soothing conversation by Mrs. Duckert, though she did leave out the dash of booze.

"They quite simply don't benefit from a drop of the hard stuff," she often said. "It makes them ill."

Karen Borg had listened to the voice at the other end of the phone line for quite some time. The man was agitated, and it would be best to let him finish talking. Eventually he had calmed down somewhat.

"I can well understand that you find it unpleasant, Gagliostro," she said calmly. "But this is not in fact your private business. You can either answer me now or wait until the Probate and Bankruptcy Court asks you."

Gagliostro was working himself up into a frenzy again, and Karen Borg was forced to interrupt.

"You can't just say that everything belongs to you, in actual fact," she said in the same calm tone. "It's not acceptable. As his spouse, Vilde has the right to access her husband's finances. It's the law, Gagliostro. I can—"

A vehement diatribe forced her to hold the receiver twenty centimeters from her ear.

"Listen to me."

She sat up straight in her chair and raised her voice. That helped.

"If you mean that you own all the shares, can't you just fax me proof of that? If the situation is as you claim, then surely there's no reason to make such a song and dance about it? Fine. Then we'll leave it at that."

Karen Borg keyed in another number.

"Johanne, can you come in with the fax from Entré as soon as it arrives?"

She kicked off her shoes and began to pull off her tights as she scanned the papers on the desk. She had only just put on the new tights when Vilde Veierland Ziegler knocked on the door.

The young widow seemed unusually pale, even taking the time of year into consideration. Karen thought she must have lost weight in the four days that had passed since they had last met. She poured a cup of tea from a thermos flask and dipped a little wooden spoon into a pot of honey.

"Here," she said, stirring it thoroughly. "Drink this."

Vilde stared apathetically at the cup, without making any move to accept it. Karen understood that she should not make any attempt to console the girl. That would make her fall to pieces. It was doubtful if the diminutive woman in the visitor's chair was in any fit state to receive information. She would have to keep things simple.

"Chin up. This doesn't look too bad. Firstly, there's the apartment at Sinsen. That seems to belong to the Entré restaurant business."

Vilde looked at her for the first time.

"Then … then I don't have anywhere to live."

Karen raised her hand and smiled encouragingly.

"You've got the apartment in Niels Juels gate of course and—"

"I *don't* want to live there. I *hate* that apartment!"

Her voice cracked and her tears threatened to spill over.

"Take it easy now. Just relax until I've explained all this to you. It will take some time to obtain an overview of the entire estate, but what I can tell you for certain …" Karen pushed the teacup toward her once more. "… is that you'll inherit a lot of money."

Vilde Veierland Ziegler curled her hand slowly around the hot cup.

"Will *I* inherit a lot of money?"

Two red patches grew visible on her cheeks, and Karen thought she could discern the suggestion of a smile on Vilde's face.

"It was obvious that your husband had intended for you to have separate ownership of his estate. I've spoken to his attorney, an old colleague of mine. He had been given the task of drawing up a marriage settlement, but Brede had not yet made an appointment to come and sign the documents. So it's all very straightforward. If the marriage settlement hasn't been signed by both of you, then it's not valid. Therefore you have joint ownership."

Karen flipped through the papers. For some reason she found it objectionable to see how her client's demeanor had altered.

"Since Brede did not have any children, you are his sole heir. As far as the restaurant is concerned ... Entré is a limited company. Brede and Claudio owned approximately half each. They had an agreement about who should decide what in the business. Moreover, it is provided for that if one of them dies, the other is to take over the whole enterprise."

She glanced again at her client, whose introspective expression was on its way back.

"But such an agreement is not necessarily binding. An agreement in which you ... If you want to decide what will happen with your possessions when you die, that's called a testamentary disposition. There are certain formal requirements for that. It means that you must write a will. Brede had not done that. A partnership agreement is not any kind of will. That probably means that you inherit Brede's shares in Entré as well as the apartment in Niels Juels gate. Although there is some outstanding debt in both places, it should still amount to a considerable sum of money. Several million kroner."

Karen continued to thumb through the bundle of papers. Out of the corner of her eye she could see that Vilde had lifted the cup to her mouth.

"And besides ... There are a lot of other assets here. That is to say, things ... valuables. Including quite a number of shares in an Italian company. Do you know anything about that?"

Vilde shook her head. She was far too young. She could not hide the fact that she was biting her lip to stop herself smiling. Karen gave a slight shudder. It had crossed her mind as soon as their first meeting a few days earlier: there was something about this young woman that did not add up.

"Then we'll discuss all this in the near future."

Karen forced out a smile.

When Vilde Veierland Ziegler left the office, Mrs. Duckert brought in a cup of coffee.

"You must have done wonders for that young lady," she said, pouring milk from a porcelain jug. "When she arrived she looked like a ghost. By the time she left, well, she gave a lovely smile when she said goodbye."

25

"I was crazy and had decided to recover my health."

Suzanne put down her spoon and flashed a smile at Idun Franck. The publishing editor had not touched her food. Why she had been invited to dinner was still a mystery to Suzanne Klavenæs. They had both worked together on the Ziegler book for several months now, without any kind of personal exchange beyond the purely trivial. Now, when it looked as if the book project might be shelved, Idun had suddenly invited her for bouillabaisse. Suzanne's initial impulse was to decline with thanks. But Idun had said they could combine the meal with work, and anyway, there was something about her. Idun was just as Suzanne remembered – or, more to the point, imagined – her real-life fellow-citizens: friendly in a reserved way, smilingly formal, and professionally attentive. On a personal level she kept her distance, and Suzanne had no need to fear a stream of invasive questions. Idun Franck was nothing like the woman at passport control at Gardermoen airport – Tone something-or-other. Delightedly, she had recognized Suzanne and begun to chatter about the old days at the Cathedral School. The queue had grown longer behind Suzanne, who had been unable to tear herself away until she finally had her passport returned and literally stumbled into Norway.

"I was ill as a teenager. Very ill. I was admitted to a closed ward at Gaustad Hospital for six months. I needed to get away to regain my health."

She was surprised at herself. Admittedly it was no secret that she had been crazy. All her friends in France knew that – at least the ones who knew her well enough for it to be natural to talk to them about something that had happened more than fifteen years ago. But she spoke increasingly seldom about it. Idun's question about why she had moved to France had been so unexpected that the answer simply spilled out unbidden.

"I'm actually half-French," she added by way of explanation. "I got my surname from my father. My mother was French. Even though she died when I was little, I had family and friends there, so it was natural to go when I first started traveling."

She helped herself to more bouillabaisse. Obviously home-made, it tasted of Marseilles.

"This is really delicious," Suzanne said. "I don't look as if I eat very much, but that's wrong. I love food. I've just been very lucky with my … What's it called in Norwegian again … metabolics?"

"Metabolism. Wish I was."

When Suzanne had received a request from the publishing company to take the pictures for their book about Brede Ziegler and his kitchen, she had mulled it over for twenty-four hours. From the publisher's point of view, the approach was virtually a shot in the dark; Suzanne Klavenæs was a regular supplier of photo-reportage for *Paris Match* and had also created a ten-page illustrated story for *National Geographic* about the flood of refugees from Central Africa. She was accustomed to major assignments, and remuneration to match.

"Home," Suzanne said out of the blue. "For some reason I always call Norway 'home'. I accepted this job because I wanted to see if it was possible for me to be here. After what had happened. After … When my father died, I arrived here on the morning plane and left an hour after the funeral. My relatives have never forgiven me, I think. But when … At that precise moment I didn't know whether I would be able to tolerate this country. Whether I'd got over it all."

"Is it possible, do you think?"

Idun Franck poured out more wine for them both and sat spinning her own glass in her hand.

"I don't really know what you've been through, and I don't mean to pry. But ... Women like the ones you spoke of from Bosnia. Raped and ... And the refugees in Africa who lost their children on the way, one by one, through illness and hunger and ... Is it possible to flee from these things, do you think? Can people really have the strength to go on living? A genuine, full life?"

Suzanne suddenly noticed that it was Sarah Brightman's voice she could hear from the loudspeakers in the living room. She could not square the torch singer with the rest of Idun Franck. Admittedly the decor in the apartment was not especially well coordinated, but the mixture of antiques and IKEA furniture created an overall impression that indicated a sure touch in matters of taste, all the same.

"I've read," Idun continued, with a brief burst of laughter, "that the liver is the only organ in the body that can renew itself completely. It's formed of so many new cells that over a five-year period we end up with an entirely new liver. If we don't drink too much, that is."

She raised her glass.

"Is it like that with a human soul, do you think?"

Without waiting for a reply, she stood up abruptly and cleared the plates.

"We need to work. We'll have coffee in the living room. Do you have the pictures with you?"

Suzanne followed her and sat down on the leather settee. When she arrived she had left her portfolio of photographs on the coffee table and she was taken aback that Idun had not noticed.

"Where did I put that manuscript?" Idun Franck murmured, inspecting the magazine rack and behind the TV set. "I must have mislaid it. I *know* I brought it from the office."

The search was futile: Idun Franck lifted chair cushions and peered inside two empty decorative vases. Suzanne poured coffee for herself from a ceramic pot, speculating that Idun must be one of those people whose sense of order is depleted during their work day.

"We'll have to manage without it," Idun said feebly. "Let me see the photos, please."

Concentrating intently, they worked without a break for two hours.

"The food and landscapes are obviously no problem," Idun Franck concluded as she ran her fingers though her hair. "I suggest you continue. I'll speak to Claudio and tell him you need to photograph the dishes described in the text."

"Does that mean you've decided to publish the book?" Suzanne asked, drinking coffee number four. "To some extent, it's fine to make plans based on what we already have, but should I *go on* taking photos?"

"We won't decide about actual publication until the investigation is over. But we've established that we'll try to run with the book for as long as possible, until we come to that decision. Not my choice. I'm subject to a boss who is … Forget it! Sorry. I'll count the dishes described in the text and give you an updated list. That one's marvelous, by the way!"

She fished out a black-and-white photo of Brede Ziegler.

"It's so … Spontaneous, in a sense! Didn't he see you?"

"No. I agree. It's excellent, if not exactly flattering."

Suzanne began to gather the photos, painstakingly ensuring that the various Post-it notes were attached to the reverse of the appropriate images. Idun snatched up the notes she had made in the course of the evening and stashed them inside Unni Lindell's latest crime novel, left lying on a sideboard beside the TV.

"Then I certainly won't forget them," she said, smiling faintly. "By the way ..."

She glanced at the book, as if it had jogged her memory.

"Have the police spoken to you?"

"The police? No. I must be very far down their list of interesting witnesses ... Why do you ask? Have they spoken to you?"

Suzanne closed the folio of photos and headed for the door. When Idun made no sign of following, she turned round.

"Yes," Idun said. "They have spoken to me. I'm in dispute with them about access to unpublished material. Confidentiality of sources. It's like talking to a brick wall. Do you know that police officers nowadays don't look like police officers? This policeman I spoke to claimed to have only a first name. He looked like a ... neo-Nazi! Inverted cross on his ear and ..."

Idun ran her hand over her head with a smooth motion, almost as if she were shaving off her hair. Suzanne narrowly avoided dropping the photograph portfolio as she leaned on the door-frame for support.

"*Mon Dieu*," she said softly. "This country is really like a ... village?"

"Do you know who I'm talking about?"

"B.T. He's called ... I always called him B.T."

"No. His name is Bobby or Billy, or something like that. Can it be the same person? Do you know him?"

"He was one of the people I wanted to flee from. That time when I was crazy and had decided to regain my health."

Suzanne Klavenæs headed for the hallway, where she put on her coat, and Idun followed. The two women stood at either end of the long corridor, one tall, dark and almost skinny, the other small, plump, with ash-blond hair.

"Thanks for coming," Idun said in a whisper. "Will I phone for a taxi?"

Suzanne said she would prefer to walk. When she had reached thirty meters along Myklegårdsgate, approaching the path through the park down to Grønlandsleiret, she turned to see all the lights in Idun's apartment switched off. Only at the kitchen window could she make out the glimmer of a candle. For a moment she thought she spotted Idun Franck's face at the window, but it might have been her imagination. All the same she shivered, and it struck her that Idun Franck was the only person she had ever met whose photograph she had never considered taking. She couldn't work it out. She simply couldn't fathom it.

26

Five people swarmed in the kitchen, their movements brisk and efficient. All the same, it was surprisingly quiet in the room, with only the occasional clunk of metal against metal disturbing the faint susurration of the colossal extractor hood above the gas cooker. Billy T. had been in the Navy. He had served in the Coastguards aboard a fisheries protection vessel in the Norwegian Sea. Entré's kitchen reminded him of a ship's galley. Slightly larger of course, but nevertheless cramped, with a preponderance of stainless steel.

"Today's lunch," one of the chefs said cheerfully, flipping a steaming dish out of the oven. "Arctic char. We'll lay them on a bed of scrambled eggs cooked in a bain-marie with finely chopped truffles."

He pointed at an apprentice who stood lost in concentration, whisking something in a massive stainless-steel bowl. Billy T. leaned slightly over its rim and sniffed.

"Smells good already," he said. "Aren't truffles absurdly expensive?"

"Here," said the chef, using a knife to point at a little clump on a chopping board. "That lot there cost one hundred and sixty kroner. But it goes a long way, in return."

Billy T. had decided to regrow the moustache that Tone-Marit had implored him to get rid of six months earlier. Scratching the stubble, he wondered whether he should perhaps change his mind.

"Looks like hash. The same price too. But where's Claudio?"

The chef shrugged indifferently.

"Is he here or isn't he?"

No one answered. No one seemed abashed at not saying anything. Each and every one of the five kitchen workers knew what they had to do, and they continued chopping, stirring, rinsing, and frying without so much as a glance in Billy T.'s direction. He grabbed the Arctic char-man by the arm, unnecessarily hard.

"Do you mean for me to stand here all day and watch you cooking lunch, or do you think your boss might have the courtesy to show up? Would you be kind enough to inform this Gagli-guy, wherever he might be, that it would please the police for him to show up *now*!"

He regretted his display of temper before it was over. The chef had been friendly enough, and of course he was not responsible for Claudio Gagliostro having already failed to turn up for two interview appointments. Billy T. needed to look sharp. There had been complaints. The Chief of Police had called in to his office the previous evening and made a polite request for the Chief Inspector to behave like a reasonable human being. Not in any way a warning. Just some friendly advice.

Maybe his outburst had worked, all the same. A man who could not have been more than five foot four suddenly appeared in the doorway, wearing dogtooth-check trousers under a voluminous white apron. His face seemed heavy and puffy, in stark contrast to his slight, narrow-shouldered body. His eyes looked almost as if they lacked lashes, and greasy wisps of his black hair were plastered to his forehead. It dawned on Billy T. that he had seen the guy before, the Monday after Brede Ziegler was killed, when he had bumped into Suzanne on the way out of Entré. It must have been the shock of meeting her that had caused him not to pay much attention to the peculiar figure.

"It's me you're looking for," the man said. "Come with me."

Billy T. forgot all his good intentions.

"Shouldn't you have come to see me at—"

"Shh," the man responded. "Not here. Come to my office."

Despite Claudio Gagliostro reaching no higher than Billy T.'s chest, the police officer allowed himself to be led by the arm like a child. He stared in fascination at Gagliostro's head. Something must have been wrong. Hydrocephalus, perhaps. In any case, the proportions were totally insane.

His office turned out to be a spacious square work table in the wine cellar, pushed against the wall with a high-backed chair behind it. An architect's desk lamp shed light on four thick bundles of papers, a telephone, and a glorious jumble of yellow notes and envelopes.

"Fucking cold here," Billy T. said tetchily.

"Eleven degrees Celsius. Eleven and a half, in fact."

At last Gagliostro looked more at ease. The lank wisps of hair began to release their grip on his forehead. Wiping his brow with a snow-white pocket handkerchief, he sat down on the office chair and gave a strained smile.

"I'm sorry that ..."

Billy T. looked around for another seat. There was none. Instead he tipped a crate of apple juice sideways and sat down on it, staring down between his legs.

"Do you sell this kind of thing?"

"What is it you want?"

Billy T. let his eyes make a detailed examination of the cellar walls. There must be several thousand bottles down here. Half the room was divided into shelf units running lengthwise like an old-fashioned archive, and the other half had racks from floor to ceiling. It was gloomy. He was freezing.

"I've called you in for interview twice already," he said, taking a deep breath. "And still you're wondering what I want from you. Okay then. Do you open your mail?"

He smashed his fist down on a pile of unopened envelopes.

"Anyway, I don't give a shit what you do with your letters. But when Oslo Police District is stamped on one of them, then *you open it*! You should have reported to me three hours ago!"

Gagliostro's white apron had acquired a green stain without Billy T. having any idea where it had come from. The man spat on his finger and rubbed the fabric. The stain grew larger and paler.

"I quite simply don't have the time," he muttered. "Don't you understand that? I'm doing the work of two people!"

"And I'm working for the police."

Billy T. stood up slowly. He took two steps over to the wine racks and let his index finger dance across the bottle necks.

"What you're really saying," he said dully, "is that it's more important to serve fish with truffles to those snobbish customers of yours than it is to clear up the homicide of your partner. Sweet Jesus, the Lord preserve us all."

He rubbed his face with both hands and sniffed loudly. Then he suddenly shook his head and squeezed out a smile.

"It looks as if you all don't give a shit who killed Brede Ziegler. But I have to give a shit. Do you understand that? Eh?"

He grabbed a bottle from the wall rack at random and pointed at Gagliostro with the spout.

"Most of all I'm inclined to call a Black Maria and have you driven off to police headquarters at Grønlandsleiret 44 without delay. But since you aren't obliged by law to give a statement, I'll skip that. I'm asking you nicely, one more time. Will you answer my questions, or do you want me to go to court and have you dragged in for formal interview? Then you'd be able to try and get the judge to appreciate that you *don't have time*! Then you can do the Canossa Walk over to the courthouse, surrounded by press photographers and hungry journalists. Your choice."

Gagliostro stared frantically at the wine bottle.

"Put it back," he whispered. "Please. Put it back."

"Well then?"

Billy T. raised the bottle to eye-level and squinted at the label in the gloom.

"A wee favorite, this one? Ooops ..."

He let go of the bottle with his right hand and caught it again with his left.

"That was nearly a little accident, you know."

"Is this an interview?"

Gagliostro was obviously starting to perspire again. The beads of sweat covered his forehead and Billy T. began to wonder if he was seriously ill.

"Listen here," he said in a conciliatory tone. "Let's just do a short interview here and now ..."

He produced a Dictaphone from his pocket and held it out to Gagliostro.

"Then you can give me a specific time in the course of the next twenty-four hours when you do actually have the opportunity to come down to police headquarters. Six o'clock tomorrow would suit me. Okay?"

Gagliostro fiddled with the stain on his apron, now the same size as an old banknote. It was only just possible to construe his head movement as a nod. Billy T. switched on the Dictaphone and got the learned-by-heart, rattled-off formalities out of the way. He said nothing about the interview being conducted in a wine cellar in Grünerløkka.

An hour and a half later Billy T.'s teeth were chattering. The temperature of the room was the only thing that prevented him from exploding yet again. The man on the opposite side of the vast table toyed with everything within his reach: the stain on his apron, a pen that leaked and colored his fingers blue, a glass elephant he had taken out of a drawer, and a silver penknife with red stones on the handle. The answers he gave were mostly brief, never comprehensive. Billy T. felt completely worn out when he made an effort to summarize.

"So you met Brede eleven years ago in Milan. Then you moved to Norway. By the way, your Norwegian's good. Yes, absolutely fluent."

"What?"

"You speak g-o-o-d N-o-r-w-e-g-i-a-n."

"Oh. One of my grandmothers was Norwegian. I used to come here for summer holidays when I was little."

"Brede worked at the restaurant …"

He waved his right hand to get the recalcitrant witness to help him.

"Santini."

"Santini, yes. In Milan. Then you became friends and you moved to Norway shortly afterwards. After having sold a place in Verona, is that right?"

"Mhmn."

The elephant's trunk snapped. Gagliostro looked perplexed as he sat holding the broken surfaces together, as if he expected the glass fragments to regrow, if only he was patient enough.

"Then you took your money and came to Norway to earn more. Together with Brede."

"Yes."

"But it took quite a long time, didn't it? Until you opened this place here, I mean. And in the meantime it looked as if you might have changed your mind. Because you and Brede entered into a project in Italy seven or eight years ago, correct?"

"Yes."

"Can't you just *put down* that animal!"

Nonplussed, Gagliostro put the elephant on the table with the trunk between its legs. Billy T. used one hand to rub the small of his back as he switched off the Dictaphone with the other.

"We'll swap places," he said, getting to his feet.

"What?"

"Swap places, I said. My back will break soon. Come on, then. You sit on the packing case. Give me the chair."

Gagliostro made no protest worth mentioning about relinquishing his comfortable seat. Instead of sitting on the crate of apple juice, he plonked himself down on a folding chair built into the wall, impossible to spot if you didn't know it was there. Billy T. closed his eyes. He leaned back in the chair for some time. The only sound to be heard was a distant clatter of saucepans and sudden shrill female laughter on the floor above.

"Sindre Sand," Billy T. said, without switching on the Dictaphone again. "Do you know him?"

"Yes."

"How well?"

"Slightly."

"Slightly well or you know him slightly?"

Gagliostro did not reply. He tugged at his earlobe and opened his mouth briefly, before shutting it again with a little snap. He stared at the floor.

Billy T. had hardly slept for the past four nights. Hanne Wilhelmsen's return had shaken him more than he thought possible. He had been lost in his own thoughts, still with no idea what sudden impulse had made him look up at the gallery on the sixth floor. When he saw her leaning over the banister and recognized her gaze, too far distant for him to know what it held, but fierce enough to feel the old intimacy he had spent the past six months trying to forget, he was on the point of collapse. He felt sick; really, genuinely sick. The nausea did not let up until he had vomited into the wastepaper basket in his office, behind a locked door. Since then he had made an effort to resist the thought of her. Of her smell, her fragrance, her bad habit of rubbing her right temple when she was pondering something, with one eye half-closed; he did not want to remember her hands, her thumbs that massaged between his shoulder-blades when she stood behind him in the canteen and kissed him on the head as she teased him because he groaned; he refused to hear the click-clack of her boots, always boots, on the indestructible linoleum floor in Grønlandsleiret 44; he heard the tapping of Hanne's heels on the floor, and he hated her.

He loved her, and had honestly never realized that before now.

"Do you know Sindre Sand well, fairly well, not well, or not at all? A, B, C, or D. Tick the box."

He did not have the energy to open his eyes, and knew he was losing his grip. He was sitting in a cold cellar struggling to drag the truth out of a reluctant witness who might well be the killer. He was taking no notes. He could not even bring himself to lift his arm to switch on the Dictaphone. This was not where he wanted to be. He wanted to go home.

"Sleep," he said slowly.

"Sort of fairly well," Gagliostro answered. "It was Brede who really knew him. He's smart. Steadily growing reputation. He's at Stiansen's now and is doing well there."

"The money, then. Do you know anything about that?"

Billy T.'s voice was almost inaudible.

"You mean the money that was to be invested in Italy?"

"Yes."

"I was also party to that deal. I didn't have so very much to contribute, just a couple of million kroner. It's still unclear to me how much Brede put in, but Sindre ... Of course he was just a young lad at that time. He threw four or five million into the pot. Something like that."

"Ten," Billy T. thought to himself, but said instead: "What happened?"

"Bad trip. It all went wrong, to put it bluntly. The money disappeared down the drain. Mine too. Brede came out of it pretty unscathed, I think. At least he wasn't dead-broke afterwards, like the rest of us. I had to start all over again. That's why it took a long time to get as far as Entré."

Billy T. opened his eyes. Claudio Gagliostro put his thumb in the air and smiled for the first time. His teeth were remarkably white and even in his hideous face.

"Why are you so talkative all of a sudden?" Billy T. said, struggling to raise his hand.

It was impossible. A violent attack of anxiety engulfed him. From far away he could hear Gagliostro respond: "You're not terrifying me so much any more. You can appear dangerous. Are you aware of that?"

"Do you think I could have a glass of water?" Billy T. managed to force out. "A glass of water, please."

He was not thirsty. He wanted to be alone. He thought he was going to die.

He concentrated on breathing. Relaxing.

"Breathe," he said, taking a big mouthful of air. "Breathe!"

Out with the air.

In again.

The blood rushed to his head. He was not going to die. He managed to open his eyes wide and raise his hand. When Gagliostro returned with a glass of water – Billy T. heard the clinking of ice cubes all the way from the top of the cellar steps – he was able to take it and drink it down without spilling a drop.

"Are you feeling unwell?"

"Just a bit tired. We must finish. Why did you bring Sindre Sand here, then? As some kind of compensation for all the money he lost?"

"I suggested it to Brede. He didn't want to. He was probably a bit uncomfortable about that business with Vilde. It didn't really seem like that, but maybe … Not quite sure."

The anxiety lessened slightly more. Billy T. wanted to stand up, but did not dare to.

"Will you keep Ziegler's shares now, or will you bring in another owner?"

"Keep … Well, that's exactly what's the problem! It turns out that it's *Vilde* who'll probably inherit the shares. Didn't you know that?"

Billy T. wrinkled his nose and drank some more water.

"Know what?"

"Brede and I had an agreement that was crystal-clear. Not because we thought either of us was going to die, but I mean … Plane crashes and car accidents, and that sort of thing … It happens, you know. We wanted to safeguard ourselves. Brede and I have always worked well together and the division of tasks here at Entré has always gone smoothly, but now this young girl comes along who hasn't a clue about anything at all, least of all running a restaurant, and will …"

Now it was Gagliostro who was in difficulties. He clutched his chest.

"When did you find this out?"

"Yesterday. No, last week, in actual fact. A lawyer phoned and created a huge commotion and I don't bloody know—"

"But when Brede was murdered, you were convinced you would inherit everything."

"Not everything! The restaurant. Brede owns a whole load more, and Vilde would of course have all the rest, but—"

A young man came thundering down the stairs; his chef's hat fell off as he reached the cellar floor.

"You have to come now, Claudio! The menu's wrong, and Karoline says it was you who said—"

"He'll come shortly," Billy T. said, waving the boy away. "Give us five more minutes."

"Okay by me," the boy mumbled, brushing dust off his cap as he headed back up the stairs. "I'm not the one who's responsible."

"I must just get one thing clear before we go," Billy T. said softly, leaning across the table. "On the evening of Sunday December the fifth, when Brede was murdered ... *At that time* you thought you would take over the restaurant, if Brede were to die."

"But—"

"Yes or no."

"Yes. But—"

"And where were you? On the evening of Sunday December the fifth?"

"Sunday evening. I was ... Let me think."

"Garbage!" Billy T. said calmly, trying to breathe more deeply. "Don't tell me that you have to think about where you were on the night your best friend and business partner was murdered. I still remember where I was when Olof Palme was shot. That's almost fifteen fucking years ago, and I didn't even know the guy!"

"At home."

"At home. Despite Entré being open on Sundays. Okay then."

"I hadn't had a day off for five weeks."

"What did you do?"

Gagliostro had begun to sweat again. He must suffer from some sort of illness, and it crossed Billy T.'s mind that it must be a serious handicap for a head waiter and restaurant owner to have hydrocephalus and sweat like a pig in eleven degrees of heat.

"I watched TV and went to bed early."

"On your own?"

The desperate expression on Gagliostro's face was answer enough. Billy T. ventured to rise from the chair. His legs were unsteady and he shook them tentatively, before stuffing the Dictaphone in his pocket and heading for the stairs.

"Nine o'clock tomorrow morning. On the dot. At police headquarters. Ask for Billy T."

Only now did it dawn on him that he had never actually introduced himself.

"Billy T.," he repeated. "That's me."

27

I stanbul was a gray sea of stone buildings wedged between two vivid blue dots. That was how she imagined the city. She had never been there. A span of silver between the Bosphorus Strait and the Blue Mosque, with the fragrance of spices and oriental rugs in between. That was how she pictured Istanbul.

Within this image, a woman was walking around thinking of her. Someone was strolling through the ancient city of Constantinople, perhaps wending her way through the famous bazaars, maybe wearing sunglasses against the fierce sunlight, en route to the bathhouse, to the mosaics and the health-giving waters below the sound of prayer calls from the minarets that jutted toward heaven, everywhere – and this woman was thinking of her.

Hanne Wilhelmsen opened her eyes and read the card again.

She could not fathom how it could have arrived so quickly. She did a mental calculation. Eight days had elapsed since they had parted. She knew that Nefis was returning to her homeland that same morning. Just over one week ago. The last time Hanne had received a postcard from Turkey was when Cecilie had been there on holiday with her group of female medic friends. Cecilie had been home for five days by the time the greeting had finally been delivered.

When she came across the card, she didn't believe it was meant for her. She looked at the close-up image of reddish-brown carpet with an indescribable pattern, slightly annoyed that the postal system was so inefficient, before glancing at the address. "Ms. Hanne Wilhelmsen, Norwegian Police Headquarters, Oslo, Norway, Europe." Almost like when she was a child and had gone on to say, "The World, The Milky Way, The Universe."

I live under the moon, and it is a cold planet. I can never forget, but the stars are not for us? Yours, Nefis.

The signature had made her forget that day's allocation of Ziegler case documents. She had locked herself into her office. The text was strange and beautiful, and she did not understand a word of it.

Question mark.

What did she mean?

Hanne had been in love once before in her life. When she had been in the third year at high school, she had caught sight of Cecilie and, like a semi-tame dog, had slinked about without saying anything, without giving any sign other than that she was always on the outside, but in close proximity. Then they had come together, as they should, as they were always meant to, and that was where they had remained. They stayed together until Cecilie no longer existed and Hanne thought she would die too.

With Nefis it was different. Nefis and Hanne were adults with wounds and scars and history. Cecilie was new when everything was new, when everything was untouched and they could shape themselves in each other's likeness without actually ever accomplishing that.

Hanne brushed her lips against the card. She sniffed its scent.

She would reply. She yearned to send a few words in return, and cursed herself for not being more far-sighted. For all Hanne knew, Nefis Özbabacan might be the most common name in Turkey. Istanbul was huge. How huge? Nefis had told her that she was a professor of mathematics, but she might have meant that she was a high-school teacher. There was a university in Istanbul. Hanne was certain of that when she racked her brains. But maybe there were several. Istanbul might be full of universities, high schools, educational institutions. She could not find space for them all when she shut her eyes and once again pictured in her mind's eye that broad belt of terracotta houses between the Blue Mosque and the Bosphorus Strait, but she shook her head, realizing she had never been there.

Hanne held the postcard to her lips and thought of Nefis. She thought of Cecilie. She thought of the apartment it had seemed so impossible to move back home to, with Cecilie's fingerprints everywhere: on the kitchen walls that Hanne wanted to be blue, but which had been painted yellow because that's what Cecilie wanted and Hanne never had time to do any painting anyway; on the settee they had bought with money they did not have, since Cecilie had seen it in a window on her way home from the cinema and could obtain an interest-free loan from her employer. Cecilie was everywhere, and Hanne did not even know where she was buried.

She thought of Cecilie's mother and father. They had sat together, holding hands, in the harsh light of the hospital corridor the night Cecilie had died. Their daughter. Hanne sat at her bedside, without ever considering that this was their place, the parents' place, as well.

She knew where they lived.

28

Thomas looked after Tigerboy very well. Mrs. Helmersen would not get hold of his cat this time. Helmer had normally been allowed to go out by himself, but Tigerboy had to stay inside the whole time until Thomas came home from school. Then Thomas ate the slices of bread that his mum had left on a plate in the fridge and shared some of it with Tigerboy. He wasn't allowed to do that, but the cat was so fond of liver pâté.

He was always scared when he carried Tigerboy downstairs past Mrs. Helmersen's front door. She could come out at any minute. It was almost as if she could smell him scuttling past. Quite often she would stick her head out to see who it was. Even though he crept as quietly as he could.

Thomas stood on the landing on the second floor, craning carefully over the railing. He mustn't lose Tigerboy. He could hear nothing except the traffic on Kirkeveien. He kicked off his wellington boots. They made a terrible squeaking noise, so he carried them in one hand and clamped Tigerboy tightly to his body with the other.

Halfway down the stairs he saw that Mrs. Helmersen's door was ajar. He wanted to turn tail, but had so much to carry that he let go of Tigerboy. The skittish kitten jumped, landing softly, and bounded down the steps to disappear into Mrs. Helmersen's apartment.

Thomas felt tears spring to his eyes and a sudden urge to pee again. He really needed to go, though he had just been to the toilet.

He sat transfixed on the stair, hardly daring to breathe. Nothing happened.

Maybe Mrs. Helmersen was not at home. Maybe she had gone out for a walk and had just forgotten to close the door. Dad always called her a senile old hag, when he thought Thomas out of earshot. Senile meant forgetful, and someone who was forgetful might easily leave a front door open when they went out. Thomas did it himself quite often, and he wasn't even senile.

Cautiously, he inched his way down the last few steps and across to the door.

"Hello," he whispered. "Tigerboy ..."

Neither Tigerboy nor Mrs. Helmersen made a sound.

Thomas pushed the door gingerly, ever so slightly, and it slid open. There was a really odd smell in the apartment. Not a nasty smell, really, just very strong. Food and perfume and old things. It smelled a bit like Grandma, but not as nice.

Although Thomas was frightened, it was also pretty exciting to be in Mrs. Helmersen's apartment. He had never seen anything like it before. In the hallway there were so many things that he almost had to shrink into himself to avoid knocking anything over. Four mirrors in large ornate frames hung on the walls. He could barely see the wallpaper because where there were no mirrors, there were pictures. And lamps, the kind attached to the wall with two arms and fabric shades with little soft bobbles along the edge that Mum thought ghastly.

The double doors into the living room were also open slightly. The gap was big enough for Tigerboy, anyway. Thomas stuck his head into the spacious room.

"Tigerboy," he said joyfully.

The kitten was perched on top of an old dresser, washing himself. Thomas zigzagged between massive tables and chairs that did not budge an inch and lifted the animal.

"Tigerboy," he whispered into the warm fur.

Then he surveyed the room.

He had never ever seen so much medicine. Apart from at the pharmacy, that is, having been there twice with his grandma. At home in his apartment his mum and dad kept medicines in a locked cabinet in the bathroom, with a picture of a snake creeping up a sort of sword on the door. There would be no room for all this in Dad's medicine cabinet. Boxes and jars and packets were piled up on top of the dresser where Tigerboy had been sitting. Thomas grew worried in case the kitten had eaten any of it, but it looked as if all the lids were in place. He glanced around the living room and saw even more medicines on a table in the corner beside the TV. And on the dining table. And on the radio. All over the place.

Thomas did not want to be here. The odor was too strong, and Mrs. Helmersen might come back at any minute. He retraced his steps to the entrance. Then he noticed the pictures. Not the kind of framed family photos that hung on the wall in the hallway, but pictures of people from the newspapers, fixed to the wallpaper with thumb tacks. He recognized some of them. Thorbjørn Jagland had been Prime Minister when Thomas was a toddler. The picture was not particularly good, and someone had written something across his face that Thomas wasn't able to read. Crown Prince Haakon had been cut out of a weekly magazine. The color photo showed him on skis.

Thomas wanted to leave. He no longer needed to pee, but Tigerboy needed to go outside. For a moment or two he wondered whether he should slam the door behind him. It would be best to leave it open. Maybe Mrs. Helmersen had left it like that on purpose.

29

S indre Sand was not so sure what he had actually expected. However, it certainly wasn't this. When he entered the tiny bedsit, he smelled the aroma of roast lamb and sage. Vilde was wearing black trousers and a gray chenille sweater with a plunging neckline. Tea lights, almost certainly twenty of them, in little glass pots scattered throughout the room made him feel that the clock had been turned back. Nothing had happened. Vilde had just found herself a new place to live, but everything was temporary and they would be married in the summer.

"I just needed to finish before I let you in," she said, offering him red wine in an enormous stemmed glass. "Sit down."

He said nothing about how beautiful it was. He did not even ask how she could know he was going to ring the doorbell on this particular night at this exact time. He took off his jacket, the smart one Vilde had given him a long time ago, before Brede.

She continued undressing him. He undressed her.

Nothing had changed, and afterwards they fell asleep.

"Fuck! The lamb roulade!"

She leapt up out of bed in the little alcove and dashed over to the kitchenette. When the jet of water from the tap hit the cast-iron casserole with its incinerated contents, clouds of smoke belched out into the room. The smoke alarm screeched.

"Open the window," she yelled, laughing, and flapped a newspaper for all she was worth at the noisy device. "Air! Help!"

He threw the window open wide and she shivered in the

ferocious draft that gusted into the room. The casserole was left in the sink and she rushed back across the floor to wrap herself in the quilt. Still laughing, she waved him over to her with one finger poking over the edge.

Sindre did not even smile. He began to pull on the clothes strewn over the floor.

"What's wrong with you, Vilde?"

His voice was sullen, as if it had suddenly struck him that in actual fact nothing was different from the way it had been since Brede had arrived on the scene and helped himself to what belonged to Sindre.

"You're behaving like the Merry Widow, I must say."

He snatched his sweater from a chair and struggled to force the tight neck over his head.

"Come and sit down, then. Let's talk."

She too was serious now. Although he hesitated, he hauled on his trousers.

"We don't really have anything to talk about. What's done is done. What's eaten is eaten."

"We didn't do much eating, did we?" she said. "Why did you come, then, if you don't want to talk to me?"

"To see how you were. How you're … coping with it all."

The words hung in the air before him like an accusation, and he stared into space.

"I see you're fine," he said all of a sudden, tightening his belt. "But I hadn't exactly expected to be invited to … a party tonight."

He crouched down to retrieve his socks. When he stood up again, it looked as if Vilde's head had receded into the quilt.

"But the money, Sindre! Don't you understand that everything's okay now, and we have money and can …"

He hooked his jacket over his arm and left.

30

The hire car was an automatic. She was not used to that: even in the USA she normally insisted on a manual gear shift. En route through Oslo she braked suddenly every time she intended to depress the clutch. A hot-tempered Opel Omega nearly crashed into her, and she thought she felt a faint bump on the fender. Perhaps that was a signal. However, she refused to turn back.

She kept to eighty kilometers per hour in the ninety zone on highway E18. She was in no hurry. She parked the vehicle less than half an hour after she had collected it at Bislett. Not directly beside the property in the spot obviously meant for visitors, but a hundred meters farther down the quiet cul-de-sac. Candelabras and plastic stars shone between the curtains in the windows of the villa; a couple of Christmas trees wrapped in plastic netting were already propped up against the walls of the house, awaiting the festivities. Smoke rose from the Vibe family's chimneystack.

Hanne Wilhelmsen hovered at the gate.

She had been there before. Many times. Cecilie had chosen the world's longest journey to school: she wanted to go to Katta, the Cathedral School in Oslo, despite having to get up at six o'clock every morning to catch the train from Drammen. Hanne had once asked her how it had all been arranged, as far as formalities were concerned. Cecilie had smiled and shrugged. Her father was the Director of Education in Buskerud County, and Hanne had never asked again.

She glanced up at the only dark window. The unoiled hinges protested in the cold. She closed the gate carefully behind her. The temperature had crept down to minus ten degrees Celsius, and the gravel crunched on the soles of her shoes. A holly garland with red berries and a silk ribbon embellished with the word "Welcome" decorated the front door. Before she had summoned the courage to ring the bell, the door opened.

"Hanne," Inger Vibe said amiably, as if Hanne were a daily visitor. "I heard you in the driveway. Well, not you exactly, but ..."

She laughed softly, laughter that Hanne had to close her eyes to withstand; she stood there, motionless, for so long that Inger Vibe finally placed her hand on Hanne's arm to encourage her to step inside.

"We've been waiting for you," Cecilie's mother said. "Come in."

Her back was Cecilie's back. The way she moved her feet, soundlessly, with short steps, as if unintentionally stealthy, was Cecilie's gait. There was a fragrance of oranges in the living room, and from the window ledge Hanne heard the delicate sound of miniature cherubs swimming in the hot air above a lighted candle; they struck tiny brass bells, rhythmic and almost inaudible.

"Is it you, Hanne? Take a seat."

Cecilie's father laid down his book and stood up, hesitantly offering her his hand.

"It's been such a long time."

Hanne sank into a deep armchair. The scent of oranges increased in intensity.

"Where have you been?"

For a moment she was unsure who was asking. She let her eyes leap from one to the other, feeling hot and sticky. A huge bowl on the coffee table overflowed with brightly colored fruit. Hanne blinked fiercely, desperate for someone to dim the light.

"I came to give you this."

She fiddled with the catch at her neck.

"Am I to have that?"

Inger Vibe held the palm of her hand up to her mouth, as if she had just won the lottery. The gesture irritated Hanne. When she handed over the necklace, her movements were more abrupt than she had intended.

"I gave this to Cecilie years ago. One birthday. She loved it, I think, and—"

"She always wore that necklace," Arne Vibe said. "Always."

"It's not right for me to wear it myself. It was Cecilie's necklace. You can have it."

Neither said thank you. They looked at each other with eyes that made Hanne feel undecided. Her discomfort made her perspire even more, and she opened her mouth to breathe more easily. Inger Vibe went into the kitchen. Her husband toyed with his book, taking his glasses off and on and continuing to smile without saying a word. His smile was friendly enough, but at the same time contained a sort of neutrality, a kind of distance that made her want to leave. She had done what she had to do. She had given them the jewelry.

This wasn't what she wanted.

Eventually Inger Vibe returned. Placing a coffee cup made of old fine porcelain in front of Hanne, she poured coffee into it and offered her cakes from a stemmed dish.

"I really came to thank you. To say ... I wasn't entirely—"

"To apologize, perhaps?"

Arne Vibe was no longer smiling. Nevertheless his face displayed a gentleness on its strong features, in the gaze now directed at her for the first time.

"Maybe you came to apologize. I would think so."

There was a strong scent of Christmas. The sound of the brass seraphim's never-ending dance at the window seemed louder now. Snow had begun to settle along the windowpanes. She began to cry. Cecilie's parents drank coffee with milk. They drank two cups each, and still Hanne wept.

"I don't entirely know," she finally said softly. "Perhaps."

Two hours later, each of the Vibes had a drop of liqueur in a glass. Hanne had switched to tea. She drank it out of a large mug adorned with a half-faded picture of the Eiffel Tower, aware that the tea leaves must be old. The brown liquid tasted of onion and pepper and oatmeal. She hugged the mug as she tucked her feet underneath herself.

"Are you cold?" Inger asked, settling a blanket round Hanne's shoulders.

"No."

"It was good of you to come. Maybe you could have come sooner. That would've been better for us all."

Arne suddenly stretched out across the armrest and prized Hanne's left hand from the mug. He held it in his own, and ran his thumb over her skin. As far as she could remember, it was the first time he had touched her, apart from shaking her hand.

"Our problem," he began slowly, "is that ... We've found it so difficult to understand. We've never rejected Cecilie. We've never rejected you. On the contrary."

"My fault. Everything's my fault. Everything, always."

Inger Vibe got up and stood in front of the enormous picture window. She rested her forehead on the glass and continued to stand like that, leaning against the window with her hands by her sides until she suddenly turned round and said: "That's your biggest mistake, Hanne. That's how you've failed."

"I know that."

"No. You don't know that. That's the problem. You always believe everything's your fault. If only you can take on the guilt, you feel that exonerates you from everything. Sorry, you say, and then think that makes everything okay. Your feeling of guilt has been your shield against your surroundings. You've been ..."

She flung out her arms with a gesture that made Hanne hide her face behind the mug of tea and close her eyes.

"You've protected yourself for too long. You've decked yourself out with guilt. You've slung it around you like a ... dark cloak. To keep people away."

"Cecilie didn't keep herself away."

Inger smiled and turned back to the window. The reflection in the dark glass magnified her.

"But then Cecilie was quite special too."

Her laughter was high-pitched and prolonged, as if she had said something really amusing, as if Cecilie was expected at some point, any moment; Hanne had to force herself not to turn to the door where Cecilie might be.

"It's absolutely ridiculous of you to stay at a hotel."

Inger's voice had taken on a determined note. She ran her hands over her skirt and lifted the necklace up to her eyes.

"You've a really splendid apartment. Do you want me to come with you to tidy it?"

"No!"

The reply came too quickly. Maybe Inger wanted to come with her. It might mean something for her to sort out her daughter's belongings.

"Cecilie isn't going to be cleared away," Hanne explained hesitantly. "She should stay there. I just have to—"

"Stuff and nonsense. Of course things have to be tidied away, now she's gone. She has clothes and suchlike that have to go. What about the Salvation Army?"

"Later. Perhaps. First of all I have to—"

"Do you want *me* to come with you?"

Arne was still stroking the back of her hand with his thumb.

"I need to go."

She rose from the deep armchair. Her legs had gone to sleep under her, and she nearly fell over. Arne caught her.

"It's okay," she said. "It's okay now."

"Just one more thing," Inger said. Hanne had opened the front door and was shivering in the icy draft. "Seize whatever you can from life. We don't live so very long, Hanne. We can't afford to squander the important things."

With a shrug, Hanne closed the door behind her without hugging either of them; not even a handshake did she manage to offer. When she reached the car, she turned round. Lights still shone in every room, bar one, in the attic.

It was now Tuesday night, December 14, 1999.

31

The truck ahead of her blocked most of her view. With no load, it clattered along from Tollbugata to Prinsens gate, with Hanne Wilhelmsen bringing up the rear. From old habit, she longed to note the registration number. She peered at the dashboard, but the hire car was not equipped with an easily accessible notepad. Anyway, the truck driver was not doing anything illegal, even though this was his third time cruising around the block in Kvadraturen. He should have parked down at the Havnelager building on the harborside long ago, to catch his regulation hours of sleep according to the rest-time regulations. Instead he was clogging up the whole street and taking his time studying the sparse selection on the sidewalk.

Every time the truck braked, Hanne also stole a glance at the silhouettes outlined in the yellow glare of the street lamps. The girls she had seen until now were too young. Most of them might be considered juveniles. She turned into the curb and stopped the car. The rattle of the truck had given her a headache. She wound down the window and lit a cigarette.

She should have visited Cecilie's parents ages ago. She had forgotten to ask about the funeral. She still did not know where Cecilie's gravestone was located.

She looked at her watch. Quarter past one.

"Girls' night?"

She jumped, suddenly gazing into a face smaller than the gruff voice would suggest. The person who had thrust almost an entire head into the car was having wig problems. It had slipped down as far as the eyes.

"Looking for company?"

The accent grated. The smile revealed a row of teeth bought a short time before, or more likely stolen. The denture was badly fitting. The words had a slurping time-lag.

"Do you speak Norwegian?" Hanne asked, leaning away; the smell of bad breath mixed with a profusion of cheap perfume forced its way into the car.

"I speak all languages."

Hanne noticed a faint trace of stubble under the brown cream. She shook her head and produced a 100-kroner bill from her jacket pocket.

"Here. I'm not interested. Not in you."

She started the engine. The transvestite snatched the banknote, with a wiggle of the backside to demonstrate pique. In the rear-view mirror, Hanne could see the long legs toddle away on ten-centimeter-high heels.

Like everyone else in the police, Hanne had begun her career on street patrol. From that time she was well aware that it was useless to ask. Whores could kill one another to secure a regular spot on a street corner, but information did not come free of charge to anyone who smelled like a cop.

Hanne smelled like a cop, and she knew it. She drove on in the tracks churned by the enormous truck. Fortunately the guy had got a nibble. Only a Volvo estate car with a child's seat visible was lurching around now in the red-light area; it was approaching some sort of closing time. The vehicle stopped quietly in Myntgata and a tiny figure in fake fur sneaked in on the passenger side after a brief discussion about price and product. The young girl would probably fit into the child's seat.

A solitary shadow limped off toward Bankplassen. The lights

on the façade of Gamle Logen reflected faintly on a short silver-lamé jacket. Hanne dropped her speed, rolled down the window once again, and said: "Hey. Hey, you!"

The woman turned and took a few seconds to focus properly.

"No time," she said abruptly.

Hanne stopped the car and made to step out.

"Don't talk to cops."

The woman continued her pig-headed monologue, walking oddly, as if half-turning with every second step she took.

"No time, don't want to."

"Hairy Mary!"

Although the woman gave no sign of responding to the name, Hanne knew she had found the object of her search. That same morning she had run a background check on Hairy Mary. The hooker would turn fifty-five in January. This person looked almost eighty. All the same there was a remarkable strength in her move-ments, a kind of against-all-the-odds defiance that had kept her upright long past her time. Hanne tried to place her hand on the woman's shoulder.

"Let go!"

Hairy Mary growled as her pace quickened. Her limp became more pronounced; the socket of her right hip might be damaged.

"Would you like some food? Are you hungry?"

Hairy Mary stopped at last, squinting at Hanne with an expres-sion that might indicate bafflement.

"Food?"

She seemed to savor the word, smacking her lips lightly and scratching her thigh. Hanne had to avert her eyes when she saw the inflamed scabs, gouged open by her dirty long nails, through the fishnet stockings.

"Food. Okay then."

Hairy Mary did not waste anything, not even her consonants.

Hanne knew her success was more through good luck than good management. It was idiotic to use nourishment to entice the woman. Hairy Mary could just as easily have felt insulted and made herself scarce. Now Hanne's greatest problem was to find something for a worn-out hooker to eat in the middle of the night. Of course she could drive to a gas station, but those gargantuan floodlit kiosks were hardly the place for a conversation with Hairy Mary.

Hairy Mary nodded in the direction of Dronningens gate and began to walk off. Relieved, Hanne assumed she knew where she wanted to go. A few minutes later they were sitting on red plastic chairs in a cafeteria bereft of other customers. Hanne smoked, Hairy Mary ate. Pink sauce dripped from the corners of her mouth. Her eyes roamed constantly to the cook behind the counter, as if to make sure there was more where that kebab had come from. She swallowed cola in a single greedy gulp.

"More. Thanks."

Hanne lit another cigarette and waited patiently until yet another kebab was served, with accompaniments. Hairy Mary belched behind a closed fist, and stared for the first time at her benefactor. Her eyes were brown with yellow flecks on the iris. Less becoming was the distinct yellow hue of the whites of her eyes, barely visible behind the heavy locks of hair.

"You were the one who phoned," Hanne said.

It was more an assertion than a question, and she regretted it immediately.

"Haven't done anything wrong."

"I know that."

Restless, Hairy Mary looked keen to leave, as if the meal had drained her of any ability to concentrate that she might still possess.

"Need to work. Bye."

"Wait a minute. If you had done anything wrong, I'd have hauled you in long ago. You know that perfectly well. I just want to know what you saw."

The food had almost done for Hairy Mary. Her eyes slid shut and her whole figure crumpled into something resembling sleep. The scraping sounds of a spatula on the grill plate woke her and she nabbed a cigarette from the pack on the table.

"That was good."

She talked down at the leftover food, and took a really deep drag before her eyes slid closed again.

"I need to know what you saw. Whether there was anyone else there. Whether you ... Did you find anything? Something you took with you?"

"Dead man and piles of garbage. Need to sleep soon."

Hairy Mary snuffled from her jacket lapel and gave a hacking cough. Hanne weighed up the possibility of getting this exhausted woman towed off to the car she had left in Myntgata.

"Where do you live, Hairy Mary?"

The question was so absurd that it momentarily shook Hairy Mary awake. Her eyes blinked against the flickering of the fluorescent lights on the ceiling.

"Live? Right now, I live here."

Then she fell asleep. Soft snoring sounds jerked in her throat; her lips smacked against each other in short snorts that brought a smile to Hanne's face. The half-dead shape sat awkwardly, resting against the windowpane, with her hands folded neatly on her lap, the cigarette balanced between two fingers. Hanne teased it out carefully and extinguished the glowing embers in the ashtray.

"She can't sleep here," the cook said in an amalgam of Turkish and Swedish. "You'll have to take her with you."

"I'll just go and get my car – is that okay?"

Hairy Mary had plenty of experience of clambering in and out of cars. Like a sleepwalker, she settled into the passenger seat and continued snoring until they passed police headquarters.

"Where are we going?"

"Home," Hanne said. "I'm going home, and you're coming with me."

When she parked the car outside the low-rise apartment block in Tøyen, it was past two o'clock on Tuesday night. Fortunately all the windows were in darkness.

32

"Felice. With an Italian *c*. Like in cello. Not Felise."

"Apologies, Dr. Felice."

Billy T. rubbed his arm and rolled down his shirt sleeve.

"Strange name. Øystein Felice. A bit ... of a mixture, so to speak."

The doctor dropped the syringe into a cardboard container, before washing his hands thoroughly under the tap.

"So your trip wasn't *entirely* wasted, then. Now you should at least avoid coming down with this winter's influenza. My mother's Norwegian. My father's Italian. I should really be called Umberto after my father's father, but I got my mother's father's name instead. He was from Valdres."

He smiled distractedly, as if so used to explaining his unusual name that he spoke on autopilot. He dried his hands diligently with a paper towel and put the edited folder into a plastic wallet.

"Here," he said, handing it to Billy T. "This is what I can tell you. Since the patient is dead, he can't release me from my duty of confidentiality. It's then up to me and my discretion. From what you told me on the phone, there's nothing in Brede Ziegler's medical history of any interest. To the police, I mean."

"You know," Billy T. said grumpily, snatching the folder with its sparse contents, "you would think there was a duty of confidentiality attached to knowing this guy Ziegler at all."

"What?"

"I don't give a shit. But ..."

He skimmed through the papers.

"The man was plagued by headaches and had a gammy knee," he summarized. "Nothing else."

"I've most certainly not said that. Neither have I said the opposite. All I'm saying is ..."

Billy T. groaned loudly and leaned forward in the cramped chair, holding his head in his hands as he rocked back and forth, moaning softly.

"Unfortunately I'm not a psychiatrist," Dr. Felice said drily. "But I can recommend a really capable man if you—"

Billy T. sat up straight and took a deep breath.

"So the headache wasn't migraine," he said despondently. "And he didn't take any medication."

"No. He was perhaps the nearest I've come to a fanatical resister of pills. His knee bothered him even more than the headache, which could be absent for months at a stretch. However the meniscus tear should really have been operated on. He refused. He wouldn't take painkillers, either."

A woman popped her head round the door.

"We're now half an hour behind with appointments," she said tartly, glaring at Billy T. before she slammed the door shut without waiting for a response.

"When did you see him last?"

Billy T. struggled to find a more comfortable position on the chair, in order to make a show of telling the doctor that he intended to take as much time as he required. Since Dr. Felice had so arrogantly refused to visit police headquarters until he had received a formal request, his patients would have to tolerate an extra hour in the waiting room. Dr. Felice opened a packet of pastilles and offered him one.

"It's quite odd that you should ask. He hasn't been here for eight months. At that time he had a laceration. He had cut himself when opening an oyster and, stupidly enough, had not gone to Accident & Emergency right away. Instead he came here the next day. He was given a tetanus injection and a course of antibiotics. Not of any interest to you, of course, but ..."

He picked a pastille out of the box and sat twiddling it between thumb and forefinger.

"What *is* interesting, I expect, is that he phoned me the Sunday he was killed."

Billy T. swallowed his pastille whole.

"He phoned you," he repeated tritely. "On Sunday the fifth. Well, well. What did he want?"

"I don't know, in fact. He called me at home. My personal number. He's never done that before. I wasn't at home, but he left a message on the answering machine. He asked me to phone him on ..."

Dr. Felice gazed across the massive office desk that displayed signs of a remarkable sense of order. Three stacks of paper sat neatly side by side below paperweights in the shape of monkeys that could not see, hear, or speak.

"Two-two, nine-eight, five-three, nine-nine," he read from a note. "Later I discovered that's his home phone number."

"When did he phone?"

"I don't know. I have an ordinary answering machine, and it doesn't record the time. He didn't say himself. He didn't say what it was about. Just that I must call him before eight o'clock. 'Before eight tonight.' That was what he said. Since I was out from two o'clock on Sunday afternoon and wasn't back until the next afternoon, I can't be more specific about the time of his call."

Billy T. produced a notepad from his voluminous jacket and made apathetic notes.

"He said 'before eight'? Not 'when you come home'?"

"No. 'Before eight.'"

"Can we have the tape?"

"Sorry, no. It's been wiped. By complete accident. Naturally I would have kept it, since I read about Brede Ziegler's death on Monday morning and was quite shocked when I heard the message from him that same afternoon. I must have touched a button in my confusion. But I remember the message clearly."

The ill-tempered nurse came in again, this time without even knocking. She banged a ring binder down on the desk in front of Dr. Felice and stamped out of the room without closing the door behind her.

"That was a bit much," Billy T. commented. "Do you find it acceptable for her to behave like that, or what?"

Dr. Felice did not reply. He pinched his eyes between thumb and index finger and forced out an abrupt smile.

"She's very efficient. She's the one who has to take the flak out there."

Billy T. buttoned his jacket on his way out.

"It's entirely possible that we'll call you in for formal interview," he said. "We'll see. In the meantime, if anything else that might be of interest springs to mind, then phone. Billy T.'s enough. That's me."

"I had understood that," Øystein Felice said. "From that point of view, we've got something in common."

"Eh?"

Half-turning, Billy T. bumped into a box of disposable gloves that fell on the floor.

"Strange name."

"Exactly."

He crouched down and gathered up the gloves, covering his fingers in talcum powder and brushing them vigorously on his trousers.

"There could be one thing."

Dr. Felice looked exhausted. For the first time Billy T. noticed that his short dark hair had a sprinkling of gray at the temples, and copious beard growth was starting to show. Billy T. fished out his pocket watch and cursed when he saw that it was already half past four.

"What is it, then?" he said brusquely.

"I ... In that folder I gave you, there's nothing about ..."

Dr. Felice helped himself to another pastille. He didn't put that one in his mouth either, but instead rolled it into a soft green pea.

"Brede Ziegler was sterilized. Of course that would emerge from the postmortem anyway. Or ... He must already have been autopsied. I wasn't sure if it was of any possible relevance for the case, so I didn't include it in the—"

He waved uncertainly at the folder Billy T. held in his right hand.

"Anyway. He wanted to be sterilized before he got married. Of course I spoke to him in detail about it before the procedure, but he was extremely set in his decision. His age would normally mean that I wouldn't have any objections, but he was childless and about to get married to a young and presumably fertile woman, so I—"

He broke off. Again he pressed his fingers against his eyes, as if struggling to focus.

"It's probably of no interest whatsoever."

"Yes, it is," Billy T. said. "I need to go now, but if you don't phone me in the next few days, then I'll call you. Okay?"

Dr. Felice did not answer. The phone rang; a modern, digital chime. He grasped the receiver as Billy T. closed the door behind him.

"That woman who always asks for Dr. Happy is on the line," he heard the receptionist say. "Shall I ask her to call back later?"

Happy. Billy T. flashed a crooked smile at a black woman with a whimpering two-year-old as it suddenly dawned on him what "*felice*" actually meant.

"Dr. Happy," he murmured. "What a name for a doctor!"

He completely forgot to pay for his vaccination.

33

In two hours' time she had to be at theater rehearsals. She still had little idea how she would actually interpret her role. As usual she had learned the words quickly but naturally – that was not where the problem lay. The difficulty radiated toward her from the very cover of the manuscript, now dog-eared and soiled with coffee stains.

"Narcissus at the Late-Night Party."

Nonsense! Thale had spent weeks analyzing the text, but the words remained inconsequential hypotheses on a piece of paper. Her role was a paradoxical parody, though that was not what the playwright had in mind; she was to play a lovesick Greek nymph in a luxury apartment in affluent Aker Brygge.

The theater manager had agreed to stage the production from some sense of duty to contemporary Norwegian drama. Why not something by Jon Fosse? Admittedly she had already acted in two of his plays, but at least he gave her something to work on, a personality to delve into. They had advertised a competition to commemorate the National Theater's centenary. A know-all crime novelist – who'd had great success with a host of murder mystery books – had won. The play was, and remained, dreadful. At the last rehearsal Thale had got it in spades from the director. He was fed up, he said, with her using their scant allocation of rehearsal time to complain about the text, instead of trying to make something of it. *Commitment*, he had yelled, as he kicked a floodlight. He had fractured his little toe. Now he was hobbling around on crutches, grumpier than ever.

Stretching out on the settee, Thale pulled up the blanket and closed her eyes. Commitment. She had to struggle to find some commitment to a play in which the Greek myth of Narcissus had been transposed to a nouveau-riche Norwegian setting in the year 2000. Apparently prosperous characters wandered around on stage, cultivating vacuity and avoiding the love of anyone other than themselves. Thale could almost hear the laughter from the audience when they were introduced to a stockbroker called Narcissus. The tragedy of it all was that the play was not meant to be a farce. That she herself, named Echo, would roam around in a Spice Girl costume would occasion nothing other than a smile of pity.

She made an effort to concentrate and distance herself from her contempt for the play, to no avail. No matter how hard she tried, she could not see the connection between the moving Narcissus myth and drinking whisky for five hours at a stretch in a postmodern apartment. The original Narcissus fell in love with his own reflection and rejected Echo's love. Since the reflection was a lover Narcissus could never possess, his self-love became his misfortune and downfall. The stockbroker, on the other hand, was basically quite happy to be in love with himself. The analogy was illogical. All the same, the liberties the writer had taken with Echo were the worst aspect of the play. In the myth, she wasted away in sorrow over her lost love, but her lament – the echo – lingered with humanity for all eternity. In the modern version Echo had become a feminist. Thale shuddered at the thought of how, in the final act, she had to rape Narcissus in his bathtub. Everyone had to get what they wanted, by force if necessary.

It enraged her that a writer who obviously hadn't understood his material should coerce her into expressing his warped ideas.

She had to turn her mind to something else. She fell asleep.

A dream woke her twenty minutes later. Sweaty and breathless, she recalled being at Daniel's bedsit to help him hang pictures. A large damp patch was horribly outlined on one wall and she concealed it with a photograph. As soon as she had hung it, cracks appeared on the wall beside it. Another picture, another crack. She kept running, faster and faster, but the entire room had begun to fall apart, all the same.

Thale sat up and checked the time. She would make herself a cup of coffee before walking to the theater.

She was deeply anxious about her boy.

Nothing had gone the way she had planned. Daniel had not received what he was due. She could see there was something wrong with the boy. He spent more time on meaningless part-time jobs than on his studies, and he seemed unhappy. She had a hunch that it had to do with something far more serious than his enforced move from Bogstadveien to that mold-infested bedsit with no bathroom. When he had tried to speak to her last Saturday, she had dismissed him. She hadn't really wanted to, but his questions were too obvious, too painful to countenance. She had been reluctant to deal with them. It was not her fault that Daniel had been let down. Thale had no wish for her son to dwell on everything that had already transpired. She was keen to help him look forward. That was what she had always done.

She sipped half a cup of coffee before going to the bathroom. The nightmare's dank miasma still pervaded her clothes: she tore them off and stuffed them into the laundry basket. Scalding hot water cascading down her back made her feel better.

It really all came down to money.

Daniel had not received the inheritance he was entitled to, the inheritance that she and Idun had agreed would go to Daniel. Daniel would be his grandfather's heir. Idun, whom Daniel ludicrously enough still called Taffa as he had done since a toddler, had no children of her own. Idun loved Daniel as if he were her own child. They had both come to an agreement. Thale had never let herself be ruled by money or the opportunity to possess it. Since the age of seventeen she had managed by herself. Never, not once, had she asked her father for money. Nevertheless, there had always been a certain security there. The villa at Heggeli was a family insurance policy, held in common, that would come to Daniel at the end of the day. It had never occurred to her that her father, a Supreme Court advocate, might have financial problems. When he died after a short illness at the age of eighty, the estate was insolvent. The villa was worth six million kroner, but the mortgage on it was almost six and a half. Thale had not been able to muster the energy to make an effort to find out what had happened. It was Idun who had uncovered it all. Their father had been a notorious gambler and the opportunity to speculate on the Internet had wiped him out completely.

She struggled with the mixer taps. Probably something wrong with a gasket: the pipes rumbled and the tap dripped constantly, no matter how hard she turned it. She punched the wall and almost toppled over.

Daniel had lost his inheritance and it was a real problem for her to accept that.

His inheritance.

She hesitated as she stepped out of the bathtub. That it had not crossed her mind earlier must be because she had tried to push it all away. She always wanted to look forward – only forward.

The thought was entirely unfamiliar, and she slowly ran her hands over her wet hair.

34

The technique of freezing her out was carefully planned, thoroughly implemented, and obviously universally accepted. In any case, no one batted an eyelid when she turned up after the meeting had started and sat at the end of the massive conference table with three empty chairs separating her from her neighbor. Hanne Wilhelmsen tried to restrain a discouraged sigh. For the first time it struck her that she did not deserve this treatment, regardless of what she might have done.

It was tedious to arrive late at this major run-through of the Ziegler case, but waking with Hairy Mary in her apartment had been like suddenly having a baby in the house. The woman had eaten more than her fill of lamb stew at half past seven that morning. There was nothing apart from canned food in the house, and Hanne had woken to the sound of Hairy Mary spewing her guts, her head down the toilet pan.

"My God, that was good," Hairy Mary said, wiping her slaver with the sleeve of a pair of pajamas that had belonged to Cecilie.

Hanne had to spend an extra half-hour going over the ground rules: no drugs, no stealing. No rummaging through closets and drawers, except in the kitchen. Eat whatever you want that you can find, but have a care for your stomach. When Hanne stepped out of the shower, Hairy Mary had a broad, triumphant grin on her face.

"Lovely sweater, isn't it?"

The garment reached to her knees, making her head stick up

like the neck of a chicken from an enormous egg; it had been a gift from Cecilie for Hanne's thirtieth birthday.

"The character of the laceration in the chest indicates that the stab wound was inflicted from slightly below."

Hanne struggled to concentrate on Severin Heger's report. She would have to scoot home at lunch break and check on how things were going.

"Which means one of two things," Severin went on: he was standing beside a flip chart, waving a marker pen in the air. "The perpetrator may have been shorter than Brede Ziegler, who was five foot ten, or else …"

He drew a staircase, and placed a stick-man on the second step.

"… Ziegler may have been standing on the stairs, and the perpetrator here, down below."

Yet another stick-man was marked on the paper, equipped with a knife, its size and shape more like a sword.

"As far as footprints are concerned, those were substantially degraded as a result of the mild weather that set in on the night of the murder. Admittedly, this staircase is pretty pointless—"

"What is it actually used for?" Silje Sørensen interrupted. "Honestly, I must admit that I never even knew about it. It seems odd that we have some sort of back stairway into the building that's never been used."

"… but it's obviously regularly frequented," Severin completed his sentence, without answering her.

Silje used her mouth to hide her diamond ring as she looked down at the floor.

"There's a brick wall just here," he continued, drawing a bird's-eye view of the flight of steps. "Of course, that functions as some kind of shelter if the wind is blowing from this direction …"

He outlined an arrow coming from Åkebergveien.

"… which happens only seldom. But the place was covered in

footprints of all shapes and sizes. The two trainees who ran round to check the tip-off about a dead man on the stairs, for instance, left their own clear marks on the site. To put it that way."

He fell silent and stared vacantly ahead, as if considering how useful it would be to repeat the tongue-lashing he had given the two trainee officers. He took a deep breath and shook his head.

"There were a few clumps of snow here and there, and they have given us some help, at least. To sum it all up ..."

Once again he began to sketch, this time the soles of shoes. Three of them were placed side by side on the sheet of paper. He wrote the number forty-four on the first, thirty-eight on the next, and forty-two on the last, before using the marker pen to point to the largest one.

"This imprint is Ziegler's own. These two ..."

He slammed the palm of his hand on the flip chart and turned to face the others in the room.

"... are probably the freshest footprints in the area. A lady's shoe size thirty-eight and a boot in size forty-two that was presumably worn by a man."

"A small man," Billy T. muttered.

"Or a teenager. Not a full-grown man."

"Or a woman with big feet."

Silje made another attempt, and her eyes leapt audaciously from Billy T. to Severin Heger.

"Or a girl in borrowed footwear," Klaus Veierød said grouchily. "Who are the people who hang about in that park of ours? Hookers and other riff-raff. They don't exactly pay much attention to what's going on."

"The depth of the footprints suggests a body weight of around seventy kilos for the woman's shoes, considerably less in the bigger boots. Luckily, we had Brede Ziegler's prints for comparison purposes."

"A well-rounded, plump lady," Billy T. concluded. "And a light, bantam-weight man. What a pair."

"Two perpetrators? Are we now talking about two murderers all of a sudden?"

Silje Sørensen tucked her hair behind her ear.

"Don't you hear what I'm saying?"

Severin took a seat and drummed his fingers on the table.

"The crime scene was a fucking mess. Loads of footprints. Loads of shit. If these prints are relevant at all, we don't really have any idea. But out of all the muddle I've got from the technicians, this seems the closest we can come to footprints that were left on the night of Sunday December the fifth. It could be right. It could just as easily be wrong."

"Have the witnesses been asked their shoe size?"

Hanne Wilhelmsen's question was self-assured, though not addressed to anyone in particular. No one answered. No one looked in her direction. In the end Karianne Holbeck shook her head slowly, blushing to the roots of her hair. Billy T. raised his hand as a sign that Severin Heger should continue.

"The really astounding information in this case is something we learned fairly early in the proceedings," he said. "Two attempts were made on Brede Ziegler's life. The one – the stabbing – killed him. The other – the poisoning – he would probably have died of anyway."

He got to his feet again, this time to take an empty Paracet packet from his back pocket. He unfolded it and held it up to the others.

"This item here is left lying in most Norwegian homes. But have you ever tried to buy two packs at the pharmacist's? It's not possible. You'll get only one. It is in fact a poison, folks. As you see ..."

His index finger smacked against the black lettering on the orange background.

"Five hundred milligrams. That's the dose of paracetamol in every pill. As for myself, I usually take two at a time. That's one gram, isn't it?"

Everyone around the table nodded in attentive silence; this was a sum they could follow.

"Very few of us *read* these warnings on the medicines we use. Permit me to entertain you: 'The recommended dose must not be exceeded without consulting a doctor. High doses or prolonged use can cause serious liver damage.' You can certainly say that again! If you consume this whole packet – that is to say, twenty tablets – you can die! That would amount to ten grams of paracetamol. If you've gone to another pharmacy and got hold of another pack, you can definitely say goodbye to your family. If you mix all of it with large quantities of alcohol or other stimulants, you need less. Then this one packet would be more than enough."

From time to time Hanne had used one packet of Paracet in a week. Unconsciously she touched her liver.

"If you don't receive treatment fairly quickly after ingesting large doses of this poison, it'll be too late. Then you'll die, no matter what. Brede Ziegler was stuffed full of paracetamol, and what's more his blood alcohol count was 0.3 when he died. That could mean he'd consumed one glass of wine earlier that evening."

"What does the postmortem indicate?" Hanne Wilhelmsen asked.

Severin did not answer but glanced across at Billy T.

"As far as I can see," Hanne continued, "there's nothing in Brede Ziegler's stomach contents to suggest he'd drunk wine before he died. Which leads us to a pretty logical conclusion. He'd been on a real bender the night before. Such a hell of a booze-up that he was still intoxicated on Sunday night. Maybe he was with someone. The killer, for example. One of them, at least. To me it sounds strange that Brede Ziegler had drunk wine on Sunday afternoon or evening. He must have had quite a stomach ache. It's true that some of the information in this case indicates that Ziegler had an unusually high pain threshold, but drinking wine if you've got a pain in your gut? Think not. Do we know anything about Brede Ziegler's whereabouts on Saturday evening?"

The room went totally quiet. Billy T. had not looked in Hanne's direction since she had entered the room. Now he stared demonstratively in the opposite direction. Karianne Holbeck's face took on a fascinating shade of puce.

"We've mostly, most of all, we've …"

She tried to obtain help from Billy T. as she scratched her ear and studied the shoe soles on the flip chart.

"We don't yet know where Brede was on Sunday evening before he was murdered," Karianne continued, stuttering. "We've been concentrating on that. Sort of. It's a mystery. No one has seen him, no one knows where he was. The only thing we do know is that he left his apartment at five to eight that evening. That's according to the alarm system. The CCTV was switched off on that particular evening. There was some confusion about changing the cassette, so we don't know anything about who went in and out of the apartment block after five o'clock that afternoon until late on Monday morning. We've concentrated on the Sunday, you see. That seemed to be more … pressing, in a sense. Most important to find out where he was and what he did on Sunday afternoon. Just before he died."

Her voice gathered strength as she spoke and broke into falsetto at "died."

"Billy T.?"

He had no help to offer.

"The body takes about an hour to eliminate an alcohol count of 0.3 in the blood," Hanne said emphatically.

She shouldn't really lecture. Billy T. twisted round in his seat. Karianne could blush as much as she wanted; she was not responsible for this case going right down the pan. Billy T. took the blame for that.

"It varies a little," Hanne went on. "Depending on the speed of an individual's metabolism, tolerance of alcohol, and that sort of thing. From the interviews I've gone through, it's difficult to form an impression of Brede Ziegler's relationship to alcohol. In any case, he was a fully grown man and we must assume that he had a certain tolerance. Let's say, then, that at five o'clock, just by way of example, on Sunday morning ..."

She tilted her head to one side, looking reflective. Silje Sørensen was the only one looking at her. The others sat like pillars of salt with their faces averted. For a moment she was unsure whether they were actually listening.

"At five o'clock on Sunday morning he must have had an alcohol count of 2.5 in his blood. Wasted, in other words. Then he would not be free of alcohol until very late on Sunday night. That reinforces your theory, Severin. About the Paracet definitely going to kill him, I mean. Besides, it makes us look like idiots for not finding out what the guy was doing on Saturday and Friday and Thursday ... the entire week before he died."

Since no one spoke, she did not give a damn and pressed on: "We can outline a number of scenarios. Of course we could be talking about the most premeditated murder in the history of Norwegian crime. Somebody has got a whole lot of Paracet into Ziegler. The perpetrator becomes impatient because it actually takes time to die of paracetamol poisoning, and stabs the knife into him to hasten his death. Well."

She crossed over to the flip chart and tore off the sheet depicting the shoe soles.

"Each and every one of you can decide for yourself the likelihood of such a modus. As for myself, I discard that theory right away. It's too crazy. The combination of strength of purpose and almost childish impatience doesn't add up. On the other hand, if we ..."

Silje Sørensen smiled. Hanne fixed her gaze on Silje's mouth and felt her anger rise. It was one thing that Billy T. had more than good enough reason to be furious. It was another thing altogether to turn the whole team against her. Silje had obviously been immune. Her smile expressed a mixture of genuine interest and something approaching admiration. Hanne wheeled round and drew two genderless figures on the rough paper.

"To some extent it's pretty sensational that *two people* at one and the same time should get it into their heads that Ziegler must die. But taking the man's extremely prominent media profile into consideration, compared with all the half-dead characters left at the roadside where this chef has driven past ..."

She stopped and clicked the fingers of her left hand.

"Hello. Hel-lo!"

Still only Silje looked up. Hanne let the seconds tick by. Severin Heger finally raised his face to hers. No one else.

"Fine," Hanne Wilhelmsen said crossly. "You take over, Billy T. I'll keep my mouth shut."

She took her time resuming her seat. All the way down to the very foot of the table, on her own, with three empty chairs between her and Klaus Veierød, where she sat with her arms folded, eyeballing Billy T.

"Well, well," Severin Heger said with feigned cheerfulness. "Let's take a closer look at our suspects, then."

"But, Annmari," Silje said, obliging the Police Prosecutor to tear herself away from her notes for a moment or two. "If Hanne is right and we're dealing with two different perpetrators here ... The one behind the poisoning: can he be convicted of homicide? Brede Ziegler in actual fact died from the knife wound, and then of course the poisoning would only be an attempted murder or a—"

"The finer legal points we can take up later," Billy T. broke in. "Klaus! Have you discovered whether anyone's missing a knife, one of these Masa ... Masa-something-or-others?"

"But shouldn't we look at these first?" Silje ventured. "Shouldn't we take a look at these suspects and—"

"Have you?"

Billy T. nodded at Klaus Veierød, who shook his head, obviously feeling extremely uncomfortable.

"No one's missing a knife like that so far. No one at Entré, anyway. I've checked eleven other restaurants as well. *Nada*. Everything points to the murder weapon actually being the knife Brede Ziegler himself bought on Saturday. But we must bear in mind that there are in fact a lot of ordinary people who also own such knives. They're on sale to the public. Fucking expensive, but available on the open market."

"So, we've got a poison that's accessible in every home, and a knife available on the open market," Billy T. said in a sullen voice. "Bloody great! Anyone else with any valuable information to share with me?"

Severin put his hand on Billy T.'s shoulder, but he dodged away.

"We could just have a squint at the suspects," Severin insisted, writing three headings on the flip chart. "Vilde. V-i-l-d-e."

"It's beginning to dawn on her that she's going to inherit a small fortune," Karianne Holbeck said. "The little widow has been in touch with a lawyer, and there's a bit of a rumpus about that partnership agreement we spoke about earlier. Apparently her rights are more extensive than we first thought."

"I know that," Billy T. said. "I've talked to Claudio Gagliostro."

"In fact, I was the one who advised Vilde to contact a lawyer," Karianne said quietly. "She was so desperate and—"

"Maybe you could put off giving advice without thinking, until you're dry behind the ears," Billy T. commented. "Lawyers are the bloody last thing we need in this damn case. Anyway, I've spoken to Karen Borg myself."

At the mention of the lawyer's name, he looked at Hanne Wilhelmsen for the first time: in undisguised triumph, since he was not alone among her former friends to turn his back on her. The truth was that he had not alluded to Hanne at all. It was a long time since the old gang of friends had stopped discussing her disappearing trick. Karen had no idea that Hanne had returned to Norway.

"She came out with the same fucking mantra as all the other witnesses in this case. *Duty of confidentiality.*"

His mouth twisted in an ugly grimace. His moustache had become more prominent in the past few days. Hanne noticed it had acquired a gray streak under his nose.

"All in all, we can sum up by saying that Vilde Veierland Ziegler inherits the lot. The net proceeds, as Karen Borg called it, will be considerable."

"Okay then. Suspect number one."

Severin Heger drew a question mark at the end of Vilde's name.

"Motive? Yes. Alibi?"

"She says she was in town with a girlfriend," Karianne said. "That's confirmed. They were at the Smuget nightclub from just before nine until around midnight. After that they went together to the bar at Tostrupkjelleren. Her friend went home at ten to one and Vilde stayed on for a while."

"That's fine, then," Severin said lamely. "So she's got an alibi. And that's been checked thoroughly?"

"Well, I'm not sure about that," Karianne said, drawing on a blank sheet of paper in exasperation. "I've spoken to her friend, and she confirms all of it."

"Confirms," Billy T. roared. "What the fuck does that mean? Have you had this girlfriend – this ... *alleged* girlfriend – in for questioning?"

"I phoned her."

"Phoned?"

Karianne tossed her pen down and roared back at him: "Now you'd better just cut it out, Billy T.! You need to stop talking to me as if I'm a second-rate piece of shit you're forced to lug around with you! It might have been easier for all of us if we had a boss who knew his job. Have you, for example, told anyone that you've spoken to Karen Borg, until now, at this meeting? Up till now you've mentioned in passing that you've conducted an interview with Gagliostro, but *where is it*? Not in any of my paperwork, at least. I haven't had a glimpse of any special report about the visit you and Severin paid to Niels Juels gate, either! Have you given me the slightest reason to concentrate the investigation on a skinny girl that the rest of us up till now haven't been able to link to very much of a motive, apart from the unspecified value of a mort-gaged apartment? You fool around with your own stuff and aren't the tiniest bit interested in what the rest of us have found out. Yesterday, for example ..."

Now she turned to the others, as if giving testimony in a closed sect for unsuccessful police officers.

"My group found out that the Alexander Schultz painting, which Mummy Johansen was so grateful her son had removed for aesthetic reasons, was subsequently sold at the Blomquist auction house. For one hundred and ninety thousand kroner. By Brede Ziegler. I submitted a special report on that to you, and you haven't even mentioned it. Some boss and source of inspiration you are!"

Now she was staring rebelliously at Billy T. and her cheeks were no longer red. Instead they were as white as a sheet and her eyes were shining. Her mouth trembled furiously as if she was about to burst into tears at any moment. Instead she ploughed on. Her rage was not simply a reaction to her superior officer's surly behavior during the past hour. Billy T. had been a shitbag for more than six months, and Karianne Holbeck had reached saturation point.

"This whole investigation is a scandal! I know that, you know that. Everybody in here knows that. *Bloody hell*, it won't be long until everybody else knows that too. Do you read newspapers, Billy T.?"

Hearing Karianne Holbeck swear was almost as shocking as her giving her superior officer a bawling-out in the presence of the entire team. Severin Heger sat with his mouth open. Klaus Veierød shuffled his feet on the floor and fiddled furiously with an unsightly wart on his left thumb. It started to bleed. Silje Sørensen looked down her nose at the spectacle and glanced slightly maliciously across at Hanne Wilhelmsen, who was still sitting with her arms crossed, not saying a word. Annmari Skar looked as if she wanted more than anything to pack up her papers and leave. The rest of the assembled company sat with their heads down, waiting for the storm to blow over.

"Obviously not," Karianne barked, holding that day's copy of the *VG* newspaper in front of his face.

The entire front page was dominated by a quote from a "centrally placed police source": "*We're fumbling around aimlessly!*"

"They're taking the piss out of us. And I really mean *taking the piss out of us!* With good reason, if I say so myself."

Karianne crashed back down on her chair, out of breath and deathly pale.

Hanne Wilhelmsen was the only one who looked at Billy T. Age had added a bloated flabbiness to his face and shoulders. They had grown rounder and, paradoxically enough, his chest seemed less prominent under the slightly too-tight sweater. She tried to catch his eye, the way she always used to do at the time when everything was as it should be, and they were both for one and one for both. She wanted a truce. She wanted more than that and knew it was impossible; but a truce would help them both, and him not least. Here and now he was the one who needed her. He did not fix his eyes on anything in particular, only straight ahead in a silence you would think there was no room for, in this space where ten detectives and one police prosecutor struggled to grasp an investigation that had long ago run away from them. Ten days had elapsed since Brede Ziegler was killed, and the case was never going to be solved. Not like this. Not under Billy T.'s vacillating leadership and haphazard control. Hanne Wilhelmsen was the only person who looked at Billy T. He never lifted his eyes to meet hers.

Thirty seconds ticked by, and then a minute.

Hanne slowly rose to her feet. She walked behind the backs of Severin Heger, Klaus Veierød, and Billy T., hugging the wall to avoid touching any of them. Then she leaned down to Silje Sørensen's ear. The young police officer listened intently, nodded, and disappeared out of the room at top speed. The noise when the door slammed behind her sliced brutally through the oppressive silence and made them all close their eyes. When they opened them again, Hanne had sat down on the back of a chair at the top of the table with her feet on the seat; she rested her elbows on her knees and stared earnestly at Severin Heger.

"I've gone through all the papers in the case," she said softly. "Read all the interviews, all the reports, gone through all the lists. I've been in Niels Juels gate. My special report is included as attachment sixteen-two in the case file. When I say this, it's not to put anyone down. I'm saying it to encourage you. There's a lot of good police work here. What's gone wrong or ..."

The chair back creaked, but she remained seated. She formed a circle with her hands and held them up to her face.

"The problem is *focus*. This case distinguishes itself from all others. As, of course, all cases do."

She tried to smile, but no one smiled back.

"You ... We have concentrated on establishing a motive. That's usually a good idea. But in a case where we're tripping over convincing motives wherever we turn, it might be a smart move to shift our focus. Instead of asking *why*, to get the answer *who*, we should really ask: *why that particular place?* Then we come closer to the answer *who*, by approaching it from a different angle."

"Eh?" Karl Sommarøy exclaimed, sucking on his dry pipe and putting down the knife he was continually playing with.

"We ought to ask ourselves: why was Brede Ziegler murdered outside police headquarters? What was he doing there? Nothing indicates that the man was brought there after being killed. He died there and then. On the back steps of police headquarters. So he has gone there – gone into a park where very few of us would set foot after dark, gone into this park late on a Sunday night when he also, to all appearances, must have had severe stomach ache. Isn't that really bloody *weird*?"

Karianne Holbeck was the next one who caved in. She wrinkled her nose as she cocked her head.

"Weird, yes ... But there must be a logical explanation, if we can just find out who did it. Don't you think?"

"Definitely!"

Hanne, no longer looking at Billy T., clapped her hands lightly, as if in ill-concealed glee at having an audience at last.

"This Brede," she continued, jumping down to the floor. "He's a man ... a man with no echo, none at all."

"With no echo?"

Karianne shook her head, perplexed.

"Yes! You can see it, Karianne! Think about it! You're the one who's had responsibility for coordinating these witness interviews, and you've actually done a pretty good job of that, but you have to ..."

Leaning over the table toward Karianne, she lowered her voice.

"Look at the big picture. You're frustrated because you *can't find a big picture*. Everything's spread out. Some people idolized Ziegler. Others detested him. Some hated him, some admired him. Some individuals claim he was a cynical, evil alcoholic. Others say he was cultured, well educated, and competent. You've dug down into all of this and let yourself become frustrated. Instead of that, lift your eyes! What sort of profile is it that we can actually see? A man with no sounding board! A man who ... If you call out to him, you get—"

"No response," Klaus Veierød said thoughtfully. "But that hardly leads us any closer to an answer as to what the fuck the guy was doing on our back stairs late one freezing-cold Sunday night."

"Maybe not," Hanne said. "But maybe, all the same. My point is first and foremost that it's about time to conclude. At least as far as concerns what sort of guy this famous chef really was. What do we call people who are characterized in such widely diverging descriptions as Brede Ziegler?"

She looked from one to the other and threw out her arms in expectation of an answer.

"An exciting sort," Karianne said tentatively, and Hanne shrugged.

"Psychopath," Severin Heger added in a quizzical tone.

"Erratic," Klaus Veierød stipulated, more enthusiastic now, and he had begun to make notes for the first time during the meeting.

"Unpredictable," suggested a police trainee who had not uttered a word until now, but who had just completed a course in psychology.

"Where are you going with this, Hanne?"

Annmari Skar scrutinized her.

"This is where I'm going," she replied, turning to the flip chart and leafing back to Severin's aerial view of the back steps. "I'm reaching the conclusion that Brede Ziegler would never have been in this particular spot late on a Sunday night unless it was in his interests to be there. He's a man who apparently *never* did anything except in his own self-interest. Those who describe him in glowing terms are people whose good opinion he has *benefited* from! When we consider that the man in all probability must have been in pain – maybe not too severe, but all the same … Somehow or other it must have been important for him to be in that exact spot. He must have had an appointment. He was going to meet someone."

They all turned round abruptly as Silje Sørensen returned, breathless and carrying a bag she held out to Hanne.

"Afterwards," Hanne said with a smile. "Sit down in the meantime."

"Brede Ziegler could also have been *threatened* into going there," Klaus Veierød said. "Isn't that actually more likely? Somebody might have forced him to go there, either directly by holding him at knifepoint, or indirectly by having something on him. Blackmail?"

Hanne outlined a big circle around the drawing of the flight of steps, and turned round to face Klaus as she put the lid back on the felt-tip pen.

"Agreed," she said slowly. "He could have been forced to come. Probably not with a weapon. His car was tidily parked in Sverres gate. That anyone could have threatened him first to park legitimately a good distance away from the park, then to walk all the way to the back steps, all this without anyone seeing anything, hearing anything, noticing anything … well, hardly. But of course you're right. He may have been threatened in other ways. That he *had* to come, or else: the usual. Which does not alter my main point: he was going to meet someone. He had an appointment, an appointment he was extremely reluctant to break. And listen to this … Pass me my papers, please."

She was speaking over Billy T., who was still staring at something nobody else could see, but at least he had not left the room. Klaus Veierød grabbed the thick bundle of documents and passed them along the table.

"Here," Hanne said, withdrawing a sheet of paper. "The report of my visit to Niels Juels gate. Did you notice anything special about the bathroom, Severin?"

"The bathroom?"

Severin pondered the question as he took off his glasses.

"I ... We weren't in the bathroom. Some folk from Securitas turned up and it—"

"Anyway, I went into the bathroom," Hanne interrupted him. "And found an unusually attractive, spacious wetroom with no notable personal effects. No medicines. Toothpaste, shaving gear. One toothbrush. I'll come back to that. But the wall, guys – the wall above the bath tub, that was very unusual."

It stung her when Billy T. finally looked in her direction. He tried to assume an expression of semi-interested indifference. Simultaneously he tried to obscure his eyes by knitting his brows, something that made him remind her of a disgruntled little boy.

"The wall was decorated with a beautiful mosaic. It was quite simply a miniature version of the façade on the mosque in Åkebergveien. The spitting image. I took a Polaroid photograph and have compared them. Absolutely, completely identical. As far as I can judge, anyway."

"And what about it?"

Karl Sommarøy yawned, pinching his tiny chin between thumb and forefinger.

"Agreed," Karianne said in a whisper; it seemed as if she had pulled herself together somewhat after her violent outburst. "What has that got to do with the inquiry?"

"Maybe nothing. Maybe it's sheer chance that the man was murdered only fifty meters away from the original of the image on his bathroom wall. On the other hand, maybe not."

She put her palms down on the table top as she went on: her voice was different now, more impassioned, more desperate to convince.

"Brede Ziegler was a show-off. A vain, shallow, and extremely competent show-off. If I had paid a visit to Ziegler's apartment while he lived, I would have been blown away by that bathroom wall. I would have praised it to the skies. Someone may have done exactly that. And then he wanted to show them the original, because it ..."

She had lost her hold on them. Karianne cast her eyes down, Severin had put down his glasses for good. Klaus had tossed aside his pen and was staring at the clock.

"Okay," Hanne Wilhelmsen said, attempting to smile, but rapidly realizing that it simply turned into an unbecoming grimace. "We'll leave it at that. But there was one more thing that struck me about that apartment. Severin, what was the most striking thing about it, from your perspective?"

"That it was stylish, of course. Impersonal, but stylish. The guy was morbidly fixated on celebrities. And not particularly fond of his wife."

He gave a broad grin.

"At least she wasn't allowed to leave much of a mark on the place."

"Exactly!"

Hanne clambered up on the chair back again, and sat wagging the toes of her boots on the edge of the table.

"One toothbrush. No perfumes, no Ladyshave. One bed with no bed linen, neatly made as if in a hotel where the guests are not expected for another week. According to the notes, Vilde was informed of her husband's death at five o'clock in the morning and then apparently *stripped off the bed linen* before going down to Oslo Central Station to catch the first train to Hamar."

"You're going to fall soon," Silje Sørensen said. "I'm getting really nervous with you sitting like that."

"How did you actually get hold of Vilde, Karianne?"

"First I rang her home number, but no one answered. Then I called the cellphone registered to Vilde Veierland Ziegler. She took the call, clearly half-asleep. I said that we'd like to talk to her about something serious, and that we could be in Niels Juels gate in half an hour. I had to follow procedure and find a clergy-man first, so it was closer to an hour before we set off. When we arrived, she was wide-awake and had her clothes on."

"And why had she not answered the first time you phoned?"

Karianne's eyes wandered.

"Maybe she didn't hear it. She was sleeping and had been out on the town. As I said. She was asleep. Tired."

"Or maybe she quite simply wasn't there," Hanne said quietly. "For my part, I believe she lives somewhere else. Not in Niels Juels gate, at least. There's not a single female in the world who leaves so little trace behind."

Billy T. shifted in his seat. He moved his head from side to side as if he had just been roused. He scratched his chin and opened his mouth several times, as if he wanted to come out with some-thing, but wasn't quite sure what he wanted to say.

"It's starting to get terribly stuffy in here," Hanne said. "Maybe we could take a break. But before that … I've got something I'd like to show you. If that's all right with you, Billy T.?"

He did not look at her, but nodded faintly.

Hanne gave a sign to Silje, who emptied the contents of the plastic bag on the table. They all leaned forward to see the items, neatly packaged in individual airtight plastic bags.

"These are the articles found at the crime scene," Silje said. "Some are still with Forensics, for instance the cigarette butts. So I just tipped out an ashtray, myself. For illustration purposes, so to speak."

Hanne gave a burst of laughter and swept her fingers along Silje's arm, encouragingly. Silje smiled broadly and glanced at the others to see if they had noticed the acknowledgment.

"Kim's Game, in a sense. What is it that's odd here?"

"Beer cans," Karl mumbled, fingering one of the bags. "An ice-cream paper from last summer. Cigarette butts. Condoms. A handkerchief. Used and disgusting."

"The gift wrap," Karianne said loudly. "The gift wrap doesn't belong with all the other stuff. It doesn't look faded, either."

"Now we'll take that break."

They all turned to face Billy T.

"But we—"

"We're stopping now. We've kept this going for three hours. It's almost impossible to breathe in here."

Karianne asked when they should reconvene the meeting.

"Tomorrow," Billy T. said. "I'll give you further instructions."

With that, he left. He turned his back on them all and stomped out of the room. The others collected the papers and empty soft-drinks cans. Silje returned the crime-scene finds to the carrier bag, and Karl arranged to have lunch with Klaus and Karianne.

They had not gathered the threads. They had not allocated the assignments. They had only just begun to look more closely at all the material they had accumulated, despite everything, in the course of the previous days' fumbling investigations. Hanne thought about the threatening letters, about Claudio Gagliostro and Sindre Sand. They had not even touched on the curious fact that Brede Ziegler was found with more than 16,000 kroner in his wallet. She thought about Hairy Mary. Only the gods knew what she was getting up to now.

Silje took her time with the carrier bag, slowly inserting one item on top of the other in a tidy system, as if packing eggs.

"We didn't really finish," she said. "You know, we haven't even talked about—"

"No," Hanne said, wrapping an elastic band around the documents before cramming them into a seventies mailbag.

"We didn't. Not by a long chalk. But Billy T.'s the one who decides. He's the Chief Inspector in charge."

"It should have been you," Silje whispered.

Hanne pretended not to hear. She had to go home to check whether her apartment was still in the same place. She should have told Billy T. about her new lodger. She had intended to do that. It just hadn't been possible. Now it would become even more difficult.

* * *

Interview with Idun Franck

Interviewed by Chief Inspector Hanne Wilhelmsen. Transcript typed by office colleague Beate Steinsholt. There is one tape of this interview. The interview was recorded on tape on Wednesday December 15, 1999 at 15.30 hours at Oslo police headquarters.

Witness:

**Franck, Idun, ID number 060545 32033
Address: Myklegårdsgate 12, 0656 Oslo
Employment: Publishing House, Mariboesgate 13, Oslo
Home phone no.: 22 68 39 80; work no.: 22 98 53 56
Informed about witness rights and responsibilities, willing to give statement.**

The witness was informed that the interview would be taped, and that a transcript would later be produced. Statement as follows:

Interviewer:

That takes care of the formalities. I see you are one of the youngest people who can call themselves "war children."

Witness:

Sorry?

Interviewer:

You were born two days before peace was declared. Your infancy can't have conformed exactly with child-welfare recommendations. *(Laughter.)*

Witness:

Is this included in the interview?

Interviewer:

Everything's included in the interview, big and small, important and unimportant. That's the point of using the tape. So that we know afterwards what was said – not merely what the police choose to include in a report. *(Pause.)* Up till now I've managed to document that I'm trying to make light conversation with a witness. Did that disturb you?

Witness:

(Cough.) No … Apologies, it wasn't meant like that. I was just taken aback that we started by mentioning the war. *(Laughter.)* When I was little, all events were designated as either "before the war" or "after the war." The war was the great watershed. It

was just bizarre that you should think like that, in 1999, I mean. But it's not my date of birth that's the reason for me being here, is it?

Interviewer:

No, of course not. We have not conducted any formal questioning of you as yet. You've only had an informal conversation with the police. A report of that conversation has been written by Chief Inspector Billy T. *(Paper rustling.)*

Witness:

So he does have a title, then, even though he doesn't have a surname? Is that the report you have there? Then you're well acquainted with the fact that I can't actually tell you very much about Brede Ziegler. I've taken a principled stand about confidentiality of sources. Yes, I'm sure you've read my reasons for that, or do I have to repeat them now? Is that the point of this interview, that I should repeat them, formally and on the record? Then I'd like to say that I have spoken to the Senior Manager of the publishing house and he is—

Interviewer *(interrupts)*:

No, it's not necessary for you to repeat all that. We have a note of it here in the report. *(Clears throat ... violent sneeze, blows nose.)* Sorry, it's obviously the season for this sort of thing. Would you like a pastille? Where were we ... ? Oh yes. It's quite peculiar, what you've said about protecting a chef as a source for a cookery book. We've cracked a few jokes about that here at headquarters. That we're looking forward to the secret recipes coming out in the book, I mean. But what I should say is that in this interview we've decided to respect your point of view, as far as confidentiality of sources is concerned. We're not entirely sure whether you're right about that, but the Police Prosecutor is working on it. We'll come back to that. In this interview we're dropping everything you've got to know from Brede Ziegler in your capacity as book editor. That's something we'll take up with the court in the fullness of time. But what I'm wondering about is whether … *(Brief pause.)* Tell me, have you studied law?

Witness:

What?

Interviewer:

Have you studied law?

Witness:

No, of course not. I'm an Arts graduate, and studied literature, ethnology, and English.

Interviewer:

Exactly. Ethnology. That's research into folklore or something of that nature? *(Pause.)* Fascinating! Then I wonder how you know all that legal stuff. You know, everything you pointed out when Billy T. was talking to you. *Criminal Procedure Act*, section 125, and the *European Convention on Human Rights*, and suchlike. In the past few days I've asked all the lawyers I've met what they think of the *Criminal Procedure Act*, section 125, and they haven't had a clue what I'm talking about. Where have you learned all that?

Witness:

Yes, erm, well … *(Laughter.)* Oh, I see, I understand what you're getting at. It's perhaps a bit odd. But I've got a good friend that I have dinner with now and again, he's a lawyer and an expert on defamation proceedings and that kind of thing. He has a number of newspapers as clients. We've discussed it a little. That's how you pick up bits and pieces.

Interviewer:

Impressively precise knowledge. Is it long since you learned all this?

Witness:

Long since? No … I don't know. A while ago.

Interviewer:

Have there been many occasions when you, as a publishing editor, have refused to give information to the police about an author? With reference to the confidentiality of sources, or for that matter any other reason?

Witness:

No. *(Brief pause.)* Not really.

Interviewer:

Has it ever happened before that someone outside the publishing company has asked you about what an author has divulged to you?

Witness:

No, well … I'm not quite sure … Yes, at parties and that sort of thing it sometimes happens that people ask what famous writers are really like, whether they're difficult and … that kind of thing.

Interviewer:

What's the name of this lawyer of yours? Could I have his name?

Witness:

Well, yes ... But is it necessary? These dinners ... *(Clears throat, inaudible speech.)* I don't think he exactly says anything about them to his wife. Well, it's not as if we ... Don't misunderstand, but I'd really prefer not ...

Interviewer:

Yes, I appreciate that *(Coughs.)* ... But could I have the name?

Witness:

Karl Skiold, of Skiold, Kefrat & Co.

Interviewer:

That's fine, thanks. It's helpful to have that on record. Then we can draw a line under that. Are you married? Divorced?

Witness:

Divorced. Years ago.

Interviewer:

Children?

Witness:

No, no children. But is this important? Can you really ask me about such things?

Interviewer:

Does it embarrass you? In principle, we can ask anything we want, you know. Then it's up to you whether or not to give an answer.

Witness:

I'm childless. Is this important, I asked you?

Interviewer:

No, it's not important. Just good to know. Let's talk about Brede Ziegler.

Witness:

Yes, but I already said ... The terms of this interview—

Interviewer *(interrupts)*:

We're still in agreement about the terms. I'd just like to know how well you knew Brede before you started work on this book?

Witness:

I didn't know him at all. That is to say ... just by reputation. Who didn't?

Interviewer:

Had you any personal dealings with him after you started working with him?

Witness:

No, absolutely not. It was a purely professional contact in connection with my work on the book. We always worked in my office. Yes, as a matter of fact ... Apart from one time. I was with the photographer when she took some photographs at Entré. Afterwards Brede and I stayed on and talked for a good while. We had something to eat, but the restaurant was closed. That was the only time we weren't at the publishing house, as far as I can remember.

Interviewer:

Photographer, I see. What's the name of the photographer?

Interviewer:

Suzanne Klavenæs. Wait a minute ... *(Rustling, pause.)* Here's her card.

Interviewer:

Thanks. If I've understood you correctly, all the conversations you've had with Brede in connection with the book, with one exception, have taken place in your office. Is that right?

Witness:

Yes.

Interviewer:

And it's these conversations you mean that, as an editor, you're duty-bound not to give a statement about?

Witness:

Yes, that's right.

Interviewer:

Can you think very carefully about this now? Was there any other occasion when you've been somewhere else to work with Brede?

Witness:

No! I've already answered you on that point. We always worked in my office, apart from that one time at Entré. By the way, that was in October, I think.

Interviewer:

And you were never together in a personal capacity? Do you smoke? We can smoke here, if you like.

Witness:

Yes, please, I'd like that … No, thanks, I prefer to smoke my own. *(Rustling, repeated clicks from a lighter?)* I have already answered what you're asking. I didn't have any personal dealings with Brede Ziegler. I came into contact with him in order to do a job. That was all. Period. I answered that earlier. *(Violent sneezing, three times, presumably from the interviewer.)*

Interviewer:

Excuse me, I think I'm coming down with a cold. You must also forgive me for asking three times, but I simply must know how far this duty of confidentiality, in your opinion, extends.

Witness:

I don't understand where you're going with this.

Interviewer:

Going? I just want you to answer. *(Indistinct, sniffing?)* I'm sorry, but I think it might be best if you don't smoke after all. I'm coming down with something. Thanks. Yes, you understand, we have of course examined everything in Brede's apartment very thoroughly. He lives on the fourth floor with an elevator that goes all the way up to his apartment. Did you know that?

Witness:

Yes. In Niels Juels gate.

Interviewer:

Okay. You really ought to know that. As I said, we've examined everything extremely thoroughly, and in the stairway and elevator there's a CCTV system. A video camera that monitors the comings and goings in the block. We've watched these films to find out who has visited Brede Ziegler's apartment in the past few weeks, before he died. According to the video footage, you took the elevator in Niels Juels gate on Tuesday November 23 at 20.23 precisely. Sometime later that same evening there's a clear picture of you walking toward the exit door. 21.13 hours. Do you know anyone else in that apartment block?

Witness:

Anyone else? Is there a picture of me in Niels Juels gate? I don't understand … *(Pause.)*

Interviewer:

I'd like you to answer me. According to what you've told me up till now, you don't have any duty of confidentiality about what I'm asking you now. Did you visit Brede Ziegler's apartment on Tuesday November 23?

Witness:

That was stupid of me … It was so insignificant that I had completely forgotten about it. I don't understand how I could …

Interviewer:

Could what? Lie to the police?

Witness:

Lie? No, do you know what! First you send a man up to my office who didn't introduce himself properly, and then you accuse me of lying? *(Raised tone of voice.)* I'm sorry I made a mistake, but you're stretching it a bit to call that a lie. Here I am being questioned about something that seemed totally unimportant when it took place, and suddenly it's a crime to forget about it afterwards!

Interviewer:

Am I now to understand that you were at Brede Ziegler's apartment on Tuesday November 23?

Witness:

Yes, I've said that. I'd just forgotten about it. It was the photographs. I was to deliver some suggested photos to him – it had just completely slipped my mind, and I apologize for that. I appreciate that it seems a bit strange, I'm honestly … It's awkward, but I had quite simply forgotten all about it.

Interviewer:

You were there for about three-quarters of an hour. What were you doing there, can you remember that? It was only three weeks ago.

Witness:

Was it as long as three-quarters of an hour? It didn't seem as long as that. I recall it as quite a short visit. We just talked for a bit about the pictures … Yes, now I remember that I had a cup of tea. There was a lot of fuss about that tea. That must have been what took so much time. It was some kind of Tsar Alexander tea, which had to be served in a Russian cup. No, you see, there wasn't anything in particular. It was just the tea that must have taken such a lot of time.

Interviewer:

How did Brede seem? Was he pleased that you had paid him a visit? What was the atmosphere like between you?

Witness:

I've already said, you know, that I don't consider it right to talk about what Ziegler said to me in connection with our work. I must ask for—

Interviewer *(interrupts)*:

Respect? I would like to remind you that you ought to show respect for the police. You've come here with an entirely new piece of information only after *(thumping noise, hand on table top?)* I confront you with evidence that what you've said earlier is incorrect. Can you be so kind as to tell me about your visit to Brede Ziegler's apartment on Tuesday November 23? What did you talk about?

Witness:

Nothing special … *(Lengthy pause.)* Yes, a lot about the tea, I suppose. Brede gave me a sort of lecture about all the different types of tea in the world. And yes, about the cups. He wanted the photographer to take pictures of them – they apparently came from Tsar Alexander's royal household. But just because I had forgotten about that, I'd really prefer not to talk about the book … It's not so risky, that about the cups, but a principle is a principle after all.

Interviewer:

Is there anyone who can confirm that you went to Brede Ziegler's apartment on November 23 to give him some photographs?

Witness:

It's not exactly the sort of thing you obtain an alibi for. Dropping off some photos, I mean. As I said, it didn't seem such a big thing when it happened, but ... *(Pause.)* No, I don't think anyone can confirm that I went there for the purpose of delivering photos. Is that really so strange?

Interviewer:

Then we'll leave it at that. As far as alibis are concerned. Where were you on the evening of Sunday December the fifth this year? Can you remember that?

Witness:

Where I was? *(Pause.)* I was at the cinema. *Shakespeare in Love.* At the nine o'clock showing. The film lasts two hours and five minutes.

Interviewer:

So you remember that precisely. How long the film lasted.

Witness:

Yes, I remember it quite well. I remember that I went to the nine o'clock showing. I had arranged with my sister that I would call in on her, if the film was finished before eleven o'clock. I remember that I looked at my watch when I came out after the film. It was ten past eleven, and I decided to go straight home.

Interviewer:

Were you with anyone?

Witness:

With anyone? No. Oh yes. I understand. No, I wasn't with anyone. But there was someone else there, somebody I know.

Samir Zeta. He works with us. We chatted a bit about the film
the next day. At work.

Interviewer:

How long did it take you to go home? Where do you live, by
the way? Oh yes, now I see it. Myklegårdsgate, that's right
across from here, isn't it? In the Old Town, yes?

Witness:

I don't remember exactly when I got home. It wasn't important to remember that, you see. But I took the tram, the Ljabru
tram. I normally take that to the intersection at Schweigaards
gate and Oslogate. From there it's two minutes on foot to my
home. I think I waited a while for the tram that night.

Interviewer:

Have you anything more to add? Is there anything else that you've
thought of, in the course of this interview?

Witness:

No, I don't think so. I'd just like to say … *(Lengthy pause.)* About
forgetting that I was at Brede's apartment … I see that it was
extremely regrettable. It's just that I had forgotten all about it.
You must believe me.

Interviewer:

You'll be called in for another interview. Thank you for coming as
arranged. The interview concluded at … *(pause)* 16.10.

*Interviewer's note: The interview was conducted without any
breaks and coffee was served. The witness clearly reacted to
what she was confronted with, regarding the contents of the*

video footage from Niels Juels gate. When she was lighting the cigarette, her hand was trembling. During this part of the interview she had a hectic flush-patch on her neck. Otherwise the witness gave a reasonable account of herself. The witness should be recalled and the questioning expanded as soon as the legal circumstances concerning her duty to provide a statement are cleared up. Judicial examination should be considered.

35

Billy T. had been walking for four hours. He began his foot-slogging as soon as he could reasonably leave: around two o'clock there had been a hiatus when it seemed all the others were busy with their own pursuits. With no idea where he was headed, he had set off in a northerly direction, past the tower blocks in Enerhaugen. At Tøyen Park he had made up his mind to go for a swim, but he could not bear the thought of all those people. Instead he plodded on, and not until he was quite far along Hovinveien did he realize that he was en route to Hanne Wilhelmsen's apartment. He about-turned to head north-west, past the nursing home in Tøyen, and did not halt until he had put all of Nydalen behind him and was only ten minutes away from Maridalsvannet lake. After that he went south-west through the districts of Nordberg and Sogn. In the end he stood bewildered and exhausted, with soaking wet feet, in front of the low-rise block in Huseby where his youngest son lived. The boy's mother was surprised to see him. The visit was outwith all his appointed times, and a worried frown appeared between her eyes when he asked politely to have Truls until tomorrow. He would take the boy to school. Truls was pleased to see his father, and even more delighted when he discovered that he would spend the night with his grandma and dad all by himself, without any of his siblings, and without Tone-Marit. His dad's wife was nice enough, but she always had that howling baby girl in tow.

It was night time now and Truls was fast asleep.

The boy's grandmother came into the bedroom. She too had been taken aback by Billy T.'s request: he wanted to spend the night there with the boy. Without saying very much, she had put clean bed linen on her own bed. Billy T. made no protest, not even when his mother showed obvious signs of being badly bothered by arthritic pain. The weather was wet and the settee was hard and narrow.

"Is something wrong?"

He did not answer, just curled his body even more tightly around the boy and pulled the quilt snugly around them both.

"Okay then. Tone-Marit phoned. She was worried. I said you were tired and had fallen asleep without realizing. Everything was fine. Jenny's over her cold."

His mother let her fingertips brush his head: he felt the warmth on his vulnerable skin, still sensitive after all these years with a bare skull. He held his breath to avoid saying anything.

She closed the door behind her, and it grew dark. Billy T. pressed his nostrils down into the boy's curly dark-brown hair. He smelled of child: soap, milk, and fresh air. Billy T. shut his eyes and felt himself falling. He held the little body so hard that the boy whimpered in his sleep. It was almost three o'clock before Billy T. finally fell into a dreamless slumber. The last thing he thought about was Suzanne: her voice when she had phoned that very last time and begged for his help.

36

It was four o'clock in the morning, and Sebastian Kvie felt fairly safe. As he walked down Toftes gate there was hardly anyone in sight. Sofienberg Park, wet and threatening, lay to the east. He crossed the road to distance himself from the dark shadows under the maple trees. He had deliberately avoided Thorvald Meyers gate: even at this time of night, several hours after the last bar had closed, you might risk coming across acquaintances in Grünerløkka's busiest areas. He rounded the corner at Sofienberggata and tried to steer clear of the light from the unmanned gas station.

"Pull yourself together," he said through gritted teeth. "Pull yourself together and breathe calmly."

When he had first discovered that Claudio was cheating on the wine, Brede was still alive. That was the reason Sebastian hadn't said anything. Even though he had difficulty believing it, there was always a chance that Brede was in on it all. Admittedly, Sebastian had never seen Brede anywhere near the wine cellar: that was Claudio's domain. But they could have had an arrangement. Sebastian would never have done anything to hurt Brede. If Brede was in on the scam, then Sebastian would keep his mouth shut.

Then Brede was murdered.

Entré was renowned for Brede's food. But the wine cellar had gradually also begun to receive recognition. In the last three months alone, journalists from one French and two German wine magazines had come to check out the selection. Claudio had a nose for those who knew their stuff. He could smell a wine connoisseur from a long way off. Even though Entré of course had its own sommelier, he was elegantly sidelined on special occasions.

Sebastian had heard that many of the bottles in the cellar were worth up to 20,000 kroner. The cheapest bottle they sold cost the restaurant guests 450 kroner per bottle. People paid that willingly. People were idiots.

In a way Sebastian had been quite impressed by Claudio's audacity. When he changed the labels on the bottles, so that the contents were in no way compatible with the price, he ran a huge risk. The system was extremely vulnerable. In the first place Claudio had to keep everything in order inside the actual wine cellar; he had to know which bottles were genuine and which ones contained the cheaper wine. Those had to be reasonably good as well. It had to be more difficult to ensure that the sommelier did not see through the scam. Kolbjørn Hammer, a seventy-year-old man who resembled a British butler from a boring old film, was certainly both servile and silent and, what's more, not the cleverest person Sebastian had met. But he knew his wine. He knew a whole *fucking* lot about wine. If a guest complained, either because he actually knew his stuff or because he wanted to make an impression on his lady companion, there was always a danger that Hammer would be called upon to taste it. *He* would discover on the spot whether the label matched the contents.

Sebastian could not comprehend how the system worked. He could not fathom how Claudio dared. What's more, it was difficult to grasp where the money actually lay in the scheme. If Entré bought in and charged for costly wine, then exchanged it for cheaper wine and charged it at the expensive price, then of course that would pay. But anyway it could not be a matter of such very large quantities. Sebastian assumed that Claudio could not implement the deception consistently: far from it. And the proceeds would go to Entré anyway. Not to Claudio.

All the uncertainty had made Sebastian keep quiet about it. He had surprised Claudio one night after closing time last summer. Claudio muttered something about the label having fallen off. But the equipment in the cellar seemed fairly advanced, though Sebastian did not know much about it. Besides, it seemed remarkable that twenty bottles of wine should have lost their labels, all at the same time. However, Sebastian had smiled, shrugged, and said goodnight. Since then he had kept his mouth shut.

When Brede died, everything changed.

Sebastian peered in every direction before slipping into the entrance. He let himself into the restaurant and switched off the alarm. Quite often he was first to arrive for work. Every fortnight the new code was whispered into his ear by Kolbjørn Hammer.

Sebastian had become convinced that Brede had not had anything to do with the wine scam. He was not like that. He worked hard for what he wanted and did not cut corners, like Claudio. Brede could have seen through it all. That chimed. The problem was solved. Brede had discovered the deception and threatened Claudio with either packing his bags and leaving or being reported to the police.

Claudio had murdered Brede.

Sebastian would find the equipment he had spotted in the cellar when Claudio claimed that the label had fallen off. He would solve a case in which the police were just wandering about, understanding none of it. Sebastian had read about the homicide and investigation in the newspapers, and had cut out the articles and taken good care of them all.

Entré looked completely different in the dark. Only the signs that marked the emergency exits at either end of the premises

shed a dim green light on the adjacent white tablecloths. The
street lighting outside hardly filtered through the curtains and
Sebastian tripped over a chair.

Suddenly he felt foolish.

He stood stock still, listening to his pulse hammer in his eardrums. Now, when his eyes had grown accustomed to the gloom,
he could see that the metal door to the wine cellar was locked with
a bolt and two padlocks. Twice he opened his eyes and squeezed
them shut again, then crept over to the bar counter. The freezers
stared at him with their tiny green eyes. His breathing was rapid
as he crouched down beside the shelf where the wine coolers were
located. It was a tight fit when he squeezed his fingers in behind
the woodwork. Claudio's hands were smaller than his. The keys
were not there.

"*Fuck!*"

He bit his tongue and swore again. He had a better feel around
and used a cigarette lighter to afford some illumination to peer in
behind the shelves. He did not keep a close enough eye on it and
ended up burning his chin.

"*Bloody hell!*"

The keys to the wine cellar were gone. They were always
placed exactly here. Claudio obviously thought it his little secret.
Sebastian had never told anyone else about it, but he assumed he
was not the only one who had noticed Claudio's daily trip down
beside the wine coolers, several hours before the first customer
arrived.

He stood up to his full height.

His first thought, that everything was now a waste of time, disappeared just as fast as it had struck him. This was the proof he
needed. At least for himself. Claudio always put the keys right here.
The fact that they were now gone could only mean that Sebastian
was right. Claudio had panicked. He had looked terror-stricken

the day that big guy from the police had paid a visit, and had not recovered his composure until much later that night.

Sebastian wanted to go home. He would try in the morning. He would pay more attention to what happened to the keys. It might be difficult, since he was in the kitchen all evening, but he would dawdle after closing time and be the last to leave. Together with Claudio, perhaps.

He switched the alarm on again, and closed the back door behind him.

The headlights that suddenly pierced the darkness, dazzling him, made him press himself back, quick as a flash, into the little recess in the entrance where the door was inset. The entranceway was narrow, and fortunately the vehicle had to reverse out again into the street to get space. The driver could not have seen him.

Sebastian stood silent, with his mouth against the dirty timber. He did not even dare to breathe before the engine stopped, the car door slammed, and the light footsteps disappeared. Slowly, expelling the breath from his lungs, he relaxed.

When he peeked out from the recess, he recognized Claudio's car in the back yard. A Volvo estate. The rear doors were open. Sebastian jogged over to the garbage bins: five enormous, stinking plastic containers. He did not need to wait long.

The short figure with the large head emerged through the open cellar trapdoor, carrying a case and moving slowly. When he let the case slide carefully into place in the trunk of the car, Sebastian could barely hear a sound. Only a faint clink, like full bottles hitting against one another.

Five cases were carried out of Entré's wine cellar. Sebastian was too far away to see if there was anything written on the wood.

Claudio put the trapdoor back into place and locked it with a hefty padlock. He slammed shut the vehicle's rear doors and drove out slowly through the entrance. Not until Claudio had stepped from the car and closed the actual gate did Sebastian dare to quit his hiding place. His clothes stank. He had just seen Claudio steal five cases of wine from himself. He understood none of it.

37

Silje Sørensen was nursing a secret. Although she should share it with Tom, she hesitated. When she came home yesterday evening, she had not felt like eating the food he had prepared. He had waited so long with dinner that a skin had formed on the casserole. It made her feel sick, and she pushed the plate away with an apology and a protracted yawn. Tom was worried. He had been worried for some time. As a stockbroker in an asset-management company, he had long work days too, and was aware that Silje had been given a fantastic opportunity by participating in a homicide investigation so early in her career. But she had lost weight. The dark circles under her eyes had become more obvious in the past few weeks. What's more, she was always feeling sick: he had heard her throwing up in the mornings, behind a locked bathroom door. He could not understand why it was necessary to work for twelve hours every day, especially when her remuneration consisted of peanuts and churlish media reports. As if money had ever been a problem, she had said – and left the table.

They had not quarreled. It had merely been a serious discussion. She should have told him about it then, although she knew he would put his foot down. They had tried for a baby for eighteen months. Silje knew that was not really a long time. Tom was more impatient. If she told him she was about eight weeks gone, he would wrap her in so much cloying solicitude that she would hardly be allowed to continue her job. It would have to wait.

Anyway, she had slept well last night. The atmosphere between them had not been improved by yesterday evening's unfortunate meal, but he had at least put on a smile when she told him she was having a long lie-in. It was Friday December 17 and she did not have to report for work until noon. The overtime budget had been breached as early as July, and as the turn of the year approached, they were all instructed to take as much time off in lieu as possible.

"Good morning!"

Silje glanced at the alarm clock. Ten past ten. She struggled up out of the quilts and placed a pillow at her back.

"How lovely," she sighed over the tray he laid in front of her.

Tea, juice, milk. Two halves of ciabatta with Gorgonzola cheese and Italian salami. A cod-liver oil pill and two multivitamins rolled around on the tray. Tom had bought today's newspapers and a red rose, with the leaves neatly picked off, inserted into a tall vase that threatened to capsize as he crept up on to the bed and kissed her on the forehead.

"How lovely," she repeated, and threw up.

38

Even though Dr. Felice had only just made a start on his work day, he felt exhausted. The influenza epidemic was raging and he had fallen behind with his paperwork. His shirt had sweat stains in the armpits. Two clean, freshly ironed garments were hanging in the closet. The first one he grabbed had lost a button, and he crossly pulled on the other one, breathing through his nose, feeling as if he could smell his own patients right through the door.

He ought to phone that Billy T. The more he thought about it, the surer he felt that phoning would be the appropriate thing to do. When he had first gone through the records, after the police had rung, he had thought the information insignificant. He had not included it in the edited version of the papers he had handed over to the burly policeman. At the time the application had not led to anything, and it could hardly be thought to have any relevance to the murder inquiry. Besides, it had been years ago. Strictly speaking, he did not even know what it had all been about. All the same, he had a suspicion that it might be important.

A father came in, holding a bewildered child by the hand. The five-year-old stopped just inside the threshold and started howling. Snot mixed with tears and candy slavers that ran from the corners of his mouth. The father swore. He coaxed and scolded, but nothing worked. The boy stood rooted to the spot, his legs straddled, screaming at the top of his lungs, and Øystein Felice was unable even to approach him.

"We're falling behind with the appointments," Mrs. Hagtvedt said crankily, shaking her head as she passed the stubborn youngster. "Fathers ..."

Øystein Felice took a toy fire engine from the closet, gave the child a strained smile, and prepared himself for yet another ten-hour work day.

39

He fed her with a spoon. The oatmeal porridge tasted of suffocating childhood, and she twisted away after only three spoonfuls.

"You must eat something," Tom said firmly. "A bit more."

She refused and stood up abruptly.

"This was exactly what I feared," she said, sounding discouraged. "You're going to wrap me in cotton wool for the next seven months. I'm an adult, Tom. I'm pregnant, not ill. You really must give over!"

He was half-sitting, half-lying on the bed, with a bowl of oatmeal porridge in one hand and a spoon in the other. He had taken off his tie and rolled up his shirt sleeves. His face shone, his cheeks were flushed, and the grin that spread across his face might imply that the baby had already been born just a couple of minutes earlier. It was astonishing enough in itself that he had postponed going to work until she was awake. That he had just phoned the office and taken the whole day off was revolutionary. Tom was never unwell; never absent from work, apart from three weeks every summer and a couple of days at Christmas.

"Do you know whether it's a boy or a girl?" he asked, laughing. "It's all the same to me, but do you know?"

"Nitwit," Silje said, peeved. "I'm only seven or eight weeks gone."

When she returned from the shower, with dripping hair, wearing a silk dressing gown, he had changed the bedclothes and aired the room thoroughly. The single rose was lying neatly on her pillow. She crossed to the French doors and tied her belt. One door was still gaping, and she opened it wide. Goosebumps appeared on her skin and, without knowing why, she began to cry. In the distance, down the slope, behind the massive oak tree that leaned to the east and brushed the garage roof with its branches, she could hear Oslo. She had never regarded the house in Dr. Holms vei as part of the city. When she had been given the property by her father as a present for her twentieth birthday, she had felt shame more than anything. She'd had a long time to grow accustomed to the idea; that was the way it had always been. She was an only child, and would take over her grandparents' gigantic villa. Her father had renovated the house before she moved in. He himself lived in a detached house farther down; the family owned a couple of magnificent hectares in that location and had never contemplated selling.

When she had attended police college, she had never brought anyone home. She muttered about her address and complained that it was so far away. She did not want anyone to discover that her bedroom was approximately double the size of the bedsits belonging to her student friends. And that she had five of them.

Fortunately her name, Sørensen, was quite common. It was not so obvious that her father owned the Soerensen Cruise Line. It would have been much worse to be called Kloster or Reksten. Or Wilhelmsen, for that matter. Silje dried her tears, thought of Hanne, and decided to get dressed and go to work.

When she and Tom had married, she had kept the name Sørensen. Tom's full identity was Thomas Fredrik Preben Løvenskiold. Although his father had originally come from Denmark and had nothing to do with the landowning family in Oslo, the name was linked to an image that Silje wanted nothing to do with.

"What about Catharina Løvenskiold?" Tom asked. He had come in with freshly brewed tea and had two newspapers tucked under his arm; only the copy of *Aftenposten* had landed in the trash, after having cushioned the worst of the vomit. "Sit up in bed, sweetheart. My father's mother was called Catharina. Or Flemming, what do you think of that? If it's a boy, I mean. Flemming Løvenskiold. There's a certain panache about that, don't you think, darling? Or what? Sit down now."

"I was thinking more in the direction of Ola Sørensen," Silje said grumpily.

He stiffened momentarily, before his face broke into a huge smile that made his eyes disappear above his unusually high cheekbones.

"We'll talk about that later, my dear. Here! Newspapers and tea. The papers might smell a bit of puke, but the tea's fresh and delicious."

Silje reluctantly stretched out on the bed and picked up the *VG* newspaper. Tom just managed to save the rose from being crushed. He closed the French doors and went over to a panel on the wall beside the bathroom. A gas fire in the soapstone-and-brass fireplace blazed and he dimmed the ceiling light before switching on her bedside lamp.

"Real Christmas atmosphere," he said cheerfully, lying down beside her and opening the copy of *Dagbladet*.

The nausea had gone. In fact, it was not really troublesome. Only in the mornings, and in the evening if she had slept badly the night before. Maybe she was mistaken. Tom was exasperatingly solicitous but, all the same, it would be a relief not to have to dissemble. Besides, he was unbelievably sweet. His enthusiasm about the expected baby was even greater than the exhilaration he had exhibited when he had proposed to her two years ago, with a diamond ring and a bouquet of fifty roses and two plane tickets to Rome in his inside pocket.

"Listen to this," she giggled. "I just love these readers' letters."

"Love? You've got a real hang-up! What about Johannes?" He nibbled his index finger as he shut his eyes. "Or Christopher? I was really fond of *Winnie-the-Pooh* when I was little."

"Listen to this, won't you!"

She sat up straight and read aloud from the "Say it with *VG*" column.

"The heading is 'Mother Monsen's Cake and the Mormons'. Fantastic! Listen":

*Our country is inundated with foreign customs. In a gener-
ation or two there will be nobody who knows what it means to
be Norwegian. We must fight back and preserve what our
forefathers spent thousands of years building up.*

"No," Tom groaned. "Not one of those. Please!" He tried to put his arm around her stomach but she brushed him off and continued:

*During the war we wore paperclips as a mark of resistance.
Let us now pin a white feather to our lapels, a white feather
that symbolizes what is pure, what is Norwegian, what is
uninfected.*

"That is sheer racism, Silje. It's not the least bit funny."
"The funny part comes next, just wait."

*Take food, for example. Food is an important aspect of every
culture and way of life. Now kebabs and hamburgers lie in
wait on every street corner. The enemy has besieged us! During
this precious Christmas season, the aroma of pickled cabbage
and Christmas baking should emanate from homes and
kitchens. I myself live in Majorstuen, and here one morning,*

when I was baking my traditional Mother Monsen's Cake, the doorbell rang. Two Mormons wanted to "save" me. They couldn't even speak Norwegian! Like any polite person, I offered my uninvited guests some freshly baked cake. When they asked whether there was alcohol in the cake, I realized that the culture battle must be conducted on every front. Are we to have polygamy and temperance fanatics in Norwegian housing cooperatives? The recipe for Mother Monsen's Cake specifies two tablespoons of cognac, as well as sixteen good, NORWEGIAN eggs!

Join me! Wear the white feather!

Silje laughed and slapped the newspaper on her thigh.

"Someone should write a book!"

"That's already been done."

Tom attempted to pull the quilt over her. She shoved him away yet again and squinted at the reader's comment.

"'Iron Fist.' She … This was obviously written by a woman, and yet she calls herself *iron fist*. What did you mean when you said it's already been done?"

"There is a book like that with horrendous reader contributions. It came out not so many years ago."

"Then it ought to be done again," Silje said decidedly. "What does *iron fist* really mean?"

Discouraged, Tom turned over on his back and puffed out his cheeks.

"Can't we talk about the baby?" he complained. "It's three-quarters of an hour since you told me I'm going to be a dad, and then you want to amuse yourself with readers' letters from God-awful racists."

Silje sprang up, leaving Tom buried in quilts.

"Iron Fist! I *knew* I'd seen that expression recently!"

Five minutes later she was dressed. She felt wide-awake, fresh, and in good shape. Tom was still lying in bed, sulky and sullen.

"I won't be late today. Promise. But right now I absolutely *must* go to work."

She kissed him on the nose, and a couple of minutes later he heard the car start. Why she insisted on driving a Skoda Octavia was something he had never understood. As for himself, he had two cars: an Audi A8 and a neat two-seater BMW.

"I'm going to be a daddy," he said slowly. "I need an estate car."

Then he laughed: happy, prolonged, joyous laughter.

Thanks to his mother, Billy T. had managed to get up in time to drop Truls off at school. Afterwards, he had bought Christmas presents. There were still eight days left before Christmas, and the thought of all the stress of gifts being out of the way made him a touch more light-hearted. All the boys got the same thing. Toolboxes in different colors, filled with hammers and fretsaws, folding rulers, screws, nails, and screwdrivers. They would be occupied until late on Boxing Day. Tone-Marit would have to be content with a bottle of perfume, and for Jenny he had quite simply bought a new baby-seat for the car. He had 3,300 kroner left in his bank account. That would have to last until the new millennium. It would never stretch.

He turned off the road and into the driveway leading to the apartment block where Hanne Wilhelmsen lived. The last time he had been here, no one had opened the door. The apartment had been empty, and the neighbors had not seen Hanne for a fortnight. Since she had not even come to Cecilie's funeral, the others had advised him to leave her be. Give up, Tone-Marit said; you can't get hold of her. Give up. He could not do it. Not until he had been there one last time and had confirmation of her disappearing act. The HR office had received a letter; he discovered that two days later. He had considered posting her missing, but the letter had finally persuaded him to follow Tone-Marit's advice. They had postponed their wedding until August, both out of respect for Cecilie and because Billy T. had never heard from Hanne. She was to have been his best woman.

It had started to snow again, gigantic wet flakes that melted as they reached the ground. In the past few days the weather had alternated between cold and mild. Now the temperature was around zero Celsius and the heating was not working. It couldn't be turned off, either. Unpleasant chill air blasted from the ventilation system. He stopped the car and sat peering up at the window on the third floor.

He would never manage to let her go. Not as long as she was in Norway, in Oslo. In the police force. The time she had been gone had been a relief, in a way. In the beginning, the first couple of months after she had vanished, she had been omnipresent. Everything he said and did, every discussion and every decision, had been filtered through his idea of what Hanne would have done and said. They talked together, long conversations, usually in an undertone when he believed himself alone. Eventually he had reached a stage where he did not think about her so much. At least not continually, and he no longer talked to himself. He still carried a nameless loss, but she stopped haunting his dreams. All the same, she was still there.

Like someone dead, he had thought. It was possible to live with the thought that Hanne was dead. In fact it was best like that, and he no longer dreamed of her. Then she simply turned up again. The pain of knowing that Hanne was back was greater and more unwieldy than the anguish that had paralyzed him when she disappeared.

It was half past three and he could turn round. He could send Silje and Karianne on a hunt for Iron Fist. Or Klaus. He was experienced enough. Billy T. started the engine, glanced again at the window on the third floor, and put the car into reverse. Then he changed his mind yet again. The gearbox whined as he crunched back into first without depressing the clutch.

Hanne was the best officer he had, and his case was as good as

ruined. Without her it was all going to collapse. She had called in
sick that morning. Maybe she had a cold. Maybe she just wanted
to avoid that day's meeting. He no longer knew her. Hanne would
never have humiliated him. Not before. Not the way she used to
be, previously. She had often put him down, yes she had, teased
and tormented him; sometimes Hanne Wilhelmsen had been a
real pain in the neck. But she had never humiliated him. Not like
yesterday. He no longer knew her. He needed her, and he would
have to lift his finger and ring the doorbell.

"What do you want?"

The apparition that opened the door had obviously just woken
up. Lank, colorless hair was sticking out in all directions and
the face was like a dried-up riverbed. Around her body she had
swathed a dressing gown that was far too big for her, the tartan
one that Billy T. knew belonged to Hanne.

"Are you going to answer, or are you waiting till you pick up
your old-age pension?"

Hairy Mary winked at her own joke, and her grimace exposed
the stumps of her teeth. Billy T. could not get a word out. An
automatic reflex made him produce his police ID from his inside
pocket. Forty-eight hours of abundant access to food had had a
staggering effect on Hairy Mary's gift of the gab.

"Is it me or her you want? I'm not coming of my own free will,
and Hanne doesn't look as if she's very keen to get up, either."

She shuffled back inside the hallway.

Billy T. followed her hesitantly.

"Who is it?" he heard a nasal voice shout from the living room.

"A raid," Hairy Mary screeched, padding into the bathroom.

Hanne was stretched out on the settee, covered in a blanket
and with a cup of coffee in her hand. A sea of used paper tissues
was strewn across the coffee table.

"Hi," she said softly. "Hi, Billy T. So … nice. That you popped in."

"That friend of yours is not really normal," they heard the muffled voice say through the bathroom door. "She's not like other police folk."

"Who the fuck *is* that banshee?" he whispered as loudly as he dared. "Have you gone totally mad?"

"Shh."

Hanne put her finger on her mouth.

"She's got ears like an owl, and—"

"She's not mad," was the shriek from the bathroom. "She's kind. I'm going soon. Relax."

"Remember to take a key," Hanne said.

Hairy Mary had put on a new face and work outfit in record time. The lamé jacket had been exchanged for something in black leather, and her skirt was so short that Hanne could see a big hole in the crotch of her tights. Hairy Mary had wound a scarf twice around her throat, and without asking had helped herself to a pair of dress shoes belonging to Hanne. She held out the key that was hanging from a chain around her neck and stuffed it well down inside her bra, before pulling on a pair of gloves that were far too large. Then she gave a farewell salute and limped out of the apartment without looking at Billy T.

"Does she live here? Have you let that bloody awful whore *move in*?"

He plumped down in the armchair and leapt up again quick as a flash when he discovered a lacy salmon-pink pair of panties hanging to dry on the wing of the chair.

"They're clean," Hanne said. "And Hairy Mary is no bloody awful whore. Whore, of course, but not bloody awful."

"For fuck's sake," Billy T. said. "What sort of life are you actually living?"

He used his finger and thumb to pick up the panties and threw them into a corner before resuming his seat. Then he peered skeptically around, as if to make sure that no more surprises would emerge from the walls.

"Are you sick?" he asked into thin air.

"Sort of. Just a cold. Had a bit of a temperature this morning, but I think it's gone down now. Stuffed up. Runny nose. It didn't seem as if you were very keen to have me on the case, so I thought I'd—"

"We've found an Iron Fist."

"The threatening letters."

Hanne blew her nose energetically and began to collect the used hankies into a plastic bag.

"Yes. We ... Silje read a reader's letter with the same signature. She phoned *VG*, but of course they invoke confidentiality of sources. What else! In this case they all say that ... However that may be ..."

He rubbed his face and snorted like a horse. His eyes were dull; he could hardly have had a wink of sleep. Hanne pulled the blanket up under her chin and lay back on the settee.

"We've got help to search," Billy T. said. "For other readers' contributions where this lady has—"

"We know that it's a woman?"

"It's obvious from a number of the pieces. She's prolific. Fortunately we also came across her address. Two years ago she wrote to *Dagsavisen* about children living in the inner city. She's against that sort of thing, of course. Oddly enough, she also mentions where she lives. In Jacob Aalls gate. Here."

He placed a scrap of paper on the table, without pushing it toward her.

"If you feel fit enough, you can take Silje with you. If not, I'll send someone else. It should be done today."

"Billy T.," Hanne said.

"Yes?"

Faltering, he turned in the doorway.

"Thank you so much. I'll be at headquarters in less than an hour."

For a moment it looked as if he was going to say something. His mouth opened slightly. Then he shrugged one shoulder and went on his way. She only just heard when the door closed behind him.

She still had not told Billy T. who Hairy Mary actually was. Now it would be almost impossible to say anything.

41

Daniel had lit a joss stick to suppress the persistent odor of stale dampness. It did not help much. Sweet, nauseating air clung to his body, making him want to peel off his shirt. He needed a shower, but was not permitted to use the bathroom for more than half an hour in the morning and fifteen minutes at night.

"I must have that money now, Daniel. You're just messing me around. A thousand kroner here and a couple of thousand there … It's just not on."

Eskild hadn't even sat down. Daniel cleared the dirty clothes off an armchair.

"Have a seat, won't you?"

"No. I need to go. But you look completely spaced out. Are you on something? Fucking hell, I need that money. Now. I have to pay my course fees before New Year's Eve. As far as you're concerned, it's only twenty-four thousand kroner. To me, it's six months' studies. You can't expect me just to nod and say that's fine, pal. That wasn't what we agreed."

Daniel knew very well what a semester's studies meant to Eskild. He had worked to gain entry to medicine for as long as Daniel could remember. Thale had called him Dr. Eskild since he was thirteen. Even though he was weak in the sciences, he had fought his way through to a university place in Hungary by repeating four subjects at Bjørknes College. At the same time he had worked at Horgans restaurant in the evenings, and Daniel had barely seen anything of his friend for a whole year. When the letter from Budapest finally arrived and Eskild could at last embark on a five-year course of studies abroad, they had celebrated for four days.

Daniel had agreed to repay everything he had borrowed when Eskild came home for the Christmas holidays. He had arrived a bit early. He had turned up as early as December 2; he had had his tonsils extracted at Ullevål Hospital after being on the waiting list for more than a year. He was out of sorts because of the pain in his throat and did not seem too perturbed when the money wasn't available at once. Now Christmas was fast approaching and Eskild was really pissed off.

"This money's peanuts to grown-ups. Can't you ask your mum or your aunt? Three more days, Daniel. Three days. If you haven't coughed up the rest by then, I'm going straight to Thale or Taffa."

Eskild adjusted the lapels of his jacket. A touch of sympathy was apparent in his eyes when he saw how Daniel flinched at the thought of his mother or aunt finding out about the impasse he had landed himself in. Then he pulled a grimace and muttered: "Three days, then. Monday."

He was gone.

Daniel had to get hold of the money. He could sell one of Grandfather's books. He did not want to: he pictured in his mind's eye the old man in his armchair, with bushy eyebrows like miniature horns above the gimlet ice-blue eyes. "Whatever you do, Daniel, never sell my books. Do whatever you want, but you must never, ever sell my books."

Daniel closed his eyes and could feel the old man's dry fingers tenderly caress him on the cheek. The stench of sweat combined with the cold and cloying incense forced him out of bed, and he staggered over to the wall beside the front door, where five cartons of his grandfather's books sat. They really shouldn't be here at all: the door of the bedsit was fitted with an old-fashioned Yale lock that could be slid open with a credit card or a fish slice. Also, the landlady had her own key.

He picked up the first book he found in the second box.

Hamsun's *Hunger* in an almost immaculate first edition. Not that one. Grandfather had been especially fond of Hamsun. Now and then Daniel had suspected it was not only Hamsun's literary works that the old man had admired. He had not taken up the subject. Daniel had never discussed politics with his grandfather.

In a separate little box, neatly packaged in plastic, was *The Song of the Red Ruby* by Norwegian author Agnar Mykle. Grandfather had told him never to touch the slipcover. It was the paper cover's spotless condition, together with the distinctive dedication, that made this first edition so special. The sketch of a woman peeping though a narrow gap at the reader: Daniel had never quite understood the symbolism. On the title page the novelist had written, "To Ruth, from Agnar."

Grandfather had never liked *The Song of the Red Ruby*, in actual fact.

Daniel had no idea what it was worth. But he had recently read the major Mykle biography that had been published that autumn, and realized that the dedication was more special than he had previously surmised.

He put the book aside and carefully closed the lid of the box. Although it was no later than half past four, he really had to take a shower. The landlady could say whatever she liked.

When he had first decided to sell one or two of his grandfather's books, he had expected to feel some sense of relief, but it did not come. All the same, he stuck to his guns. He needed 24,000 kroner, and he knew how he could obtain that sum.

42

The courtyard was spacious, bright, and airy. The strips of earth that were probably well-tended rosebeds in summer were now covered with sacking and a thin layer of dirty snow. Here and there, a thorny twig thrust its way through the coarse fabric. Hanne Wilhelmsen surveyed the façade of the inner block and exclaimed: "Well, Iron Fist certainly lives in well-ordered surroundings. These apartment blocks are built to a British architectural design. Nationalists have a tendency to cultivate the foreign, as long as it's prestigious enough. Shall we take stairway A, B, or C first?"

"C," Silje said firmly. "We'll start at the back."

People were obviously still out shopping. This was the last Friday before Christmas, and it was not yet five o'clock. No one answered when Hanne rang the first doorbells. After a brief push on the seventh, a deep male voice responded.

"What is it?"

"We're from the police," Hanne Wilhelmsen replied. "We're trying to track down a woman who … There's a woman in this block, getting on in years, presumably. We just want to have a chat with her, she's a prolific letter-writer and—"

"Tussi Helmersen," the man said. "Stairway B. Good luck, by the way. She'll chew your ears off!"

A click told them that the man was more taciturn than his neighbor.

"Yesss!" Silje exclaimed. "Bullseye at the first attempt!"

"We shall see," Hanne said in a more subdued tone, jogging behind her colleague across to the next stairway.

The residents' names were embossed in white letters on small black plates beside the doorbells. Tussi Gruer Helmersen must have stayed there longer than anyone else in the entire complex. Her name was partially erased, and Hanne could not quite make out whether her middle name was Gruer or Gruse.

"Gruer," Silje said. "It must be Gruer. The last letter's an R, anyway."

She rang the doorbell. No one answered. Hanne pressed the button. Still no answer.

"Heavens above," Silje said, disappointed.

"What had you expected? That she would be sitting here all nice and tidy, waiting for us?"

Hanne tried the rest of the doorbells in the block. A child's voice answered.

"Hello," Hanne said. "Is Mummy at home?"

"Mhmn."

"Are you saying yes or no?"

"Yes."

"Do you think I could have a word with her?"

"Why's that?"

"Hello?"

A woman had taken the microphone from the boy. She buzzed them in and had opened her door and was waiting for them when they arrived at the fourth floor. A little boy stood shy and curious at her back, peering out from behind his mother's hip.

Hanne produced her police ID and introduced both herself and her colleague. The boy gave a broad smile and let go of his mother's thigh.

"Are you real police?"

"Absolutely," Hanne Wilhelmsen replied, taking a toy police car from her jacket pocket. "Here. You can have this."

Silje looked at her in surprise. The boy dashed into the apartment making nee-naw noises. The car whizzed through the air like a plane.

"Be prepared," Hanne murmured. "We're actually looking for Mrs. Helmersen. Do you know her?"

"Do I know her …?"

The woman rolled her eyes as she wiped her hands on her apron and invited them in. The living room showed signs that the mother and son were looking forward to Christmas. The dining table was covered in red-and-green wrapping paper, scissors, glue, and bags of nuts. When the light from the ceiling lamp caught her face, Hanne could see that the woman had traces of golden glitter on her chin. The boy sat on the floor teasing a little cat with part of a Jacob's ladder toy. He had parked the police car in a loosely plaited Christmas basket.

"Sorry about the mess," the mother said, asking them to sit down. "Tea? I've already made some, so it's no bother. My name's Sonja, by the way. Sonja Gråfjell. That's Thomas."

She smiled in the direction of the youngster.

"And Tigerboy," Thomas said, lifting the cat up by its front paws.

"Tussi Helmersen," Sonja Gråfjell said slowly. "It's quite peculiar that you should be asking about her. I've actually been thinking of contacting the police. About Mrs. Helmersen, I mean. But then it felt a bit sort of … stupid."

"I see," Hanne Wilhelmsen said. "Why's that?"

"Why was it a bit stupid? Well, I think—"

"No. Why would you speak to the police about Mrs. Helmersen?" Sonja Gråfjell raised her voice and looked in the boy's direction.

"Thomas! Can you go into the kitchen and give Tigerboy some food and milk? It's in an opened tin in the fridge."

The boy grumbled and turned away, showing no sign of wanting to leave.

"Thomas. You heard what Mummy said."

He got to his feet slowly and reluctantly, tucked the cat under his arm, and padded over to a door at the opposite end of the room.

"She killed Thomas's pet cat," the mother said softly. "She used poison to kill Helmer."

Swallowing, Hanne glanced at Silje. She looked at the kitchen door in confusion.

"Not Tigerboy," Sonja Gråfjell eagerly explained. "He's a new cat. Mrs. Helmersen killed Helmer. The previous cat. Thomas had come home from school and ... He's terrified of Mrs. Helmersen – that woman's the terror of the whole block, at least for the young ones. He saw her put out a saucer of milk, or maybe it was something else. I was at work and came home ... Helmer was dead, and I said to my husband that ... Bjørn, that's my husband, he said that we didn't have any proof, and that it would be ... Is it a crime to kill somebody's cat?"

She talked with each inhalation and exhalation of breath, as if it were an enormous relief finally to be able to share her annoyance with others. She ran her hand over her forehead, and glanced from the one to the other in search of an answer.

"We'll take this from the beginning," Hanne said with a smile. "Thomas came home from school. So then what happened?"

It took more than ten minutes to gather all the threads in the story. Thomas came in again from the kitchen, only to have his outdoor clothes forced on him, as he was sent out to the back yard with Tigerboy.

"It is actually a punishable offense," Silje said without conviction. "To kill other people's cats, I mean."

"It's covered by the animal-protection law," Hanne said. "Moreover, it's definitely a violation of someone else's property. Do you know, by any chance, where this Tussi is at present?"

"I haven't seen her for a few days. I hope she's gone on holiday."

Sonja Gråfjell shuddered, toying with an angel fashioned from a toilet roll. The halo of gilded pipe-cleaners fell to the floor.

"That woman is downright scary."

"I think so too, Mummy. Mrs. Helmersen is really scary."

The boy had obviously done an about-turn on the stairs.

"I think she catches cats. Maybe she's one of those ... A kind of witch that eats animals. I rescued Tigerboy from in there. He ran in because the door—"

He swallowed the last word, and blushed slightly.

"Thomas," his mother said, sounding tense. "Have you been *inside* Mrs. Helmersen's?"

The boy nodded gingerly.

"But it was only because Tigerboy ran in there. I didn't want Mrs. Helmersen to catch him. But she wasn't at home."

The boy was no longer so shamefaced. The two policewomen would listen to what he had to say – he could see that from their faces. He smiled triumphantly, exposing a big gap in his upper jaw where his front teeth had recently fallen out.

"Mrs. Helmersen has loads of medicines all over the place," he lisped earnestly. "More than Grandma. Much more than at ... the pharmacist's shop, even. All over the place. On the table and on the TV and the dresser and everywhere."

He let go of the cat and took three tentative steps into the living room as he glanced up at his mother.

"We only have a medicine cabinet. With a snake on it. That means that medicine is dangerous. The snake."

Thomas pulled down the zip on his quilted anorak. Hanne Wilhelmsen hunkered down, resting her elbows on her knees.

"Are you quite sure of that, Thomas? That there's loads of medicines at Mrs. Helmersen's?"

"Yes."

He nodded energetically.

"Are they just in the living room? In the open?"

"Hmmn. Just like ..."

He looked over at the TV set and pointed to three sparrows made of art glass.

"Like those birds there. Almost like ornaments, sort of thing."

Hanne stood up abruptly and approached the boy. She had not touched her tea. She stroked the boy's head.

"You can become a policeman when you grow up, Thomas. A really good policeman. Thanks for telling us!"

She nodded at Sonja Gråfjell and gave a sign to Silje to come with her. When they had gone all the way down to the court-yard, Hanne tapped in the number for police headquarters on her cellphone. After a brief conversation, she clicked off the call and shook her head despondently.

"Annmari Skar refuses permission to break down the door. She doesn't see that it's urgent enough. What does she know about it? As a rule, lawyers have strange notions of what's urgent."

She blew her nose into a paper hankie and smeared Mentholatum salve on her lips.

"We need to find this Tussi. And ask nicely for permission. I *will* get into that apartment. Won't I, Silje?"

She clapped the young officer between the shoulder-blades.

"Yes, I guess so," Silje Sørensen said. "It can't be *so* difficult to find somebody like Tussi Gruer Helmersen."

There was exactly one week left until Christmas Eve and the soft breeze might mean that a spell of mild weather was just around the corner.

43

The other guests had finished their evening meal some time ago. At the long table of rough pine in the center of the room, there was a limited selection of food: herbal extract, oatmeal porridge, and fruit. Tussi Gruer Helmersen was on a special diet and could only have potato extract. The cup in front of her was half-full and the contents lukewarm. A huge pile of newspapers lay beside her plate. Mrs. Helmersen put on her glasses, which made her eyes look absurdly large in her narrow face. She took no notice of the staff clearing away the debris from a meal that cost more than the most extravagant hotel buffet. The health farm offered its guests very little food and a great deal of exercise and demanded an exorbitant price for both.

Tussi Helmersen had finished with the readers' contributions and now turned to the crime reports. The newspapers at dinner time could still offer two or three pages of Ziegler coverage daily. An armed mail-robbery in Stavanger was relegated to roughly half a page well inside the newspapers, and a nasty rape in Enerhaugen only got a passing mention.

Mrs. Helmersen squinted down at *Dagbladet*:

Well-informed sources ... [she mumbled as her finger ran along the lines of text] *have confirmed to* Dagbladet *that Brede Ziegler had strong ties and financial interests in Italy. His ownership interests in Italian investment companies are difficult to follow at present.*

Hah!

She peered around in confusion as if looking for a conversation partner. The staff had disappeared. Outside the picture windows she could see three of the guests in the subdued evening light moving toward a forest path at the end of an open meadow. She began to stand up, but changed her mind and read on:

> The Chief of Police in Oslo is not willing to comment on rumors that the deceased was involved in money-laundering. Hans Christian Mykland dismisses the issue as speculative.

I should think so!

A young girl entered with a damp cloth in her hand. With little enthusiasm, she let the rag dance along the buffet table, without looking in Mrs. Helmersen's direction.

> From sources in INTERPOL, it has been confirmed to Dagbladet that Mafia killings are often characterized by symbolic acts. These sources do not discount the possibility that the scene of Brede Ziegler's homicide can be interpreted as a warning to Norwegian police. The Ministry of Justice, in close cooperation with ØKOKRIM, the financial branch of the Norwegian police, has been in the vanguard of several international initiatives to fight the laundering of money originating in criminal activity.

Tussi smiled broadly at the cleaner, who was dressed in clinical white.

"Look at this," she said, agitated. "The Mafia. That's what I've always said."

The girl shrugged and shook the cloth into a massive fireplace of coarse granite.

"The import of food. You don't get away from the Mafia. What do you think about our Crown Prince, young lady?"

"He's quite nice," the girl said, taken aback.

"Nice! Don't you read the newspapers? Norway risks being without a queen! The Crown Prince has been to a bar with *homosexuals*!"

"Most of the articles are about the women he goes out with," the girl answered, becoming more enthusiastic about her cleaning.

"You shouldn't take it so lightly, young lady."

Tussi adjusted the lilac woolen turban she was wearing.

"The Crown Prince should have gone into the Army, like his father. Think about it – educating a Crown Prince in America. Soon he might as well go on a study visit to ... Pakistan! The boy looks as if he's more concerned about these groups of immigrants rather than about us, the old folks who built this country."

"I need to get on with my work," the girl said sharply.

"Yes, there's a lot of work still to be done."

Her hat was sliding steadily down over her eyes. Mrs. Helmersen tugged it much farther back. Her hair came into sight, red at the ends, gray closer to her scalp.

"The phone line for tip-offs," she muttered as she riffled angrily through the copy of *VG*. "As if that's going to help the police in the least."

She was starving, and rejoiced at the thought of the chocolate she had hidden in her clothes closet. Tonight, on top of that, she would indulge in half a packet of potato crisps.

And an ever-so-tiny dram, just for the sake of her heart. And to celebrate a little. That was something she really deserved.

44

When the idea had first entered her head, she had come up with absolutely no objections. In principle, she was on holiday. She could do whatever she wanted. The journey had taken only eleven hours, though it felt as if she had been away from home for years.

The cold water made her skin contract. On the way out of the bathtub she almost fell over. She grabbed the shower curtain and pulled it down. Bewildered, she had stood holding the cheerful yellow plastic sheet in her hands.

The practical preparations had been undertaken within two hours: ordering the ticket and writing a hastily scribbled message to the home help. Not until she phoned her parents in Izmir to tell them she was not coming home for the holidays did she feel a prick of conscience. She gave an international conference as her excuse. Nefis had never lied to her parents before. Now it felt frighteningly easy. She was forty-two years old and a professor of mathematics at the University of Istanbul, but could still feel like a little girl disappointing her mum and dad. When she had turned thirty-five they had given up on the idea of seeing her married. Since she had seven brothers, all with wives who constantly gave birth to children, her parents had eventually learned to live with their *little professor*. Three times a year she dutifully traveled home to fulfill the role of submissive daughter in the huge house that was always full of people and endless meals. The family celebrated all the Muslim festivals, but more as the bearers of tradition than from any particular religious commitment. Nefis enjoyed being at home: she was happy in the role of only daughter, and aunt to sixteen nieces and five nephews. This was one of Nefis's lives.

The other was in Istanbul.

She finally put down the shower curtain and left it crumpled behind the toilet. The room was expensive enough not to make any great fuss about the damage. She wrapped a towel around her body and crossed to the window.

From the thirteenth floor of the Oslo Plaza Hotel the city looked like a cobbled-together patchwork. It looked as if the streets had been under water recently; a dank gray veil overlaid everything and made even the neon signs look colorless.

Nefis Özbabacan had two lives.

In Izmir, she was the daughter of the house.

In Istanbul, she was the internationally renowned scholar with her own apartment in the modern part of the city. Friends and acquaintances came from the university milieu, like herself, in addition to a couple of diplomats at foreign embassies. They never asked her why she was unmarried. Since she was used to living two lives, it had been astonishingly uncomplicated to discover a third space in her existence.

She dressed at a leisurely pace.

They had explained to her at the reception desk that this was the last Saturday before Christmas Eve and apparently high season for restaurants. It might be difficult to get hold of a taxi. However, they had found the address for her, no problem. She shuddered a little when she was forced to acknowledge yet again that she had traveled all the way from Istanbul with nothing to go on other than one beautiful night in Verona and the name of a woman who lived in Oslo.

She had just completed her make-up when the phone rang.

Her taxi had arrived.

45

Vilde Veierland Ziegler was listening so intently to the trick-ling water that she did not catch the waiter's question. Only when he spoke to her for the third time did she look up in confusion.

"Oh, sorry. I'd rather wait until my associate arrives. By the way ..."

The waiter had already turned away.

"Could I have a glass of iced water?"

It was Vilde who had suggested they meet at Blom. The restaurant was a place where they could talk in peace without imminent danger of meeting anyone they knew. The other customers were mainly foreign business people. They had let themselves be tempted by a Norwegian artists' restaurant that Norwegian artists could no longer afford to patronize. The tables were well spaced out and she had a feeling that someone had turned up the volume on the fountain in the center of the room. The sound of running water was so loud that she could not think clearly.

Claudio was four minutes late. When he sat down, it was as if someone had suddenly turned off the noise of the fountain.

"What is it we're actually going to talk about?"

"Saying hello would be a good start!"

"Hello."

He squirmed in his seat and avoided her eye. He was already sweating profusely, even though he did not seem out of breath.

When he looked up at last from the yellow damask tablecloth, his gaze was fixed somewhere between her mouth and nose.

"Have you been looking forward to this?"

The waiter appeared with a carafe of iced water. He poured for them both and recommended the sandwich buffet. Vilde ordered two with prawns, without asking Claudio.

"No."

She drank an entire glass of water and then let the ice cubes clink slowly from side to side.

"I've not been looking forward to it. But I have to sort things out. Since Brede can no longer decide everything for me. That's how it is for you too, isn't it? Brede's no longer the one who decides."

"Listen to me now!"

He wiped his forehead with an immaculate white handkerchief, before looking up at the tip of her nose.

"You should perhaps be a bit more concerned about what Brede has decided. Is it not usual for a widow to respect her husband's last wishes? Brede wanted me to take over Entré if anything happened to him. That was the way he wanted it."

Vilde was used to Claudio's hostility. They had never got on. Eventually a silent pact had arisen between them: they would avoid each other. That was no longer possible. Brede was dead, and Claudio was not only affected by his usual surliness. He was also afraid.

"It suited you nicely that Brede died, then."

She pierced a prawn with her fork and held it up in front of her mouth.

"So you'd get your hands on all of it. But then we both got a surprise."

The prawn disappeared between her lips, and she chewed for a long time. Claudio Gagliostro fingered a sprig of dill without showing any sign of hunger.

"Although you think so, Claudio, I'm not stupid. You should know that I'm not going to give away what's mine. Without so much as a by your leave, I mean."

"I don't think you're stupid."

He glanced over at two men who had just sat down a few tables away. It was as if he was not quite sure whether he knew them, and could not entirely make up his mind whether it was pleasant to have something else to look at apart from Vilde, who was tucking her hair slowly behind her ears as she ate the prawns one by one, leaving the bread.

"You're not stupid," he repeated. "But you can't run a restaurant. You know absolutely nothing about that. And I still don't know why you want to talk to me."

"Just that."

He did not recognize Vilde. The arrogant smile made her eyes hard. He had never understood why Brede had chosen Vilde. Of course she was pretty, but Brede had always had access to pretty girls. Beautiful, young, and usually stupid. In the beginning, when Brede had just begun to show more than a passing interest in the girl, Claudio had thought that his partner was going through a phase. He was nearing fifty years of age. Since he had never had a mid-life crisis, Claudio had thought that Brede's relationship with Vilde was nothing other than a symptom of his delayed anxiety about aging. But why they should get married was a mystery. Brede definitely did not want children. Once, late at night, after closing time, when the two partners had partaken of a glass or two in the semi-darkness at the bar, Brede had told him he was sterile. He had got himself fixed, he had said, laughing. The laughter was strange, almost spiteful, as if the man had played a grim joke on his situation and could finally talk about it.

"Exactly."

Claudio jumped, dropping the lemon slice he had been fingering.

"What?"

"That's exactly what I wanted to talk to you about. You're right. I haven't a clue about running a restaurant. That's why I want to offer you an arrangement. A settlement, if you like."

Claudio leaned back in his chair and squinted at Vilde. He really did not recognize her. The few times she had come into the restaurant, she had behaved like a self-conscious young girl. They had barely exchanged a word, but from the little they had spoken, he had concluded that the girl was more or less not up to scratch.

"I've talked to my lawyer," Vilde said, unruffled. "She's explained it all to me. Since we're going to be joint owners of Entré, I'm quite dependent on you continuing to run the business. As you say yourself: I don't have a clue about running a restaurant."

She contorted her voice into a faint Italian accent. Then she giggled softly, as if all of a sudden she was falling back into an old, memorized role.

"But I want my share of the money. I've actually worked hard for that place too. In my own way."

Again she giggled. Claudio felt puzzled, and was suffused with a sudden rage that made him finally seek direct eye contact. He leaned over the table.

"What do you mean?" he spluttered. "Have you …? I don't give a flying fuck what you've done. What is it you want? Or should I perhaps ask what your lawyer wants?"

Vilde composed her face into demonstratively thoughtful furrows.

"You're playing games with me," Claudio snarled. "You're damn well sitting there *playing games with me!*"

He stood up so abruptly that the chair toppled. He stood in disarray, staring down at the floor.

"Take it easy," Vilde said quietly. "I'm not playing games. Sit down."

He felt as if she had him by the balls, so literally that he held his crotch. Then he picked up the chair and sat down falteringly, snatching a glimpse of the exit.

"I need money," Vilde said. "And I need it now. According to my lawyer, winding up an estate takes an eternity. Several months, at least. I haven't time to wait."

Claudio did not speak. She looked at him, for a long time, as if waiting for him to be the one to cough up a solution to the problem in which they were both entangled.

"My lawyer says that Entré is worth around five million kroner," she said in the end, with a loud sigh. "That means that I can demand two and a half, if you want it all for yourself. At least."

"Two and a half ..."

He rolled his eyes in agitation and threw out his arms expressively.

"How the hell am I going to come up with—"

"I've got a suggestion," she interrupted. "You give me one and a half million now. For that sum you get two percent of my shares. That means you're the boss. That gives you fifty-one per cent."

"One and a half million for two percent? When the whole shebang is worth five? I think you're—"

She broke in again, angrier now: "We'll draw up an agreement. In three years, it's all yours. All my shares are transferred to you. On condition that I get one million more next year, and yet another divided over the next two years. In total three and a half million."

She raised her glass in a toast.

"And ta-da, Entré is all yours!"

A group of Japanese men in gray suits entered the restaurant, all wearing small name badges on their chests. The waiter, two heads higher than his guests, ushered them to a table immediately behind Vilde's back. She lowered her voice.

"Or else we can sell Entré at once. That would produce a good chunk for each of us." She smiled broadly and poured out more water. The ice cubes had almost completely melted.

Claudio could not sell Entré. He knew it was too late to start all over again. He would soon be fifty, and had lost everything he owned once too often. It had almost finished him off. Nevertheless he had got up again, fought on, and in the end got cracking on a venture that amounted to something. Entré was his goal, and the only thing he wanted.

Claudio Gagliostro had literally been born and brought up in the restaurant trade. He had come into the world on the kitchen floor in his uncle's restaurant in Milan. Both his parents had died before he was two, paradoxically enough of food poisoning. They had eaten tainted mussels in a dive in Venice during their extremely delayed honeymoon, and little Claudio had continued to live with his mother's brother. His uncle had gone bankrupt when the boy was fourteen, and since then Claudio had fended for himself. With varying fortunes, admittedly, and with the benefit of a morality that was the result of his upbringing as the ugliest boy in the street. But he had benefited from something that none of the others had: his annual trip to Norway. His mother's mother, who originally came from Holmestrand, had left her Italian husband and therefore also her children after years of ill treatment, three years before the Second World War. Her grandson was her pride and joy, even though she had been required to give up her battle for parental rights after a brief, expensive fight through the courts. His uncle had been magnanimous enough to send Claudio to Norway for the summer holidays, even though for his part he had never forgiven Claudio's mother for leaving him as a child. The boy knew how to make good use of his summer language. Even as an eight-year-old he had stood in the Piazza del Duomo, picking out Norwegian tourists through a combination of intuition and a sharp ear. He was remarkably patient. Days could go by between victims. The little dark-haired boy with the peculiar head, who amazingly enough spoke perfect Norwegian, was the most expensive tour guide in Milan. Neither did he turn down the opportunity to rob his clients, though they never reported him.

Claudio Gagliostro could not lose Entré.

"I must have the money by Christmas," Vilde said. "You don't have many days left."

When she raised her eyes and looked at him, she shuddered.

"You'll get your money," he said contemptuously. "Brede's dead. That he made the mistake of marrying you is not going to destroy me. Let that lawyer of yours set up an arrangement. I'll call you."

When he stood up again, this time actually to leave, he was calmer.

"You'll get your money," he said curtly. "Even though it doesn't belong to you."

46

The apartment made her think of an explosion in a bordello. Hanne was placidly resigned about the description being so apt, at least to some extent. Despite her embargo on making a mess anywhere other than the kitchen, Hairy Mary had obviously made herself at home and taken the law into her own hands. Clothes and possessions were scattered across the floor and furnishings, and the washing machine was making noises that indicated something was seriously wrong. Soap was oozing out along the seals. A river of white foam ran between the glass on the drum and the shower. Hanne put her nose closer to it and shut her eyes in despair when she caught sight of the bottle of Zalo washing-up liquid, upset and empty on the tumble drier.

Her cold was worse. She could not muster the energy to tidy. Instead she contributed to the chaos by clearing out a cupboard in search of an old tracksuit. There had to be something on TV. Something that would send her to sleep. The doorbell rang.

"Bloody hell!"

Hanne had repeatedly badgered Hairy Mary about the key. She hauled herself up from the settee and shuffled out to the hallway. Without asking who it was, she pressed the button on the intercom and left the front door open slightly. She hurried back to the settee, since she was halfway through a cheesy crime-drama on TV.

The noises from the hallway were unfamiliar. Someone was making a real effort to be quiet. It couldn't be Hairy Mary; she sounded like a traveling children's orchestra, complete with pots and pans. Hanne sat up, aware of a stab of anxiety as she yelled: "Hello? Who is it?"

No one answered.

She was out in the hallway in one bound.

The woman in front of her, wearing an ankle-length suede coat and bright-red gloves, looked worried. When she saw Hanne, she held out her hand.

"I found you," she said softly.

There was an explosion in the bathroom. It sounded as if the washing machine had blown up.

47

His headache had returned. Billy T. wandered around the apartment with a gurgling, contented daughter in his arms and an old-fashioned oatmeal poultice around his head. Shrieking, Jenny snatched at the topknot, tearing a hole in the plastic bag he had painstakingly wrapped in a dish towel, as he tried to wriggle away. The little girl happily slurped the oatmeal on her fingers.

"Dada," Jenny said.

"Dada, my ass," Billy T. said in an unctuous tone, grabbing the phone that had been ringing for ages.

"Yes!"

Jenny daubed oatmeal on the receiver. He tried to make her sit on the settee, but she howled and tugged at his arm.

"Ma-ma," Jenny screamed, spitting out gray puke.

"Just a minute," Billy T. groaned, hoping that the caller was patient. "Mummy's not here, silly-billy. Come here."

Finally he distracted her with a rag doll.

"Hello? Are you there?"

"Hi there. This is Dr. Felice here. You've obviously got your hands full."

"It's just my daughter wanting to join the conversation. She's nine months old, so I don't suppose there's any breach of confidentiality if she hears what you say."

Øystein Felice did not laugh.

"I don't know if this is even important."

He hesitated for so long, Billy T. thought the call had been disconnected.

"Hello?"

"Yes, I'm still here. I just want to tell you something that came to me since your visit. Something that's not mentioned in those papers I gave you. As I said, I'm not sure whether it's important, but I—"

"Just a tiny second."

Billy T. tore off his compress and touched his cheek. Jenny had given up on the rag doll and was wriggling down from the settee. She lost her balance and fell to the floor and pulled the poultice bag down with her in the fall. She was lying with her bare bottom in the cold porridge, her face turning a dark shade of red. Billy T. held his breath, waiting for the scream. It took him two minutes to calm her down, and she did not produce a smile until he had ripped the paper off a licorice stick that the boys had left behind. Tone-Marit would kill him.

"At last," he said glumly to Dr. Felice. "I'm sorry."

"Quite all right. That's what I have to put up with nearly all day long."

"What was it about, did you say?"

"A communication came from Ullevål Hospital a number of years ago. That had to do with Brede Ziegler, I mean. It might have been in '93 or '94. I thought it pretty strange at the time, since strictly speaking it wasn't procedure to send it to me. It had to do with a preliminary investigation about donation."

"Eh?"

"Now and again people get enquiries about whether they are willing to participate in organ donation. Or bone marrow, for that matter. Never before in my experience has the application come through me. However, one or two of my regular patients have had questions in that regard."

"But why—"

"I was a bit surprised, as I said, and made contact with Ziegler immediately. He was angry, and it …"

Jenny had gobbled down the top of the licorice stick. She had only two teeth as yet: twin pearls twinkling white in all the black gunge. Like a beaver with an underbite, she was grinding her way effectively down the stick of candy, babbling and grinning all the while.

"Yes," Billy T. said.

"It was a bit odd. That he was so furious, I mean. People usually take such requests extremely seriously. In fact it can be a question of saving another person's life."

"Did he say anything?"

"Only something along the lines of there must be some misunderstanding, and I should turn down the whole business. That was all."

Billy T. put Jenny down on the floor, letting her crawl to her heart's content, closed his eyes, and made up his mind to clean the whole apartment later.

"I don't think I entirely understand," he said into the receiver. "It's good of you to phone about this, of course, but what you're saying doesn't really tell me anything more than we already know. Ziegler was a fucking egotistical bag of shit, pardon my French!"

"That may be. I don't have an opinion on that."

"But—"

"I don't mean anything other than that such requests almost always come on behalf of a relative. A close relative. Since Ziegler did not have any siblings and, despite everything, was on speaking terms with his mother, it might mean—"

"Jenny!"

The licorice stick could be used as a crayon. The living-room wall was white. He shouted so loudly that he terrified her, and a puddle of pee flowed slowly out from under the bare bottom.

"But what does it *mean*, then!"

"It's not my task to be a detective. My … unqualified impression, you might say … is that Brede Ziegler may have a child."

"*Child?*"

"Yes, a child. But I don't know, of course."

Billy T. did not say anything, and there was also silence at the other end of the line.

"Thanks," Billy T. said finally, giving a slow whistle. "Vilde."

"I beg your pardon?"

"You said the man had been sterilized. Despite being about to marry a young fertile woman."

"Yes, but I don't quite comprehend what that—"

"You don't need to, either. Thanks very much for phoning. I'll call you again. Fairly soon."

He put the phone down on the living-room table and picked up his daughter. She was wet and smelled of pee, licorice, and stale porridge. When he threw her up in the air and caught her again, she shrieked with delight.

"Dada," Jenny said.

"Dada will be gone from now until Christmas, sure as shooting," Billy T. said, deciding not to phone Hanne.

48

"Daddy! Catch me!"

The boy, about six years old, was swinging by the knees from a branch not really strong enough to bear his weight. He sank slowly to the ground. A man of medium height in a red anorak and no-longer-fashionable glasses took hold of the boy and swung him over his shoulder. A toddler in a green snowsuit clung to the man's leg, desperate to be carried too. On the asphalt path ten meters away a woman stood holding an empty pushchair while talking on a cellphone.

The Akerselva river, sparse in winter, ran under the Bentsebrua bridge, drawing with it an unpleasant gray mist that spread over the level expanse below Sagene church. The area was almost deserted. The time was just past eleven on Sunday morning, December 19, and Hanne came to a sudden halt.

"Shit!" she muttered under her breath.

"What?"

It had seemed a good idea to take a taxi to the lake at Maridalsvannet and walk all the way along the river down to Vaterland. It would take about an hour at a brisk pace, and then they could eat lunch in town. Put the night at a distance, Hanne thought. At least the final part of it.

When Nefis had come back from the bathroom around four o'clock in the morning and had reported in a matter-of-fact tone that there was an old woman sitting on the toilet behind an unlocked door, shooting up, Hanne began to cry. Then she roared. Hairy Mary sat, eyes glazed, her hands over her ears, smiling blissfully.

When Hanne had taken Hairy Mary in for an unspecified period, she had reckoned on her stealing from her. Oddly enough, nothing had disappeared. Hairy Mary took great liberties as far as borrowing was concerned, but she returned everything. The most important thing for Hanne, all the same, was that Hairy Mary appreciated the seriousness of the embargo against drugs in the apartment.

"I'm a police officer. You *mustn't* keep or use anything here inside this building. Okay?"

Hairy Mary had nodded, crossed her heart, and mumbled all sorts of holy oaths when the rule was repeated at regular intervals in the first three days. Of course she did not keep her word. Hanne had not discovered this until that night. Hairy Mary held her ears. Everything would have gone fine, if only that Turkish baggage hadn't had different toilet habits from Hanne – and how in hell was Hairy Mary supposed to know that!

Nefis had taken it well. She smiled wanly, accepting Hanne's stuttered explanation of Hairy Mary's presence in the household with no more than a resigned rubbing of her eyes.

Hanne, however, threw Hairy Mary out with the few belongings she possessed. Admittedly she did not confiscate the key, but the temporary expulsion was at least some kind of marker. Afterwards she turned the house inside-out searching for illegal substances. There were two user doses, wrapped in plastic, inside the cistern, and behind the bookcase in the guest bedroom she found four sterile needles. She flushed the heroin down the toilet and rinsed it with bleach. The needles were locked inside the medicine cabinet. After that, Nefis and Hanne ate an exceptionally early breakfast.

A walk would blow away the cobwebs.

"Shit!" Hanne repeated.

It was impossible to avoid the family of four: Håkon Sand, Karen Borg, and their children. Hanne spotted them before they caught sight of her. She fleetingly considered pulling Nefis down to the river, desperately using her eyes to search for something down there that might prompt a sudden swerve across the muddy grass. She spotted nothing except a pair of sleeping mallards.

"Hi," Håkon said dully.

It looked as though he wanted to give Hanne a hug. He took an almost imperceptible step forward as he raised his arm, but stiffened. His glasses steamed up from the bridge of his nose all the way over the large lenses. His eyes disappeared, and he turned his face to Karen.

"It's been a long time," Karen said obstinately as she installed a protesting Liv in the pushchair.

Hans Wilhelm hid behind his father.

"Hi, Hans Wilhelm! How big you've grown. Do you recognize me?"

Hanne crouched down, mostly as a means of escape. The boy stared shyly at the ground and made no sign of being keen to talk to her. She straightened up again and used her hand to indicate Nefis.

"This is Nefis. A ... an acquaintance of mine from Istanbul. She has ... never been in Norway before."

Håkon and Karen nodded formally at the woman in the suede coat, red gloves, and clumsy mountain boots that were far too big for her.

"We really have to get a move on," Karen said, trying to walk past them on the path. "Bye."

Hanne did not budge. She smiled at Liv, who returned a broad smile as she thrust a dirty spade into her mouth.

These were people who had once been very close. Håkon was so different from Billy T., more sincere, more direct in his affection, and far less competitive than their swaggering friend. More forgiving. She missed him. It struck her when she saw him standing, bewildered, clutching his son's mitten, in a shabby, idiotic anorak, jeans that were slightly too short with baggy knees, steamed-up glasses and traces of a receding hairline: she really yearned for him. Not the way it was with Billy T.. A reconciliation between them, as she wished and intended, would have to include an acknowledgment on his part that he too bore some responsibility for what had happened. In Cecilie's bed, with Cecilie in hospital, dying; they had committed an offence against her, and Hanne barely remembered anything except scrubbing her skin until it bled in the shower afterwards.

Hanne had done an injustice to everyone in her circle, and she was well aware of that. No one would let her forget it, either, it seemed. With Håkon it was different. She could sit down with him one evening and explain it all. Not apologize – just tell him how everything had been, why she had had to do as she did, what had driven her, forced her. He would nod and maybe adjust his glasses. Håkon would make a fresh pot of coffee and quaff it with an unhealthy amount of sugar. She would touch him, hold him, tell him that she dreamed about him, often. She would see him smile, and everything would be the way it had been before.

"Excuse me," Karen said sharply. "I want to pass."

Karen belonged to Cecilie. More to Cecilie than to Hanne, and Hanne stepped aside without taking her eyes off Håkon. As he passed, she saw his eyes through the dull lenses of his glasses. He gave an almost invisible shrug and made a tentative sign with his thumb to his ear and his little finger to his mouth – a telephone, inconspicuous; Hanne was not even sure she could believe her eyes.

"Some friends!" Nefis murmured. "Who are they?"

When Nefis had turned up yesterday evening, the apartment had become Italian. The chaos surrounding them had become

Latin and eccentric. The slices of bread with Jarlsberg cheese and liver pâté had turned into delicacies. The wine from a cardboard box tasted sunny and exclusive. From then on, until the episode with Hairy Mary, the night was a reliving of Verona, but closer now, as it should be: at home, in Oslo, among Hanne's belongings and in her world.

Now she did not know whether she had the strength.

Her feet were glued to the asphalt, and her shoulders ached. She turned toward the little family who were disappearing in the direction of Bentsebrua bridge, would soon be out of sight, and saw fragments of her own dismal story.

"I barely know them," she said, and added: "It was all a long, long time ago. Let's go."

In less than five minutes she had not only denied her friends. The words she had used to introduce Nefis were left hanging like a bitter, burning lump in her throat.

"Damn!" she said softly as she began to walk. "Damn and bloody, bloody blast."

"I hate these boots of yours," Nefis said, gazing down at the borrowed mountain boots, before hurrying after Hanne. "And I don't exactly like your friends, either."

If only Hairy Mary would stay away for a while.

49

The apartment block at Bidenkapsgate was undergoing renovation. Scaffolding stretched from ground level to well above the roof ridge. The iron construction was covered with green tarpaulin that rustled faintly in the night wind. Sebastian Kvie peered under the rough plastic, ascertaining that the scaffolding was fully secured and the work on installing new windows was well under way. Curls of pink mastic were scattered everywhere and, even in the semi-darkness, the newly painted, pristine white window frames were obvious. Sebastian was in luck. He immediately devised a new plan. Instead of ringing the doorbell and confronting Claudio with everything he knew, he would climb up to the apartment and see if it was possible to get in through the window. What he would do after that was still not quite clear in his mind. Anyway, he had six half-liters on board, as well as two shots of Gammel Dansk bitters that a friend had bought for him because it was his birthday. The planned showdown with his boss was a totally impulsive act. But it was a brilliant impulse, to Sebastian's mind. It was about time someone did something to force Claudio to confess his crimes. The police were all at sea. He'd read that in the newspaper. They'd soon have something else to write about.

"Criii-mes," Sebastian hiccuped contentedly.

The tarpaulin made it impossible to see where he was going. Once he had started climbing, it would become easier. At least he knew which of the apartments belonged to Claudio. Brede had once brought him here to fetch something at his friend's house.

Since Claudio lived on the fourth floor with no elevator, Sebastian had offered to run upstairs while Brede waited in the car.

Although the building workers had removed the ladder from street level to the first landing of the scaffolding, it was a simple matter to swing himself up. Sebastian went to the gym twice a week at the SATS training center; he did not want a chef's pot belly by the time he was thirty. The planks creaked under his feet and he tried to stand as still as possible. Only the incessant rustling of the tarpaulin could be heard above the sound of the occasional vehicle passing on Ullevålsveien, a hundred meters to the north-east. The windows of the apartment he was now facing were covered in thick plastic. Sebastian climbed higher.

All the way up at the fourth floor, he panted for breath. His pulse hammered in his eardrums, and when he discovered the tarpaulin was only fixed to the metal braces with small nylon clasps that would loosen at the slightest provocation, he grew scared. For one reason or other he had until then considered the green plastic to be a solid wall. It no longer felt so reassuring. Sebastian swayed.

Light shone from a window at the far end.

Sebastian took a good grip of the metal bar and tried to creep across the planking. There was a terrible screech of metal against metal on the suspension. The windows up here had not yet been replaced. He pressed his nose against the first one. In the interior darkness he could make out the outlines of a worktop and, when he looked more closely, he caught sight of a fridge. According to his calculations, this should be Claudio's apartment. He pressed his fist against the window frame but it would not budge.

"What the hell was I thinking?" he muttered, desperately longing to be down on terra firma again. The wind had picked up and he was freezing.

The next window was larger. He stepped over a knee-high crossbar and struggled to remove his Swiss Army knife from his pocket. He was sure he had remembered to bring it with him. He always carried that knife; it had belonged to his grandfather and was in use nearly every single day.

He just managed to spot a shadow in the room before he fell. The window may not have opened with tremendous force, but it was sudden. The frame struck Sebastian's left shoulder and he fell back with all his weight. His upper torso tipped over the framework to the tarpaulin, yanking his leg with it. He hit his head off the railing on the next floor and fractured his arm when he tried to seize hold of the third. On the first-floor exterior of the apartment block in Bidenkapsgate the tarpaulin was particularly firmly attached, and his fall was checked to some degree before it all collapsed and Sebastian fell shoulder-first on to the asphalt below.

"*Santa Maria!*" Claudio exclaimed, racing down the stairs in only his pajamas, screaming the whole time: "An accident! An accident! Fell from my scaffolding – a burglar!"

He lifted the tarpaulin.

A trickle of blood ran from the corner of Sebastian's mouth. The boy was unconscious, maybe even dead.

"He's breathing," Claudio cried hysterically to a neighbor in a blue dressing gown who was holding a cordless phone in his right hand. "He's breathing – Sebastian! We need to call an ambulance!"

"I've phoned everyone who needs to be phoned," his neighbor whispered. "Is he dead?"

"No, he's breathing, I tell you! He … I saw somebody outside the window, outside my window, and …"

Claudio pointed up excitedly at the apartments, as if his neighbor did not know where he lived. A woman in her twenties with piercings in her nose and both lips crossed the street and leaned inquisitively over Sebastian. The sound of sirens came steadily closer.

"For fuck's sake, look how pale he is," she said, impressed. "Did you see it? Did he fall?"

She put her head back and tugged at the tarpaulin.

"Away," Claudio yelled. "Go away!"

An ambulance, police patrol car, and two fire engines rounded the corner at approximately the same time. The little street was bathed in blue light and by now everyone was wide awake. People were hanging out of windows in neighboring blocks, and eight night-walkers had already huddled around Sebastian. The boy was still breathing and still unconscious.

It took the police five minutes to establish that nothing was burning, dispatch the red vehicles, and move people away. Only Claudio and his dressing-gown-clad neighbor were allowed to remain inside the cordon of red-and-white plastic tape. Another patrol car parked in the middle of the road, and a uniformed man in his thirties drew Claudio farther back.

"Were you the one who phoned?"

"Is he alive?"

Claudio tore himself free from the firm grip on his arm and ran back to Sebastian. Three men in white coats were crouched over the boy. The policeman enlisted help from a colleague and attempted to drag Claudio away.

"Is he alive?" he repeated, striking out wildly. "Is Sebastian alive?"

Sebastian regained consciousness. He opened his eyes, obviously struggling to focus. He did not whimper, did not complain; merely stared in surprise as if he could not fathom what all these people were actually doing. Then he spotted Claudio.

"He pushed me," he said in a loud whisper.

The paramedics froze.

"Claudio pushed me down."

His eyes slid shut and the paramedics managed to attach the neck brace.

"Do you live here?"

The policeman was no longer quite so friendly. Claudio nodded and swallowed and nodded again as he pointed up into the air, as if he lived in the sky.

"Let's go up to your place," the policeman said firmly.

"Up to my place?"

"Yes. What's your name?"

Claudio apathetically reeled off his name and – quite unnecessarily – his address. He hardly noticed the policeman repeating it all into his police radio.

The ambulance was about to turn into Wessels gate and disappear.

Claudio was no longer sweating. His teeth chattered and his whole body was shaking.

"I don't want to go up," he whined. "We can talk here."

The police did not accede to his request.

"Here?"

The older police officer, out of breath from virtually dragging the Italian up four flights of stairs, pointed at the double windows in Claudio's living room. A colleague stood in the doorway, as if to prevent any possible attempt to flee. Claudio Gagliostro did not seem accustomed to that sort of thing. He sat lethargically in a ladder-back chair wearing a pair of pajamas with horizontal stripes that, taking the circumstances into consideration, made him look like a jailbird.

"Mmm. Yes."

"What happened?"

Claudio did not answer.

"Hel-looo!"

"I was asleep."

Claudio tugged at his flannel pajamas as if to prove he was telling the truth.

"I was asleep," he reiterated. "Then I heard some noises. The company that … We got a note in the mail to tell us to be on our guard against burglars, now that the scaffolding is up. Noises woke me and I came out here to check. Then I opened the window and …"

He gasped, and shook his head ever so slightly.

The policeman leaned out of the open window without touching anything.

"Can you explain why the boy said you pushed him?"

The man was speaking out of the window, and Claudio was unsure whether he had heard him right.

"I know him," he said out loud. "Sebastian works for me!"

"These cases of wine," said a plain-clothes officer from the hallway; he just popped his head round the door and looked at Claudio without introducing himself. "Why do you have so much wine stored here?"

Claudio had clung to a forlorn hope. The long wall in the hallway was almost papered with wine cases. Displayed like that, they might with luck be taken for some kind of interior decor. The cases were made of wood, and several of them were extremely old.

"I think we'll take a trip down to the station, Kaglistro."

The policeman at the window approached him, talking non-stop into a radio fastened to a strap across his shoulder.

"Gagliostro," Claudio muttered. "Can I … can I put on something else?"

"Of course."

Fifteen minutes later Claudio Gagliostro was in a patrol car en route to Grønlandsleiret 44. He still had no idea whether he was charged with anything. He had dressed in a pair of jeans and a linen shirt, the armpits already wet. His socks were too thick for his elegant shoes, but he did not notice them pinching his toes. He looked at his watch, hoping to finish at police headquarters in

time to grab at least a couple of hours' sleep before Monday was
properly under way.

What he did not know, either, was that the police had been
granted the necessary authority by the duty officer and were in
the process of turning his apartment upside-down.

50

From time to time she felt some sort of awareness. Then she saw herself from the outside, a bird's-eye view, as if perched high on the opposite wall, indifferently watching herself. The floor was green. She tried to clutch the grass, but only scraped her fingers until they bled. Something told her the green stuff was concrete, but she could not manage to hold that realization long enough to understand where she was. Her brain sloshed from side to side inside her skull. At first it felt quite pleasant, but then she grew afraid that her brains would leak out. She thrust a finger in each ear, before promptly taking them out again. They screamed. Her fingers had screamed and she struggled to focus on her own fingerprints. She put them to her lips to comfort them.

"Ecstasy," one custody officer said to the other. "Fucking hell! Can't figure out how they dare."

It was Monday morning, December 20, and the police had set up a major drink-driving checkpoint at Sinsenlokket. When Vilde Veierland Ziegler had tumbled out of the driving seat of her car, the police officers could barely understand how she had been able to keep the vehicle on the road at all.

The custody suite was full to overflowing. The perspiring police prosecutor on duty was seated in a spartan room doing his level best to deal with the repeat-offender fines. Some stood head down, cap in hand, quite literally, while others screamed and sniveled and shouted for a lawyer.

"The doctor will be here soon," the custody officer yelled at Vilde, before turning to his colleague. "Hardly any point in taking a blood sample from this one. We could just take a video of the lady."

Vilde was driving a car. She made broom-broom noises and kept tight hold of an imaginary steering wheel. Claudio's face expanded in front of her. She switched on the windscreen wipers and tried to think of Sindre, but he slipped away. Claudio grew larger. His eyes ran over with black gunge, which disintegrated and spilled down his cheeks like hot asphalt.

Vilde shrieked.

The shriek drowned out every other sound in the custody suite and encouraged a few other prisoners to join in. A cacophony of howls, yells, and piercing screams ricocheted off the concrete walls, causing the understaffed custody team to call for reinforcements. The Custody Sergeant grabbed the phone as he barked at two trainee officers: "For God's sake get hold of a psychiatrist from Accident & Emergency! We need to get that werewolf in number twenty out of here!"

He glanced at his watch: not yet 9 a.m.

"Happy Christmas," he groaned, buttoning his trousers. "Happy bloody Christmas!"

51

"With his *daughter*? Was he a *pervert*?"

Karl Sommarøy grimaced as his mind turned to his own small daughters.

"But *why*?"

Billy T. flung out his arms in consternation.

"It all fits! Question: why would a childless guy who's about to embark on marriage with a young woman in the prime of life let himself be sterilized? Answer: because he doesn't want a grotesque child."

"Or because he doesn't want children at all," Karl said, looking skeptical as he ruminatively rubbed the smooth bowl of his pipe on his cheek.

"Question," Billy T. went on, unaffected by his colleague's objection. "Why was his wife living in a bedsit when they had an apartment as big as a football pitch in the middle of the city? Answer: because Brede Ziegler actually found it quite repulsive to have his daughter in his marital bed. Despite everything."

"But you haven't yet given me any motive."

Billy T. tugged at his earlobe.

"No idea," he said lightly. "But I'll find out. We'll haul in that young widow and hear what she knows about it. Come with me, then. It took us far too long to find that bedsit in Sinsen. On the other hand: what the hell would we want with that address before now?"

He smiled. Karl Sommarøy had not seen anything like it for ages. At least not since Hanne Wilhelmsen's return.

"Can't," he said tersely. "I've more than three hundred hours of overtime due, and I promised the wife we'd go shopping. I won't have long to live if I'm not home in half an hour. You'll have to take someone else with you."

Billy T. went to Sinsen on his own.

* * *

Interview with Tussi Gruer Helmersen

Interviewed by Chief Inspector Hanne Wilhelmsen. Transcript typed by office colleague Rita Lyngåsen. There is one tape of this interview. The interview was recorded on tape on Monday December 20, 1999 at 12.30 hours at Oslo police headquarters.

Witness:

Helmersen, Tussi Gruer, ID number 110529 23789
Address: Jacob Aalls gate 3, 0368 Oslo
Retired, phone no.: 22 63 87 19
Given information about witness rights and responsibilities, willing to give a statement.
The witness was informed that the interview would be taped, and a transcript later produced.
Witness informed that she is giving a statement as part of the investigation into the homicide of Brede Ziegler. She explained as follows:

Interviewer:

I've switched on the tape now. Before we get properly started, I'd like you to confirm some personal details. Tussi is your real name, is that right? That's how you're listed in the Population Register?

Witness:

Yes. You see, I was born at a time when the authorities left
law-abiding people in peace to take care of their own business. My name is as my parents wanted it to be. There weren't
any kind of departments and that sort of thing then. Or
whoever it is that decides these things nowadays. You see, I
was born in May. When my mother came home from the hospital with me, my father had decorated the living room with
coltsfoot flowers. To celebrate the great occasion, you understand. My father didn't have much money, but he had
imagination. *Tussilago farfara* is the Latin name for coltsfoot.
Coltsfoot from *far*, the Norwegian name for father. Do you get
it? It's as simple as that, for heaven's sake—

Interviewer *(interrupts)*:

Thanks, that's fine. It's just that we have to be sure we get
accurate details. It was good of you to come here so quickly, I
will—

Witness *(interrupts)*:

It's the least I could do! The minute I saw the note on the door,
I came right down here. Please make contact with the police,
it said. Extremely polite! Yes, you know I only came back to
Oslo on the Valdres Express this morning, but as soon as I saw
that note, I came along here. I only stopped to put my luggage
in the hallway. I didn't even attend to my potted plants, even
though they're sure to be terribly thirsty, and yes ... *(Sounds of
a door banging? Pause.)* Here I am!

Interviewer:

Fine. Do you know why the police want to talk to you?

Witness:

Why? Well, it's probably because the police believe I might know one or two things of interest.

Interviewer:

I see. But do you know what the police want to talk to you about?

Witness:

What? Well, there are so many things. I keep my wits about me, I can tell you that. Very much so. And then you pick up a few things. Could I have another cup of this delicious coffee of yours?

Interviewer:

Coffee? Yes, of course. Here you are. *(Crackle, pause.)* The police have received information that you have a great deal of medicine stored at home. Is there any particular reason for that?

Witness:

That's the most impudent thing I've ever heard! Has someone told the police about my home? There's never anybody in my home apart from me, so what you've heard is absolute twaddle! If you ask me, you'll get an answer.

Interviewer:

We are in fact extremely interested in taking a closer look at your apartment, Mrs. Helmersen. Does that mean you agree to a search?

Witness:

Search? That's a bit extreme, is it not? But you can just enter my home whenever you want, young lady. I'll offer you some

coffee and some Mother Monsen's cake. I've plenty of that sort
of thing in my freezer. You know, I keep up the old traditions
and bake for Christmas, I—

Interviewer *(interrupts)*:

Does that mean you have no objection to a search? *(Rustling
paper, brief pause.)* Would you be so kind as to sign here?

Witness:

Yes, of course. That makes it almost like a written invitation.
Doesn't it? *(Brief pause, laughter.)*

Interviewer:

Thanks. But this about the medicine – is that true? Do you
take a lot of pills?

Witness:

Yes, unfortunately. At my age—

Interviewer *(interrupts)*:

Mrs. Helmersen, it's helpful that you came so quickly. But it
would be a great advantage if you'd keep your responses brief.
Try to concentrate on what I'm asking you. Who is your
doctor? Because I assume you get these medicines of yours
from a doctor?

Witness:

My doctor? I can tell you it's far from easy to find a competent
doctor these days. So I go to a few different ones. You could
say I'm on the lookout for the very best. Do you know what:
the other day I had booked an appointment at Bentsebro
medical center. The doctor was as black as coal! As if I would

let myself be treated by a hula-hula medicine man like that! If it hadn't been for—

Interviewer *(interrupts)***:**

Does that mean you get medicine prescribed by a number of doctors?

Witness:

Yes, but I already told you that. Young woman, perhaps you ought to pay better attention.

Interviewer:

I assure you I'm paying a great deal of attention. Iron Fist – does that mean something to you?

Witness:

Yes, of course. Such a splendid expression, don't you think? Hard-hitting and yet refined, in a sense. In all modesty … *(faint laughter)* a bit like myself.

Interviewer:

A bit like yourself? Tell me, do you write letters that you sign Iron Fist?

Witness:

I'm a person who likes writing. I can tell you that. There's so much in this society of ours that people need to be warned about. Of course I don't know how well you have followed them, but these school reforms, not to mention the absurd idea of a National Police Directorate. Something like that will inevitably lead to—

Interviewer *(interrupts)*:

Mrs. Helmersen! *(Pause.)* I'm a bit fed up with ... Do you think you could try to answer the questions I'm asking you? This is a police interview. Do you understand that? Can you answer me why you sign yourself Iron Fist?

Witness:

Don't take that tone with me, young lady. Not now, when we've been having such a pleasant ... *(Pause, lengthy rustling of paper.)* Yes, of course. Iron Fist is my alias. I think you know that. I've written a lot for the newspapers – I could almost be considered a regular writer, in the Oslo newspapers. That's why you're asking of course, isn't it? Because you recognize Iron Fist as a well-known commentator?

Interviewer:

I can assure you, Mrs. Helmersen, that the police don't normally call in cultural personages for a chat. I would like to show you some letters. The question is whether they were written by you. Wait a minute ... *(Longish pause.)* The interviewer is showing the witness evidence bags containing documents 17/10/3, 17/10/4, and 17/10/5. Do you recognize any of these? This one, for example, here where it says "The chef's goose is cooked".

Witness:

No, but my goodness, how exciting! Do you think somebody's stolen my alias?

Interviewer:

I don't think anything. I just want to know if it was you who produced this letter.

Witness:

It's quite elegant. The wording, I mean. Don't you agree? But do you know what – I write in the newspapers. That certainly wasn't me. But it is a famous pseudonym, of course. Somebody may have stolen it. Do you think I should report it? *(Laughter.)* Theft of intellectual copyright, what do you say, Mrs. Policewoman?

Interviewer:

(Pronounced sigh, pause.) I say that you should answer … *(sharp noise, striking the table?)* my questions, Mrs. Helmersen. Did you know Brede Ziegler?

Witness:

A highly disagreeable person! But I didn't really know him … People in the public eye do know one another to some degree, of course, you know.

Interviewer:

Now I'm going to ask you a very precise question, and I want a very precise answer. Have you met Brede Ziegler?

Witness:

I wouldn't dream of going into his restaurant, I'll have you know. This so-called nouvelle cuisine that doesn't have the least respect for—

Interviewer (*interrupts*):

I'm warning you, Mrs. Helmersen. If you don't give me a reasonable answer now, I'm going to draw a halt to this interview and apply for formal questioning in a court of law.

Witness:

Am I to go to court? I'd really like to do that. What do you say to judges these days? In my youth, when I actually worked as a lay judge on a number of occasions, people said Most Honorable—

Interviewer *(interrupts)*:

(Loud voice.) Mrs. Helmersen! Have you met Brede Ziegler, or have you not?

Witness:

But my dear! No need to be so indignant. Everything will run much more smoothly if you pay attention. I have already told you that I haven't met him.

Interviewer:

So you've never met Brede Ziegler?

Witness:

No. But not so many years ago I had the pleasure of spending a weekend with—

Interviewer *(interrupts)*:

That's been noted, Mrs. Helmersen. So I'd like to know where you were on the evening of Sunday December the fifth.

Witness:

December the fifth? *(Pause.)* That's the evening Mr. Ziegler was murdered, isn't it? Young lady, do you suspect me of something? Or do you just want to eliminate me from your inquiry? As you can probably hear, I know my police jargon.

Interviewer:

(Drumming noise, like fingers on a table? Pause.) Where were you on Sunday evening? Answer!

Witness:

Well, for heaven's sake! I'm doing as best I can, Mrs. Policewoman! Sunday, Sunday ... *(Pause, light coughing.)* Two weeks ago. Let me see ... *(Pause.)* Yes, I can tell you in fact, young lady. I was doing something extremely unusual. I went for a long walk that evening. I was sitting writing an article about Muslims. You probably agree with me that the advance of Muslims in this country is a danger to our culture and established Christian values. I ... Could I have some water, do you think? I've been talking so much now. Yes, thank you, thank you. *(Pause, distinct sounds of drinking.)* Then I found it necessary to have a closer look at the monstrosity. This building that so much was written about at one time, you know. So I took a stroll from my home – exercise is good for you, you know – all the way to Åkebergveien. But I took the bus back again. The weather was really nasty that evening. The cold wind made it necessary for me to have an ever-so-tiny drop of cognac when—

Interviewer *(interrupts)*:

What monstrosity?

Witness:

The mosque, that ghastly mosque, you know.

Interviewer:

The mosque in Åkebergveien. I see. And what time was that then?

Witness:

Well, I can't really say for certain. But it was late. Quite late, I'd expect. You understand, I have problems sleeping. So I thought an evening stroll to help me sleep would do me good. And then I could have a look at that eyesore at the same time.

Interviewer:

What do you mean by late? Was it after midnight?

Witness:

Well, now you're asking a difficult question. It must have been somewhere between ... *(pause)* ten o'clock and midnight. Something like that.

Interviewer:

And approximately how long were you at this mosque?

Witness:

That's impossible to say.

Interviewer:

Try.

Witness:

I detect a hint of sarcasm in your voice, young Mrs. Policewoman. It doesn't become you, if I can allow myself to say so.

Interviewer:

Try to estimate how long you spent outside the mosque in Åkebergveien between twenty-two hours and midnight on December the fifth.

Witness:

Quarter of an hour, perhaps? That's a pure guess. I can't understand—

Interviewer *(interrupts)*:

Did you see anyone there?

Witness:

See anyone? But my dear, we're talking about the worst area in the east end! People loiter in those parts to such an extent that you'd think they had no home to go to.

Interviewer:

Did you see many *(distinct raising of the voice at "many")* people there?

Witness:

(Mumbles indistinctly.) Not so sure *(inaudible)* … took a taxi home.

Interviewer:

You said bus.

Witness:

Bus or taxi, it's all the same. The main thing is I got home safely.

Interviewer:

We need to take a little break, Mrs. Helmersen. The time is 13.35. *(Scraping of chairs, the tape is switched off.)*

Interviewer:

The time is now 13.55. The interview is resumed. What kind of knives do you have at home?

Witness:

Knives? That's a strange question. Naturally, I have a number of different ones. A good knife can never be underestimated in a kitchen. Good food demands good ingredients, but also adequate equipment, as I say. For filleting I use one I inherited from my father, he was such a—

Interviewer *(interrupts)*:

Do you know what a Masahiro is?

Witness:

Yes, you know what? That's the very jewel in the crown, if I can put it that way. Unfortunately my pitifully small pension doesn't stretch to the purchase of such a piece of equipment, but everyone who … By the way, it's Japanese. Those Japanese folks! In truth, they're people who know what they want. And then they stay at home, at least. They come here on holiday, but they go straight home. Like a civilized island in the midst of the barbarians, they have—

Interviewer *(interrupts)*:

Sorry, we need to take another little break.

Witness:

It's terrible how restless you are, Mrs. Policewoman! You ought to try St. John's Wort and—

Interviewer *(interrupts)*:

The time is 14.05. *(The tape is switched off.)*

Interviewer:

The time is now 14.23. Do you like cats, Mrs. Helmersen?

Witness:

Well, that's a strange question. From knives to cats, and with constant breaks in between. But if you want my honest opinion, then you can have it. Cats are dreadful creatures. In apartment blocks it should be absolutely forbidden to keep pet animals, I have often—

Interviewer *(interrupts)*:

Have you killed your neighbor's cat? The Gråfjell Berntsen family's cat?

Witness:

No, do you know what? Are you accusing me of murder? The Berntsen family, yes. I know what to expect from certain people. But killing ... Now you need to take care, Mrs. Policewoman. I wouldn't dream of killing a living soul. Not even a cat.

Interviewer:

Now I must make you aware that you are no longer being interviewed as a witness in the investigation of Brede Ziegler's homicide. You have, in the course of this interview, given such specific information that the police find sufficient grounds to suspect you of having something to do with the actual murder. You are charged with homicide and/or attempted homicide, or having been an accessory to the crime. This is the provisional charge. It was drawn up at the last break we took.

To the report: the accused was shown—

Witness *(interrupts):*

Charged … Does that mean that I'm suspected? But we were talking about cats, and now all of a sudden you're talking about Ziegler!

Interviewer:

I repeat, the accused is shown the charge. You do not have to give a statement. Do you still wish to give a statement, with the status of accused?

Witness:

But, my dear, I'm happy to give a statement – I've been talking for hours now!

Interviewer:

As the accused, you have the right to have a lawyer present during the interview. Do you wish to have a lawyer present, or shall we continue? I have a few supplementary questions.

Witness:

Of course I will give a statement, but I have most certainly not killed Brede Ziegler. It's the cat you really want to know about, isn't it? I did the whole block a favor, the day I took the poor creature's life. It was the best thing for everybody.

Interviewer:

How did you kill the cat, then?

Witness:

Arsenic. I use it for the rats in the basement too. Extremely effective, if I may say so.

Interviewer:

Arsenic?! *(Extremely loud voice.)* Surely none of your doctors have given you arsenic?

Witness:

You wouldn't believe you were a member of the police force. You don't get arsenic from doctors – you get it from a vet. You just have to say you're looking after a horse and that its coat's a bit dull, and hey presto: you get some arsenic. The pharmacy at Ås is absolutely first-class.

Interviewer:

That's a piece of unusually interesting information. We'll come back to that later. But I'd like to go back to Brede Ziegler. Have you, or have you not, sent Brede Ziegler threatening letters, signed Iron Fist? I would remind you that this is a serious situation, Mrs. Helmersen.

Witness:

No, do you know what? I have admitted killing the cat – that's all I have to say. Now I want to go home. I'm an old lady, you can't go on tormenting me in this way!

Interviewer:

Does that mean you no longer wish to give a statement?

Witness:

Not another word will pass my lips! I want to go home. I'm getting treatment and I want to take my herbal tea.

Interviewer:

Unfortunately that's not possible. You have the charge in front of
you. As you see, it states on that sheet of paper that this is a decision to take you into custody. We are going to put you in the
custody suite until we have searched your home. The police consider there to be a danger of contamination of evidence. When
we have gone through your apartment, we will decide whether
you can be released. I'm sorry, but I have to take you down to the
custody suite now, Mrs. Helmersen. *(Commotion, witness
repeats several times, "Do you know what?")*

*Interviewer's note: The interview ended at 14.50. The witness
was served coffee and water during the interview. The interview was interrupted several times in order to consult a
lawyer. The accused was led down to the custody suite. The
interviewer will ensure that the accused receives any necessary medical attention, as she has indicated that she requires
medical treatment. A patrol car has been sent to the accused's
residence in order to conduct the search.*

52

It was as if a curse lay on Grandfather's books. Daniel had spent the weekend sorting them into some kind of system. With each title he touched, he felt his grandfather's eyes on his neck. Though the old man had gambled away all his possessions, the books had obviously been sacrosanct. It must have been very tempting for the old man to cash in some of his leather-bound assets. Especially when the debt began to creep up to the chimney of the house where his children had grown up, and where his wife had cultivated the garden into a delightful, successful botanical masterpiece. It had taken her more than thirty years. The buyer of the property was a developer who had reduced both house and garden to rubble in order to fire up a row of four detached houses.

Daniel had made up his mind.

He stood just inside the door of Ringstrøms' antiquarian bookshop. The vinyl record department was on his right. Daniel could go to the Beatles section, pick out the *White Album*, buy the disc, and go home with Grandfather's two books tucked under his arm. Once again he had made a choice.

A man with well-worn jeans appeared behind a curtain at the far end of the premises. The handwritten sign with 'No Admittance for Customers' was about to detach from the thick curtain. The man looked as though he had hardly been out of this place for his entire life. His complexion was sallow and he did not seem to mind that the ribbed cuffs of his sweater were unraveling.

The shop assistant glanced indifferently at Daniel before serving an old lady who was looking for Garborg's *Peasant Students*. Daniel continued to stand, at a loss, watching them both. Once the woman had shuffled off with her book buried deep inside a capacious wheeled shopper, there were no other customers left in the shop.

"And you, sir," the man said in a friendly tone. "How can I help you?"

"I've got a couple of books," Daniel mumbled, aware he was blushing. "I just wondered if ... I thought I might ... The value. How much are they worth?"

"Let me see them, then."

Daniel fished out the flat box propped against the back of his rucksack to avoid damage. He lifted the lid with care and unwrapped the top book from its plastic cover.

"Here," he said softly.

"Aha, yes."

The shop assistant drew his glasses from their perch on top of his head. His hands were long, with narrow, practiced fingers that trailed over the immaculate binding.

"*Farthest North*," he said chattily, mostly to himself. "From 1897. Lovely little book. Very handsome copy. It is actually ..."

He dried up. The book he held in his hand was number eight in a numbered special edition of 100 books. The shop assistant was well acquainted with this series, but had never seen any examples. When he found the dedication, he squinted at Daniel, before he looked down again and read: "To Hjalmar Johansen, with sincere thanks for courageously joining the expedition. Fridtjof Nansen."

Daniel stared at the book, as if he had only just discovered it and didn't quite understand to whom it belonged.

"Let me see the other one," the shop assistant said brusquely, almost snatching the book underneath.

"*The Road Leads On*," he said harshly. "Knut Hamsun, 1933. Beautiful specimen. Let's see what sort of inscription you've come up with here, then!"

Although the shop assistant seemed rather angry for some reason – his nostrils vibrated slightly and a mauve patch had begun to spread under each eye – his hands were soft, almost loving, as he handled the book.

"Herr Imperial Commissioner Josef Terboven; accept this book, with thanks and hope for help in the future. Nørholm, January 1941. Knut Hamsun."

Daniel smiled timidly.

"Are you aware what you have done?" the shop assistant bellowed, brandishing the book in the air, as if he were thinking of slapping Daniel with it.

"Done?"

"You've ruined an absolutely magnificent first edition with these scribblings of yours! And where did you get these books, in point of fact? Eh?"

"I have … It was my grandfather who …"

Daniel was sweating. The odor of dust and books made him want to sneeze, but he did not dare, and he had to sniff loudly instead.

"Amateur!" the man barked. "Hamsun would have written a greeting like that in German! He spoke excellent German, and in January 1941 he had just been to see Terboven to ask for—"

All of a sudden, he fell silent. He opened the book again and held the dedication up to his eyes while tilting the page in the light from the ceiling lamp. Daniel felt the perspiration streaming from his armpits, and his nose tickled unbearably. He sneezed loudly, several times over. His nose was running, and he wiped it with the sleeve of his sweater. The shop assistant slammed the Hamsun book shut, picked up *Farthest North*, and scrutinized it also for several minutes. His voice was totally different when he finally exclaimed: "These books are worth a small fortune, young man. Please wait for a moment, and I'll fetch some of the necessary paperwork."

Daniel could barely breathe. He rooted around in his rucksack to find his asthma medication. He must have left his inhaler at home, and he found it increasingly difficult to draw breath. The man was taking a long time. Daniel wanted to leave, he needed air. The dust was coating his mouth and throat, making it completely impossible to inhale in anything other than short gasps. However, the shop assistant had taken Grandfather's books with him. Daniel needed to get them back and he forced out a hoarse: "Hello! I must … have … my books … back."

Only when two uniformed police officers came into sight in the doorway did Daniel understand why it was all taking so much time. The shop assistant stepped forward at last from the inner recesses and handed the books over to one of the policemen.

"There have to be limits," he said indignantly as Daniel was led out to the waiting patrol car. "I'm not *so* easily fooled, you know!"

53

"There you are!"

Annmari Skar sat on her own in the canteen. A Christmas tree that might well have been from last year was leaning sadly over the chair opposite. Someone had amused himself by filling the decorative baskets at the top with condoms. Others had gone to the bother of drawing faces with Tippex on the red baubles; one of them looked remarkably like the Police Chief.

"I've been looking everywhere for you!"

Silje Sørensen brushed spruce branches and needles off the chair and sat immediately opposite the Police Prosecutor.

"You simply won't believe what I've got to tell you. I can't find Billy T., but this is so important that—"

"Not another one," Annmari Skar sighed in dismay.

"Another one?"

"Forget it. For the moment. What's it about?"

Wiping her mouth, she pushed the rest of the unappetizing omelet away and grimaced into her cup.

"This coffee is bad enough when it's freshly made. At this time—"

"Sindre Sand is really up shit creek," Silje Sørensen broke in. "I've just done an interview with him, in the old way, that is – I just can't wait for … It takes so long with these printouts and … He's lied about …"

She took a breath and chuckled.

"So," she began over again. "I have interviewed Sindre Sand. That earlier statement of his leaks like a sieve."

"I see."

Annmari Skar gave herself a neck massage.

"There's a hole in his alibi! Like a barn door. It's totally absurd that we haven't discovered it before now. I have ..."

She thrust the interview sheet at the Police Prosecutor. One minute later the interest shown by her opposite number had increased considerably.

"Had he near enough *forgotten* that he left the NRK studios for more than half an hour?"

"He claims a maximum of twenty minutes. Others say about an hour. As you see, they had a break in the filming. He jumped on to his Vespa to buy some cigarettes at the gas station in Suhms gate. There he apparently met an old pal from his schooldays who—"

"Whose name he doesn't remember, of course," Annmari said, smiling faintly. "We've heard this story a few times, haven't we?"

"The first name, then. Lars. Or Petter. 'Or something like that,' according to him."

Silje laughed uproariously and added: "He said it was so embarrassing not to remember his name that he didn't like to ask. They were in parallel classes at elementary school. We'll check it out, of course, but that takes time. I thought first we could get some useful information from the CCTV footage at the gas station, but that only shows Sindre entering at twenty to eleven and leaving again two minutes later. This alleged friend of his must have been standing outside that area. However that may be, all the same ..."

"... Sindre Sand has a barn door in his alibi."

Annmari Skar swept her dark hair behind her ears. Silje noticed for the first time that the dour Police Prosecutor was pretty. There was a touch of something un-Norwegian about her: big brown eyes and Latin coloring. Silje cocked her head and continued hesitantly: "Though it does seem excessively cold-blooded to buy cigarettes before you go to kill a guy, and then head back to a TV recording nonetheless ..."

"The person who murdered Brede Ziegler may well have been cold-blooded," Annmari Skar said pointedly. "But you've got more here!"

Her eyebrows rose slightly as she browsed the interview report. Silje observed a scar above Annmari's eye: it gave her brow an unfortunate tilt that made her look anxious rather than actually surprised.

"This is really good, Silje," she said gravely.

Silje Sørensen beamed. It had been Hanne Wilhelmsen who had whispered in her ear that it might be worth taking a closer look at Sindre Sand.

"Not that I think he's actually done it," she had said with a shrug on Friday evening. "But I've read his interview notes a few times. And it *stinks*. Far too much of a smart-ass. Far too cock-sure. If you've got time at the weekend, and don't mind working for nothing, then check that guy out. While we're waiting for Tussi, anyway. Good police work is keeping all possibilities open. Remember that, Silje!"

Silje had nothing against unpaid work. After a half-hearted attempt to get hold of Billy T. on Saturday morning, she had got cracking without his say-so. After two days of investigating on her own, which had mainly consisted of phoning people they had already spoken to, her conscience was far less troublesome. Billy T. would only have stopped her. If for no other reason, then out of consideration for the overtime budget. Silje could not care less about budgets. The nausea was no longer bothering her. On the contrary, she had felt on top of the world on Sunday evening when she had written a special report of five pages, with nine appendices, neatly printed out and placed in a green folder with a meticulously handwritten list of contents. She had run her hand gently over the green paper and laughed out loud. Silje Sørensen liked being in the police. She enjoyed it hugely and fell into a deep sleep when she finally got home and stumbled into bed beside her increasingly anxious husband. Fortunately he did not realize that she had set the alarm for four o'clock.

Sindre Sand had not only lied about his movements on the evening of Sunday December 5. The man at the gas station might well exist. It was precisely such things that witnesses had a sorry tendency to forget. Fair enough. In itself.

What was worse for the young man was that he had been observed in Brede Ziegler's company on Saturday evening.

"A number of places!"

Annmari Skar smacked her hand on her forehead.

"How did this get past us? How the *hell* did we manage to overlook this?"

"Don't you remember what Hanne Wilhelmsen said when we—"

Annmari peered at Silje in displeasure.

"Hanne says so many things," she said crossly. "You should be careful with that lady, Silje. She's not all good, in fact."

"But she is good."

Annmari did not answer.

"Honestly," Silje said in an unusually loud voice. "Don't you see that you're being manipulated by Billy T.? What has Hanne Wilhelmsen actually done to you?"

"Forget it."

"No! I'm *pissed off* with everybody going around treating Hanne as if she had … AIDS or something. I'm not so stupid that I don't understand that she and Billy T. have some kind of unfinished business, but that doesn't have anything to do with the rest of us!"

"Everybody falls for Hanne Wilhelmsen," Annmari Skar said. "Everybody gets a little ..."

She hesitated. Suddenly her face opened out into an unfamiliar smile.

"Everybody quite simply falls a bit in love with her."

"In love!"

Silje felt hot and cold in turn, and began to rise from her seat.

"Yes, in love," Annmari said obstinately. "Hanne Wilhelmsen is outstandingly clever. From a purely police point of view, I mean. Maybe the best. What's more, she has a special flair for impressing the youngest members of the force. They feel privileged, flattered even. It's as if the queen herself had—"

"I'll tell you one thing, Prosecutor Skar!"

Silje had stood up to her full height now, and leaned across the table as she used the heels of her hands to support herself.

"I'm a happily married and, into the bargain, *pregnant* woman. I love my husband and feel nothing, and I emphasize *nothing* ..."

The table reverberated as she smacked it. The glass bauble that looked like the Police Chief wobbled in terror, and a canteen employee, about to lift a tray with used coffee cups, suddenly stopped in his tracks.

"You are totally ... You are ..."

She straightened her back. All of a sudden she felt exhausted. Nausea coursed through her body and she swallowed audibly.

"... old," she added. "You are quite simply too old, Annmari."

"I'm not forty yet."

They both turned to the cleaning operative, as if at a secret signal. He stood, open-mouthed, with the tray in his hands. Annmari burst out laughing. She laughed loudly, and then louder, for a long time. Silje stared in consternation at her and seemed uncertain whether or not to sit down again. Her back was aching, and she sank back on to the chair.

"Sorry," Annmari said in the end. "But you don't know Billy T. the way I do. He was so shattered when Hanne left. Totally destroyed. Did you know, for instance, that she was to be best woman at his wedding, but didn't get in touch with him at all? He waited an incredibly long time. The day before he was to marry, he asked his sister instead."

Silje shook her head slowly and held up her hands, as if reluctant to hear any more.

"You are right," Annmari repeated. "It's none of our business. But it's more difficult for me than it is for you. Okay? Fine. And what was it she said, in fact?"

"Said? Who?"

"Hanne. You started this ball rolling by saying she was the one who—"

"Oh yes. Yes. She said that we had stared at Sunday the fifth until we went blind. That we should have been more scrupulous about Saturday and Friday and Thursday ... About the week, and weeks, prior to the murder. We weren't. Not until Hanne came back. That's why we didn't get this information before now."

She pointed at the closed folder.

"I considered applying for a blue form tonight. But then I decided to take a perhaps slightly original approach."

Embarrassed, she looked away, as if she had been guilty of gross neglect of duty.

"I phoned Sindre Sand this morning at five o'clock and asked him to come for interview."

"You did what?"

"Is that forbidden?"

"No."

Annmari Skar fiddled with her coffee cup.

"So he came then," Silje went on lightly. "And there we sat. He did not admit to seeing Brede on Saturday evening until I had laid it on thick. It's a bit hazy as to where and why, but ... He has lied about Vilde as well, and I had to—"

"Listen," Annmari Skar said, looking at her watch. "Now I really *must* go. But I promise I'll ... Where is he now?"

"Round the back. I thought you could write me a blue form and then—"

"I'll tell you something," Annmari said, leaning over the table.

The cleaner had taken his tray and disappeared. Silje and Annmari were on their own in the huge canteen. From the kitchen they could hear distant sounds of a dishwasher and utensils being returned to their places.

"At the moment our back office is looking like an overheated waiting room for various witnesses in this Ziegler case."

"What do you mean?"

Annmari took out a list from her jacket pocket and read out: "Claudio Gagliostro: *Criminal Procedure Act*, section 233, cf. section twenty-nine. Plus 257, alternatively 317."

She glanced up from the paper, producing a pair of reading glasses from her handbag as she explained.

"Attempted homicide and theft, alternatively handling stolen goods. Vilde Veierland Ziegler: *Road Traffic Act*, section twenty-one, cf. section twenty-two, cf. section thirty-one. Driving under the influence, in other words. Tussi Gruer Helmersen: section ..."

Slapping down on the table the list of the people arrested that day, she rolled her eyes.

"That lady, in any case, is off her rocker. Your friend ... Sorry, Hanne ... She just shakes her head and says, to be on the safe side, we should go through her apartment, but that the old hag is probably just trying to make herself seem interesting. In the meantime, she's sitting round the back on a fairly contrived charge, but what the hell are we going to do when—"

"Are all these people in custody? What on earth has happened? Sindre Sand, Claudio, Vilde, and—"

"And that Tussi-character of theirs. I've got a headache at the thought of tomorrow. We can hardly present them all for jailing at the same time, of course. It—"

"But you'll hold Sindre?"

"Yes. I'll hold Sindre. At least in the meantime."

"You're a peach," Silje said, picking up the documents. "I'll put a set of copies on your desk. Bye!"

She dashed off, not noticing that her hair was sprinkled with spruce needles. It was five o'clock on Monday afternoon and she would have to phone Tom to tell him she would not be home for dinner. Not today, either.

54

"No, I fucking won't! I want my shoes!"

One of Hairy Mary's colleagues curled her bare toes on the concrete floor, as if clinging on for dear life. The mink coat from Fretex, the Salvation Army's second-hand outlet, was covered in bald patches. She had already been given the brown carrier bag containing her personal belongings. In her case, this held three packets of condoms and a small photo album. An officer was trying to eject her forcibly from the custody-suite reception.

"Shoes," she roared, hanging on stubbornly. "I want my shoes!"

A man was hunched over the red guard-rail, throwing up.

"Fucking pig," the Custody Sergeant spluttered.

It seemed the staff were losing control. Hanne Wilhelmsen touched her ears and leaned over the counter.

"Is there nobody who can give this woman a pair of shoes? She's going to freeze to death!"

She knew the Duty Sergeant as a level-headed man. Now he threw his clipboard on the floor and raged, "This is *not* a branch of the Salvation Army, Chief Inspector! That woman had no shoes on when she came here, and she's not getting any shoes now that she's leaving. Understood?"

He bellowed at the officer who still had hold of the fur-clad hooker.

"Get that bloody old bag out of here! And you ..." He took a breath and directed his index finger straight at Hanne Wilhelmsen, as if thinking of shooting her: "Please don't poke your nose into my business! This is not a damn custody suite any more, it's hell's waiting room on the devil's day off!"

The eruption helped. He ran his hand over his bald pate and muttered something inaudible, before dropping his voice and adding, in a discouraged tone: "Hanne, can't you calm down that prisoner of yours in number seven? She's causing a riot in there."

Hanne decided it was more important to stay on good terms with the Duty Sergeant than to find shoes for a frozen prostitute. When the massive iron door between reception and the custody suite opened, she was assailed by noise and smells. A sweaty young custody officer, obviously on the verge of tears, squeezed past Hanne as if he had spotted the opportunity to flee at last.

Five hours in a bare cell had left its mark on Tussi Gruer Helmersen. Her lipstick had bled into her wrinkles, forming a red star pattern around her narrow lips. The lilac turban had been used as a handkerchief and was smeared with black make-up stains. Mixed remains of mascara, eyeliner, and shadow had congealed below her eyes.

"Friends!" she screamed in falsetto with her face pressed against the bars on the door. "Guilty and innocent! Let us unite in a common …"

Although she could not see her audience, they responded with emphatic noises. Some begged for quiet. Others joined in with cheers of encouragement. One guy who was absolutely smashed messed his pants and had a great time describing his artistic efforts. At the far end of the corridor, a deep bass note could be heard, rhythmic and repeated: "Fucking cops. Fucking cops."

Once Hanne Wilhelmsen had let herself into Tussi's cell, the old woman ceased the political pleas to her fellow-prisoners.

"You have to let me out of here," she whispered in despair. "This is too much for me. Please, Mrs. Policewoman!"

Hanne explained that they were only waiting for one or two interviews with her neighbors.

"It'll soon be over, Mrs. Helmersen. An hour or so, and then you'll certainly get permission to leave."

"An hour—"

"On condition that you sit nicely on that bunk there and keep quiet for a while."

Tussi shuffled across the concrete floor and sat erect with her hands on her lap. Her eyes were hopelessly confused, and Hanne faltered slightly as she locked the cell door behind her. It should be against the law to arrest old people.

Children too, she thought when she glanced into the next cell.

The boy was adult enough, at least physically. The face that turned to her made her stop all the same. The boy must be about twenty. He was weeping silently.

"What's your name?" Hanne asked, without knowing why.

"Daniel Åsmundsen," he sobbed, wiping his runny nose with his sleeve. "Can you help me?"

"What kind of help do you need?"

"Can you phone someone for me?"

"Phone someone," Hanne repeated, looking around for a custody officer. "You have the right to let your family know you've been arrested. Has nobody told you that?"

"No."

He sniffed and rose stiffly from the concrete bunk. He seemed unsure whether he was allowed to cross to the cell door.

"I'll call your parents," Hanne said crisply. "What's their name? Have you got a phone number for me?"

"No!"

The boy was right beside the door. Hanne saw that she had been mistaken about his age; the boy must be nearer twenty-five.

He had big blue eyes in a round face, but a five o'clock shadow was conspicuous on his jaw.

"Don't phone my mother! Phone … If you could phone my aunt, Idun Franck. Her phone number is two-two—"

"Idun Franck? Do you know …? Is Idun Franck your aunt?"

"Yes. Do you know her?"

The boy attempted the suggestion of a smile. Hanne unlocked the cell door and took Daniel Åsmundsen with her through the crossfire of shouts and shrieks from the other prisoners. Now they all had aunts they wanted her to phone.

"I'm taking number eight with me for interview," she said brusquely to the Duty Sergeant.

"Take ten of them, for all I care," he replied, turning to a trainee officer. "Where the hell is that duty psychiatrist?"

The shoeless hooker was still standing in the middle of the floor, screaming for footwear. She had scraped her toes on the floor until they bled. Officers walked round her in wide body-swerves. She had become part of the furniture, an awkward pillar in the middle of the floor and a hindrance to them all, but no one now felt compelled to do anything about it.

"Here," Hanne said. "Take mine."

She pulled off her own boots, the Texan ones with silver spurs and heel studs.

"Thanks," the woman in the fur coat murmured, taken aback. "These are brilliant, by the way!"

She pulled them on with a strenuous effort and smiled triumphantly at the Duty Sergeant behind the counter. He did not even look in her direction. The woman gave a sigh of contentment and trudged out into the night, just before Christmas, with a brown paper bag under her arm, proudly holding her head up high. Hardly anyone noticed her disappear.

55

Hanne Wilhelmsen had not really envisaged Idun Franck's apartment as it appeared late on the evening of Monday December 20, 1999. When the publishing editor had been interviewed five days earlier, her clothes had been in matching colors, her hair clean and shining; there was altogether something delicately attractive about the middle-aged woman. Moreover she had, despite the unpleasant line of questioning, conveyed a mental strength that underscored her appeal.

The Christmas cactus at the window would have been better suited to the desert. It hung sadly with its bushy head, surrounded by faded dried flowers. The air in the apartment was stuffy and there was a fair sprinkling of dirty clothes all over the place. Idun Franck had a hectic flush on her cheeks when Hanne and Silje Sørensen ascended the stairs to the second floor. She had obviously used the few seconds from the time they had rung the doorbell until they arrived at the door to remove the worst of the mess. There was still a dirty cup on the coffee table. The ashtray smelled foul and should have been emptied two days earlier.

"Have a seat," Idun Franck said, looking glumly at the living room without making any move to lift the voluminous handbag from one chair or the stack of newspapers from the other.

Hanne and Silje sat side by side on the settee.

"Coffee?" Idun Franck suddenly blurted out and disappeared into the kitchen.

"Won't it take far too long?" Silje whispered. "Coffee, I mean."

She scratched her stomach.

"Unfortunately, I don't have any milk," Idun Franck said in a loud voice as she placed three cups on the table. "I didn't manage to do any shopping on the way home today. Now there's only eleven days to go."

"Eleven days?"

Hanne Wilhelmsen picked up a copy of Unni Lindell's *The Dream Catcher* from the sideboard and leafed aimlessly through it.

"Till the end of the world," Idun Franck said, laughing. "If we're to believe these prophets of doom. Maybe we shouldn't. Have you read it?"

Hanne shook her head.

"No. I don't have time for that sort of thing."

"I've often wondered whether police officers read crime fiction," Idun Franck said; there was a different tone in her voice now, a strained inflection that made her sound younger. "Or whether you get enough of that stuff at work. What is it you want actually?"

Silje picked up the empty cup and rotated it between her hands. The coffee machine gurgled loudly from the kitchen and they could just hear the strains of "O Holy Night" from the neighbor's apartment below.

"Jussi Björling," she said softly.

"Are we to talk about Jussi Björling?"

Without waiting for a response, Idun disappeared into the kitchen again.

"There's not much Christmas spirit here," Silje said in a hushed voice. "It's sometimes a bit untidy in our house, but not so ..."

She ran a finger over the coffee table.

"... *filthy!*"

Three of the walls in the living room were covered in bookcases from floor to ceiling, wall-to-wall. Nevertheless there was barely space for them all; beside the door to the small balcony there were three tall piles of excess books.

"Books create dust," Hanne said, shrugging; she thought in alarm about what her own apartment had looked like when Nefis had arrived on Friday night.

"Here," Idun Franck said, pouring. "No milk, sorry, as I said. Sugar?"

She lifted the bundle of newspapers and sat down.

"I see you have lots of books," Hanne said, looking round with a smile. "Are any of them valuable?"

"Do you mean from a purely literary point of view? Yes, definitely."

Idun smiled wanly and waved her right hand apologetically.

"*Mea Culpa*. No, I probably own a few copies that might raise a couple of thousand kroner at auction. No more than that."

Hanne raised her backside and produced a yellow note from her pocket.

"Is there anyone else in your family who collects books? I mean really valuable books? Antiquarian."

Idun Franck obviously apprehended very little. Her face showed traces of genuine astonishment, quite a different expression from the strained, watchful gaze with which she had greeted them.

"My father," she ventured tentatively. "He had an extremely valuable collection. We don't really know exactly *how* valuable, but it's probably worth many hundred thousand kroner. If not more. It's Daniel, my nephew, who—"

She closed off the remainder of the sentence by fiercely biting her bottom lip. A faint blush grew visible above her low-necked sweater.

"It's actually Daniel we've come to talk about," Hanne said lightly, smiling.

"Daniel? *Daniel?*"

Idun held her cup tightly without lifting it to her mouth.

"Has something happened to Daniel? Where is he? Is he—"

All of a sudden there were tears in her eyes and her lips were quivering.

"Relax," Hanne said, and it crossed her mind that this reaction was excessively protective for an aunt. "Daniel's fit as a fiddle."

Silje pulled out two transparent bags marked "Evidence 1" and "Evidence 2" from a voluminous handbag.

"Did these belong to your father?" Hanne asked as Silje placed the books neatly side by side on the table, as if they were being sold to a less-than-enthusiastic purchaser.

Idun Franck shot a brief glance at the packages.

"I do believe so. Can I open them?"

Hanne nodded and, taking the books out of their bags, Silje handed them to Idun.

"The Hamsun has a singular background," she said, closing the book. "My father was a Supreme Court advocate. He defended Justice Minister Riisnæs at his trial for treason. The man was absolutely stark staring mad and was found criminally insane. As far as I know, he remained in Reitgjerdet Psychiatric Hospital until the seventies. He gave my father that book in '46. We never found out how he himself had laid hands on it. We've never been in any doubt that it was valuable. In fact, my father was slightly doubtful about whether he should keep it. It might even be stolen. But ..."

She shrugged.

"... it's so long ago now. This one here ..."

Gingerly, she opened *Farthest North*.

"Yes. My father bought this when I was a young girl. A long time ago as well. Time marches on."

Her smile was deferential, but her shoulders had slumped. She seemed relieved in a way, without daring to show it.

"Then everything's perfectly all right," Hanne said, slapping her thighs. "Daniel was hauled in when he tried to sell these books today. However ..."

She held out her arms and gave Idun Franck a broad smile.

"Now that you've confirmed that Daniel has neither attempted to sell stolen goods nor tried his hand at forgery, then we're the ones who owe him a substantial apology."

"Is Daniel ...? Have you *arrested* Daniel?"

"Relax. Just a little misunderstanding. I'll go straight to police headquarters now and release your nephew."

Hanne and Silje had gone out to the hallway before Idun Franck said anything more.

"Is it usual—" she asked, and broke off. "When you've done something like this, arresting a young man for—"

"Theft, receiving, and/or criminal deception," Hanne helped her out.

"Exactly. Do you send out two officers to question witnesses so late in the evening? Usually, I mean?"

"Service," Hanne said curtly. "The boy doesn't have a record. It's absurd for him to spend time locked up with us in the midst of the Christmas rush for something he hasn't done."

"But couldn't you ..." Hanne nudged Silje, and they had both already reached the next landing when they faintly heard her continue: "... just have phoned?"

Neither of them answered, but once they were out in the street, Hanne punched the air in annoyance.

"Shit! I forgot something!"

She pressed the intercom button.

"Has Daniel spent a lot of money lately?" she asked when Idun finally answered.

"No ... Daniel is very careful with money. But he did splash out on a trip to Paris for me a few months ago. He said he had been saving for a long time to give me an extra-special present. It was just the two of us, and we had such a ..."

Idun Franck broke down in tears. The sound turned into dull crackling over the intercom, and Hanne muttered a half-hearted excuse, before running after Silje.

"The woman's blubbering," Hanne said morosely as she wound her scarf an extra turn around her neck.

"I can well understand it," Silje said. "I agree with her. What really was the reason for us to go storming into her home ... Two of us! You could just have phoned, Hanne. It was no big deal."

She looked askance at her colleague.

"You promised me you'd look at everything I've got on Sindre Sand," she said. "You said you'd look at it tonight. It's quite amazing, he—"

"Annmari said he would be brought to court tomorrow."

"Yes! You're going to—"

"We'll wait," Hanne said, putting her arm around Silje's shoulders. "If he's to be brought to court, then you've had a response and you don't need my opinion, do you? Okay?"

Silje Sørensen wriggled free.

"No," she said, offended. "It's not okay at all. We could have spent this past hour on ... I can't fathom why we had to waste valuable time on—"

"There's something about Idun Franck," Hanne interrupted again. "Or perhaps—"

She stopped abruptly. They had entered the park west of Oslo Prison, south of police headquarters. A thick snowfall had cloaked the previous day's open muddy expanse. Hanne scanned the prison wall and her eyes did not pause until she caught sight of the back steps where Brede Ziegler had been found murdered fifteen days earlier.

"Or ..."

Silje had stopped. Hunching her shoulders against the cold and shuffling her feet, she gave a lengthy yawn.

"Maybe it's really Daniel there's something about," Hanne said. "Something or other. I just can't work out what it is. If … I'll race you!"

They ran, laughing, stumbling, and jostling each other, throwing snow and tripping up all the way, until Silje slapped her mitten on the metal doors into Oslo Police District Headquarters.

"I'm getting old," Hanne complained, gasping for breath. "You go home! I never want to see you again!"

Daniel was released before midnight. He did not call his aunt or his mother before he went to bed. As he fell asleep, it dawned on him that his grandfather's books had been left behind at police headquarters. He could pick them up tomorrow. He was not going to be able to sell any of them, anyway.

At five o'clock in the morning he was awakened by his own sobbing.

56

Hairy Mary did not come crawling back, she arrived limping. It was far beyond her comprehension that Hanne could make such a fuss over a measly syringe.

"I don't deal with shit," she muttered, shuffling on toward Lille Tøyen all the same.

It was a long way from Bankplassen to Hanne's apartment. Hairy Mary had no money for a taxi. Her welfare remittance was delayed, which is to say that the payment form was drifting between addresses she had left behind long ago. It was early on Monday evening. The two nights she had spent in the open had been harder to bear than any Hairy Mary could bring to mind. On Saturday night she had located a heating duct behind the garbage at a gas station at about five o'clock in the morning. She had hallucinated about clean sheets and hot food, and for the first time in her life had been really scared of dying. That syringe in the bathroom at Hanne's had been a mistake. Next time she would take care to go down to the basement. The key hung on a hook behind the front door, inside a key cupboard in the shape of a little house with a picture of a padlock on the front. Hairy Mary had already been into the store room, where she had helped herself to a pair of winter boots, but only to borrow. They were too big, and after almost three days outside she might just as well have padded about in a pair of pumps. It was not yet nine o'clock at night. The traffic was abominable in Bankplassen. Fathers were still dillydallying about with wives and children doing Christmas shopping, and it was too early for inebriated partygoers keen to round off their festivities with a cheap shag. Some young girls had commandeered her corner. Hairy Mary didn't have the energy to argue. She was struggling to focus; it was difficult to make out whether there were three or four of them.

"No way do I deal with shit," Hairy Mary said angrily, panting for breath as, fishing out the key from her bra, she let herself in.

Making herself at home, she headed for the kitchen and opened the fridge. A bowl of black olives made her pull a face. Her gaze continued to run over the contents until she spotted a side of salmon that made her mouth, with the lamentable stubs of teeth, salivate.

After almost forty-five years on drugs, Hairy Mary's child-hood memories had vanished into a gray mist. The only thing she really remembered was the family who had looked after her from when she was seven until she was nine. They owned a smokehouse. Mummy Samuelsen was kind and round as a barrel. She had dentures bought in Tromsø and an ample lap, and had taken on four illegitimate children, for lack of any of her own. In the evenings, when Daddy Samuelsen came into the living room and filled it with the heavy aroma of smoked salmon, he had tossed the salmon skins into a frying pan on the open fire in the hearth. The children were allowed to eat their fill of crispy fish skins and oily salmon, and washed it down with hot chocolate. Hairy Mary had taught herself to read and write. Daddy Samuelsen had roared with laughter and clapped his hands when the wee girl had corrected his accounts with a copying pencil; her blue lips had smiled in delight and she got two caramels for her trouble.

Then Mummy Samuelsen had died, and the children had to leave. Daddy Samuelsen had made a fuss, but the authorities would not relent. Hairy Mary had experienced two good years in her life, from the age of seven until two days before her ninth birthday.

Hairy Mary piled the salmon, four potatoes, two eggs, one onion, and half a cup of crème fraiche on the kitchen worktop. She was still wearing the synthetic fur coat. And she was still freezing like a dog.

"Blabbermouth," she muttered when she caught sight of Nefis in the doorway.

"Hello. How are you?"

Hairy Mary merely shook her head. It had been a sheer stroke of luck that no one had been home when she arrived. She had hoped to get fed and maybe heated before being ejected again. Pleasures were things that came and went in Hairy Mary's life, and never lasted long.

"Fortune gives and fortune takes away," she said, deciding to pretend that nothing was amiss.

The lady sat down at the kitchen table. Hairy Mary turned her back on her and rattled pots and pans without forcing the darkie woman to retreat. The fish skin sizzled in the butter in the pan. Hairy Mary poured milk into a pot and found cocoa powder in a top cupboard. She cracked two eggs into the strips of salmon skin.

"Smells good," Nefis commented.

"What does the woman want? She's not getting any. Brazen hussy!"

Hairy Mary smirked at the eggs and scooped a mountain of potato salad and three pieces of fish sprinkled with crisply fried skin on the plate, before crowning it all with two fried eggs. When she sat down to eat, Nefis left the kitchen. The food was delicious: the best Hairy Mary had tasted since she was nine years old, short of two days.

"And I made it all myself," she sighed in contentment, dozing off with food in her mouth.

"Fuck!" she mumbled when Nefis came back, waking her.

The sleeve of the faux-fur coat was in the middle of the potato salad. Nefis took a firm hold of her and escorted her out to the bathroom, where she began to strip off Hairy Mary's clothes.

"But you're not making me into a dyke," Hairy Mary protested, sinking naked into the bathtub.

The bubbles covered her up to her neck. She noticed an unfamiliar warmth, quite different from the sensation heroin gave her. She closed her eyes, but opened them again when it had obviously not entered the shameless woman's head to make herself scarce. She was sorting clothes. Suddenly she held up a pair of soft jeans to her. Hairy Mary nodded apathetically. She did not understand any of it, but the lady could do what she wanted as long as she left her in peace. Now it was a blouse Nefis was showing her. Hairy Mary nodded and smiled lamely, before shutting her eyes again.

"What about this?"

Hairy Mary raised one eyelid. Nefis was showing her a beautiful set of underwear. The bra was lacy and the high-cut panties snowy-white.

"Yesss," Hairy Mary said, finally understanding the woman's intentions.

Nefis pointed at the pile of Hairy Mary's dirty clothing on the floor and let her finger wander across to the washing machine.

"Wash," she said, using exaggerated mouth movements as she spoke. "Tomorrow: Shopping!"

Shopping. At last a word that meant something. Christmas had come early this year, and Hairy Mary smiled happily as Nefis triumphantly held up the outfit they had decided upon: elegant designer jeans, mauve blouse with gray sweater on top, and underneath, the whitest underwear in the world. Nefis shot a glance at the fake-fur jacket on the floor. The corner of a silk scarf was protruding from the sleeve.

"Nice. Same color as the blouse."

The scarf was green and mauve, a perfect match.

Hairy Mary looked at Nefis, captivated. The bath was warm. The water was clean and smelled of summer. She wanted to put on the new clothes at once, but didn't have the strength to move. Instead she lifted her gaze to Nefis's face. Nefis was the prettiest woman Hairy Mary had ever seen. At least since, two days away from turning nine years of age, she had been forced to leave Daddy Samuelsen. That was so long ago. That was another life entirely, and Hairy Mary regretted that Nefis had not got to taste any of the food.

"A-i lo-ove yew," she said in a low voice.

It was Hairy Mary's very first sentence in English. She was sure this was the right thing to say to her new friend.

57

When Judge Bengt Lund entered the crowded courtroom at Oslo Courthouse on Tuesday December 21 at 13.27 precisely, it seemed as if the journalists had decided to do a Mexican wave. Behind the low barrier dividing the few public benches from the courtroom itself, the sweaty media representatives were packed like sardines in a tin. It was making a virtue of necessity when they all stood up together, in order to be able to show the administrator of justice the deference he demanded.

Judge Lund did not raise his eyes. Instead, staring intently at the recessed computer screen on the table, he discreetly cleared his throat and read in a loud, ponderous voice: "Oslo Courthouse hereby decrees: this hearing will take place behind closed doors. I will permit photographs for three minutes before closing the doors. Meanwhile I will leave the room. Three minutes."

When one of the two defense lawyers, Advocate Osvald Becker, crossed to Annmari Skar, the Police Prosecutor busied herself flicking through the thick folders of documents piled up between her and Billy T.

"Prosecutor," Advocate Becker said loudly, smiling in the flurry of camera flashes. "When was this Tussi Gruer Helmersen released?"

The advocate's voice had a remarkably high pitch. Osvald Becker squeaked: he had eventually become notorious for his annoying, shrill speech. It contrasted strangely with his bulky appearance. Annmari Skar tried to fix her eyes on a neutral point. She found a stain on Becker's dark jacket and replied, unflustered: "Yesterday. At seventeen-thirty. She is above suspicion."

Raising his eyebrows, Advocate Becker turned his face partially toward the journalists, who were busy jotting notes, and the photographers, who for lack of the accused's presence in court were firing off all the film they had on this relatively uninteresting subject.

"Released? Well, well. Good grief!"

His laughter was just as nerve-racking as his voice. He placed one palm brashly on the barrier and used the other to smooth the top of his head.

"So she is above suspicion. Otherwise I would have thought the police were having some fun in this case, by throwing as many suspects as possible into prison. Odd that there's only two brought before the court today. Very odd."

Annmari Skar had never been able to stand the man. Privately, she wished Claudio Gagliostro had an advocate who was not quite so obsessed with posing for the newspapers. Accused number two had been far more fortunate. Advocate Ola Johan Boe had been a permanent defense lawyer in the Supreme Court for years and confined himself to a thoroughly matter-of-fact tone. The man had a gentle manner, though no one harbored any doubts about the alertness in his small, almost twinkling eyes.

Finally the room had emptied of everyone except the court secretary, the two defense counsel, Police Prosecutor Skar, Billy T., and a court functionary who spent the waiting time on replenishing plastic jugs with water. The air was stuffy and depleted, despite the proceedings until now having lasted less than half an hour. The courtroom had no windows. Annmari Skar felt a headache starting. Judge Lund returned, signaling for the participants to remain seated, before sitting down energetically at the judge's table, rolling up his shirt sleeves and getting the formalities out of the way.

"This case represents," said Becker, who had got to his feet without asking for permission to speak, "an investigation the like of which I have never seen in my entire career, and I underline *my entire career*."

He raised his hand dramatically before pressing it to his heart, as if swearing the veracity of his pronouncement.

"I consider there are already grounds to bring to the court's attention that there is reason to direct strong criticism at the police. *Strong* criticism. I must—"

Judge Lund interrupted him.

"Advocate Becker, permit me to warn you now ..."

He drummed his fingers lightly on the table.

"No lengthy speeches, thank you. This court *is* aware of your long career. You refer to it in almost every hearing you have presented to yours truly. Nevertheless, I assume that you, too, were young once upon a time ..."

Annmari exchanged looks with Advocate Boe. She could swear that the eminent older advocate cracked a smile.

"... and so my predecessors may have been spared hearing about the length of your career as an absolute and – if I may say so – fairly irrelevant argument for the benefit of your clients. I also have it on good authority that you're not yet forty years old."

Advocate Boe still had a barely perceptible smile on his lips. Out of loyalty to his unfortunate colleague, however, he asked for latitude for defense lawyers to be permitted the opportunity for criticism of the progress of police work. Judge Lund grunted and turned his face to Annmari.

"With reference to that, Police Prosecutor Skar ..."

His gaze was penetrating, and he seemed almost sarcastic.

"Let me just assure myself that I have read the documents

correctly. There are apparently two accused in the same case. Both are charged with killing the same man, but at different times. Is that how I am to understand the police allegation?"

Annmari Skar never blushed. Now she felt the heat burn underneath her skin. She started to rise, but could not quite make up her mind. She remained on her feet with a strange kink in her hips.

"Accused number two is only charged with attempted," she said in an undertone, blowing at her fringe. "Attempted homicide, I mean. But if the deceased had lived long enough, he would none-theless have died of the first attempt that was not fulfilled because he later, afterwards, the man – the deceased, that is ... He was later ..." She sat down abruptly and continued more succinctly: "I shall come back to that when I go through the petition."

"I sincerely hope so," Judge Lund said curtly. "In fact, I'm looking forward to it. Can we get accused number one, Claudio Gagliostro, up from the basement?"

After a few minutes Claudio entered the courtroom, escorted by two uniformed police officers. He stumbled forward in con-fusion to the witness box, his eyes flickering from side to side. Perspiration ran down his forehead and he panted as if an asthma attack was imminent.

Judge Lund gave him an appraising look, with an expression of friendly interest.

"You are accused of..." he began: and so followed references to various paragraphs at breakneck speed until he glanced up and took off his glasses. "That means you are accused of intention-ally inflicting a fatal stab wound on Brede Ziegler in the area of his heart on the night between December the fifth and sixth of this year. Moreover, that you, in the early hours of the morning of Monday December the twentieth – that is, yesterday – attempted to cause the death of Sebastian Kvie by using physical force to dislodge him from a scaffolding at Bidenkapsgate number two. In addition you are charged with misappropriation and/or handling of an indeterminate quantity of vintage wine."

Nibbling the arm of his glasses, Judge Lund squinted at the prisoner.

"Do you plead guilty or not guilty?"

"My client pleads not guilty, he—"

Advocate Becker was on his feet before Claudio had absorbed the judge's question. Judge Lund did not let him finish and waved his left hand in irritation as he barked: "I assume that your client has the power of speech, Advocate Becker!"

"Innocent!"

Claudio almost shouted. His voice was gravelly and thick, as if he had just woken.

"Not guilty," the judge corrected him, and nodded at the court secretary.

"He *looks* bloody guilty," Billy T. whispered in Annmari Skar's ear. "I'll be damned if I know whether he *is* guilty, but look at him!"

"Cut it out," she snarled back. "Shut up and give me each document I need *before* I need it."

Once the formalities were done and dusted, the Police Prosecutor was given the floor to interrogate the accused. The judge raised his eyebrows slightly when Annmari abstained. She calculated that Claudio's own advocate would do the job for her. That proved correct. Even in response to the simplest and most well-disposed leading question from Advocate Becker, Claudio Gagliostro managed to contradict himself. He stammered, stuttered, and dabbed his forehead. His Norwegian language skills deteriorated steadily, and toward the end of the examination you would think he had arrived in the country only a few months ago. It was as if his entire being was in the process of disintegration.

Bodily fluids poured down his shirt front: snot, tears, and sweat combined into a viscous mess that made Claudio's face shine and the judge blatantly look down at his documents in embarrassment.

"He's probably seen it before," Billy T. muttered, almost inaudible.

He felt uncomfortable himself. Not because he was witness to the painful humiliation of a fellow-human being, but because he did not believe in the guilt of the accused. At least not as far as the murder of Brede Ziegler was concerned. There was too much that did not add up. Claudio Gagliostro was an amoral corner-cutter. He would probably not have had any particular objection to swindling his own brother, if he had one. But murder? Too weak, Billy T. thought as he drank a glass of water. Too weak. Besides, it was Brede who was the actual attraction at Entré. Hardly anyone knew who Claudio Gagliostro was. Although the Italian must have harbored the delusion that he would inherit his partner's share of the restaurant on Brede's death, he would lose on the swings what he gained on the roundabout. Entré was not yet a year old, and even though the place had built up a fantastic reputation in record time, most of that would fall apart without Brede Ziegler's name and presence. Claudio was a swindler. Billy T. was sure of that much. But the guy was far from stupid. And almost certainly no killer.

Annmari Skar thought differently.

"I'm telling the truth," Claudio sobbed, thrusting a soaking ball of tissue at his nose. "I was definitely not at police headquarters that Sunday. I was at home! At home! And this other thing, with Sebastian … It was an accident! *Accidente!*"

The words came out in fits and starts. He gasped for breath and closed his eyes as he turned his face to the ceiling. His Adam's apple danced up and down, and for a moment Billy T. was afraid that the man would choke.

"But, Gagliostro ..."

Judge Lund leafed forward to a document he had obviously marked in advance. He put on his glasses and stared at the Italian in the witness box.

"It appears from the documents that a not inconsiderable sum of money was found in your apartment and seized as evidence. Fourteen thousand two hundred and fifty kroner, to be exact. The fourteen thousand-notes were new and bore consecutive serial numbers. It says here that ..."

He let his stubby finger find the text, and quoted.

"... 'Serial numbers on the fourteen thousand-kroner banknotes found at the accused's apartment on Monday December the twentieth are the subsequent serial numbers to the sixteen thousand-kroner notes found on the body of the deceased, Brede Ziegler, on the night of Sunday December the fifth.' Rather clumsily expressed, you might say, but both you and I understand what the police mean. Do you have an explanation for this, Gagliostro?"

The prisoner experienced a sudden transformation. It was as if he had at last found the strength to pull himself together. Perhaps his body had drained of all fluid. He hoisted his shoulders and leaned forward aggressively. Even his voice seemed more composed: it deepened as his language grew more fluent.

"I see, Your Honor. An ever-so-little case of tax evasion. It happened now and again that Brede or I would withdraw money from the bank. So we would write a false invoice for 'paid cash' ..."

Claudio waved two fingers angrily in the air.

"... and then split the money. I might as well admit that. But I have not, I most certainly have *not* ..."

He slammed both fists down on the witness box. The thump was more powerful than he had intended, and he flinched at his own outburst.

"... killed anyone," he added submissively.

The monetary evidence had been Annmari's ace of trumps the evening before. She had clapped her hands in glee when Klaus Veierød had come breathlessly in to her with the report about the serial numbers on the banknotes. Billy T. had merely shrugged. That two close colleagues both had money obviously withdrawn from the same bank at the same time meant nothing at all. He had mocked the theory that Claudio had murdered Brede in order to help himself to less than half the money his friend had in his possession. Annmari had thrown him out when he insisted that Claudio was a red herring. He was ordered to turn up fit and refreshed at seven o'clock the following morning, *without* that reversed cross in his ear and *with* a tie. That would give him six hours to learn the documents by heart before the remand hearing.

"By heart," she had spluttered three times over and slammed the door behind him.

Billy T. had his own theory about the money. The more he thought about it, the better it seemed. Police Prosecutor Skar could paddle her own canoe. Billy T. might just as well sit as her assistant and puppet in Oslo Courthouse for a few hours. He would spend the night on his own work.

At length Annmari Skar stood up to summarize the police application for a remand in custody. Her voice was always pitched lower than usual when speaking in court. She spoke slowly, as if she imagined that the court secretary was noting every single word she said. She held forth for forty-five minutes. The content demanded barely five minutes of the court's time.

"The police support the application," she rounded off and knocked the desktop back into its normal position before resuming her seat.

Advocate Becker tossed his tie over his shoulder, as if to give the impression of being in a hurry. He spoke fast, and so loudly that after a few minutes Judge Lund interrupted him to draw his attention to the fact that there was barely a meter between the desk and the judge's table: could the lawyer please lower his voice? Obviously he couldn't, and his colleague Boe shifted three places farther along the lengthy desk. All the same, he held his hand discreetly to his right ear.

"The police application is a shot in the dark," Becker screeched. "It is obvious that after more than a fortnight's investigation, they're desperate for tangible results. Christmas is approaching, Your Honor, and the press are drooling. Drooling!"

He made an eloquent gesture toward the exit door. Billy T. wondered whether the advocate was speaking so loudly in the hope that the journalists outside could hear him.

"Strands of hair!" Becker said, smiling broadly at Judge Lund. "The police have found strands of hair belonging to my client on the deceased's clothing. Aha! I am fairly certain, Your Honor, that if you ask the police to examine your own coat, then strands of hair would turn up from most of the people with whom you share a cloakroom. A cloakroom!"

He clicked the fingers of his right hand and suddenly added a clarifying expression.

"Aha! So simple!"

He raised the plastic tumbler to his mouth, no longer in so much of a rush. When he had drained the glass, he poured more into it from a plastic jug. He smiled again, a broad smile that revealed a set of unusually white, even teeth in his round, almost childishly soft face.

Now at last he had dropped his voice a notch or two.

"So we see, Your Honor, we see that the police are undertaking a truly remarkable maneuver in an attempt to establish reasonable grounds for suspicion. Truly remarkable. So my client, in addition to stabbing Brede Ziegler to death a fortnight ago, is supposed to have tried to take the life of Sebastian Kvie the night before last ..."

Once again he smiled, this time followed by a chuckle.

"Stuff and nonsense. I repeat—"

"You do *not* need to repeat 'stuff and nonsense', Advocate Becker. It would also be an advantage if you adopted a somewhat calmer demeanor while you are speaking."

Advocate Becker had begun to wander around, but he accepted the reproof and instead stood in a pose that resembled a soldier standing to attention. Slowly he drew his tie down from his shoulder and studied the pattern for several seconds before placing it neatly on his chest.

"*Self-defense!*" he screamed so suddenly that even the two uniformed policemen who had been sitting with their eyes half-shut, obviously not bothering about what was said, nearly jumped out of their skins. "Yes, the incident that took place the night before last on scaffolding in Oslo city center was probably nothing more than a sheer accident, but if it really *is* the case that my client pushed Sebastian Kvie, then we're talking about a textbook example of self-defense. Because what is it that the Prosecutor alleges? Yes, she claims that my client sat in the middle of the night, dressed in his striped flannel pajamas, and waited for his victim to climb up scaffolding and place himself outside his window on the fourth floor. The fourth floor! Is this normal behavior for a victim? Climbing up house walls to place himself in a convenient position for a push? Eh?"

One of the men in uniform tried to stifle his laughter. He leaned down recklessly in his chair, resting his lower arms on his sprawling thighs, and let his head drop to his crotch. His shoulders shook soundlessly.

"See," Advocate Becker said, pointing at the young man. "This is so ridiculous that even your own police officers can't believe it! Your own officers!"

Advocate Becker had become flushed with agitation. His client, on the other hand, seemed calmer now. He glanced up at his lawyer in admiration and had stopped perspiring.

Advocate Becker spoke for a long time. Annmari was amazed that he was allowed to continue. Admittedly he had a good case, but in his delight at having so much to go on, he completely lost the ability to restrain himself. When he began to repeat his cloak-room theory for the third time, in order to undermine the police's strand of hair evidence, Judge Lund had at long last had enough.

"I think, then, that the court feels thoroughly enlightened," he said firmly.

When Sindre Sand entered the witness box after the break, it struck both Annmari and Billy T. that the boy looked in unusually good shape for someone who had been awake most of the night, and had for that matter spent thirty-six hours in a bare cell. His shirt still looked freshly ironed, and somebody must have seen to it that the young man had the opportunity to shave.

"Not guilty," he said decisively after the introductory formalities. "But I am willing to give a statement."

"In the course of the past few weeks you have given several statements to the police," Annmari Skar ventured. "Among other things, you have explained that you … couldn't stand Brede Ziegler?"

She looked at Sand for confirmation of her wording. He shrugged indifferently.

"That was apparently the reason for not having any contact with him for a long time," she continued. "Furthermore, you have stated that you were the boyfriend of – virtually engaged to – Ziegler's widow, Vilde Veierland. You haven't spoken to her for ages, you claimed in your interview."

"I said that—"

"Just a minute. Both the court and I know what you said, Sand. You yourself signed these transcripts."

Under her breath, Annmari conveyed a request to Billy T. and received a document in return. Then she stroked her nose with her forefinger and thumb and lingered for some time in her seat.

"Why did you lie?" she said all at once.

"I haven't lied. I haven't seen Vilde in a really long time. Not since ... I don't know."

"Why?"

Leaning back in her chair, she folded her arms.

"Why is it so dangerous to admit that you've seen Vilde several times recently?"

"I have *not* seen her," Sindre Sand said defiantly.

Annmari asked Billy T. for another document and quoted a few lines from a paper in which Egon Larsen, one of Vilde Veierland Ziegler's neighbors at Sinsen, said that he had observed the accused in the area on three occasions. In one case Sindre Sand had been seen entering the apartment block where Vilde lived.

"Egon Larsen is the catering manager at Sogn High School, Sand. He knows what you look like."

"He must have been mistaken. There are hundreds of students up there. I left Sogn the year before last. He's made a mistake."

Annmari leaned forward over the desk and tried to catch his eye. He still had an air of superiority about him, as if he either had not appreciated the gravity of the situation he faced or else quite simply couldn't care less. Annmari Skar had come across this before. She knew that the cockiness in the sullen look he gave her was only superficial. The young lad could potentially keep up this façade for his entire court appearance. However, he could just as easily break down completely in a few seconds.

"Are all the other witnesses mistaken then, Sand? Let me see ..."

She took time locating the document, even though it had already been taken out of the ring binder and left in plain sight before her.

"... one, two, three, four ... five. Five witnesses say that you were out of the NRK recording studio in Marienlyst at the time Brede Ziegler was murdered. Some claim that you were absent for as long as an hour. Is it the case that—"

Advocate Boe rarely interrupted his opponent in court. Remarkably enough, his voice was also unusually reedy.

"One moment, please," he said imperiously. "Perhaps the Prosecutor could stop here and clarify for us where she is actually going with all this? She has just very forcefully argued that it is the accused, Gagliostro, whom there are reasonable grounds to suspect of stabbing Ziegler to death. I have difficulty understanding how it is then defensible to take up the court's time establishing that it is also probable that my client was present at the crime scene. Sindre Sand is surely not charged with the murder?"

His voice was low. His face always wore an expression of surprise, with wide-open eyes behind his gold-rimmed glasses. Now he looked more astonished than ever.

Judge Lund looked at Annmari.

"I am inclined to agree with Advocate Boe. This seems rather peculiar. You must either explain what you want to achieve with this line of questioning or else restrict yourself to what the charge obviously refers to. If you intend to introduce something new into the case, then the police must investigate that outside this court. We do not conduct investigations here."

He concluded by staring in resignation at his wristwatch. It was 6.30 p.m.

Annmari was furious. It was objectionable to be interrupted in the middle of questioning an accused, and she had really not expected that. Not from Advocate Boe.

"Okay then. I shall give an explanation. I hope I may be permitted to emphasize that this is a very serious case," she said shrilly. "However, if the court and defense counsel do not understand ..."

She got a warning finger from the judge's desk. Judge Lund obviously would not tolerate an insinuation that he did not understand. Especially not from a prosecutor who was thirty years his junior. Annmari took a deep breath and pressed on.

"Sindre Sand is accused of attempted homicide. He has, in the opinion of the police, fed Brede Ziegler a large amount of poison in the form of paracetamol. This poisoning would almost certainly have led to his death. In this very unusual situation, we assert that the victim was stabbed before he—"

"Yes, I understand that."

Judge Lund scratched his head.

"What I do not understand, on the other hand, is why you insist on asking questions about where *this* accused ..."

He pointed abruptly at Sindre Sand.

"... was located while *another* person killed Ziegler? Because you surely can't mean that I should hold Gagliostro on remand if at the same time you are of the opinion that Sand here killed the man?"

"The prosecution's theory," Annmari began; now she was speaking so slowly that it must of necessity be considered a provocation, "is built on a chain of circumstantial evidence. I would like, through my examination, to establish that the accused, Sindre Sand, has consistently given erroneous information to the police. For the present, my point is therefore simply that *the man has lied!*"

She struck the table lightly with her hand, gazing at Judge Lund as if he were an obstinate child who absolutely refused to understand. The judge raised his hand inconspicuously in a fresh warning.

"As far as the charge of attempted homicide is concerned," she went on without looking at the judge, "then that is based in the first place on the fact that the accused has a strong motive.

He has admitted that. From the accused's point of view, Brede Ziegler fleeced him of a fortune, a girlfriend, and possibly also career opportunities. Secondly, Sand has lied about his contact with Vilde Veierland Ziegler. We can prove that he has seen Vilde several times in the past few weeks and furthermore that he ..."

She eagerly picked up the paper that Billy T. had located.

"... has lied consistently about the simple fact that he spent a considerable part of the evening and night between December the fourth and fifth in Brede Ziegler's company. That is to say, during the period when it is very probable that Ziegler ingested the poison that would later have caused his death."

Judge Lund sat motionless. Annmari had gone further than giving an explanation. She had gone some distance with the case for the prosecution. The judge looked as if he would let it pass.

"When all these circumstances are taken together," she added, much faster now, "they cannot simply be brushed aside as coincidence. They form a pattern in which there is one, and only one, person who had both motive and opportunity to poison the deceased."

She returned the papers to Billy T. and reclined in her chair. Then she smoothed her hair back from her forehead and said, "May I ask my question now?"

Advocate Boe stood up slowly before the judge had time to answer.

"If it may please the court," he began, "I would like to attach a number of comments to what the Prosecutor has just said. Since Judge Lund was so willing to let my honorable adversary interpose a procedure somewhat beyond the normal order of business, then I assume that I may also steal a few minutes of the court's time."

He smiled faintly in the direction of the judge's table and lifted a paper, before continuing.

"The documents from the investigation show clearly that Brede Ziegler was a man with a large circle of acquaintances, but few or no close friends. He was a ..."

Stroking his beard gently, the advocate gave the impression that he was unsure which word to choose.

"... disliked man," he said in the end. "In addition, he had a strange marriage, to put it mildly. As I understand it, it can't be entirely excluded that the murder victim was also a candidate for suicide. He could quite simply have taken an overdose of paracetamol of his own free will."

Annmari opened her mouth to protest. A look from the judge made her jaw snap shut.

"The Prosecutor makes an extremely pertinent point of my client having lied," Advocate Boe continued. "That is understandable, although the representatives of the police should also have gained the knowledge that people are not necessarily criminals because they tell lies. In fact we humans lie very often. Not commendable of course, but that is nevertheless how it is. My client has admitted he told lies about his contact with Brede Ziegler on that particular Saturday evening. To put it simply, he was terrified. Naive and stupid. We can all agree about that. But to illustrate my point, I would like to refer to Document 324."

The sound of rustling paper swept through the room.

"It has to do with this Mrs. Helmersen. When questioned yesterday, Monday, she insisted that she had been in the vicinity of the crime scene at the time of the murder. Closer investigation undertaken by the police shows that, not to put too fine a point on it, she is telling tall tales. One of her neighbors quarreled with her several times that evening, because she was playing ..."

He lifted the top sheet of paper and let his finger run down the page.

"*Summer in Tyrol.* So there we have it. The witness rang the doorbell a total of four times at the period in question because Mrs. Helmersen was playing it so loudly that he could follow the libretto in his own living room. Probably very annoying. So Mrs. Helmersen was lying. However, that is no reason to claim that she killed Ziegler."

Advocate Becker got to his feet as soon as his colleague sat down.

"Your Honor. Your Honor, I beg leave to speak."

"I am not minded to allow that, to be honest. This is not your client."

"But it's important, Your Honor. What's taking place here is nothing short of a scandal. A scandal that now impinges also on my client. It *must* be highlighted. The police are thrashing about in all directions! It is about time that we asked what has happened to Vilde Veierland Ziegler. She is the one it is claimed the accused has lied about! Why isn't she here? After all, isn't it common knowledge that this young woman inherits all Ziegler's money and thus has the best motive of all?"

"I agree with Mr. Becker," Judge Lund said slowly. "It would be interesting to learn more about this widow. Is there a more recent statement from her? One in which she might possibly refute the accused's assertion that they have not seen each other for some considerable time?"

A report about Vilde Veierland's breakdown had not yet been compiled. The omission could still be defended to some degree.

"She is … indisposed."

Annmari cleared her throat and gave an almost undetectable shrug. Billy T. did not know whether the gesture was meant apologetically. Perhaps she was attempting to minimize its importance.

"Vilde Veierland Ziegler was arrested at a random traffic checkpoint. Yesterday morning. She is charged with driving a vehicle in a severe state of intoxication. Narcotics. After that she was held in custody at police headquarters, waiting for a doctor to take a blood sample."

Billy T. fiddled with his tie and cast his eyes down. He had wasted four valuable hours of working time searching for Vilde the previous day. So she had already been under arrest. He had built up a frantic rage that he was going to unleash on the first poor soul he encountered, when he discovered the blunder. On further thought, he had realized that coordination was actually one of his own responsibilities and had kept his mouth shut.

"During the period spent waiting, she suffered a psychotic breakdown," Annmari continued in a quiet voice. "And she has now been admitted to a psychiatric hospital. The doctor treating her informs us that she is in no fit condition to give a statement. Not at present, and not for some time. We would of course have liked—"

Advocate Becker interrupted in a falsetto: "Exactly! That is exactly what I said! It's a scandal. The police now come out with a sensational piece of information that has been suppressed until ..."

He drew back his suit jacket sleeve and stared frantically at his watch.

"... eight o'clock. It's eight p.m. on Tuesday, it will soon be Christmas, and I repeat: the police have suppressed crucial information. We have therefore a drug-addicted widow who is the sole heir, and whom the police have entirely ignored. All this while the full force of their suspicion is cast on my client, without so much as a *fingerprint* linking him to the murder. A fingerprint!"

Judge Lund gave him a frosty look and gestured for him to sit down.

"But we have a strand of hair," he said sharply. "That's surely more than we can say about Mrs. Ziegler."

"With all respect, Your Honor, but this is now being ..."

Advocate Ole Johan Boe shook his head gently. A fine network of red veins had started to appear on the skin above his well-tended beard.

"You were actually the one who started this," Annmari Skar let slip. "I was about to—"

A commotion caused them all finally to glance over at Sindre Sand, who had been standing still in the witness box for more than half an hour. No one had thought to offer the man a chair, despite the court secretary at least having noticed that he had grown noticeably paler. Now he sank slowly to the floor and took the witness box with him in his fall. The two police officers reached him in one synchronized leap and managed to prevent the large wooden box from falling on top of him. A moment or two later Sindre was sitting on the floor with his head between his knees.

"Water," one of the policemen offered. "Don't get up yet."

Sindre murmured, "I don't give a damn about anything. Let me go. You don't give a shit about me anyway."

The judge looked quizzically at Advocate Boe, who hesitated for a few seconds before nodding. The judge's gavel banged on the table. They all stood up.

The break did not have a refreshing effect on any of them. Judge Lund had rolled down his sleeves when he returned and straightened the tie under his dark jacket. It was half past nine before they were finally finished with the remand hearing.

Advocate Boe's argument had been deadly. He had not raised his voice like Becker, and he never repeated the points he made. They were too good for that sort of thing, and Annmari felt exhausted and drained when Judge Lund eventually concluded the proceedings by declaring that a verdict would be delivered the following morning.

She turned to Billy T.

"If the two of them are released, it's *your* fault," she snarled through gritted teeth. "You and that *hellishly* confused investigation of yours. I hope you've learned a thing or two today!"

She marched out with only her bag slung over her shoulder. Billy T. could attend to the task of bringing the pitiful detritus of the investigation back to the station. Nearly two thousand pages of documents.

He knew she was right. He did not have an overview of what was written there, and there was no red thread running through the material. No all-encompassing theories. A whole load of shots in the dark, as Becker had quite rightly screamed. Billy T. nevertheless tried to return all the documents to their rightful places, as if some sort of sense of order would shed fresh light on the case.

His painful tooth was throbbing like mad.

58

Billy T. stared at the young woman in the bed, whose face almost merged into the white sheets, making it difficult to see whether she was breathing at all. The room was dim. Only a faint bluish-white light filtered from the corridor through the half-open door. He picked up a chair and sat down. A wall clock with oversized numbers on a white background told him that it was already two hours into the wee small hours of Wednesday December 22. There were now two days left until Christmas Eve. He had almost given up on sleeping.

The doctor had burst into dry, irritating laughter. Vilde Veierland Ziegler was not going to be able to make a statement. Not for a long time. Guards outside her door would be completely out of the question. As far as the doctor could understand, Vilde was not remanded in custody. A charge of driving under the influence could hardly legitimize either the police squandering resources or the substantial increase in workload it would involve for both patients and staff to have to put up with uniformed police officers cluttering the corridors. When Billy T. had asked to be allowed to see Vilde, the doctor refused. The patient needed rest. Billy T. had shrugged, pretended to head for the sealed door leading from the locked ward, but instead did a U-turn in the corridor as soon as the doctor was out of sight. A nurse had asked him brusquely what he wanted, but she had backed down when he showed her his police ID and muttered something about permission from Dr. Frisak.

Billy T. did not want guards in the corridor to keep watch over Vilde. He wanted to have them there to pick up every single sign of improvement. He simply *must* have an interview. He needed one *now*.

Vilde Veierland Ziegler was Brede's daughter. Billy T. was convinced of that. The doctor had refused to answer questions about Vilde's medical history – whether she had ever, for example, needed an organ donation. There was no authority for that, Dr. Frisak had asserted bombastically. Deep inside, Billy T. swore that as soon as this inquiry was over, he would take up law. Obviously everyone else had. He sat on a chair at the woman's bedside, but most of all what he wanted was to search her body for scars. He moved his arm over to the thin quilt, but let it drop.

Everything had unraveled. At least, most of it had.

The Italian trail had led nowhere. The report from Økokrim, the financial branch of the police, had decided that a preliminary examination of Brede Ziegler's business interests in Italy had not given them any grounds for further investigation on the part of the Norwegians. Of course there were limits as to how far they had been able to check matters, because of both time and legal constraints. Nevertheless, everything appeared in order.

Nothing to note.

That was how it was written, at the foot of a four-page-long report that had arrived in the internal mail that morning.

Then it must be Vilde.

Brede inhabited a strange marriage. When the police had first discovered the bedsit in Siloveien, it was quickly established that in the main Vilde was never in Niels Juels gate. The spouses saw very little of each other, even though their wedding was less than six months ago. Also, Brede had chosen to be sterilized. Only twenty-four, Vilde was hardly capable of making such a serious decision about the future. In all likelihood she had not even known about the procedure. Brede had ensured, entirely off his own bat, that he would not father his own grandchildren.

But why?

"Why?" Billy T. whispered, trying to force some moisture into his dry eyes. "Why marry your own daughter?"

Brede Ziegler had been notorious as a young man. Women had dangled from his every finger. He did not want children. He did not want a wife, either: at least, that was how it had looked. Then all of a sudden he marries his own daughter.

"Fuck!" Billy T. muttered, yawning; it did not help much to counteract the feeling of having sandpaper behind his eyelids.

Claudio had discovered the secret. Billy T. did not know how, and had not yet dared to question the guy about the matter. Gagliostro had attempted blackmail. That must be how it had been. The money had not gone from Claudio to Brede, as the Italian claimed. It had gone in the other direction. Brede had paid Claudio to keep his mouth shut. That would make the serial numbers logical. Billy T. would interview the guy until he broke down. But not yet. First he needed to talk to Vilde.

The question was whether she had known all along. That the man she had married was her own father. Probably not. Something must have happened. Something must have come up. Brede Ziegler had been exposed.

How?

Was it Vilde who had murdered Brede? During a late-evening stroll to clear it all up? The Masahiro knife was light, the stabbing had been sudden. She could have done it. Her alibi could be false. Her friend could be lying. Everybody can tell lies. Vilde could have persuaded someone else to do it. Sindre Sand could have done it. Anyone at all could have done it. Annmari was a shit. Hanne was a traitor. Jenny was crying, and everything had gone red: he would have to hurry if he were to catch the train to the Bahamas. He was not wearing any clothes. He tried to run for the train, where he could hear Jenny crying, but his legs would not move and everything was red and he saw Hanne and Annmari at a window, laughing at him. Suzanne stood in front of the train. She had captured Jenny and dropped the child down between the rails, before jumping down herself.

"This is really extremely serious, Chief Inspector."

Billy T., rudely awakened, rubbed his face.

"Harrumph," he cleared his throat. "Sorry."

"I made it pretty clear that the patient should not be disturbed," Dr. Frisak said. "But obviously that wasn't sufficient. I consider it necessary to report you. Could you at least be kind enough to leave the hospital grounds? This is a closed ward, and you are here without permission."

Billy T. stood up stiffly and without a word walked past the doctor and disappeared. He might as well go to Grønlandsleiret 44.

59

As a rule, Annmari Skar expressed anger with an exaggerated show of self-control. She spoke if possible even more slowly than in court, as if the words came out of her mouth in enormous, easily read letters. Now she was speaking slowly, admittedly, but her self-control was less well handled.

"Have you been in Vilde's bedsit in Sinsen *without* a blue form? Have you gone *sta-rk ... rav-ing ... mad?*"

She looked daggers at Billy T. and took a deep breath, three times over. Then she slumped back heavily in the chair and gazed challengingly at the Police Chief. When he did not say anything, she suddenly leaned forward again and raised the blue sheet into the air. She held it by the outer edge between thumb and index finger, as if the paper was a foul-smelling dishcloth.

"I refuse to sign. I don't make use of trickery and deceit."

She slapped the paper down in front of the Police Chief.

"And to *top it all off*," she continued, "the first thing that greeted me this morning was a detailed and extremely formal complaint from a Dr. Frifant or Frilynt—"

"Frisak," Billy T. said.

"I don't give *two hoots* what he's called! The point is that you quite illegally went in to see a patient in the middle of the night, in total contravention of the hospital's instructions and without so much as the shadow of a court order. What are you giving me?"

The last sentence was spoken to the Chief of Police. Annmari reclined in her chair, arms crossed on her chest. Her gaze rested on the completed search warrant on blue paper. Only the lawyer's signature was missing. Annmari's breathing was labored, before she suddenly cut through the oppressive silence in the Police Chief's office once again.

"And only *now*," she said; her voice was quivering and Hanne could swear that her eyes were shining with tears. "Now, *today*, you tell me that some things indicate Brede Ziegler has a child. Let me see ..."

She counted on her fingers with strenuous movements.

"Saturday, Sunday, Monday, Tuesday, Wednesday. Five days. Five days and a bloody *horr-en-dous* meeting in court, after you had received information that, to put it at its mildest, has significance for the case, you consider it a good idea to share your knowledge with me. With all the rest of us."

"I spoke to Karl," Billy T. said sullenly.

"Karl! *Karl!* Hah. *I'm* the one who's the lawyer appointed to this case. It is in fact *moi* ..."

She struck herself on the chest with her fist.

"... who has to bear the brunt of your ... your—"

"Honestly!"

Billy T. raised his voice, his red-rimmed eyes blinking repeatedly.

"It's hardly the first time an investigator has asked to have a blue form post-dated! It surely can't be worth making such a bloody fuss over!"

Annmari put her face in her hands and rocked slowly from side to side. They all stared at her, as if unsure whether she was thinking or crying. Hanne thought she could hear some faint snorts, as if she were actually laughing at the whole situation. The Police Chief ought to say something soon. Hans Christian Mykland kept silent. He did not take his eyes off Annmari. Finally she looked up and drew a breath. "Chief – I would like to give you a report of yesterday's court hearing. It was a nightmare."

Mykland's eyes blinked. "But it went okay ... Four weeks' remand, with an embargo on letters and visitors for both the accused, was exactly what we had requested."

"We got it by the skin of our teeth, and really only because one of the accused was demonstrably lying and the other sweating so much, as if he had a dammed ocean of guilty conscience that simply had to pour forth at that very moment. Anyway, the ruling has been appealed. God only knows what the Appeal Court will say. But it was ..."

She gasped for breath and swallowed noisily.

"*Shameful!* It was absolutely agonizing to present such a poor investigation and such an inadequate chain of circumstantial evidence. It took the defense counsel no time to find out that we have arrested and charged people at random. There's only one thing we can do now. Quite simply not put another foot wrong. When you ..."

Once again her forefinger was trembling in the direction of Billy T.

"... wander around at night to prove that Vilde is behind her husband's murder because he's actually her father, at the same time as you sit beside me when I'm demanding custody on homicide charges for two other people, I lose my last scrap of confidence in ..."

She gasped for air.

"... you."

It began to dawn on Hanne Wilhelmsen why Annmari had phoned for her. She felt hot and cold by turns, and crossed her legs to prevent herself from getting to her feet and leaving the room.

"This is not a social club," Annmari said; for the first time there was a note of regret in her voice. "We have to be professional.

At present you're not professional enough, Billy T. I request that you step down as leader of this investigation in favor of Hanne Wilhelmsen."

Hanne had been tricked. She gazed at Billy T. to signal that she had known nothing about this in advance. He had closed his eyes and was barely recognizable. The moustache under his nose was pitifully unkempt and he had obviously not had time to shave his head for several weeks, either. A gray-flecked ring of hair around the crown made him look ten years older than he was.

"That's out of the question," Hanne said, unruffled. "End of discussion. Absolutely impossible.'

The Police Chief looked as if it had only just occurred to him that he was the one who was supposed to chair this meeting, and that they were sitting in his office. Cupping one hand in front of his mouth, he cleared his throat.

"Police Prosecutor Skar and I have discussed the situation," he said in a quiet voice. "And I agree it would be advantageous if you resume your old post now. It would have happened anyway, of course, in the New Year. There's only a week or so until then. Actually, it's entirely undramatic. And that is a request, Hanne. Not an order."

"I see," Hanne said, standing up. "Cannot comply with the request."

Before she had reached the door, she turned quickly on her heel.

"Do you know what's wrong with you?"

She stared alternately at Annmari and the Police Chief.

"When something gets so difficult that your feet are on fire, you look for a scapegoat. I've seen it before, and will probably see it again. You ought to support Billy T. He has a difficult job. Besides ..."

She threw a penetrating look in the direction of the blue form that had ended up in the center of the oval table.

"... somebody should sign that blue form. Now."

She left without even glancing at Billy T.

60

"Did anything new emerge from that coordination meeting this morning?"

Silje Sørensen waved her hand to disperse the cloud of smoke in Hanne's office, but sat down all the same with her feet planked unceremoniously on the table.

"Nothing special. How is Sindre Sand doing?"

"Refuses to give a statement. That's become so fashionable these days ..."

Silje picked up the cigarette packet and read out loud: "Tobacco causes serious damage to your health."

"Tell me something I don't know," Hanne said, slightly miffed, and snatched the packet. "What about the investigation into the paracetamol?"

"A team of technicians are going through his apartment with a fine-tooth comb, and a whole group of police trainees are trawling all the pharmacies in the city to see if they can come up with anything. Something they almost certainly won't do. Sales of Paracet aren't registered. It's well known that it's a prescription-free medicine."

She yawned behind a slender hand with dark-red nails.

"Things take time. But we'll get the better of him sooner or later. We'll see how he reacts to being locked up for four weeks with no visitors."

"I would last for around half an hour precisely," Hanne said, offering her a pastille from a squashed packet. "Poor Tussi

Helmersen will never be herself again after her six hours round the back."

"We'll all be happy about that," Silje said. "At least, little Thomas will. His mother phoned me this morning to say thank you. Mrs. Helmersen has been in touch with an estate agent. She wants to move to the countryside, she says now. So it was good for something, all that. By the way, she *was* the one who had written those threatening letters. Fingerprints all over them, as it turned out. She had a nice little wall of hate in her living room, with pictures cut from newspapers of all the people in the public eye who had ever made a positive comment about anything whatsoever from beyond Norway's borders. Thorbjørn Jagland, for instance, had been given a horn in the middle of his forehead. She'll get away with a fine. Or a waiver of prosecution, as Annmari put it. No point in persecuting the lady for killing a cat, which she admits, and a few ridiculous threatening letters. What *I* have learned from this is that our biggest problem in each investigation is all the dead ends we get trapped in. Is it always like that?"

"Always. Everyone has something to hide. Everyone tells lies, at least in the sense that they never tell us the whole truth. If everyone apart from the guilty party told the truth in every case, then we'd have the easiest job in the world. And then perhaps it wouldn't be such fun any more."

Silje chuckled and scratched her stomach discreetly.

"But now Tussi's going to move away. Good for Thomas. Amazing what a stay in a bare cell can lead to. That Daniel boy of yours wasn't so very sure of himself, either."

Hanne did not reply. She tapped an unlit cigarette on the table top as if she had not quite made up her mind whether to light it.

"All the same, there is something about that Idun Franck," Silje said, grabbing the matches. "It was as if she were ..."

Hanne was not sure whether it was intentional. When Silje Sørensen tilted her head and looked askance at the ceiling, she looked like a thoughtful little child.

"... keeping a secret!"

"A secret," Hanne repeated, holding out her hand. "The matches, please. Everybody has secrets."

"Don't smoke."

"Come on. Let me have them. Don't you have any secrets?"

"Smoking's dangerous. Besides, it's forbidden here."

"That's certainly not a secret. Come on, now. Give me the matches."

Hanne half-rose from her chair and tried to grab Silje's wrist. Her young colleague stretched her arm above her head and laughed as she shook the box.

"I have two," she said. "First of all, I'm rich."

Hanne sat down again, opened a drawer, took out a lighter, and lit the cigarette.

"Rich? I see."

"Loaded," Silje whispered, giggling. "I mean, I really do have loads of money. But I don't tell anyone. Not here at police head-quarters, I mean."

"No, I suppose not," Hanne said drily. "You just go round in clothes that cost ten thousand kroner, shoes for almost half that, and jewelry we could have sold and used to build a new national prison. What is your second secret? Are you pregnant?"

Silje Sørensen was a pretty woman. She was small, almost petite. Hanne had previously wondered whether her colleague had been measured in her high heels to achieve the regulation height at police college. Her facial features were regular, and her nose had a slight kink that emphasized the inquisitive expression in her eyes.

"Now you look retarded," Hanne Wilhelmsen said.

"But," Silje began, and closed her mouth.

"You're scratching your belly. Buy a good cream and apply it often. Besides, there was a smell of vomit after you'd been to the toilet yesterday morning. Bulimic? I don't think so ... Pregnant? Probably. Elementary, my dear Silje. But ..."

It was as if the information about Silje's pregnancy had suddenly struck Hanne as a catastrophe. She stiffened entirely, with her hand halfway to her mouth, the cigarette still bobbing between her lips. In the end she had to close her eyes on the smoke and exclaimed: "Have you seen Daniel Åsmundsen, Silje?"

"Seen him? Wasn't he released yesterday?"

"I mean *seen!*"

Hanne stubbed out the cigarette in the foul-smelling ashtray and headed for the door. When she returned three minutes later, she was holding something behind her back. She leaned toward Silje. Their faces were only a fraction apart when she repeated, forcefully: "Have you ever in your life clapped eyes on Daniel Åsmundsen?"

Silje drew back without thinking.

"I don't think so," she said slowly. "Why do you ask?"

"Thank goodness they had the wit to record the boy on file. I don't have a bloody clue whether they took his prints, but his photo was in the case files anyway."

She plumped down in her own chair and slapped a photo of a young man's face in front of Silje.

"Look at this boy. Is there anything familiar about him?"

Silje stared at the photo for a long time. Daniel Åsmundsen looked young. She knew he was more than twenty, but judging from the photograph he could easily pass for a teenager. Maybe it was the roundness of his cheeks that made him look younger, or possibly his eyes that gazed wide-open into the camera lens.

She raised the photo to her face and squinted.

"There *is* something familiar about this face," she said hesitantly. "I'm pretty sure I haven't seen him before, but all the same there's something ..."

She put her knuckle into her mouth and sucked loudly.

"Look here," Hanne said, turning to the computer screen, which had finally been connected by one of the dilatory IT assistants. "If it's as I believe, then the information in the Population Register will show that ... Bingo!"

"What is it?"

"Daniel Åsmundsen's mother's name is Thale Åsmundsen. Isn't she the actress, by the way? The one at the National Theater? Never mind ... Look here. Father: Unknown!"

She clenched her fists and banged them on the keyboard in her enthusiasm. The details disappeared in a chaos of indecipherable symbols.

"At the morning meeting with the Chief it emerged that Brede probably has a child somewhere. Billy T. had spoken to ... Doesn't matter a damn. And if you look at this picture here, then—"

"Honestly. You just told me that nothing exciting happened at that meeting, and then you say that—"

"Look! Take another peek at this photo!"

Silje picked up the picture again and lightly smacked her lips.

"Brede Ziegler," she said. "Daniel Åsmundsen looks like Brede Ziegler. But ..."

She continued to stare at the picture. The same round face as his father, the same nose: slightly too broad, slightly too large, but wide, oval nostrils.

"How does this help us?" she asked meekly and looked up. "So Daniel may be Brede Ziegler's son, but what has that to do with the murder?"

"No idea," Hanne said, grinning broadly. "But get that millionaire fur coat of yours. We're going out."

61

Billy T. sat with his knees tucked under the table for fear that the chair would not bear his 107 kilos of weight. He got cramp in his thighs from trying to make himself lighter. Besides, he was not hungry.

"Why would they call a Norwegian restaurant 'Frankie's'?" he asked crossly as he sipped his beer; the froth settled on his moustache and made him reluctant to lick his lips. "Can't they think of something Norwegian? Like 'Hunger', for example? Hunger is good."

"If we'd gone there, we'd still not have a table. They try to make the queuing arrangements seem hip. Urban and young and democratic, and that sort of drivel. The truth is that they make a fortune out of people hardly having wiped their chins before the next customer pokes you on the shoulder. Here at Frankie's, on the other hand ..."

Severin Heger smiled at the proprietor, a good-looking woman from Bergen who was sashaying between the tables.

"*Carpaccio* and *spaghetti alla vongole* for both of us," he ordered, putting down the menu.

"I don't want any fucking vongley spaghetti," Billy T. said.

"Yes, you do. And a white Italian."

The woman suggested a type, and Severin was drawn into a lengthy discussion. Billy T. yawned. He tried to forget the morning meeting, but it was impossible. He had walked around in a daze all day long. If Hanne had not reacted as she had, he would have handed in his resignation. Unequivocally. Then his children could starve to death. What Tone-Marit would have said about it, he could barely imagine. He had hardly spoken to her for several weeks. He came home late, grunted at both her and the baby, and was up and out before the first morning feed.

"I can't afford this," he complained when the woman left.

"My treat," Severin said, raising his glass in a toast. "Shitty day? Something you want to talk about?"

"White Christmas," Billy T. said, nodding apathetically at the massive windows, where big flakes of snow were drifting past.

If the low temperature held out, even the inner city would be blanketed in snow in a few hours. Billy T. yawned again, regretting the toolboxes he had bought for the boys. They were going to be disappointed. Also he would have to get Jenny another present. A fucking car seat was not enough.

"You're wrong," Severin Heger said all of a sudden, as if he had been standing beside a cold fjord in May and had at last decided to dive in. "Vilde can't be Brede's daughter."

Billy T. drained the rest of his glass. When he put it down again, he shook his head slowly.

"And you've found that out?" he asked tersely.

"Yes."

"How?"

Severin picked up a Parmesan shaving and placed it on his tongue.

"Vilde's father is called Viktor Veierland. Engineer. He's still married to Vilde's mother. Vivian Veierland is her name."

"Do they have an obsession with the letter V in that family, then? And what about it, anyway? A marriage has never stopped people having children. With someone else, I mean."

The waiter poured their wine and removed their beer glasses.

"But listen to this," Severin said, discouraged. "Vilde was born in 1975. In Osaka in Japan, of all places. Her father had a job there from 1974 to 1977. At that time they were never in Norway. They saved money, the man explained. The entire point of their stay was to pile up money for a house here in Norway. Incidentally, the guy was quite down-in-the-mouth about my questions. They were never in Norway at that time, Billy T. You know as well as I do what that means. To be on the safe side, and for *your* sake, I checked whether there was anything at all that might indicate that Ziegler had made a detour to Japan at that time. Nix. He has never been to Asia at all."

The spaghetti arrived at the table.

"Okay, okay!"

Billy T. held his hands in the air and rolled his eyes.

"You don't need to rub it in, then. My theory has collapsed like a—"

He dropped his fork in his food and threw the linen napkin on the floor in irritation.

Severin's cellphone played a digital version of a Norwegian folk tune.

"Hello?"

Billy T. was tired out. His eyes slid shut. The room seemed to spin round on its axis. The snow outside the window changed color: now the swirling flakes seemed violet in the harsh street lighting. He gasped for air. The money, he thought lethargically. Why does a guy walk around in Oslo with 16,000 kroner on him, in the middle of the night? Why was he walking around in Oslo at all? He was in pain, and it was Sunday night. Brede Ziegler should have been at hospital. Or at home. Hanne was right. He must have met someone. A prearranged meeting. Billy T. tried to eat, but the spaghetti slid off his fork. He made an attempt to help out with the spoon, but his hands were behaving as if they no longer belonged to him. He sat there gaping at the almost untouched plate.

"It was Karianne," Severin said, crestfallen, stuffing the cell-phone back into his brown shoulder-bag. "Sebastian Kvie died three-quarters of an hour ago. Poor, unlucky bastard."

It was exactly forty-eight hours till Christmas Eve. Billy T. could think of nothing except that the toolboxes for the boys were totally, totally wrong.

62

When the woman opened the door, it seemed as though she had been expecting them. Or, more to the point, was *waiting* for them. Although the apartment was furnished as if it had been preserved at some time in 1974, it was clean and tidy. A hollow on one of the armchairs revealed that someone had just been sitting there, but the TV was switched off. It was totally silent in the apartment, and there were no books or newspapers lying around. Just as if she had known they were on their way and was simply sitting here waiting. When Hanne Wilhelmsen showed her police ID, the woman nodded gently and brushed away invisible dust from her trouser leg.

"I have tried to do the right thing, but I was wrong."

It was the very first thing she said. Not hello. She did not invite them in, either. She simply headed for the living room and took it for granted that they would follow. The settee was a DIY construction, covered in floral Marimekko fabric. The petals had once been deep purple. Now they were faded to a pale shade of lilac, and the stuffing had leaked through in a number of places. An enormous yucca plant in the corner facing the street served as a Christmas tree, decorated with handcrafted Christmas baskets, two blue glass baubles with artificial snow, and festooned with lights that did not work. Beyond the living room, Silje Sørensen could make out a kitchen with orange walls and green appliances.

"If you hadn't come to me, I would have paid you a visit," the woman said calmly. "It's not fair to Daniel, how it's all turned out."

Hanne's look made Silje shut her mouth on the questions that sat on the tip of her tongue. Instead, she leaned back on the settee, fingering her diamond ring.

Thale Åsmundsen appeared unaffected by the ensuing silence. It seemed that she had left her features behind at the theater and had no expressions left for personal use. She curled up in the armchair with her legs tucked underneath her. Her mid-length hair was smooth, but not anywhere near what you would call a hairstyle. She lifted a teacup to her mouth. It took some time before she finally put it down again.

"It began when I met Freddy," she said, composed. "You know of course that that was Brede Ziegler's real name. Freddy Johansen. I didn't really like him."

For the first time some kind of expression appeared on her scrubbed, shiny face; a touch of something Hanne interpreted as self-mocking irony.

"But I was only eighteen. It was all some sort of protest. Against my father, and also against Idun. She is much older than me and had already graduated from university. Father wanted me to study law. So I applied for drama school instead. And got involved with someone who ... wasn't academic. It became something of a scandal at home in Heggeli. Which I was exceptionally pleased about."

The irony had gone. All the same, Hanne was puzzled. It might seem as if the woman in the green flannel trousers was reliving an old sorrow, but then she shrugged and went on: "That was how it was. Actually it had all been over between us for a while before I fell pregnant. I just didn't understand it. Freddy was, to put it mildly ..."

A smile drifted across her mouth and she hid her face in her cup for a moment.

"... not interested, you might say. Well. I couldn't care less. I wanted to have the baby. The last time I met Brede at that time was in 1977, on the street. I was heavily pregnant. He said hello and walked on. Without asking. He never phoned me. Never tried to find out whether he had fathered a boy or a girl. I sent him a letter, to keep things above board. Told him that the boy had been born. And that his name was Daniel. He never replied. It was all the same to me. Freddy was never preoccupied about who he was. He was preoccupied about who he was going to be. I had understood that long ago. Would you ... would you like a cup?"

She held her own up to them in the form of a question. Silje nodded, but Hanne waved her hand dismissively and lied: "We've already had a bucketful of coffee. No, thanks."

"At the time I dumped Freddy, he had actually also dumped himself."

Thale Åsmundsen gave a short burst of mirthless laughter. Hanne was not even sure that she had meant to laugh. Maybe she had just snorted.

"He had started as an apprentice chef in order to go to sea. But then he discovered the sophisticated restaurant life. He wanted to be elegant too. He reinvented himself. That was when he became Brede Ziegler."

Now her laughter sounded more genuine.

"Just think! Freddy Johansen became Brede Ziegler. You would think he was the one who was the actor, rather than me. I've actually seen it myself ..."

She stretched out her leg and pulled a grimace, as if her legs had gone to sleep.

"I've seen how he could stand in front of the mirror and try out different roles. Have you seen that Woody Allen film? *Zelig*?"

Hanne nodded, Silje shook her head.

"That was what Brede was like. Some evenings at the Young Conservatives' meeting: one of the jet set with a loden coat and beautiful sweater. A night at Club Seven, and hey presto ... he turned into a sensitive member of the avant-garde. His best role, all the same, was the man-of-the-world with artistic talents. Little by little, he became really good at that. Fucking poser!"

It seemed surprising that she swore. It did not seem appropriate to the flat, deadpan way she had of expressing herself. Hanne Wilhelmsen asked carefully, "But weren't you sad that he didn't bother in the slightest about the child?"

Now Thale Åsmundsen looked genuinely taken aback.

"Sad? Why would I be? I didn't want Freddy Johansen – and I wouldn't have touched Brede Ziegler with a bargepole. Freddy was like ... Do you know the myth of Narcissus?"

She fixed her eyes on Hanne as if she had given up on Silje Sørensen. Hanne shrugged.

"Sort of. That's the one who falls in love with his own reflection, isn't it?"

"Exactly. That's just what he was like. And I had no interest in being Freddy's Echo. Besides, I had Idun. She was the only person who seemed genuinely happy when Daniel was born. He called her Taffa, almost before he said 'Mummy' to me."

She stood up abruptly.

"I'm hungry," she said casually. "I usually eat at this time. After the performance. Yes ... whether I'm performing or not. I'm off this evening, but I'm hungry ..."

She gave a faint smile and padded barefoot out to the kitchen. Silje grabbed Hanne's foot.

"She ought to have a lawyer, we should—"

"Shh. We're eating."

The kitchen table was painted orange, like the walls. Thale Åsmundsen put out a teapot and three rough ceramic cups.

"I can't be bothered spending time looking for new things. I like routine. Things being where they've always been."

Silje stared at her in fascination. Not only her home, but her entire being seemed like a throwback to her hippy days. Although Thale Åsmundsen clearly had a pretty face, she wore no make-up, she was dowdy, with baggy flannel trousers, bare toes, and a wide Indian batik shirt. Silje had seen her play Miss Julie in a Swedish television production, and could hardly grasp that this was the same person.

"You could well say that Idun and I shared the job of mothering," Thale Åsmundsen said, cracking three eggs into a pan. "Daniel and I always eat fried eggs and drink hot chocolate. It's become a sort of … Well. Although Daniel lived here, of course, he spent almost as much time at her place. As soon as I dared to let him out on his own, he took the tram to the Old Town by himself. And when Daniel was ill …"

She smoothed her hair from her forehead with the back of her hand: she had grease on her fingers.

"She was the one who took time off when I couldn't. It was actually quite … okay?"

She looked at them both with her eyebrows slightly puckered, as if wondering whether they thought her unfeeling.

"But Freddy – or Brede Ziegler as he was by that time – I didn't give him a thought until I was forced to. Daniel needed a kidney. Mine was not suitable."

The eggs were sizzling in the pan. She found a packet of cigarettes in her breast pocket and lit a cigarette without asking if anyone minded. Hanne took out her own packet and kept her company.

"Actually," Thale said pensively. "Actually it was the only time I had anything that might resemble true feelings for him. I hated him. For a fortnight. We sent a request through the hospital and his doctor, to see if he would allow himself to be examined with a view to organ donation. He turned it all down. Point-blank. Did not even get in touch. But …"

She flipped the eggs on to three slices of bread. The cocoa was about to boil over.

"But it turned out all right," she said lightly, and rescued the brown milk. "Idun's kidney suited. Daniel received Taffa's kidney and he's healthy today. Daniel knows about it all. When he turned eighteen, I told him who his father was. And how he had behaved. That he's not someone worth having. Here you are."

They ate. Thale had ketchup on her fried egg, and Silje had to swallow to avoid throwing up. She pushed her plate away with a mumbled apology.

"To be honest, I don't give a damn whether you catch the person who killed Freddy," Thale Åsmundsen said. "But I want Daniel to have the money. His inheritance. He has a right to that, don't you think?"

Once again she looked at Hanne.

Silje could not understand any of it. She cleared her throat and draped her napkin over her food. She noticed that Hanne's eyes did not waver from Thale. Finding the silence extremely uncomfortable, Silje tapped her knife against the edge of the table without thinking. Thale, on the other hand, lit another cigarette and inhaled deeply, before blowing a perfect smoke ring up at the ceiling.

"Am I callous, do you think?"

"You understand that I have to ask," Hanne Wilhelmsen said. "Where were you on the evening of Sunday December the fifth of this year?"

Thale smiled vaguely, as if finding the question totally irrelevant.

"I was toastmaster at a fiftieth birthday party," she parried calmly. "There's no performance on a Sunday, and my colleague Lotte Schweigler was celebrating her birthday with twenty-odd guests at her home. The party began at seven o'clock and I didn't go home until five o'clock the next morning. She lives at Tanum in Bærum. It's quite far to there. From the police station, I mean."

Silje had produced a notepad and tried to be discreet. It was difficult; the silence in the room made it possible to hear the almost dry felt-tip pen on the paper. Hanne glanced surreptitiously at her watch. Almost half past ten. She got to her feet as if to signal that she had reached her final question.

"I don't quite understand all this about the inheritance," she said. "You've obviously not bothered about money before now. Brede Ziegler has hardly paid any maintenance, since you never named him as the father. Why is it so important now? So important that you had considered coming to us to tell us about this ... this secret?"

"Daniel is worried about not having any money. I can see that in him. Idun told me that you arrested him the other day."

There was no recrimination in her voice, rather a brief statement of fact; as if it did not trouble her in the least that her son had been unlawfully held for hours in a bare cell.

"Daniel would never have tried to sell his grandfather's books unless he really needed money. Besides ..."

She began to head for the front door, as if she regarded the visit as over.

"... it's about time Freddy paid his share. Don't you agree?"

This time she gazed at Silje Sørensen. The young policewoman muttered something inaudible and crammed her notepad into her handbag. She almost knocked over a little bronze figure of a baby curled in a fetal position; it was sitting on a lye-washed sideboard in the hallway.

"Beautiful," Hanne said, running her fingers gingerly over the egg-shaped child. "Lovely sculpture."

Thale Åsmundsen gave her one of her infrequent, warm smiles.

"Yes, isn't it? I got it from Idun when I was expecting Daniel."

Hanne noticed a family photograph beside the mirror above the sideboard. An elderly man in an armchair was seated in the middle, flanked by two women and a young man. Thale, Idun, and Daniel smiled at the photographer, but the old man's gaze was sad and serious.

"Family photograph?"

Hanne tapped her finger lightly on the glass.

"Yes. It's actually the very last picture we have of us all together. It was taken on Father's eightieth birthday last winter, just before he died."

Hanne leaned forward and studied the picture. Silje had already opened the front door and, tripping with impatience, had her back half-turned as she buttoned her jacket.

"So this was taken less than a year ago," Hanne said softly, without taking her eyes off the photo.

"Yes."

Hanne Wilhelmsen did not feel relieved. A faint glow burned below her complexion. She tried to straighten her back, but continued to stand, bent at the hips, studying the barely year-old image. Daniel was smiling broadly as if nothing could hurt him. He was young, strong, and surrounded by people he loved. Hanne let her finger slide over the frame, a black, narrow molding around a sheet of glass that was cracked in one corner. Maybe the picture had once fallen on the floor. It hung slightly crooked and she adjusted it carefully. In the end she stood up, stretching to her full height. She turned to face Thale. Hanne ought to feel relieved. Instead she was engulfed by a sense of great, inexplicable disappointment.

Even though the case was now solved.

63

It was two o'clock on the morning of December 23, 1999 and snow blanketed the streets. The occasional flake still whirled in the air, but the sky had cleared in the last hour. Markveien had been decorated for Christmas for a couple of months now, with transverse garlands of lights between the lamp posts. Artificial stars and plastic moons, however, could not outshine the real thing; Hanne Wilhelmsen looked up and caught sight of the Plough, trundling slowly above Torshov. Out of habit, she let her eye locate the Pole Star, only just visible in the northern sky. Department stores were unstinting with electricity. The snow appeared golden yellow, bathed in all the light. Tomorrow it would vanish into gray, wet slush.

Billy T. was no longer grumpy. Instead, he seemed apathetic. When she phoned to talk to him, he was not dismissive. Only indifferent. She was not permitted to visit him at home. Tone-Marit and Jenny were asleep. She had the impression that he had given up on that sort of thing. He did not want to meet at police headquarters, either. When she suggested a stroll through Løkka, she was met with a barely audible *yes*, before the conversation was disconnected.

He did not say hello. A faint head movement when he emerged from his own front gate showed that he had seen her, across the road, under a street lamp. He did not approach her. Instead he shuffled along the sidewalk on the opposite side. She had to jog to catch up with him. It was the middle of the night and he did not even ask what it was about. He was well wrapped up. The collar of his pea-jacket was turned up and his cap was pulled down over his eyes. Around it all he had wound a huge red scarf. He thrust his hands deep inside his pockets and did not say a word.

"You can't stop being a policeman," Hanne said.

A one-and-a-half-meter-tall porcelain hound stared blankly at them from an over-decorated window; a red-clad Melchior sat astride a reindeer with elk antlers. Hanne tried to slow the pace.

"You can be angry at me. I can't deny you that. But don't give up everything else just because of me."

He stopped suddenly.

"Because of *you*?"

He sniffed and had to wipe his nose with his jacket sleeve.

"That's rich. As if you mean anything at all in this context."

Again he started to walk. He strode out over the pedestrian crossing in Sofienberggata without looking. A taxi tooted, skidding badly. Billy T. paid no attention. He cut diagonally across Olaf Ryes plass.

"Can't we sit down?"

Hanne took hold of his jacket. They were standing beside the circular pond in the middle of the square, half-filled with snow and garbage. A stray dog loped toward them. The boxer was shivering with cold as it wagged its tail optimistically and thrust its squat face up between Hanne's legs.

"Shoo!" she said, waving it away. "Here. I brought these with me."

She put two thick newspapers on the bench.

"Always prepared," Billy T. said, patting the dog. "Our own Girl Scout."

But he sat down. First he pushed his mat farther away. Then he turned from Hanne. He stared at Entré. The scraggy winter trees blocked some of the view, but he could see someone switching off all the lights after a long night. So they were still open. Despite one of the owners being murdered and the other locked up in jail, charged with the murder. Billy T. sniffed again, and he followed the boxer with his eyes as it scurried from bush to bush, whimpering painfully and trembling all the way to the tip of its tail. It caught the scent of something and trotted off along Thorvald Meyers gate, before turning the corner and disappearing into Grüners gate in the direction of Sofienberg Park.

"Can't we ever be friends again?"

Hanne let him sit at the far end of the bench. She wanted to move closer, but let him be. She did not even look at him, but threw the question out into empty space along with a gray-white cloud that quickly dispersed. Maybe he shrugged. It was not easy to say.

"Of course, I can say sorry one more time," she said. "But it's probably no use. All I can say in my defense is that I realize I treated you badly. And that I didn't do it to hurt you. I just couldn't do anything else. I was in no fit state to ..."

She held it in. Billy T. was not listening. He had closed his eyes and his lips were moving soundlessly and almost imperceptibly, as if in the middle of a contemplative prayer.

"Have you *never* done anything you regret, Billy T.? Have you never betrayed anyone? I mean, *really* betrayed?"

Her voice broke. All the lights around her drifted together into a fog of stars, and she blinked hard. The tears stung like ice crystals on her cheeks.

Still he did not respond. However, his lips had stopped moving.

"I have regrets, Billy T. I have real regrets. So many things. But I can't just cut out my past and burn it. It is there. All the stupid things. All the times I've hurt people I care about. All ... all the anxiety. I'm always so scared, Billy T. I'm so scared that someone will ..."

She rummaged in her pocket and found a roll of paper hankies.

"I've always been afraid that someone will *see* me. Everyone goes about thinking I'm embarrassed about being a lesbian. They think I hide ... *that.* You don't understand that all the time I'm using my energies to hide my whole self. It's as if I don't dare. For me it's just as dangerous if someone gets to know that I ... like having my back scratched. Or that the best thing I know is pancakes with syrup and bacon. That's *me*, all of it, and it's mine. Mine. Mine."

Now she was sobbing. She tried to pull herself together, taking a deep breath and squeezing her thumbnail against the palm of her hand inside her mitten. The tears flowed all the same.

"What the hell," she said harshly and stood up. "The Ziegler case is solved anyway. That was why I needed to talk to you."

At last he looked at her. Slowly he lifted his face to hers and pulled the scarf away from his face. She felt a pang when she saw his eyes. It was as though they did not belong in that dirty, familiar face: pale-blue, they stared at her as if he had never clapped eyes on her before.

"What," he said hoarsely. "What do you mean by 'solved'?"

It took only five minutes to explain. It was all so obvious after all. The solution was in itself a crying denunciation of Billy T., of the way he had led the investigation, of everything he had not done. Hanne could no longer bear to look him in the eye. She noticed that she tried to put a gloss on it all, that she tried to give him credit for which there was absolutely no justification.

"That's it, then," she said finally, hitting one foot against the other, mostly out of embarrassment. "We'll make the arrest early tomorrow morning. Or what do you think?"

She forced out a smile. He staggered as he stood up. His movements were stiff as he began to walk; he obviously wanted to go home. After a couple of steps he wheeled round.

"You asked me if I had ever betrayed anyone. I have."

He wanted to tell her about Suzanne. He wanted to take her hand and sit down again on the cold bench, feel the warmth from Hanne's body and eyes and hands, and confide in her that the whole investigation had hit the skids when, less than twenty-four hours after the murder, he had bumped into a woman at the door of Entré.

Suzanne was only fifteen when he had met her. A precocious, beautiful girl from a good family. He himself was an ungainly student at police college, and had already turned twenty-two when he fell head over heels into a love greater than he could handle. One thing was that the relationship between them was a crime. That had in itself scared him to death, as soon as the first, dazzling excitement had subsided. The fear had eventually pushed him away, driven him off. He was a trainee police officer and they were smoking hash. He ran away. Changed his phone number. Moved from one address to another, and yet another, while Suzanne's health deteriorated. Between the psychotic breakdowns, she found him. He had never understood how. She phoned, usually at night. She sent him letters. Accusing, loving letters in which she begged for help. She called on him: ran away from the hospital and clawed at his bedsit door until her hands were bleeding. Billy T. moved again. At last, after two years of anxiety about being exposed, punished, dismissed from the police in disgrace, it all went quiet.

He had forgotten Suzanne because he had to. For his own sake, and he had no choice. That was how he had felt it to be.

"I have …"

It was impossible. He gasped a couple of times, desperate to talk. Hanne's face lit up in front of him: in the end it was as if her eyes were all he could see. The cold air tore at his lungs when he caught his breath, but he could not speak. He would never be able to tell anyone about Suzanne, even though for more than a fortnight he had looked over his shoulder wherever he went. The story of his betrayal of Suzanne was his own, and could not be shared with anyone. Instead he pulled Hanne close.

"Thanks," was all he managed to say, with his lips against Hanne's ice-cold left ear.

64

She had tidied the office. The superfluous books piled up all over the place were gone. Moominpappa sat on top of a shelf, propped up by a luxuriant potted plant. The desk was bare, apart from a lidless cola tin filled with pens. The notice board was empty. A dark-blue wool winter coat hung on a hook behind the door. She grabbed it as she caught sight of them. She looked better now. Her cheeks had some color, and her hair caught a faint reflection of three large candles on a table in the narrow corridor.

"Shall we go?" she asked, putting on her coat.

Billy T. and Hanne Wilhelmsen nodded.

Before she went with them, she withdrew the nameplate from the metal runners on the glass wall of the office. She stood for a moment, studying her own name. Then, letting the loose letters run down into her hand, she shoved them into her pocket.

* * *

Interview with the accused, Idun Franck

Interviewed by Chief Inspector Hanne Wilhelmsen (H.W.) and Chief Inspector Billy T. (B.T.). Transcript typed by office colleague Rita Lyngåsen. There are in total three tapes of this interview. The interview was recorded on tape on Thursday December 23, 1999 at 11.30 at Oslo police headquarters.

Witness:

Franck, Idun, ID number 060545 32033
Address: Myklegårdsgate 12, 0656 Oslo
Employment: Publishing House, Mariboesgate 13, Oslo
Telephone: 22 68 39 80
The accused agreed to the interview being taped and a
transcript later produced. Provisionally charged with
contravention of Criminal Code section 233, subsection 2.
The accused (I.F.) gave the following statement:

H.W.:

As the accused in a criminal case, you have certain rights. I
would like to record on tape that you have been made aware
of this. You have the right to refuse to give a statement. You
have the right to let yourself be assisted by a defense lawyer
during this interview. Your defense counsel, Bodil Bang-
Andersen, is present. You are also informed of the charge …
(Pause, paper rustling.) That is what you have in front of you.
You are charged with the premeditated homicide of Brede
Ziegler on the evening of Sunday December the fifth, 1999.
Do you wish to give a statement?

I.F.:

(Cough.) Yes, I am willing to give a statement. *(Cough.)* I would
only say that I don't really need a lawyer. I am happy to give a
statement, and I know what I'm doing.

Lawyer:

I don't think you fully understand what this involves. You are
charged with premeditated homicide. Say what you intend to
say, then we'll deal with the question of guilt later. I ask that

you respect that, Wilhelmsen. No questions about guilt. Just the plain facts.

I.F.:

But it's quite simple, you see ... I have ...

Lawyer:

I think we'll do it like that.

H.W.:

That's fine. We'll do as your lawyer says. But now we'll make a start. I would like to continue, without interruptions. *(Rustling at the loudspeaker, indistinct.)* The accused is being shown evidence number sixty-four. Can you tell me what this is?

I.F.:

This is ... Can I have some water? *(Clinking.)* Thanks. It's a scarf. My scarf.

H.W.:

Are you quite sure? How do you recognize it as your scarf?

I.F.:

The pattern. Indian pattern in green and mauve. I bought it in London a long time ago. But it was a while before I remembered I'd lost it. *(Barely audible, whispering.)* You found it there, didn't you?

H.W.:

We're not actually the ones answering the questions, Idun Franck. Where do you think the scarf was found?

I.F.:

Outside police headquarters, wasn't it? *(Quiet, lengthy pause.)* But I don't understand … *(indistinct speech, scraping sounds)* anything. Why didn't you arrest me before, if you had the scarf? I've been waiting for you for ages. That time you and that other woman came to my home, I thought … They've been dreadful weeks. First I just wanted to go away. That Monday night after it had all happened, I sat awake and decided to go to the police. Hand myself in. But then … it was sort of so … *unfair.* I was to be punished for something that … So I went to work, and thought that this business of confidentiality might help me not to get entangled in too many lies. Since … *(Voice disappears, pause.)* But I understood yesterday.

H.W.:

What did you understand yesterday?

I.F.:

That I was going to be arrested. Thale phoned me. She told me that you had talked about Daniel and Brede. Sooner or later you would find out the whole story. I had expected that. Thale was strangely upset by your visit. She usually takes such things so … Well, she has hardly … She was so … detailed. Recounted the entire conversation. Word for word, was the impression I got. About eggs and hot chocolate and even that … And that you stared so long at that family photograph. From Father's eightieth birthday, I mean. Then I knew that you would come. I suddenly remembered what I had been wearing that day. The gray silk dress. And the scarf.

H.W.:

Okay. Let's go back to the beginning. Were you with Brede Ziegler on the evening of December the fifth this year?

I.F.:

Yes. We had arranged to meet outside the mosque in Åkebergveien at eleven o'clock.

H.W.:

Why was that? Outside? So late on a winter's night?

I.F.:

From the outset it was an absolutely stupid arrangement. I tried to get out of it, but Brede insisted. He was most insistent that we should look at the new mosaic that's been constructed at the mosque. It gave expression to his ... "concept of beauty," as he put it. I said it didn't suit. I was going out that night. Church concert. *(Burst of laughter.)* A chance occurrence can crop up like a peculiar wild card, can't it? It wasn't true that I was at the cinema. A work colleague said he had seen me there. But he was wrong. Must have simply mistaken some-body else for me. When Billy T. asked me later where I had been that evening, I just plucked Samir Zeta's comment out of ... So I had my alibi all sorted. It crossed my mind, quite by chance. I had seen the film the previous week. I knew all about its plot, how long it was, that I was too late to visit my sister and ... Anyway ... *(Pause, sound of water poured into a glass?)* Brede did not accept that I was busy. He always wanted to make a whole performance out of the simplest thing. "The light at night time lends the building more character." *(Somewhat distorted voice.)* That was how he put it. He had a long and fairly odd theory about the building's location in relation to police headquarters and the prison, and made a song and dance out of the mosque actually being lit up by all the lights around the jail. And what's more, he had a surprise for me, he said. Yes ... so that's how it came about. We were to meet in Åkebergveien at eleven o'clock, just opposite police headquarters.

H.W.:

What happened then?

I.F.:

I didn't see him when I arrived. I was about to go home again when he shouted at me from down beside the police building. From the steps where he was found. He had stood there to shelter from the wind. Anyway, he had a strange theory that you should approach the mosaic wall from slightly below, so that ... Well. I went down to him, and we talked for a bit about the mosaic. However, he seemed quite faint. Sick, almost. He made some strange faces from time to time, as if he was in pain. He didn't come out with the ecstatic lecture I had expected. We had discussed the mosaic before, and we did not agree about it. He wanted to use it as a recurring theme in the book. A kind of symbol. That he was open to the world, the past, the future, and the spiritual. It sounds crazy, doesn't it? That was what I tried to tell him, in fine turns of phrase. For some idiotic reason he thought I would be more convinced if he was able to show me the actual building. It is impressive, but ...

H.W.:

There's something here I don't quite understand. We have ... We have reason to believe that Brede Ziegler had ... a good excuse, on health grounds, to call off the meeting. You say yourself that he seemed in a bad way. Why was it so important for him to meet you? At that particular time?

I.F.:

I think … I don't entirely know if you understand what kind of person Brede Ziegler really was. He had an absolutely extreme need to – how should I put it? – direct! Direct his own life, like in a film. If anyone had objections to his way of thinking, he wasn't able to deal with that like the rest of us. Give in, that is. Maybe occasionally admit that others are right. It seemed as if it was some kind of sport … No, more than that. It was *(noticeable raising of voice)* imperative for the man to be right. We had come so far with the pictures for the book that it was actually too late to use the mosaic as a recurring theme anyway. He understood that. He wasn't stupid, Brede Ziegler. He was just … He wanted to convince me, and he had to do it there and then. That Sunday. The following Monday we were to devise a strategy for the next stage of work that would make it impossible to make major changes. I think nothing could stop him.

H.W.:

Let's go back to what happened. You said that he had a surprise for you?

I.F.:

A surprise? *(Silence.)* That turned out to be pretty fatal. It was the knife. The knife he was killed with. *(Silence, lengthy pause, indistinct sounds, talking?)* May I smoke?

H.W.:

The accused gets cigarettes. Billy T., can you fetch an ashtray? Okay, there's one here. Then we can continue. The knife?

I.F.:

It was the knife that was the surprise. A present for me. He had it with him, wrapped up in gift paper and all that. I don't know what he imagined. It was bordering on bribery. That I should go along with the ridiculous mosaic theme, if he paid court to me with presents. The whole ... *(Lengthy pause.)*

H.W.:

The whole what?

I.F.:

It all stemmed from an incident a few days earlier. Suzanne Klavenæs had taken a photo of some raw ingredients on a flat stone on the seashore. Fish and fennel and ... well. Raw ingredients. The picture was very successful, especially the light. We discussed the possibility of using it on the endpapers of the book. The ones pasted on the inside of ... However that may be, Brede went into total reverse mode. At the far edge of the picture you could see the handle of a knife. It was apparently the wrong knife. It was hardly visible, but all the same he kicked up a terrible commotion and threatened to withdraw from the whole project if we didn't reject the picture. I grew quite impatient, to put it mildly. I mean, associating with these authors is sometimes pretty demanding and ... Anyway. He gave me chapter and verse on kitchen utensils.

B.T.:

But this was a few days earlier, you said. What happened on Sunday night?

I.F.:

He took out the parcel. Began to open it, while saying something about artists always requiring the best tools if the art is to be divine. It was absolutely insufferable to listen to – it was after all only a knife! He even made a comparison with how top-class violinists needed a Stradivarius to attain their goal. The worst of it was that I had heard it all before, of course. But I said nothing. Thought it best to get it over and done with so that I could go home. He kept going with that nonsense as he unwrapped the paper. Underneath was a golden-colored box with black Japanese symbols on it. When he lifted the lid, he held the box out to me. So that I could take the knife. He said I should feel it. Feel how light it weighed. I did as he asked.

H.W.:

So you held the knife in your hand. Were you wearing gloves?

I.F.:

Yes, I was wearing gloves. I just wanted to leave, didn't I? And I certainly didn't want that knife. But Brede had taken off one of his gloves, to untie the ribbon, most likely. He had dropped it on the ground, or on the steps, to be more precise. I was about to bend down to pick it up, but then I took hold of the knife when he held it out to me.

Lawyer:

Think carefully, Idun, before you go any further. This is an important—

B.T.:

Defense Counsel, don't interrupt the statement. You can—

I.F.:

(*Interrupts, in a loud voice.*) It's not necessary. Don't start with all that! I want to tell it as it was. I stabbed him with the knife, okay? Is that clear? I pushed the knife into him! My God, if it hadn't been for that damned knife, I'd have contented myself with slapping his face! I … We were standing on the steps and I stabbed him, he made some gurgling noises, and then he buckled. It all happened so unbelievably fast. I must have hit a really vital organ. For some reason I wiped the handle with a paper hankie. Idiotic. After all, I was wearing gloves, and I … The peculiar thing was that there was so little blood. Coming out of him, I mean. When I got home, I found specks of blood on my gloves, no more than that. I threw away those gloves. Together with the box that I had taken with me, for some strange reason. When he collapsed … I shook him. But it was too late. He was dead. He died almost instantly. *(Pause, clears throat, crying?)* Then I ran. I ran home. That was it. *(Quiet, sound of match striking.)* That must have been when I lost my scarf. When I shook him. But I didn't notice at the time.

B.T.:

But I don't entirely understand … You say that you were standing talking to Brede Ziegler. You were slightly annoyed with him. He was going to give you a present. You take the knife in your hand and you stab him with it. But why? Why did you do it? Because you were annoyed that the man wanted to show you a mosque?

I.F.:

I can't explain it. That's just how things turned out.

B.T.:

You've almost certainly been with people who weren't exactly your favorites a number of times in your life, without stabbing them for that reason. You haven't as much as a speeding fine on your record.

I.F.:

No, but there probably weren't so many people I've met in my life that I disliked as passionately as Brede. You've talked to Thale, haven't you? You know what he did to our family.

B.T.:

Yes. We understand that you were angry with him. But you've left him in peace for more than twenty years, so why did you kill him at this particular time?

I.F.:

(Extremely loud voice.) That's just how things turned out, I tell you! He stood there, in front of me … He had given me a knife, it was as if he was asking for it … *(Crying.)*

Lawyer:

I suggest we take a break. My client is completely exhausted. She must have a chance to compose herself.

H.W.:

That's fine, we'll have a break. Interview concluded – the time is … 12.47. *(The tape is switched off.)*

H.W.:

The time is now 13.43: the interview with the accused, Idun Franck, is resumed. The accused has been to the toilet. She has been offered food, but does not want to eat. Coffee has been served. Are you ready to continue?

I.F.:

Yes, I'm ready.

B.T.:

Let's go back to how you knew Brede Ziegler. When did you meet him for the first time?

I.F.:

When did I meet him for the first time? *(Laughter.)* That depends who you mean. I met Freddy Johansen nearly twenty-four years ago. Once. That was enough. I met Brede Ziegler for the first time in August this year. At the publishing house. He didn't recognize me. That was maybe not so strange. Twenty-four years leave their mark, and then I've got a different name now. I was married for a few years. I've already told you about the book. It was my idea that I should help him with the writing. The publishing firm thought it was a brilliant idea, but Brede was a bit skeptical. He had a preference for a bigger name. And someone familiar with Italy. He actually asked for Erik Fosnes Hansen. As if he'd have time for that sort of thing ... Ghostwriter for a ... Well. I asked a couple of people. Writers. In such a way that I knew they'd turn it down. So he had to make do with me. Brede had no idea that I was Thale's sister, and I didn't mention it.

B.T.:

But did you know that Brede was Daniel's father?

I.F.:

I've always known that Freddy Johansen was Daniel's father. But he disappeared off the scene, of course, and we've never missed him. When he was resurrected as Brede Ziegler, it was as if he didn't have anything to do with us. Not until Daniel fell ill.

B.T.:

Ill, in what way?

I.F.:

When Daniel was fourteen, he became seriously ill. He needed a kidney transplant in order to survive. Thale was investigated, but she wasn't suitable as a donor. *(Pause, raised voice.)* Thale's already told you all this!

H.W.:

Tell us about it all the same.

I.F.:

We were desperate. I asked the hospital to send a request to Brede Ziegler. At the same time I allowed myself to be investigated, but the chances were slight, since Thale had not been suitable. But it was okay, after all. Daniel could receive my kidney. He was restored to health. But Brede ... *(Voice disappears, crying.)* He couldn't even be bothered to reply. He couldn't be bothered to reply! I've never thought highly of either Brede Ziegler or Freddy Johansen, but that he was willing simply to let his son die ... *(Lengthy crying, mumbling, indistinct speech.)* That's something I can never forgive.

H.W.:

Tell us about Daniel.

I.F.:

I'm his aunt. He's my nephew. I love him. You've talked to Thale, so you know that we've sort of shared him between us. Brought him up together, so to speak.

H.W.:

Yes, we know that. But tell us about him. Properly. Did you speak to Daniel yesterday?

I.F.:

How do you know that? That was the worst thing. Talking to Daniel ... *(Fierce crying.)* I'm going to lose him, and he still needs me ...

Lawyer:

Idun, does this mean that you didn't sleep last night? I would like that noted in the interview transcript. That my client is suffering from severe lack of sleep. We can take another break if you need it.

I.F.:

No, I'd like to talk about it ... *(Wipes nose?)* I've often been asked if I have any children. I answer no, because I don't really. It doesn't seem appropriate to be an aunt who's totally devoted to her nephew. But I've often thought of it as Daniel having been born twice. Once to Thale, and then to me. When he got my kidney. When we were on the verge of losing him, it dawned on me that Daniel is the only person in my life that I've been really close to. Always. For as long as he's lived. I've not actually wanted another child. *(Quiet.)* I need some more water, please. But it's not just that ... That he got my kidney, and that I looked after him so much when he was small. It's ... it's like ... People usually say that a child needs a mother and a father. Two parents, isn't that so? Daniel doesn't have a father. He has Thale, but she is – how shall I put it? – extremely level-headed. Daniel has needed me, because I don't only see the world from a practical viewpoint. What soul Thale has, she puts into her roles on the stage. Apart from that, she's quite hard-nosed. At home with me, Daniel has had a chance to express his feelings. His wonderment. He's a sensitive boy and … I've tried to show him that the world is a bit more than mere practical duties and the theater. *(Burst of laughter, lengthy pause.)* I'll give you an example. Daniel knows that Brede is his father. He learned that from Thale on his eighteenth birthday. In a matter-of-fact way. She thought he had the right to know, but it was nothing to make a fuss about. Now, when Brede died, I've noticed that Daniel has been confused and unhappy. Naturally *(burst of laughter, sob?)* I haven't wanted to talk to Daniel about his father's death. But of course I've seen what it has done to him. He has seemed quite desperate, and he's too young to carry it all by himself. Thale didn't want to mention it until there was talk of an inheritance. *(Slight laughter.)* But I've been a bit too much of a mother hen as far as Daniel is concerned. What has tormented Daniel most of all lately is not his father's death. He's sorry about that, of course: Brede's death robbed him of his last hope of ever having a father. But when I spoke to him last night I managed to drag out of him why he wanted to sell my father's books. Immediately after my father's funeral, Daniel invited me to come to Paris with him. He said that it was his turn to do something for me. I realized that it was important to him for me to accept, but I didn't really think much about where he had obtained the money. He said that he had saved for a long time. It turns out that he had borrowed the money from a friend who had just had his student loan paid out, and Daniel had taken it, with no second thoughts. You see, he was so sure that his inheritance from his grandfather was right round the corner. *(Pause.)* Daniel cried a lot last night. He thought it was shameful that the first time he did anything grown-up and treated me, it had been on credit. He would never have asked me for money to pay for my own present, even though he was about to ruin his friend's studies. But I sorted it out this morning. The money was transferred to Eskild before you arrived.

B.T.:

Does Daniel know that you killed his father?

I.F.:

No. I couldn't cope with telling him. Daniel just has to live with the fact that he has parents who have made his life very difficult, and I only hope that he … *(fierce crying)* can move on.

B.T.:

But I still don't understand. You had every reason to hate Brede when he left Thale and the baby more than twenty years ago, and you had every reason to hate him when he let Daniel down when he fell ill. But why was it now that you murdered him?

I.F.:

I got to know him. He was worse than I had thought. It was my job, of course, wasn't it? To get to know him, in order to create the book. I was to sort of get under his skin. Portray the man. I should never have done it, of course. But I was curious. Remarkably enough, I also did it to give him a fair chance. I had not actually believed that he could be as cynical as my impression had been over the years. I had the idiotic idea … If I could see him from his own perspective, then I could perhaps come to understand him. It was terribly naive, but in fact …

(Crying.) It was all some kind of ... *(lengthy pause)* gift? To Daniel. I would get to know Brede so that I could convey some understanding of why his father had treated him the way he had. I couldn't believe that Daniel could have his origins in someone who lacked any good qualities. But when I probed beneath the surface, there was nothing there. Brede Ziegler had one single driving force. His own profit.

B.T.:

He had managed to achieve a great deal, then.

I.F.:

I was fundamentally impressed by what the man had achieved. He had a passionate yearning for success. Of course he had done well for himself in every way, but he always dressed it up in something ... pompous. For example, this stuff about him being an artist, and that the cookery book should express spirituality, beauty, and goodness knows what. It was as if no words were too great for him. Not when it had to do with himself. But I'll give him something: in one respect he actually showed genuine feelings. At least a trace of them. When he spoke about Italy, it was with a certain warmth. But that was really the only thing I found he bothered about that wasn't simply about himself. Fancy that! *(Laughter.)* Loving a country, when he had a son he couldn't care less about!

B.T.:

Do you know any more about Italy? About what he did there?

I.F.:

No, not much really. He just became different when he talked about Italy. Enthusiastic, in a sense, without showing any affectation. I've worked out that he went there round about the time Daniel was born. It would have been best if he'd stayed there! But then he came back, as Brede Ziegler. He had worked as a chef for a few years in a restaurant in Milan and later bought a place with the guy who's now his partner in Entré. He spoke about some investments and that he wanted to settle down near Verona. If only Entré became a success, so that he could sell it at a good profit. It has occurred to me that he liked Italy because there he was able to be Brede Ziegler in peace, without being afraid that Freddy Johansen would catch up with him. "I become a more complete person in Italy." That was a typical Brede saying. As if he had any idea what a complete person was.

H.W.:

Why did you lie about your visit to Niels Juels gate? In the interview you gave on December 15 you denied that you had visited him at home. That wasn't true. Why—

I.F. *(interrupts)*:

I didn't lie! I had quite simply forgotten all about it! I've been so scared, so dreadfully ... It had slipped my mind completely. I was telling the truth, but you didn't believe me.

B.T.:

Let's go back to that night outside police headquarters. The way you've explained it, you hadn't planned to kill Brede. You have also explained that you are worried about what will happen to Daniel now. *(Pause.)* I believe Ziegler must have said something. Done something ... I believe that ... Why did you murder him at that very moment? He must have—

I.F. *(interrupts)*:

For Daniel's sake, I really regret what I did. *(Crying.)* I don't know … *(sobbing and sniffing, mumbling/indistinct speech)* how he's going to take it. After all, I've killed his father! *(Fierce crying, crackling sounds.)*

H.W.:

Here are some paper hankies. *(Pause.)* Can you answer Billy T.'s question? You have just said that you were standing there talking, and then you stabbed him. It is important that we understand why you did it. What you were thinking about when it happened.

I.F.:

But don't you understand? I've spent ages describing the most detestable person I've ever met!

H.W.:

We understand very well that you didn't like him, but we don't understand why you killed him. Did he say something to you? Did he say something you couldn't bear to hear?

I.F.:

Yes! He did say something! He said something that was so cynical that my head began to swim! It sounds like a cliché, doesn't it? But that's exactly how it feels. I swam into a terrible, sudden darkness. I had never believed myself capable of doing anything like that – I've never as much as toyed with the idea. If it hadn't been for that *(raises voice)* damn knife, I would just have slapped him, slugged him in the belly or the face, and nothing would have …

H.W.:

(Lengthy pause, soft voice.) What did Brede Ziegler say before you killed him?

I.F.:

(Blows nose loudly, continues in a soft voice.) In fact I remember it word for word. This past fortnight, when I've been going off my head, I've thought about that conversation. It reminds me of why and how I could have killed another human being. It happened when he gave me the knife. I thought the whole ceremony was childish, and I wanted to go home. A number of times I had noticed that he was greedy, in small things really. So when he unwrapped the knife from all that beautiful gift paper, I asked him if there had been special offers in kitchenware at IKEA. I just wanted to let him know that I didn't buy his little drama. But of course I've already told you how pompous he was – it was as if he couldn't tone down a drama production. Even if the audience wasn't in the least interested. That was when he said it. The comment that sparked off all the horror. *(Voice extremely distorted, at a deeper, slower pitch.)* "If you know me well, Mrs. Franck, then you know that I never play tricks. This knife is not some IKEA rubbish. It's the best knife in the world." I became so … *(Pause.)* I replied: "I know you better than you realize, Brede. I know that you do play tricks. You tricked yourself out of fatherhood once upon a time." He looked at me with a … *(shouts)* repulsive smile and answered: "Fatherhood? Aren't we talking about knives?" I felt a completely uncontrollable rage. I've never felt anything like it before, and said something like: "Don't you remember that you're a father? It was actually drawn to your attention once that you have a son! A child who today is a young man of twenty-two and whose name is Daniel!" That was when it happened.

H.W.:

Happened? Was that when you killed him?

I.F.:

No. It was when he said *(voice distorted again)*, "Twenty-two? Well, hardly a child any longer. Over and done with!" *(Lengthy pause.)*

H.W.:

I don't think I entirely—

I.F. *(interrupts, in a very loud tone of voice)*:

Understand? He smiled! That same smile. The same repulsive, abhorrent, egotistical smile! As if his entire denial of his own son – of my Daniel – was of no consequence, since Daniel was grown-up. "Well, hardly a child any longer. Over and done with!" All of Daniel's childhood, his illness, all of his ... All of Daniel's *(shouts)* existence ... was something that could be swept away like ... *(Fierce crying, pause.)* That was when I lost it. That was when I realized that I was faced with an evil person. I can't actually express it any other way. Until then I had regarded him as shallow, superficial, unpleasant. But immediately before I stabbed him, I felt that Brede Ziegler was downright evil. *(Very lengthy pause.)* I ... *(Quiet, uncertain voice.)* It was Elie Wiesel who said it, I think. That the opposite of love is not hate, but indifference. Even toward Daniel, his own son. My Daniel. *(One minute of the tape is without sound.)*

H.W.:

Then I have only one more question at present. What size of shoe do you wear?

I.F.:

(Barely audible.) Size thirty-eight. As a rule.

H.W.:

Thanks, Idun. We'll finish the interview now. The time is 17.32.

Interviewer's note (H.W.): The accused was allowed to confer with her lawyer in an adjacent room, both before and after the interview. Defense Counsel Bodil Bang-Andersen advised that her client would agree to four weeks on remand, with an embargo on letters and visitors. The accused requests that her sister, Thale Åsmundsen, is told of her arrest. The accused was escorted to a remand cell at 18.25 hours. She will be taken to Oslo Prison as soon as a court order regarding custody is available.

65

It was the strangest Christmas tree Hanne had seen. Round as a ball, it was far too big for the living room. The top took a right-turn at the ceiling so that the star was lying sideways, pointing at an exclusive nativity scene that had pride of place on the TV set. The tree was decorated with fruit and vegetables, everything from oranges to cucumbers and a lovely bunch of grapes tucked in beside the trunk. Expensive glass figures suspended from silk loops and abortive attempts at Christmas baskets were hanging side by side. The lights gave maximum effect: the tree twinkled and shone. Nefis and Hairy Mary must have bought enough lights for five trees: the green cables were twisted round and round, making the whole tree look like a glittering gift parcel. Seven presents were arranged at the foot. It was already midnight, and they were both fast asleep.

A note from Hairy Mary was lying on the table in the living room:

Deer Hanni,

We've dekorraitit the tree an shoped til we bluddy droped. Thairs food in the frigge that Iv maid for yoo. Wev bot food for tumorro as wel. Lootfisk an porc ribb an lotss of good thing's. Neffis is reely kind. Shes a Mooslim, an hasnt a cloo abowt Krissmass. Butt nise all the saym. We need too taik cair of hur. Sleepp wel.

Mary.

Sory abowt the skarf. I shood hav tol yoo beefor. But it wos so worm an luvly in the kold.

Mary agayn.

Hanne smiled, and put the note in a drawer. She stripped off her clothes and snuggled down naked in the bed. When she felt the warmth of Nefis's back against her stomach, she began to cry; silently, so that she would not wake her. Hanne could not remember when she had last looked forward to Christmas Eve.

It was probably the first time ever.

66

H.W. Next time you are in possession of crucial evidence, could you please be kind enough to bring it with you to the station? It would simplify the investigation considerably. Furthermore, it would be a good idea not to have important witnesses staying in your home. At least not without letting the leader of the investigation know. Billy T.

Hanne Wilhelmsen tore the Post-it note off the door. She was not even angry, despite realizing the note must have hung there long enough for most of the others in the department to have seen it.

She should not have taken Hairy Mary home with her. At the very least she should have let them know. She should have towed in Hairy Mary when she found her: immediately and without further ado. Instead she had enticed and tricked her into going home with her, with food and small talk, as if Hairy Mary had been an ownerless dog to which she had taken a sudden, inexplicable liking. The woman should have been interviewed in the proper fashion. Then they would probably have noticed the scarf. They would have asked her where it had come from. A green-and-mauve silk scarf would have contrasted starkly with Hairy Mary's lamé jacket and laddered stockings. Someone would have asked her. Almost certainly, Hanne thought, biting her lip.

When she had caught sight of Idun Franck's scarf on the family photograph in Thale's apartment, she had recognized Hairy Mary's only acceptable item of clothing. At the same moment she had seen what she had done. It wasn't only Billy T.'s fault that the investigation had hit the skids. At any rate, Hanne Wilhelmsen had had the opportunity to sort it all out again. The solution was to her credit. They all knew that. They all gave her the kudos.

Billy T. had to content himself with writing sarcastic notes.

"What's done is done, after all," she muttered, stuffing the yellow note into her pocket.

"Hello, Hanne. That wasn't necessary."

Silje Sørensen nodded at her trouser pocket, where the corner of the note was still visible.

"It's been hanging there all day. We've all seen it."

Hanne pulled an indefinable, fleeting grimace.

"Don't give a damn. How are things with Sindre?"

"Confessed. At last."

"Do tell."

It was almost lunchtime on Christmas Eve 1999. Police headquarters was imbued with an unfamiliar atmosphere, as if the building itself had given a sigh of relief that it was Christmas this year once again. The aroma of mulled wine and gingerbread biscuits seemed to cling to all the people who walked to and fro in the corridors, bringing with them a delicious scent of the festivities. People had time to spare. Some smiled, others said hello. Others again exchanged small gifts. Hanne herself had received a red parcel from Erik Henriksen. She had hardly seen him since that very first day, when she had stood in front of the elevator on the ground floor, wanting more than anything else to turn and run. He grinned, wished her Merry Christmas, and more or less threw the present at her. It still lay unopened on Hanne's desk. As long as it lay there, in its bright-red glossy wrapping with golden bow and glitter, it served as a reminder that everything, once long ago, had been quite different from now.

Silje and Hanne took the stairs up to the canteen. The police orchestra was playing "A Child is Born in Bethlehem" in the foyer: harsh and beautiful, with a much too dominant cornet.

When Hanne heard how Brede Ziegler had invited Sindre Sand into the city center on Saturday December 4, it struck her that she had still not quite got to grips with the famous restaurateur. Maybe Idun Franck had been right.

Brede Ziegler might quite simply have been evil.

Hanne had seldom met evil people. Murderers and killers, rapists and fraudsters: she had wallowed in these people for more than fifteen years. Nevertheless, on reflection, she could not bring to mind having met a truly evil person.

Brede Ziegler had phoned Sindre. Effortless and easy-going. He suggested a trip into town. Not to the restaurant, not an actual invitation; it was obviously not going to cost Brede more than the drinks he bought for himself. Sindre had accepted. Mostly because some sort of curiosity had overshadowed the fury he felt: his anger and humiliation about Ziegler phoning him in a casual, everyday tone, after having squandered all his money and stolen the girl he intended to marry.

Naturally there was something behind it. After two drinks, Ziegler offered Sindre a job. Poorly paid, admittedly, but he would get an option on shares in a newly established company. Some project or other in Italy. If he got the place up and running, with a promise of substantial financial backing and a whole heap of staff, he could cash in a small fortune later on. So they'd be able to call it quits.

"Sindre says it was all typical Brede Ziegler," Silje said. "For next to nothing he would get an enthusiastic, young, and capable Norwegian to create something that would mainly serve Brede's interests."

She bristled slightly.

"The boy had actually planned it all out," she added.

Having stopped at the sixth floor, they leaned over the gallery with their arms on the railing. The police orchestra had launched into "It's Beginning to Look a Lot Like Christmas" in the foyer below. Hanne caught sight of the Police Chief down there in full uniform, handing out mandarin oranges to the staff. A photographer was tripping around him, constantly taking photos. The Police Chief seemed annoyed, and wheeled round to present a bar of chocolate to a little girl accompanied by a tall man. As he crouched down, he lost his balance and pulled down the five-year-old in the fall. The photographer went berserk with the flash.

"Yes, it's certainly beginning to look a lot like Christmas," she said tartly.

"Sindre had bought three packs of Paracet the day before," Silje went on to explain. "He knew that he needed to go to different pharmacies. An article in *Illustrert Vitenskap* magazine had told him that ..."

An article in *Illustrert Vitenskap*, Hanne thought resignedly, peering at the tumult far below. Two uniformed men had got the Police Chief back on his feet, but the youngster was screaming like crazy.

"An attempted homicide based on a highly simplified article in a popular science magazine," Hanne murmured. "They never cease to amaze us, do they?"

Sindre had begun with two pills in a gin and tonic, in the Smuget nightclub just before midnight. The pills had been pulverized in advance. Brede did not notice anything. Sindre continued. By the time morning came, on Sunday December 5, 1999, Brede Ziegler had ingested nearly thirty Paracet tablets.

"The worst thing is," Silje said, shuddering, "that he took the last five tablets voluntarily. Brede and Sindre had ended up at Sindre's place, both totally smashed. Brede was in pain. He had just said something about Vilde not being worth keeping. She was fading too fast … No, her petals were falling off! That was it. That was exactly what he said. He was sick and tired of the girl and thought she wasn't very intelligent. Got stoned too often. Did nothing."

"I'm never going to understand why he married that young girl," Hanne commented.

"He probably didn't know himself, either. Some kind of crisis, perhaps? He was approaching fifty, and Vilde was young and beautiful. Don't know."

Silje sighed and nibbled her index finger.

"Sindre, on the other hand, never got over her. Eventually he began to suspect her of being behind the murder. That was why he insisted so obstinately that he hadn't seen her for ages, despite our overwhelming evidence to the contrary. He did not want to make her more interesting for us. Naive."

"To put it mildly."

"When Brede began to bad-mouth Vilde, Sindre grew over-confident. Brede was complaining of pains in his stomach and a headache, and Sindre gave him five Paracet. Which the guy swallowed without a murmur. Washed down with whisky. It must have been almost the first time the man had taken a pill."

She shuddered again.

"Sindre was not even sure that Brede was going to die. He just wanted to torment him, he says. Torture him, in a way. The worst thing is that he is right. People react differently to paracetamol. Although Brede Ziegler must have felt quite indisposed on Sunday, he didn't necessarily suffer such terrible pain. But enough to try to get hold of a doctor, obviously. He might have thought it was all due to the awful binge-drinking of the previous night. When Monday came round and Sindre read in the newspaper that Brede had been stabbed to death the previous evening, he could hardly believe his own luck. It made him over-confident. Brazen. You saw that yourself in the first interview. And … he was telling the truth, concerning the hole in his alibi. Sindre, that is. He bought cigarettes and met an old school friend outside the gas station. We tracked the friend down in the end."

The little girl down below had been comforted by a huge bag with something exciting inside it. The orchestra was taking a break. The aroma of Christmas cake and mulled wine was over-powering now and displaced the usual reek of floor polish, stress, and police uniforms. A nun dressed in black waited at the counter for a new passport, and Hanne gave a faint smile.

"Did you know that many nuns wear gray?" she said into thin air.

"What?"

"Nothing. Whereabouts in Italy was Sindre offered that job?"

Silje wrinkled her nose.

"In Vilana … No, I'm talking nonsense. Oh … what was it called again?"

She tapped her forehead lightly with the palm of her hand.

"Verona, of course. Romeo and Juliet. Just outside Verona. It had been some kind of convent."

Hanne Wilhelmsen felt a pleasant heat course through her body. An ice-cold sensation ran down her spine in the midst of all the heat, and she felt the fresh running water in a deep pool filled with plump carp.

"What was the name of the place?" she asked softly.

"Don't remember."

"Villa Monasteria, perhaps?"

Hanne straightened her spine and massaged the small of her back with both hands.

"Yes," Silje exclaimed excitedly. "Villa Monster … yes. What you said. Brede bought it a couple of months ago and thought it had fantastic potential. Was going to spend millions renovating it and creating an exclusive hotel."

Silje twisted the diamond round to the palm of her hand and fell silent.

When Hanne closed her eyes, she could feel the anxious eyes of the nuns on her face. She heard *il direttore*'s hurried steps on the floor whenever she entered a room. She remembered that they had all stopped talking to her.

She knew they had mistaken her for someone else.

Actually she had not planned to go. Silje had insisted. Even though Billy T. was sulking and had stayed away, that was no reason for Hanne not to come. A message from the front desk had made her pay a visit to the office first.

Håkon Sand had phoned.

She phoned him back: immediately, so that her courage would not fail her. He did not want anything. Not really. He did not want to meet her, and neither did he want to invite her to the traditional Christmas breakfast that Cecilie and Hanne had always attended, on Christmas Day from twelve till twelve. He just wondered how she was. Where she had been for all that time. When he hung up, she could not really remember what they had talked about. But they *had* talked. He *had* phoned.

If there was an end to everything here on earth, Hanne thought, then there must also be new beginnings.

For once the buzz of voices did not die down when she entered the room. The faces that turned toward her were friendly, and Severin Heger drew out a chair.

"Sit down," he invited. "Annmari! Pass a mug of mulled wine!"

Several of the police's regular benefactors had sent boxes of sandwiches, Christmas cakes and two huge Lukket Valnøtt marzipan cakes. Karianne Holbeck had cream on her chin and was laughing at a joke that Karl Sommarøy had obviously spun out. Someone had brought a CD player. Anita Skorgan's voice rasped from the broken loudspeakers and Hanne bent toward Severin's ear: "Turn off the music. It sounds awful on that machine."

"No, certainly not," he said lightly, raising his mug. "Cheers! And congratulations!"

"Why the hell have you released Gagliostro?"

Klaus Veierød suddenly appeared in the doorway, dressed for a party, in a dark suit shiny at the knees. His tie hung loosely around his neck, and his hair was disheveled. He was waving a car key, but no one caught on to what he meant. He fixed his gaze on Annmari Skar. The Police Prosecutor put down her fork and swallowed carefully, before returning his smile.

"There's no longer any danger of him tampering with evidence," she said calmly. "He definitely didn't murder Brede Ziegler, and as far as Sebastian Kvie is concerned, I'm afraid it all ends with the case being dropped. His defense lawyer is right. Sebastian climbed up on scaffolding in the middle of the night. Gagliostro can hardly have sat there in his pajamas waiting for him. Doubtful case, if you ask me."

She raised her mug to her mouth.

"Do you realize one thing," Klaus spluttered, pulling a small plastic bag out of the wide pockets of his suit trousers. "Here's the tape from Brede Ziegler's answering machine. Billy T. impounded it as early as day three, when he and our friend here ..."

He glared contemptuously at Severin, who shrugged and smiled broadly.

"... were in Ziegler's apartment. Our absolutely *splendid* Chief Inspector Billy T. ..."

He scanned the room wildly. When he could not spot Billy T., he raked his hand through his hair and snorted like a horse.

"... had *forgotten* that he had taken it out of the machine. Just as he had *forgotten* to develop three rolls of film that he had ... *seized* from the deceased's fridge. But to take first things first—"

"We know that already," Annmari broke in, still completely unruffled. "There was a message from Gagliostro there. About him expecting to see Brede at eight o'clock, as arranged. The guy *was* interviewed about this. He admits it now. Brede had found out about the wine scam. Gagliostro obviously suffers from what we might call wine kleptomania. They talked to each other that Sunday evening. Brede threatened to report Claudio, and to throw him out of the whole business. In the end they came to an agreement, all the same. Claudio was to return the bottles before opening time the next day, and Brede would get some money. Some sort of compensation. He got sixteen thousand kroner as a down-payment. Claudio managed to trick him into thinking that he didn't have any more. Brede left at half past ten. You are right, of course, that we ought to have ... We should have listened to this tape earlier. But it wouldn't have mattered one way or the other, as far as solving the case is concerned. More likely the contrary. It would have reinforced our suspicions of Claudio. Considerably. And ..."

Once again she gave a faint, almost provocative smile as she looked around.

"... he had not killed his colleague. Just cheated and swindled and lied."

"And that's the guy you've *released*!"

Klaus waved the car keys frantically, still without anyone understanding why.

"Yes. He'll probably be charged with both fraud and a lot of other minor stuff. Giving false evidence, for one thing. Of course he hadn't yet been charged when he was questioned the first time. But all the evidence has been secured. His apartment has been searched. So he could be released. It's Christmas, Klaus! Sit yourself down and have some cake!"

"I'm going to my mother-in-law's," he snapped. "The car's

broken down, and my mother-in-law's waiting in Strømmen. I don't have a fucking present for my wife yet, and what's more, I'd forgotten that I was supposed to see to the turkey for tomorrow."

He glared angrily at the keys as if they were the cause of all his problems. Then he took out three envelopes from his inside pocket and threw them down on the table.

"Here are the pictures you impounded," he growled at Severin. "Just a fucking building. A gray building with little gnomes around it. And dry, yellow grass."

Then he turned on his heel and left. Both car keys and photographs were left behind. As the door slammed behind him, the buzz of voices returned. After a few minutes the festive atmosphere was back. Karianne gave a loud, protracted laugh, and Silje had her hands full struggling to turn Severin down, as he tried to ply her with mulled wine with added raisins and almonds. Anita Skorgan had reached "Silent Night" and three police trainees joined in at the far end of the table.

Hanne picked up the envelopes containing the photographs. Her fingers trembled as she opened the first one. All the others around her were left to their own devices, and she put the bundle down in front of her without quite daring to look.

The pictures must have been taken in the autumn. The grass was withered, but the occasional obstinate flower still glimmered red in all the brownish-yellow. The sky was low and gray. All the pictures must have been taken on the same day. Hanne could sense rain in the air above the graveled courtyard. The hat on the faceless gnome that stood in front of the chapel on the southern side, which she had stroked with her hand every time she walked past, was dark and damp.

The Villa Monasteria had been photographed while she was still staying there. She had never noticed anything at all. Her hands grew quieter as she leafed slowly through the bundles.

Daniel would inherit the convent. Only a DNA test remained to be done, and three-quarters of Brede's estate would be his, Annmari had explained to her that morning. Hanne had derived some kind of comfort from that, as if all the wealth in the world could make up for Taffa being in jail. The boy was inconsolable. He had sat in her office for more than two hours without saying very much, but he hadn't wanted to leave, either. In the end he had stood up stiffly and taken her hand. When he wished her Happy Christmas, she had not had the energy to answer.

Daniel Åsmundsen was not going to build a swimming pool at the Villa Monasteria. He was going to fall in love with the deep pool with its crystal-clear water. Maybe he hadn't heard of fresh-water prawns, either. He would saunter through the bamboo thicket: the green stalks on one side, black on the other. Then he would sit on the stone wall beside the oval pool and watch the carp, the indolent beasts that suddenly, quick as a flash, made a beeline for something he could barely see.

"Happy, Happy Christmas, Hanne."

Silje kissed her lightly on the hair. Hanne half-turned, and when Silje grasped her hand, she did not want to let go.

"Happy Christmas to you too," she said quietly. "Have a really lovely time."

"Are you going to be alone this evening?"

Hanne hesitated: it seemed as if the answer was sticking in her throat. Then she swallowed noisily and forced herself to speak.

"No. There'll be three of us. My girlfriend, a good friend, and myself. It's sure to be great fun."

"Sure," Silje said softly. "There's Billy T., by the way."

She let go her hand and left.

The others had stood up, some fairly unsteady on their feet. Two empty bottles of vodka sat beside the pot of mulled wine. The cake plates were empty, the candles had guttered. Billy T. looked at her over Severin's shoulder, between the heads of two drunken trainees who completely ignored him. He snaked past them and held out his hand to her.

"I thought you would like this," he said dully. "It is Christmas Eve, after all."

Then he turned round and disappeared just as abruptly as he had arrived.

Hanne Wilhelmsen waited until they were all gone and the CD player was silent. The police orchestra had long since packed up all their instruments. Even around the back of the building everything was quiet; most of them in the enormous police headquarters had gone home and left Oslo to its own devices for twenty-four hours or so.

She unfolded the sheet of paper he had handed her.

It was a detailed map of the Østre Gravlund cemetery. At the top corner, some distance from the chapel, beside a gravestone marked with a red cross and a tiny little heart, he had written:

Cecilie's grave. I've been there this morning and left flowers and lit candles. Cecilie's parents came while I was there, and they were very pleased. I hope you are too. If not, you can just throw out all the crap. Billy T.

She slowly folded the sheet again.

It was now five o'clock on Christmas Eve. The church bells began to ring, heavy and rhythmic, throughout Oslo.

She would take a detour on the way home.